A New
BEGINNING

DAVID A RUSSELL

LifeRich Publishing is a registered trademark of
The Reader's Digest Association, Inc.

This is a work of fiction. All of the characters, names, incidents,
organizations, and dialogue in this novel are either the products
of the author's imagination or are used fictitiously.

LifeRich Publishing books may be ordered
through booksellers or by contacting:

LifeRich Publishing
1663 Liberty Drive
Bloomington, IN 47403
www.liferichpublishing.com
1 (888) 238-8637

ISBN: 978-1-4897-1395-7 (sc)
ISBN: 978-1-4897-1394-0 (e)

Print information available on the last page.

LifeRich Publishing rev. date: 12/18/2017

FOREWORD

D uring the latter part of the 18th Century, Central Europe seemed in a continuous state of war. Poland, sandwiched in between Prussia, Hungary and Russia, had to defend her lands constantly. From 1784 until 1789 Poland fought numerous battles, first with Prussia on the Western front, and then on the Eastern front against Russia. The Polish soldiers, led by the Polish Cossacks, were a match for any troops the other countries could field, and time after time, threw back the invading forces. However, in 1788, the leaders of Prussia and Russia coordinated their battle plans and attacked Poland from both sides. Russia captured the Polish capital of Warsaw. The Polish Army regrouped, and after a terrible battle, retook Warsaw.

A major part of the Polish Army was decimated, leaving them so weak they could not defend against two strong armies attacking on two fronts. The Russian and Prussian armies overran the Polish troops and almost annihilated them. Few would surrender for they knew they would either be killed or have to become a soldier in the invading armies. Also to surrender meant the capture of their homeland.

Finally, the two invading armies were successful and the two countries divided Poland between them. Poland was wiped off the map and ceased to exist as a nation. It would not become Poland again until the year 1920, after the Germans and Prussians were defeated in what was known as World War I.

Those Polish troops who could manage to escape, did so, fleeing to other friendly countries. A few, like Andraui Vladimir Stanislaski, who became Andrew Stanley in our story, left Europe seeking freedom in the new world. This is primarily about his search for a new home, a new beginning.

In 1788 there could hardly have been a more degrading situation than to be thrown into debtor's prison in England. The embarrassment was enough, but the prison was as bad as any in the world. The stench of unwashed bodies, vomit and human waste combined to make the smell unbelievable. Add to this the degradation and depravity of the inmates and you had not a prison, but a hell-hole, a training ground for the young criminal and a death sentence for those who could not defend themselves from the cruel, hardened, professional criminal. It is easy to understand how anyone, slated for this fate, would choose a term of indenture rather than prison. Besides, for Catherine York, it was a way to escape the embarrassing situation she had found herself in back in England. She had never particularly liked the cold and fog of London. She was offered a chance to come to America, and rather than going to prison, she gladly accepted.

For several hundred years, slave traders of many nationalities had raided the coast of West Africa, capturing slaves from all the countries that border the ocean. Slaves from that part of Africa that today is known as Namibia, Ghana, Nigeria, Guinea, Cameroon and practically all the coastal areas experienced raids at one time or another. Most of the raids were by Arabs and other blacks who preyed on their own people. The raiders were cruel and often killed innocent children, raped the women and whipped the men into submission. If any tried to escape, they were whipped to death or mutilated as a lesson to the others. Namibia and Cameroon were two areas that were raided most often because the natives of this area were unusually large and strong. They fought fiercely but when captured, brought a larger sum in the slave markets of Casablanca, Tripoli and Alexandria. However, Casablanca was where most of the white men obtained their slaves for the new world, and they paid the highest price of all.

That is where Witambe Morandu and his people were brought and became a part of this story. As much as this is the story of Andraui Vladimir Stanislaski and Catherine York, this is also the story of Witambe Morandu, and their efforts to find a new life and freedom in a new land. While all characters in this book are purely of the author's imagination, any similarities to actual persons, living or dead are coincidental. While intended as a work of fiction, the actions and events are as close to the actual times and places of the era as we could determine by extensive research. I hope you find the reading to be both thought provoking and entertaining. If so, I have done what I set out to do.

Note: During the era in which our story occurs, the money used in the new states of America included British, Spanish, French and various other currencies, both in the form of paper and coins. Various colonies (states) also issued currencies in both paper and coin form. For simplification an ease for current day readers, we have chosen to use the term (dollars) in our story. It was all but impossible to ascertain the exact values of slaves, guns and other items mentioned in our story as they varied by types, locations and degree of scarcity. Therefore we have attempted to affix the prices as close as we could determine to those that existed during the time period in which our story occurred.

CHAPTER ONE

The soft autumn breeze kept the ships' sails full and the pressure of the mainmast caused the ship to creak and groan as it rolled on each wave. It had been a pretty good voyage since leaving Boston Harbor and the weather continued warm. It was now late August, the skies were clear and the sun bright. It had been fairly cool in Boston and a light coat felt good, but now as the ship moved south along the Virginia Coast, the days were warm enough for shirt sleeves. The further south the ship sailed, the more cheerful the crew became, and even the passengers seemed to be in somewhat better spirits.

The Sea Mistress was an old ship, but a good one. Its owners had made sure it was well built and the captain was a man who kept his crew busy. The ship was always cleaned and freshly painted. Captain Joshua Wilson, a sailor for more than 30 years, had sailed the seven seas; but the past five years, he sailed mostly between Europe and North America with an occasional trip to the Caribbean and Mediterranean.

The helmsman on board the ship yelled out, "What heading do we take this evening, Captain?"

"South by Southwest," Wilson yelled back. "We should make Charlestown by mid-day tomorrow."

* * * * *

As they skimmed across the water, the captain stood on the deck looking out to sea. There were things about this voyage that troubled him.

His mind turned back to the beginning of the current voyage which had started in Hamburg, Germany, thence to London where he had picked up 20 bonded servants. From London he had sailed south, skirting the western edge of Europe to deliver a cargo of dry goods to Casablanca on the northern coast of Africa.

There, Captain Wilson picked up a cargo that he didn't like to carry - a shipment of 110 black slaves, captured in Cameroon and Southwestern Africa. They were awaiting shipment to the new nation in North America, which had just a few years ago won its' freedom. It called itself the United States of America. Wilson disliked transporting slaves. First, on moral grounds, for he opposed slavery. Secondly, his ship had neither the accommodations, nor the crew, to take care of the needs of human passengers. However, the ship's owners did not want him sailing away half empty. Taking the slaves to America would turn a profit for them, and he would do the best he could with what he had to work with. Food and sanitation, as well as security would be a problem. Further, just a few of the slaves spoke any English; nor did he understand any of their native languages. Tales of slaves' efforts to escape forced him to keep them locked up on the entire voyage. On occasion, when left alone, a young man would jump into the sea, planning to swim back to shore. The slaves had little concept of the vastness of the sea; and if the ship did not turn around and pick them up, they would die for their efforts.

The 20 bonded servants that had boarded in London wouldn't be much of a problem. This group volunteered, more or less, for the trip. They were petty criminals, people in debt, or other similar circumstances, who aimed to avoid jail. In the 1780's, you did not want to go to prison in London. The prisons were the depth of depravity, and only the very strong survived their stay. Almost half of all who entered prison died, either at the hands of other inmates, or from dysentery, starvation, pneumonia or the likes. Many of those released had contracted leprosy or some other deadly disease. Anyone who had seen the goals of London would choose almost any alternative if given a chance. Those souls on board had chosen to bond themselves to someone in America who was willing to pay their fines or debts. There was little difference in treatment however. They were virtually slaves during their bonded period and the person, who all but owned them, often treated them cruelly. Though the bonded period might be for three, five or more years, once the period was served, the person was released and could then pursue his own life. Frequently, an unscrupulous bondholder found numerous excuses to stretch a bonding period out or deny the release altogether. But even this was better than facing debtor's prison, and the bonded people were not as likely to try to escape. In fact, some looked forward to going to the new world. Many felt this would be their chance to begin a new life. There were many tales of fabulous wealth waiting for the taking. They also spoke English, although many of those from the slums and alleys of London often had their own dialect and were difficult to understand.

With the blacks it was a different matter. They had been forcibly taken from their families, and in many instances, had seen wives and other loved ones killed. They were not very friendly to the white man in general, and would probably have to be locked in the hold and restrained on the entire journey. This group included a few who had been captured with their women, and about a dozen young boys and girls in their early and middle teens. The men with families showed more caution and were more concerned for the welfare of the women and children. The young men, on the other hand, would require leg irons most of the trip. They were more violent and determined to take vengeance on someone.

The whole business brought a strong distaste for what Joshua Wilson had to do; it went against his compassionate nature. The least he could do was try to make the trip as comfortable as possible for his cargo.

The slaves had been brought to the ships by their capturers, and as they were being off-loaded from the carts and wagons and they saw the ship, one of the women began to cry. Her eyes showed panic as she moved toward the ship she began to scream. Perhaps she had a fear of the sea. Perhaps she knew that once aboard, there was little hope of ever seeing her family again. As she cried, the younger children joined in the wailing. It was about to turn into a very ugly scene.

The slavers unlimbered their whips and moved among the slaves, slashing and striking them to get to the women. Wilson noticed one tall black man from a group of the slaves move swiftly through the other slaves. Even though he had leg irons on and shackles on his wrists, he moved with considerable speed and reached the woman before the slaver did. He spoke to the woman and children in a deep guttural voice that carried authority. Just as the whip descended, he inserted himself between the slaver and woman so that the blow fell across his back.

The whip was a cat-o-nine-tails, nine individual strips of leather, each with a small weight in the tip of the strip, and all bound to one handle. The "cat" was often used to whip slaves into submission. When wielded by someone with average strength, it could cut a person's back to shreds.

The slaver with the whip was a big burly man with snagged teeth and a shaggy beard. The blow cracked hard, and the big black man's mouth tightened. There was no other acknowledgement from him. The burly man drew back to lash out again, frustrated because he'd been prevented from reaching and striking the woman.

Wilson yelled, "You there! Belay that whip. I do not want damaged cargo when I arrive in port. These people are frightened and there is no need to abuse them further."

The burly slaver glared at the captain. He did not appreciate being deprived of one of his favorite pastimes. Then he shouted back, "All right. They are your prisoners. Sign my receipt and I'll be on my way. You can be responsible for getting them on board."

Captain Wilson answered, "Fair enough."

He turned to his first mate. "Take ten men with arms and go down the gang plank and take charge of the cargo. Quickly, man."

Then he preceded his men and walked directly to the tall black man who had become the woman's shield. The black man turned to face him. The captain spoke slowly to him, "Do not be alarmed. My men will not harm your people. Do you understand me?"

The black man did not answer or give the appearance of having heard.

Another slave to the side answered, "I speak some English and a little Spanish I learned from our captors."

Wilson turned and spoke to him, "Good! Can you speak to all of the slaves?"

The man said, "To some of them. Some come from tribes I do not know and do not understand their language. But perhaps some of the others can tell them what I say."

The captain sighed a little for this bit of luck. He observed the translator a little closer. He was not like the others. He was more brown-skinned and appeared to be an Arab. He asked the man his name.

"I have a number of names which you would find hard to speak. I am sometimes called Abdulla by the slavers, and that will be good enough."

"Very well, Abdulla. Tell these people that my job is to take them to another port. That I must do this even if it makes me unhappy. I do not believe in using the whip, and I will not treat them badly if they do not make trouble for me. If I relieve this slaver and send him on his way, they must agree to go aboard the ship peacefully without trouble. We will only use force if it becomes necessary. Tell them that."

Abdulla stared at the captain, then asked him, "Do you really expect these people to believe you? They have been stolen from their families, starved and in many cases seen their wives raped and their children killed. Do you think they will go peacefully?"

Wilson looked over the crowd which had grown totally silent now. He saw the big black man that had shielded the woman. He was looking at the Capitan with piercing dark eyes. Wilson shivered slightly. It was as if the man was looking into his soul. All of the blacks watched the big man that had shielded the woman, as if he would protect them also, as if waiting for some signal as to what they should do. One word from him and Wilson knew that all hell would break loose, and blood would be shed on that wharf that day.

He turned back to Abdulla and spoke to him again, "I doubt that most of them would trust any white man. I know that I would not. However, I can only say what I mean. I will deliver you to your destination one way or another. I prefer to do it peacefully and without force, but if force is necessary, I will use it to the extent needed. I had nothing to do with your capture, and it is not in my power to set you free. If you do not cause me any trouble, you will not be abused on board this ship. I will punish any of my men who disobey that order. Now tell them all of this." Once again Abdulla stared at the captain, then turned to the other slaves and began to speak. After several seconds; he switched to another dialect and seemed to repeat the same message. As he spoke, many turned their eyes toward the captain, showing confusion and hate for the people who captured and mistreated them. There was no doubt of their open hostility. Wilson waited, giving time for the message to sink in.

Abdulla stopped speaking and an undertone of muttering ensued, in perhaps a dozen different dialects. Although most of the slaves were in rags, some more than half naked, there was a noticeable difference in some of their appearances. Some were dressed in remnants of animal skins and others were wearing clothes made of some kind of rough cloth. Their hair styles were noticeably different, too. It was obvious that they came from different tribes.

After several minutes of talking among themselves, the tall black man took the hand of one of the women and one of the younger boys and moved toward the gangplank. The woman, in turn, reached and took the hand of a tall, thin girl, who looked to be about ten. It was as if the tall man had broken the ice. He moved aboard with, what Wilson assumed was his family, and the rest bowed their heads and followed. There were still six or eight young men tightly bound in chains. They resisted, refusing to go aboard voluntarily. Wilson cursed silently under his breath and ordered his men to separate those who continued to resist and to leave them standing on the dock. He ordered Abdulla to remain behind also.

Wilson turned to his men and told them to move the slaves aboard.

As the slaves boarded the ship, he observed each individual closely. A few resisted strongly and would have to be physically carried aboard. He made a mental note which ones would have to be forcibly restrained, not only by locking them in the hold of the ship, but would have to be kept in irons as well. Many of the slaves had already tasted the whip and would not hesitate to slit your throat or disembowel you with a spear if the opportunity presented itself.

Wilson counted to make sure of the numbers. There were 85 men and 19 women and young girls between the ages of 12 and 15, as well as 6 children. Some of the men seemed to be protecting the various women. Wilson looked each one over as the group came aboard, watched how one would interact with the others around him. And above all, Wilson watched their eyes. You can tell a lot about people, even savages, by watching their eyes. Wilson searched for one who might speak some English or might be a leader, one he could converse with.

While the rest of the slaves boarded, Wilson studied Abdulla more closely. Abdulla stood out from the rest of the lot. Short in height, he carried himself differently. And he seemed to be educated. The captain was convinced of his first impression. Surely, Abdulla must be an Arab, he thought. Wilson spoke to him again. "You are not of this group are you?"

"No. At one time I was a merchant and lived in a small village in the area you call Southern Africa. I am a Moslem and most of the blacks are not of any particular religion. They were captured. I was sold into slavery by one of my enemies. Before I opened my little shop, he was the only one in the village who sold cloth and spices and other goods. When my shop began to flourish, he didn't like the competition so he had some of his men kidnap me during the night and take me to the slave traders.

"It is a way to permanently eliminate your competition without killing someone. In our religion, a Moslem cannot draw the blood of another Moslem unless that one has drawn blood first. The Holy Koran forbids it."

Joshua asked, "Has no one come looking for you?"

Abdulla replied, "I have no family. I brought my goods south from the area known as Persia. It was my hope to establish a good business and return to marry a girl from my home town. By this time she probably thinks I am dead, so there is no one who would miss me."

Pointing to the remaining young men, Wilson spoke again. "I would like you to help me with these slaves. I must take them where they are supposed to go, but I do not like the job. I will provide them with as much food and clothing as I can and make their journey as comfortable as possible, and they will not be mistreated. However, I will not permit them to disrupt the other passengers or cause trouble. Tell them that I do not have the time or men to guard them all the time; that if one of them causes trouble I will throw him overboard to the sharks."

Abdulla raised his eyebrows, and with a smile, turned to the group of young men held together in chains. He spoke in a foreign dialect for several minutes. He paused and the blacks went silent. Abdulla turned to Captain Wilson. "I think they understood that pretty well. I don't think they will give you much trouble."

After the main bunch of salves were on board, Wilson turned to his men and told them to move the remaining slaves on board. If they resisted his men were to use what force was necessary but not to abuse them more than was necessary to get them aboard.

Once again, he turned to Abdulla. "Who is the big man that protected the woman?"

"I'm not sure; he just came in yesterday with the woman and most of the children. He carries himself with great pride and I would guess he is some sort of chief or sub-chief, for most of the other men listen to him. He is more intelligent than the others and I suspect he understands enough English to know what you are saying. For his own reasons, I guess he prefers to remain silent. I heard one of the others address him as Writable bey or something like that. Bey in Arabic means chief or ruler."

Several days out of Casablanca, the Capitan had gone down into the hold where the slaves were being held. The shabbiness of their clothes and particularly the women and girls, distressed him. They had barely enough clothing to hide their private parts. There was nothing but straw on the floors, and in one corner of the hold, there were a dozen buckets of human waste. These conditions were wretched and Wilson was unhappy about it. It was all he could do to keep form gagging from the awful stench. He came up to the deck for fresh air and called Abdulla over to him. "Bring the tall, black one out of the hold."

The brightness of the sun temporarily blinded the man when he arrived up on deck.

The captain spoke. "Abdulla, I am most unhappy that these people have to stay in those conditions. I am sorry that I have contributed to their misery. If they will cooperate, I will try to improve their conditions. Tell this man, but first, ask him what his name is."

Abdulla turned to the tall black man and hesitated. Just as he started to relay the captain's message, the black man spoke, "I understand your tongue. I can speak English."

Surprise showed on the captain's face, but Abdulla only smiled. In the days since boarding, he had learned the black man could indeed speak English. But Abdulla would not have revealed it if the man had not spoken up himself. For whatever reason, the black man had maintained his silence. It was his own business, and Abdulla would not give him away.

Wilson asked the man, "Why have you not spoken before?"

"There was no need to. No one had spoken to me that deserved an answer. Besides, one can learn more of what is planned if others think we are all a bunch of ignorant savages that can't understand what they are saying."

"What are you called?"

The man stood straight and tall. "I am Witambe Morandu. In my country I was a warrior and sub-chief of my tribe. Another tribe that we have fought for generations attacked my village while most of our warriors were away on a hunting trip. Our enemies have been capturing blacks for the slave trade for a long time. We had nothing but spears and knives. The slavers had given our enemies sticks that spout fire, what you call guns, and they overran our village. They killed my wife and two small children for there was no demand for little ones. I was struck on the head and when I came to, we were chained together. The woman is a sister to my wife and the little boy and girl, as well as some of the other children, are also from my village."

The captain listened and thought for a few moments. "Witambe, I am sorry that you have suffered at the hands of your people and mine. I had nothing to do with your capture and the killing of your wife and children. I want to help you and the rest of your people as much as I can. The conditions you are living in are horrible, and unless we do something, all of your people will be sick and suffering from sores before we reach our destination.

"We gave the indentured servants the run of the deck, and they are in much better condition than your people. If I let your people out on deck, can you control them and keep them from jumping overboard? We are far out at sea and they could never survive nor make it back to their homes. That is impossible."

Witambe nodded. "There are perhaps twenty men from my village, and maybe twenty more of the men from other tribes that know me and respect me. We could form a guard, and I think the majority of the others would follow our lead. I do not know about the younger men that are in irons. They may listen to us. We can try."

"Good. Here's what I propose. We will bring you up on deck in groups of about thirty or forty. I will have my men screen off an area on the starboard side of the deck and give you buckets. You can dip water out of the sea and wash off your bodies. I'm sorry I do not have enough fresh water to permit you to bathe, but this is better than nothing." We have some old clothes on board. I will turn them over to you to see that those who are worst in need get them. There will not be enough to go around, so some will be disgruntled. You will have to deal with them.

"You are to bring the buckets of waste up to the deck and empty them over the side. Take fresh water back to the hold and clean up as much of the mess as you can. Each group will be permitted to stay on deck one hour each day. Then another group will be brought up. You can tell your people that this is a privilege, and if any cause trouble, or attempt to jump over-board, it will be suspended and they will all have to remain in the hold for the rest of the trip. Be sure to remind them that we are far at sea and if they do go overboard, they will drown or the sharks will get them. We have a few blankets and some extra sail cloth. I will give you what we can part with. These are to be given to the women and children."

Witambe studied the captain, looked at Abdulla, and nodded in understanding, but said nothing.

The captain continued, "Abdulla told me that a number of your people are not used to the food and some are sick because it is not what they are used to. If you will tell me what they eat, I will make a stop in the Azores, which is an island we will pass, to pick up something that they are used to eating. That should lessen the number of cases of dysentery also. Do I have your word that you will cooperate with me?"

Witambe looked straight at the captain. "You are a white man. Will you take the word of a black man?"

The captain shifted his weight as the ship rolled in tune with the ocean's cadence.

"Witambe, evil is not limited to a man's color. Nor is honor restricted to the white people. You have evil men in your race who hunt their own countrymen down to be sold as slaves. You would not have been made a sub-chief if you were not an honorable man. Furthermore, as a chief it is your duty and responsibility to help your people and protect them from harm to the best of your ability. Am I wrong?"

Witambe's eyes narrowed. It was as if he stared directly into the captain's heart.

Finally he answered, "You are right captain. You are also a wise man. I will cooperate with you as will all of the people from my village. I will also do as much as I can to convince the others to take advantage of your offer."

As the captain turned to go, he had one more question. "Where did you learn to speak English? You speak it almost as good as I do."

"An English missionary came to our village when I was a little boy. My father, who was the chief, welcomed him. He thought it would be good for our people to learn something about the outside world. This missionary taught us to read and speak English. I did not do well in the writing, but I can write my name. He also taught us about your Jesus, who was full of love and kindness. We believed him and for many years he was one of our most revered people. Your God must have deserted him though, for the slavers killed him when he tried to stop them from murdering my people."

For the rest of the journey, Witambe and Abdulla moved

groups of slaves to the deck each day. They seemed to be biding their time, and the captain stayed vigilant.

True to his word, Wilson obtained more clothing and blankets in the Azores. Now, almost every one of the slaves was decently clothed, and there was one blanket for every two people. This helped them fend off the cold.

Witambe was definitely a leader. Once, when one of the young men became unruly, a swift command, from Witambe to one of his men, brought the incident to a sharp end. Four or five of them attempted to escape when they were in Boston. Also, true to his word, Wilson made all of them stay in the hold until they left the harbor. The rest of the slaves beat the ones who tried to escape and after that, there was no more trouble.

* * * * *

They reached Boston harbor after 19 days at sea. Wilson unloaded his cargo, most of the indentured servants and 25 of the slaves were off loaded also. This left a half dozen of the indentured people; some 55 men and about half of the women and children. Wilson cleared the port in Boston as quickly as possible. The rest of the slaves were bound for the Carolinas and he was anxious to get them off his ship as soon as possible.

The rest of the voyage had been without incident, and on this day, Captain Wilson stood in the wheelhouse with the helmsman. As he frequently did, he glanced at the compass to make sure the helmsman was holding a true course, south by southwest. A good wind sprang up, and if it held, they would make port in Charlestown by day-break rather than at noon as he had thought earlier.

Today was Tuesday, giving the slave auctioneers three days to clean up the slaves, feed them, clothe them and dress any sores or wounds. A sick slave or one who appeared to be half-starved did not bring a good price at the slave auction. The auction would be held Saturday morning and there would be a large gathering of rich plantation owners. The harvest would be coming up in a few months and the plantation owners would be looking for more workers. They would train the new slaves and get them accustomed to their new surroundings and establish a work routine. Not being familiar with the work on a farm they would be of only limited help with the current harvest, but they would be ready by planting time next spring. In the meantime they would be used to clear new ground during the winter and get it ready for planting in the spring.

Wilson had lived on a farm as a boy, and he knew the back-breaking work that lay ahead for the slaves. Silently, he wondered how many would submit to slavery and work for their masters and how many would attempt to run away and be killed.

There were many good masters who treated their slaves well and provided them with a decent place to live, but there were others who were cruel and often mistreated their slaves. Anyone who was bought at the slave market by one of the latter would live a miserable life. No matter, it was all out of his hands. It was the way of the times, and he couldn't change things, no matter how much he would have liked to.

CHAPTER TWO

The captain tore his thoughts away from the slaves and glanced down at the strange man at the ship's rail. Although a white man, years in the sun and weather had turned him a light brown. Standing just over six feet tall, the broad-shouldered man peered out into the vast sea. When he stood this way, staring at the sea, it was as if he was looking back, to another time, another place. Wilson judged him to be in his late twenties, but his expression indicated he might be older. Yes, either he was older, or the things he had seen and been through had aged him beyond his years.

Wilson knew the signs. He could tell his passenger was troubled. He had spoken to the man, who was a paid passenger only briefly. Should he approach him or not? Would it be rude to intrude on the man's thoughts? The reclusive man had mingled little with the other passengers during the voyage, and he gave the distinct impression that he wanted solitude. Wilson let go of the thought for now. Let him have his peace.

The captain turned to the helmsman. "I see Mr. Stanislaski is taking in the fresh air today, as usual."

"Yes sir. He spends almost all his time on deck, looking at the sea. I doubt he even sees the waves. I think his mind is many miles from here."

The helmsman changed his focus slightly upward,

toward the sky, and then continued with a question, "Where does he come from? I've seen a few people dressed like that before. Most of them were from Russia, but he doesn't seem like a Russian."

Wilson acknowledged that the troubled man, who had come aboard in Hamburg, was dressed a little strange for this part of the world. He wore black, shiny boots that always appeared to be recently polished; his trousers were tied at the waist with a combination leather belt and sash. The pant legs sort of ballooned and were tucked into the top of his boots. His white shirt, with billowy sleeves, was buttoned tightly at the wrist. Over the shirt he normally wore a black, sleeveless, sheepskin vest, but heavy-threaded, like a coat. On this day, with the weather warmed slightly, the vest was off and lying nearby. The entire apparel was not the kind of attire that you usual see people from Europe wearing.

In the earlier conversation, the Capitan had noted that while most Polish people's eyes were black, this man's eyes were light, sort of a blue-grey, an indication that perhaps some of his ancestors might have come from the Scandinavian countries. He was not unattractive, yet his sour expression made him appear so.

Wilson replied to the helmsman. "He isn't Russian, and I would be careful that you don't call him one. He is a Polish Cossack. They are ferocious soldiers, more at home on a horse than on their feet. Notice the slim waist and broad shoulders. Their legs are strong for grasping the sides of the horse, but their feet are not used to walking. Notice that from the waist up he looks very strong and well developed. I would guess he is plenty tough and not a man you would want to trifle with."

"He came aboard in Hamburg, didn't he?"

"Yes," Wilson said thoughtfully, trying to remember everyone on board, along with their particular details. "I thought he would get off in Boston, but evidently he didn't like it there. After going ashore for a few hours, he came back aboard and asked where we were going next. I told him Charlestown in the Carolinas. He wanted to book passage. When I asked him how he liked Boston, all he said was, 'Too many people. I'm used to forests and farms and open plains."

"I also ventured to ask him if he had relatives in Boston or the Carolinas. He said, 'No relatives at all. All are dead in Poland.' I didn't want to ask any more questions. He seemed not to want to talk about his past or his family. I thought it best to leave it be."

After a few minutes in thoughtful silence, Wilson spoke again, "Did you see the scar on the left cheekbone? That's a saber scar. I've seen those before on Calvary troops who have been in hand-to- hand combat. One of those military sabers can slice you up pretty good. From the look in his eyes, and the sad expression on his face, I would say he has seen his share of hell."

"Do you think he's a deserter, or on the run from the law?" The helmsman shifted the wheel slightly southwest, taking advantage of the wind.

"Maybe. From what I hear about the wars Poland has been fighting, they've been fighting on all fronts for the last 20 years. They are hemmed in by Russia on the east; Hungary to the south; and Germany and Prussia on the west. And all of these countries want a part of Poland. A couple years ago Russia attacked and took over part of Poland including their capital of Warsaw. Poland rallied and drove the Russians out of Warsaw, but they suffered heavy losses. And early last year, Prussia attacked from one side and Russia from the other. They overran the Polish Army and all but annihilated them. Then Poland was divided between the two, wiping a whole country off the map. I suspect he is one of the few Polish soldiers who escaped." Wilson rubbed his tired eyes. "All of this is just guessing though. It is a subject I don't want to ask him about."

The morning breeze caused the waves to playfully smack the bow. Stanislaski, who stood at the railing of the ship, moved in time with the ship's dance; his muscles expanded and pressed tightly against the sleeves of his shirt.

Wilson thought back to an earlier conversation he'd had with the Polish fighter, one day during their long journey at sea, before reaching Boston. The indentured people were usually kept on the forward part of the deck, and the black people on the aft section. At various times Stanislaski had walked briefly about, between the black slaves and the indentured. He seemed only slightly interested in the two groups on deck and was more interested in staring out to sea. On this particular sunny day, seeing him standing at the rail, the captain approached cautiously so as not to intrude too harshly on his thoughts.

Talking with the Polish soldier was somewhat difficult as he was very close mouthed and while he was civil, he hadn't encouraged much conversation. After exchanging pleasantries about the weather, the captain finally spoke, "These (motioning towards the slaves) people have really had it rough. I feel sorry for them but I don't know anything more I can do for them than what I have."

The soldier said, "Yes. For people like that life is a struggle from birth to death, with very little pleasure in between." "It is pretty much the same no matter where you go. In my country they would have been called serfs or peasants. Whatever they are called, their status is almost always the same. Body and soul they belong to the landowner on whose land they live and work. He might have a title such as a Duke, a Prince, or just a landholder. Whatever his position he has life or death control over those who are in his domain. The names and faces change, but the situation is about the same."

The captain spoke, "So, it is this way in your country?"

"The way it was. There is no more Poland, but those who now control my country treat my people much as these people are treated. If it were not for the fact that they are needed to work the land, they would probably have killed all the men, and taken the women into their houses as maids and concubines. Slaves are not new. They are a part of almost all societies."

Wilson asked, "I noticed that you signed the log book as Andraui Vladimir Stanislaski. Do you prefer to be called Andraui or Vladimir?"

"In English it would be Andrew, I believe."

"Were you of the landed gentry in Poland?"

Andraui laughed. "No. My father was a peasant, but through hard work he gained the respect of our master and was given the position of overseer at one of the bigger farms. He also looked after a large tract of land that the owner held. It was a tract of virgin forest and was heavily populated with stag and other game. Only the landholder and his friends were permitted to hunt in the forest. My father was well liked by the owner who was a fairly generous man. He allowed us to hunt and we lived better than most, for we always had plenty of food."

After a short pause, Andraui continued, "The owner took better care of his people than most other owners, and as a result, we defended his holdings from raids by robbers and poachers. He permitted some of us to receive some schooling and training in the art of fighting. The better fighters we were, the better we could protect his holdings. We did not know that this same training would one day be useful in defending our homeland as well."

Now that he was talking, it seemed to the captain the

man could not stop. It was as if he needed to tell someone, to try to get it straight in his own mind.

"I was 22 when we were first called up to fight in the Army. That was in '86. We had been under attack many times, but this time, we had many killed and wounded. They needed replacements. Since I had received some training with a sword and battle-axe, and was a good horseman, I was given the rank equivalent to a sergeant and told to take a group of young men from our area to the battle field. The first few battles we were lucky. The troops we encountered were no better trained than we were and we won back much of the land the Russians had taken.

"When the Russians withdrew, we thought we had beaten them and our commander transferred most of us to the southern front to meet an invasion from Hungary. Again we were victorious and the Hungarians withdrew. But while we were in the South, the Russians attacked again and took Warsaw, our capitol. Many of our soldiers were killed and our army was routed. Before we could regroup and gather replacements, Prussia attacked from the west, catching us from behind. We were sandwiched in between the two armies. Both had well-trained and well- equipped men and for the most part; we were farmers and cattle herders."

"Most of our regular troops had been killed in the battle for Warsaw. We were no match for them and they proceeded to kill as many of us as they could. Those captured were given a choice, to either swear allegiance to the captors or be executed. Of the 800 men in my troop who started out with me to recapture Warsaw in '88, only 93 were left, and many of them were wounded. Neither the thought of swearing allegiance to Russia or Prussia, nor of being executed appealed to us. So, when we saw we could fight no more and that to stay would be suicide, we decided to flee. We had no choice, can you see?"

Andraui looked forlornly out to sea.

Wilson stared out to sea alongside the man and silently nodded in understanding.

"There was no chance to regroup and form another army strong enough to stand against both the Prussians and Russians, and there was no place on Polish soil that was safe for a former soldier. To be caught was sure death. That is when I decided to come to North America. I had heard that there was freedom and opportunity here. But I do not want to work on another man's farm. If I work the land, I want it to be mine. These poor people will probably never have that opportunity, no more than the serfs who worked on the farm where I was born. But I have heard that a free man may acquire land in America and have no one to rule over him. Is this true?"

Wilson had been so engrossed in listening to the soldier talk that he was caught off guard by the question. He quickly recovered and replied, "Yes, that is true. And you are probably right about these people, motioning towards the black slaves. They are little more than cattle, however, most people in America are free to choose their own path. There is plenty of land for the settling and a free man doesn't have to answer to anyone, as long as he doesn't do harm to another or attempt to take something that belongs to someone else. If you really want a chance to start over, this will be a good place to begin."

Andraui lapsed into silence again, and from that day forward, the two men would have no further conversation on the topic.

* * * * *

Now, as they neared their final destination in Charlestown, Wilson watched Stanislaski, as he leaned against the rail.

The only time the man seemed to pay attention to anything else was when the indentured people came on deck. Wilson recalled on a couple of occasions, Stanislaski had spoken to one slender English girl, who, while one of the groups of bonded people, seemed to stand apart. She was different. It seemed she had some education and better breeding. She was a pretty girl, quite buxom under her torn woolen dress. Even its shabbiness could not hide her trim figure. Wilson guessed she stood about 5 feet 6 or 7 inches tall and weighed about 110 pounds. She had a slim waist and long, shapely legs that were exposed below the hem of her dress. All of the men paid close attention to her and some had made overt passes and whispered innuendos to her, but she ignored them and kept to herself. It was clear she was not one of those from the slums of London. Perhaps most striking about her was her hair. It was reddish, blonde and hung down to her waist. She had managed to keep it neat and clean in spite of the shortage of sanitary facilities. She usually kept it plaited and rolled on the back of her head, but when she was on deck she would undo it and let it blow in the wind. On a sunny day, it shimmered, and with the wind blowing it freely, she was a pretty picture.

Stanislaski had free run of the deck at all times, and Captain Wilson noticed that he always seemed to be on deck when the girl came up. It was one of the few times he seemed to take any interest in anything.

Although he had seen her on the deck before and had spoken to her several times, they had not talked very much. But it seemed she too looked forward to their brief talks.

Andraui was much intrigued by the young woman and today, as they sailed closer to Charlestown, she looked lovely, standing at the railing, her hair gently blowing in the wind As he moved closer and spoke to her, he greeted her with "It is a beautiful day, isn't it?

She turned slightly so as to see him better, answered pleasantly and favored him with a small smile. "It is indeed. One of the best we have had." Her eyes were a light grey and had little flecks of light in them. "It is nice, but I will be glad to get off this ship tomorrow. We have been at sea for 23 days since I boarded in London, I can't wait to have a good bath and some clean garments." Her voice was like music, and as she spoke she reminded him of the girls who lived in the castle at home. They were the daughters of the landlord and had been taught how to greet people and make them feel important. This girl had that ability.

In just a few minutes they were in a lively conversation. It was a comfortable conversation, as if the usual reticence that existed between men and women did not apply to them. Perhaps it was due to the unusual circumstances they found themselves in. There was no coyness about her and she seemed perfectly comfortable talking with a stranger

Andraui didn't speak for several seconds, and then he asked, "You will be staying in this Charlestown then?"

"Yes. My indenture is with a large plantation owner here. He wants me to tutor his three children."

"Are you a teacher?"

"Yes and no. I received my teaching certificate but could not find a teaching job. Most of the teachers are men and I could not find a teacher position."

Andraui looked puzzled. He probed further. "I don't mean to pry, but if you are a teacher, what are you doing with these prisoners and indentured people?"

"Well, it's kind of a long story. When I couldn't get a job as a teacher, I began to seek any other employment I could find. While working in a ladies clothing store, a fancy lady came in and bought several expensive dresses, lots of pretty clothes. As I was helping her dress, she mentioned that she and her husband were looking for a tutor for their little girl. I told her I had my teaching certificate but had not been able to find a position. She insisted right then that I come home to meet her husband and daughter. We left the store and went to this big house. It must have had thirty rooms. It was about the biggest thing I had ever seen. When the husband looked at me I felt uneasy, as if he was undressing me." She appeared embarrassed and almost stopped talking.

In a few seconds, she continued, as if wanting to get it out in the open and for some reason she did not want this man thinking badly of her. She probably had not had anyone to talk to about whatever it was she had been through and seemed to need to talk about it for her own benefit. "The husband appeared enthusiastic that they had found someone who could help the little girl learn to read and cipher. They hired me on the spot at a wage I couldn't refuse. "I enjoyed working with the little girl. She was a sweet child and very intelligent. We got along well together."

Again she hesitated, as if wondering whether she should tell her story to a stranger. She wasn't sure how he might judge her and for some reason, she didn't want him to think badly of her. Then, as if deciding it didn't matter for she probably would never see him again after they docked tomorrow, she plunged ahead with her story.

"I often found the husband staring at me and it made me nervous. I always made sure we were never alone together, and although he never made a movement towards me, I still felt strange around him. I worked there for almost six months and he did not bother me. Then one day he came home in the middle of the afternoon while his wife was away shopping. The little girl was taking her afternoon nap and the husband called me to come to the library. When I walked into the room he closed the door and began to put his hands on me. I resisted as politely as I could for several minutes and tried to get away from him. Finally he cornered me against the couch and pushed me back on it. Before I could recover and get up, he was on top of me. He was trying to put his hand underneath my petticoats and was squeezing me everywhere. I began to fight him, pushing him as hard as I could. I raised my knee up and got it between me and him and pushed hard. He fell off the couch and hit his head on the corner of the table. I ran from the library and to my room. I packed and was ready to leave when the wife returned. She insisted upon knowing why I was leaving without a notice. I would not give her an answer, except to say that I had a sick relative and must leave immediately. About this time her husband came out of the library wiping blood from his forehead. He made up a story for his wife that he had been missing some jewelry and other valuables around the house. He had come home early to confront me and caught me with one of his wife's rings in my pocket. He told me to return it and he would not press charges. He said I hit him with a book-end."

She paused to catch her breath.

"I tried to explain to his wife, but by then there wasn't anyone who would believe me. Perhaps if I had told her right off, she might have believed me. Anyway, when I couldn't produce the ring, they charged me before a Magistrate and he sentenced me to three years in prison. The only way I could avoid prison was to bond myself for four years, three years for the prison term and another year to pay for my transportation to the new world."

Andraui was silent for a several minutes, staring into the sea, taking it all in. Then he asked, "Who are you indentured to?"

"A man named Thomas Heyward. He has a large plantation someplace in the Carolinas. Someone is supposed to meet me at the Heyward House in Charlestown. They say it belongs to Mr. Heyward. I have instructions to register there and wait until someone comes for me."

"If I stay in the area, will I be allowed to call on you?"

"I think that will depend upon Mr. Heyward. I think under the terms of the bond, I can have some private life and my own friends, but I'm not sure how this works."

"I saw on the ships log you were registered as Catherine York. Will you be using that name here also? They won't require you to change names will they?"

"Yes, I will be using my own name. They don't require you to change your name. What makes you ask that?"

"Well, in Poland a family often adopts the last name of the lord of the manor. It is sort of a means of identifying who works for whom, or more correctly, who belongs to whom."

Catherine looked at him and caught the sadness in his eyes.

She turned to him. "I do not think it would be wise for you to come to see me. Not that I object to seeing you. It is only that with my indenture I will be at the mercy of my bond-holder and I do not know where he will take me or exactly what I will be doing. I am supposed to be a school teacher at a new school in a new town he is building somewhere in the interior of Carolina."

She turned to him. "I could not offer you any hope for anything other than friendship."

Andraui smiled. "Well, at least I would have one friend in this new country, for I know of no other than you."

Catherine thought it is a nice smile, and said, "As you wish."

Other than to wave goodbye to her the next morning as she left the ship, this was the last time Andraui would speak to Catherine for some time. Much would transpire before they were to meet again.

27

CHAPTER THREE

The ship docked early in Charlestown and deckhands began to off-load the cargo. The indentured people off-loaded first, then the balance of the cargo. The slaves were the last to come off the ship. The auctioneers came in large wagons with high sides, heavy and stoutly built, much like the Conestoga wagons common to the Pennsylvania area. Wilson had seen these type wagons before at the docks in Philadelphia. It took at least three teams of mules or two or three teams of oxen to pull them once they were loaded. The slaves were loaded into the wagons and moved to a large warehouse further down the dock.

Captain Wilson was on the dock and watched them as they left the ship. There was a noticeable difference in their eyes as they left. There was a hint of friendliness in some of them as if they wanted to thank him for the kindness he had shown them, but they didn't know how.

The last to leave were Abdulla and Witambe. Staying close to Witambe was the woman and the children. Witambe came forward and placed his hand on the shoulder of the captain. He looked him straight in the face and spoke, the words coming from deep inside him.

"You have been a kind man and have helped my people even though you did not have to do so. I may never see you again, but I will carry your face with me, and I will try to remember that there are some good people in all races. Maybe I can pass such a kind thing onto someone else sometime, some place."

Wilson was moved. He followed Witambe's example and placed his hand on the big black man's shoulder. "Witambe, this is an amazing country and there are many good men. I will pray to my God that you are bought by one of them. If you are lucky enough to be sold to the right man, you may yet find some happiness in this new land. May God be with you!"

To Abdulla, he said, "I have no doubt that you will find a new life here. You are a man with great mental capacity and your people have endured and survived more than two thousand years, under all sorts of conquerors. You, too, will survive; and I would guess you will somehow manage to obtain your freedom. If you do, you will probably become wealthy here. Always be careful who you befriend and who you do business with. Good luck to you!"

The captain stood for a long time on the deck watching them disappear in the distance. Little did he suspect then that he was to play yet another part in the lives of these slaves.

The Capitan was glad to be docked and have the slaves off his ship. This had been a hard voyage for him and his crew. As soon as the ship was cleaned and fully battened down, he was going to get roaring drunk, washing away all the unpleasantness. He vowed that this would be the last time he'd have slaves on his ship. When he arrived back in London there would be a serious talk with the ship's owners. If they didn't see it his way, he would quit. He had been on the sea too long now anyway.

He spent the rest of the morning seeing to cleaning of his ship and the unloading of the cargo, and his men. Shortly after the noon meal, he sauntered down the docks and turned left into one of the streets leading into town. He passed a number of pubs that looked like dens of inequity and moved on up the street. The bars near the docks in every port in the world always attracted the worst kind of people. Thieves, pick-pockets and murderers seemed to always hang out in the dumpiest of places. They would drug you and roll you for your poke if you gave them half an opportunity.

The street slanted up hill and the dock area gradually fell behind him. The shops appeared much cleaner and the people more civilized. He spotted a tavern that looked a cut above the rest and turned in that direction. Over the door was a sign which read, "London Pub." Wilson had been here a few times before. It was run by an Englishman by the name of "English Charlie". English Charlie had also been a sailor. He had lost a leg and now walked on a peg. Wilson suspected that the shop owner may have been on one of the pirate ships that plied the waters between America and Europe. Many would raid, rob and pillage along coasts, or take a fat merchant ship like his if they could. Then before the Navy could catch them, they would sail for the ports along the Caribbean or over into the Mediterranean. But that was none of his business; that was then and this was now. The man served a good stout of ale and didn't water it down. Neither did he allow the riff-raff and hangers-on to clutter up his tavern. It was a good place to have a drink and chat with some of his own kind. You could also get all of the information about what was happening in a town or village from a tavern. Everything that went on in a town was chewed over very well by men having a friendly drink.

Wilson stepped onto the boardwalk and was met by a wobbly individual being propelled through the door. English Charlie had the drunk by the belt and the back of his collar and literally threw him into the street. Without a word, the barman turned back into the tavern. Wilson straightened his cap, walked up to the bar.

"What'll ye have?" the bartender asked.

"Two fingers of good Irish Whiskey."

At hearing Wilson's voice, English Charlie came out of the corner and clapped his hand on the bar. "For a man who drinks Irish whiskey, the first drink is on the house."

Then he turned and held out his hand. "Good to see you again, Joshua. They told me you docked this morning. How was the trip?"

"Not too bad Charlie. We had a safe enough voyage. No trouble on the sea, but I brought over a load of slaves and I need to wash some of the stench off my soul."

"I know you don't believe in slavery Joshua, but they are just like any other cargo. You haul what you have to, to make a profit on your ship."

"Maybe so Charlie, but these people have enough misery without me adding to it. I know that if I didn't bring them, someone else would have. Still, I don't have to like it."

"Well drink up, and later I'll have my old woman fix us up a hearty meal. After all these months at sea and eating galley food, this will make you feel better."

The captain spent a pleasant evening with his friend and after a good meal; they swapped sea stories until around midnight. Finally, Joshua said goodbye and headed back to the ship. After all these years, he was unable to sleep any place except in his own bunk in his own cabin.

Wilson checked with the ship's watch to make sure nothing was amiss, and made his way to his cabin. The several tankards of ale were taking affect, and he looked forward to a good night's sleep. Strange as it might seem, his last thoughts before falling asleep were of the slaves and what would happen to them.

31

CHAPTER FOUR

C aptain Wilson had been in Charlestown port three days now, and today was the auction. He would set sail by Monday. The loading of his new cargo had progressed smoothly, and he saw no reason to hang around the ship. His crew knew what to do and would take care of everything just fine.

He was restless and couldn't get the slaves out of his mind. Finally, he left the ship and walked to the warehouse where the auction preparations were underway. He generally did not attend these boorish events, but today, he was drawn there nonetheless. Auctions attracted a lot of people, some to bid and others just to watch. A sizable crowd began to gather. Wilson had no interest in sitting down front with the bidders, and he selected a place against the wall of the warehouse. He sat on top of a wooden keg.

In addition to the slaves who had arrived aboard his ship, there were a number of others. The auctioneers knew that a man covered with scars indicated an unruly person and few would bid for him. Also, there would be little bidding for one that appeared sick. Mainly for these reasons, rather than for humanitarian reasons, the slaves were generally well treated by the auctioneers. Wilson recognized the group from his ship. They were cleaned up and provided with half-decent clothing. Those who had bruises or other injuries, or who had been sick, had been treated once they left the ship. They appeared to have bounced back to reasonably good health.

Wilson watched as the individuals came out for observation. The young bucks, defiant, were brought out first. Bidding went slowly for them and it was no wonder. Most of the plantation owners did not want slaves that would be troublesome. Spending time chasing run-away slaves, or having to use the whip on them were undesirable activities. Contrary to what many people thought, most owners were not cruel. They sought good, strong workers to do the back-breaking jobs found on their farms. Clearing the forests and getting land ready for planting was not a task for the weak bodied. Runaway slaves, or those who had to be locked away most of the time, did the owners little good.

The auctioneers were shrewd businessmen. They brought out the less impressive slaves first. Most would be sold before the bigger, stronger slaves were put on the block. If the best ones had been offered first, the less desirable slaves may likely not be bid on at all, or at the very least, would not bring a good price.

Witambe and his followers were brought out last. They huddled together as much as they could on one side of the platform. By this time, many of the owners had filled their desired number of slaves and bidding lagged. When Witambe came forward, though, the owners perked up and bidding became brisk again.

A man by the name of Charles Pickney made the high bid of $2500 for Witambe. When they attempted to separate him from the others he refused to go. The auctioneers brought out the leg irons and the rest of Witambe's men moved forward. The slaves didn't know what was happening and felt threatened again. Fear and anger showed on their faces. It appeared they were ready to fight if something wasn't done.

Wilson could see the trouble brewing. He had to do something, and do it quickly. He came down off the keg and moved toward the auctioneers' block.

"Just a minute! May I speak?"

The auctioneer in charge turned to him. "Who are you? What business do you have interfering with this auction?" he demanded.

Wilson walked toward the platform on which the slaves and the auctioneer stood.

"I am Joshua Wilson, the captain of the ship that transported these people from Africa to Charlestown. This man is a sub-chief and this woman, these children, and those 16 men are all that are left of his tribe. The rest were all killed by slave traders. If you separate them, you will never have any peace. They'll keep running away and trying to join back together until you kill them all. I have seen the whip used on them. They won't bow to the whip and harsh treatment. But if you can keep them together and treat them decently, I believe you will have a good work force that will not give you unnecessary trouble."

Then he turned to the bidders. "Is there any owner here who could use this many people?"

A low mumbling scattered across the crowd, but no one spoke up. The auctioneer sneered, "Mind your own business. We know how to handle slaves and can take care of any trouble-makers."

Wilson spoke up again. "I'm sure you can, but who wants a slave that has to be kept in leg irons all the time, or is laid up because the skin has been peeled off his back? You want workers, not people who you have to be chasing all the time."

The plantation owners grunted in agreement, but no

one came forward to accept Wilson's plea. Suddenly, from the crowd, a man arose and asked the auctioneer, "Do you have a price on the lot, sir? Including the children?"

The auctioneer knew that, except for the two teenage girls, the other children where too small to bring a big price. Quickly, he calculated the price of each man at $2,000 per head and the women and girls at $1,500 each. He looked at the man who had spoken and said, "With the exception of this big fellow, who has already been sold, I would take $2,000 a piece for the remaining 16 men; $1,500 each for the 7 women and 2 girls over 13 years old. I will take $750 each for the 6 children, just to cover the cost of their food and transportation. That is a total of $51,000."

The man who had asked for the total price spoke again. "If Mr. Pickney will sell me the big man for the $2,500 he has just bought, I will give you $1,500 for each of the men; $I,000 for the women and older girls, and you will throw in the children with the rest or you will be stuck with them to have to feed and look after."

The man who bought Witambe rose and spoke for the first time. "Sir, I understand what you are trying to do and I admire your purpose. I will release the big man to you if the auctioneer accepts your offer." He then paused for a moment, then added, "And if he does not accept your offer, there will be no more bidding here today and he will have some thirty slaves to feed and house until the next auction."

Turning to the other owners in the crowd, he said, "Am I not right gentlemen?"

They all answered in unison, "You are right. The auction is over for today."

The auctioneer knew he had no choice. He couldn't afford to hold the slaves until another auction. And after all, at these prices he would still make a small profit, albeit not as much as he had expected.

Still, he thought to dicker more, thus he complained, "At this price I will lose money. I must have at least $1800 for the men and $1400 for the women."

The tall man put on his hat as if to leave. "My final offer is $1600 for the men and $1200 for the women. Take it or leave it."

The auctioneer looked at the only man left standing in the warehouse and knew he was beat. "You win sir. The slaves are yours. In what name shall I register them?'

"The name is Thomas Sumter. They will be going to a place called Sumterville."

Witambe looked at Captain Wilson, and for the first time spoke. "Again you have helped my people by keeping us together. We will work for this man and as long as he does not mistreat us, we will cause him no trouble."

Thomas Sumter heard the exchange between Witambe and the captain. He was surprised at the big black man's use of the English language. He then looked at Wilson and said, "Sir, I thank you for speaking up for these people. I am building a new town inland and shall provide them with good food, good accommodations, and they shall be permitted to live with their families." Then he turned to the black man and asked his name.

"I am Witambe Morandu. I am a warrior and sub-chief of my tribe." He stood proudly.

"Witambe, I do not like to keep a man in chains. If I have these chains removed, will you and your people follow me and not run away?"

Witambe looked surprised. "As the chief of my people I give you my word that we will not run away." Then he turned to his people and spoke for several seconds in a guttural tongue. All of the slaves nodded their heads as if in agreement.

Sumter ordered the auctioneer to remove the shackles and chains. Then he turned to Wilson. "Captain, will you remain with these people until I can arrange transportation? I had not expected to have so many more mouths to feed. I won't be long."

After agreeing to wait with Witambe, Wilson sat down and talked about their new life. He explained about the many changes they would experience. "And I'd advise you to take your lead from Mr. Sumter. Always address him as 'Sir,' or whatever way he wants you to call him. Like it or not, he is your master now."

Witambe nodded in understanding.

They were still engaged in discussion when Mr. Sumter returned.

"I can only get one wagon which will be adequate for the women and children, but I am afraid the men will have to walk."

Witambe stood, stretched his muscles and said, "That is good. We have been too long sitting and standing. Our arms and legs are weak. Walking will do us good and help us to regain our strength."

Wilson noted Sumter had two other wagons. One was loaded to the hilt with kegs of nails, saws, hammers, pickaxes and building materials. The other wagon had kegs of meat, flour, cornmeal and food stocks. The man was definitely planning to build, and it looked like his people would eat good.

In less than an hour, Sumter and his new slaves departed. They moved down the street and headed for the forest at the edge of town. Witambe turned toward Wilson and raised his hand in final farewell. Neither man would probably ever see each other again.

Wilson tipped his hat in acknowledgement. He felt a little sad but was glad he'd come to the auction today. It felt good to help Witambe and his people one last time. Silently, he offered a prayer for their safety and happiness.

Wilson stopped for a last round with his friend, English Charlie, before heading back to the ship. Entering the bar, he noted a certain amount of tension. He had not lived all these years, and been in as many bars in as many ports as he had, not to recognize the signs of trouble. Slowly and cautiously, he made his way to the far end of the bar with his back to the wall. The bar was too quiet. The normal laughter and joviality you heard in most bars was not present.

Wilson scanned the room for Charlie, but didn't see him. He asked, and the bartender told him Charlie was uptown, bringing back some supplies.

Wilson's eyes adjusted slowly to the dim light. He looked over the customers in the tavern. He was surprised to see Stanislaski sitting at a table in the corner. The man had a drink in front of him but hadn't touched it. He seemed to be waiting for something.

Wilson had not seen the Polish man since docking, and he'd assumed the man had left the area. He decided to wait a few more minutes to see what was going on around him before walking over to talk to him.

A couple of seamen at the bar snickered and giggled loudly. They were making fun of the way Stanislaski was dressed. True in this place, his white shirt and ballooned pants made him look like a fancy Dan.

The captain thought to himself, those two are looking for a fight or somebody to bully. They are picking on the wrong person. They were too drunk to see the anger in Stanislaski's eyes.

Wilson spoke softly to the bartender, "How long has this man been here?"

Almost in a whisper, the bartender replied, "Just a little while. He came in, ordered a drink and went to the table. Just as he passed these two yokels, they began to guffaw and laugh at him. He sat down but he hasn't touched his drink.

"I think he wants to keep a clear head in case there is trouble. And there probably will be. Those two have been run out of most of the taverns up here. They normally stay down on the docks. They are rough ones; they like to use a knife in a fight."

Again, Wilson was tempted to walk over and sit down with Stanislaski. But if there was going to be a fight, it would be better to stay out of it. He was over fifty years old now and didn't need the grief of a barroom brawl. He would just wait and see what happened.

Andraui tensed up, then relaxed and put himself at ease. He picked up his drink, but he merely touched the glass to his lips. Setting the glass down, he walked over to the bar were the two drunken sailors stood. Very calmly, he spoke; and to anyone whose mind was not befuddled with drink, his tone would have been warning enough.

"Gentlemen, you seem to like my clothes. I can understand that, looking at what you are wearing. You don't know very much about how to dress. I would be glad to go to a clothing store with you and help you pick out something more suitable than what you are wearing."

The two bullies looked at each other, and then it dawned on them that he had insulted them. It was now they who were being made fun of.

Stanislaski waited calmly and studied them more closely.

The shorter of the two men stood about 5 feet 8 inches and was swarthy of complexion, probably aged 30 to 40. He had enormous shoulders and his hands looked like large hams. His nose had been broken several times and had not healed back well. It was lopsided, and he had trouble breathing. His long, shaggy, red hair matched the color of his flushed face. His eyes were a light brown and more closely resembled the color of his teeth.

The other man stood right at 6 feet, closer to Stanislaski's height, and was very thin. His yellowish skin indicated he had consumption or some kind of internal ailment. Probably a bad liver, Stansilaski thought, most likely from all his drinking. While the shorter man seemed more inclined to quick, reckless decisions, this one was more contemplative, more cautious. This one was probably the more dangerous of the two. If trouble began, Stanislaski would deal with this one first.

The short man almost exploded, "Are you trying to insult us by making fun of what we are wearing?"

The tall man grimaced. He clearly was not interested in a fight. "Let it go, Jonesy. It's time to leave anyway."

Stanislaski replied to the short man, "Isn't that what you were doing about my clothes? But of course, it is impossible to insult a jackass for they don't have enough sense to know when they have been insulted."

Before the tall man could pull Jonesy away from the bar and out the door, the short man swung a balled fist at Stanislaski, who ducked.

When the man was off balance, Stanislaski gave him a push that sent him spinning into the tables. Stanislaski was quick as a cat, and without slowing his motion, he lunged into the tall man and pinned him against the bar railing. The force of the blow knocked the breath out of the tall man, and before he could recover, Stanislaski threw a resounding blow just below and on the tip of the man's jaw. The tall man sank to the floor as if poleaxed.

Without waiting to see the results of his blow, Stanislaski turned to the short man. With those broad shoulders and muscles, it would not be good if his opponent got him from behind. The man stumbled to his feet, so mad he sputtered. He put his head down and charged like a bull. Stanislaski stepped out of the reach of his arms and, as the bully passed, hit him in the neck, driving him into the side of the bar. The thick, bulky man hit with a thud and shook the whole bar.

Stanislaski thought the fight was over, but he was wrong. The heavyset man shook his head and came at him again, swinging his big fists. Stanislaski took a blow to his left shoulder with such force that he was thrown into a table. His arm became numb. He knew then he could not slug it out with this burly bull of a man.

Dodging and weaving, he kept tables between them until the feeling returned to his left arm. The burly man raised a chair over his head as if to throw it, and Stanislaski charged underneath the chair, hitting the man square in the stomach with his head, thankful there was plenty of fat on the brute. When the wind rushed out of the bully's mouth, the air was filled with the smell of bad breath and sour ale. The chair fell to the side and the bully fell over backwards. Stanislaski jumped on him before he hit the floor. The first blow went just below the heart, and the second to the neck, right in the Adams Apple. The man gasped for breath and crawled to his knees. Stanislaski stepped back, measured his swing and hit him again just above the ear. The heavy-set man collapsed and the fight was over. The fellow never even knew his partner was also down.

Stanislaski turned, surveyed the room to see if there were any complaints and walked back to his table. He picked up his glass, looked at it thoughtfully, and finally drank it down in one swallow. Then he bid good day to the bartender and walked outside. The fight lasted less than two minutes and Stanislaski hadn't even worked up a sweat.

Wilson left the bar and approached Stanislaski. "Andraui, that was a real thorough job in there. I thought you might have been out-numbered and debated whether you would need some help. Obviously, you didn't."

Andraui smiled. "Not with the likes of those, I didn't."

"Where did you learn to fight so well?"

"We had taverns in Poland, too, and there are bullies everywhere. I'd visit the taverns and drink with all the other young soldiers. Not all people liked having us come into their towns. The girls always seemed to like the uniforms. We fought many times over little insignificant things, but mostly it was over girls."

"I thought you had left the area. What were you doing in that bar?"

"Looking for you. Your first mate said you sometimes come to this tavern."

"What did you want to see me about?"

"You are the only friend I have in this country and I need to discuss some things, to get some advice."

"Well let's head back to the ship before those two bully boys come to. You might have to do the job all over again."

Andraui smiled and said, "You know, I kind of feel good. I needed that to help clear my mind. Let's go."

CHAPTER FIVE

They walked toward the ship and Wilson noted something different about Andraui. He couldn't put his finger on it, but there was something decidedly different. He was still dressed as he had been on board ship, and his clothes were just as neat as always. Even after the scuffle in the tavern the boots didn't show a single scratch or mar on them. In fact, they were so well-shined, they reflected the sunlight

No it was something else, but the captain just could not figure exactly what it was. Crossing in front of the general store, they chatted about the day's events.

Andraui said, "I saw how you handled the auction this morning and I admire what you did for the slave, Witambe, and his people. I believe they would have put up a fight if they had been separated."

"Where were you? I did not see you at the auction."

"I was near the back with the crowd that had come just to observe how the auction was conducted. I didn't see you in the crowd until you spoke up. I had intended to approach you then, but after the slaves were sold, I saw you still talking to Witambe and the man who bought them. I decided to come down to the tavern to wait for you. I figured you might take a tankard of ale before returning to the ship."

Wilson grunted in agreement. "I usually stop off to chat with English Charlie before I turn in and before I sail. He wasn't there today, though, and probably it's just as well. He would have taken a belaying pin to those two before things got out of hand. That would have spoiled your little work-out."

Wilson kicked at a rock in his path. "However, I must warn you to be on your guard. Those two have no scruples about way-laying a body and slitting his throat. You bested both of them in a fight in front of people they know. They won't take kindly to that and may try to corner you in an alley. You need to watch yourself."

"I will. But I don't think I will stay here more than another day or two. That is part of what I want to talk with you about."

They arrived at the ship and went up the gang-plank to the deck. Darkness was a couple hours away, and the watch looked a mite thirsty. Wilson relieved the two men.

"Now you two go get something to eat and a drink, but mind you, you best return in two hours." They hurriedly headed down the gangplank. "And you better not be drunk when you return!" Wilson yelled after them. "You still have three hours left on your watch!"

Then he turned to Andraui, shaking his head in amusement. "Let's go up to the wheelhouse. We can sit down yet have a clear view of the deck and the docks. If any sneak thief tries to come aboard I will be able to see him."

They climbed the steps to the upper deck and entered the wheelhouse. They pulled the wooden deck chairs to get a good view of the lower deck and sat down.

"What was it you wanted to talk to me about?"

Andraui stalled briefly, as if he wasn't sure where to begin.

Finally, he spoke. "I have decided to stay in America, but I do not want to stay in a city such as Boston or even this Charlestown. As a boy I was raised on a farm and in the forest. That is what I want to do, where I want to go."

"I am told that far west of here there is plenty of land to

be had. All you have to do is stake out what you want and prove up on it. I think they called it homesteading. I have been talking to people who say that in some areas you can get a whole section of land for yourself. They say a section is 640 acres. Although we measured our land in hectares and meters, I believe 640 acres is quite a bit of land. If the land was good, and a person worked hard, it would be enough to raise a family on. Have you heard of this before?"

The captain smiled.

"Yes. There are vast land areas to the west that are practically for the taking. Of course, much of these lands are still occupied by the natives, the Indians, who were here long before white men came. Some are friendly, but I hear others are very mean and when they kill someone, they scalp him, cut the top of his head and pull all his hair off his head." "I have not actually seen this, but I have heard it from many people and I believe it to be true. If you plan to go into the wilderness, you will need someone who knows his way around and you will need to go well armed. You will need more than a sword to defend yourself. How much experience have you had with guns?"

"I have used a muzzle loading rifle and a big gun with a large barrel that you stuffed with shot and nails and whatever is handy. I think you call it a blunderbuss. The Prussians were a war-like people and were always finding ways to improve their weapons and means to kill people. They have a gun that you load from the breech. The barrel is longer than most guns and one of the models looks much like the Hawken Rifle with an octagon barrel that you build here in America. Although I have fired one of these rifles a few times I'm afraid I am not a good shot. We didn't get to practice much for there was a shortage of powder and shot but I can hit a target at a fair distance, even if it is moving.

"I saw one of these rifles in a store yesterday. The

storekeeper said it wasn't a popular gun here. I believe I could get it fairly cheap. One thing the Prussians were good at - they knew how to forge metal. These guns are superior, in my opinion, to those made in most countries. However, I have heard that the Pennsylvania Rifle made in America is as good as the Prussian guns. I will go tomorrow and visit a gunsmith."

Wilson acknowledged that was a good plan. And they sat in silence a bit longer. He sensed there was more that Andraui wanted to ask.

Andraui turned to face the captain, studying him. Evidently, Wilson must have passed the test for his guest launched into a new subject.

"Captain, I do not know anything about your customs and laws here and I do not want to get in trouble with the law or do anything that would put me in a bad light. Tell me, are indentured people ever re-sold? What I'm asking, is can someone buy up an indentured person's debt?"

"Oh yes, if the person who holds the bond is willing to sell. You can work out a bargain with him and pay the indenture or bond, and that indentured person would then pass to you. You can buy the bonded people almost the same as you do slaves. The key is whether the bondholder wants to sell. "Why do you ask this?" A gleam came to Wilson's eyes. He understood where the conversation would lead.

Now Andraui shuffled in his chair slightly and smiled sheepishly. "Well," he said, "You remember the English girl on the ship?"

"Yes. The one with the reddish hair and the long legs?"

"That is the one. She has been much on my mind since we have landed. I went to see her again at the hotel yesterday, and they said she had already left with the man who held her bond, a man by the name of Charles Heyward. They are going inland to a place called Orangeburg."

Andraui paused, perhaps to change the subject, but then lightly shrugged his shoulders. "I think I am in love with her. It probably seems strange to you because we have only talked a few times and we have never talked about our feelings for each other. She may not want anything to do with me, but I intend to go see her before I leave to go inland to search for some land. Does this sound like a stupid act to you?"

Wilson knew he needed to handle this very carefully lest he offend the Cossack. Quickly he spoke, "No, I don't think it is stupid at all. Sometimes on board ship I watched the two of you talking. You seemed to be very comfortable with each other. Often, that is more important than some of the things others may consider essential. You see, being able to share your thoughts, secrets, and also enjoy each other's company is a big first step towards loving someone.

"Besides, you two have some things in common. Both of you are without families. Both of you are in a strange, new country and you are both alone, without other friends and loved ones. It may be very natural for you to turn to each other. If I may offer some advice though, I would move very cautiously and get to know her better and let her get to know you better as well. Give your relationship time to develop and grow between you. If you try to push it too fast, it may cause her to put up a wall between you to protect herself from further harm or possible abuse."

Andraui nodded thoughtfully. "I can see where she would want to protect herself and she probably feels that she is all alone and has to look out for herself. Very well, I will go see her and spend a day or two there in Orangeburg before I go further inland. If the opportunity presents itself, I will tell her how I feel. If it does not, I will wait until I return."

All of a sudden, it hit the captain. Now he understood what that something was about Andraui that he could not put his finger on earlier. Andraui was more animated and less forlorn. It was as if having found a chance for a new beginning, he was throwing off the sadness and the tragedy of the past and looked forward to building a new life. This would be a new adventure for him. Joshua noted the excitement and sparkle in the man's eyes. Yes, Andraui was ready to meet the challenge of this new life. It would be a long time, and maybe never, before the tragic battle scenes would fade, but for now, this new idea was beginning to crowd them out. The thought of a young and attractive female would certainly be a part of his new adventure.

Andraui coughed to clear his throat and launched into a new subject.

"There is one other, very important thing I need your help with. This may be a big imposition upon you, but I do not know who else to trust." With this statement, he stands up, undoes the sash around his waist, pulls out his shirt tail and reaches underneath the shirt. A few seconds later, he pulls out a leather belt from around his waist. The belt is perhaps 4 or five inches wide and contains a dozen or so small pockets of about two inches by three inches. It had fit so snugly around his waist that Wilson had never suspected that it was there. Surely, no one else had noticed it either.

Andraui held the belt in his hands and sat back down.

"In the latter days of the war in Poland, we were driven back and back and back until we finally were in our own village. We were in almost constant combat and all of us, officers and men, were on the verge of exhaustion. The landowner for whom my father worked sent me a message and asked me to come to his castle as soon as I could. We were only some five kilometers from the castle so I borrowed a horse and rode to see him. When I arrived I could tell he was very agitated and seemed to be genuinely frightened. He took me into the basement and removed a stone in the wall. He reached in and pulled out a large wooden box. He set it on a stool then turned to me. He said, "Andraui, you and your family have been loyal to me and my family for many years. Now I must entrust you with the bulk of my wealth. There have already been bands of Prussians prowling the woods and forests and I fear it will only be a matter of time before they will break in and maybe kill all of us. Do you think the Army can hold back the Prussians?"

"I told him we could not. Our troops were fighting valiantly but they were out-numbered by almost 10 to 1 and both the Russian and Prussian armies had brought in new, fresh troops. We were exhausted and had been in almost constant battle for more than 20 days with very little rest. Our food supplies and our ammunition were almost out. We couldn't stand against the guns of the Prussians with swords. It would be suicide.

"At this point he opened the box and took out this belt. He selected diamonds, rubies and other gems out of the strong box and stuffed them into the belt until every pocket was full. Then he handed it to me. He said, 'This is the bulk of my fortune, except my lands and the castle. I fear for my life. My wife and the two girls left weeks ago and I believe they have made it safely to England. Now I must leave, for if the Prussians catch me here, they will surely hang me. They know that I have helped fund the detachments of the army that were sent from this area. Besides, they want our lands and they know that as long as I or any of my family live, someday we will be back to claim our property. So if I am caught, they will probably execute me, as well as you and all of the other soldiers. I want you to order your troops to withdraw during the night and try to escape. There is no need for them to fight to the last man. They have fought honorably, but there is no need for them to continue to battle against such odds. Tell them to flee and escape the country if they can.'"

Andraui paused, reliving the moment. He shuffled his feet, sighed, and then continued in a quieter voice. "He asked my help to get him out of Poland. We had to leave that night. He insisted I wear this belt and not take it off for any reason until they could reach safety. The man then pulled out a leather pouch and counted out 200 gold coins. He divided them into smaller bundles and rolled them up in strips of cloth, tying them together into a big knotted clump."

Andraui turned to the Joshua, "Capitan, I had never seen so much money in my whole life. We carried the coins in our baggage to use as travel money and to bribe the guards along the way. His final instructions were that if anything were to happen to him, I was to deliver the jewels to his wife in England. He provided me an address where he thought his family would be. And he told me to keep whatever remained of the coins, and to use that for my escape and for a new start in England."

Now agitated, Andraui stood up and looked outward towards the port.

"I returned to my troops and told them what we had been ordered to do. Some wanted to remain and fight to the end. I explained that it was much better to save ourselves in the hopes we could build another army and come back to take Poland again. Eventually they saw the wisdom of not sacrificing themselves on a lost cause and we fled. I returned to the castle and picked up the owner and we departed. On the way out, he insisted that we stop by my home and warn my family. When we arrived at my father's house, it was in smoking ruins. It looked as if a roving band of marauders had come to the house and caught my family alone. My father had evidently put up a fight and they had hanged him from a rafter in the barn."

Tears glistened in the man's eyes.

"My mother's body lay in the yard where she had been killed, and my 16-year-old sister was in the barn. She had been raped repeatedly. When they finished with her, they bayonetted her to death."

Captain Wilson listened with dismay. No wonder there had been sadness in this man's eyes. As he watched him now, he could see the tightness of his mouth and the rigid line of his jaw.

Andraui regained his composure, and through half-clenched teeth, he continued. "We loaded their bodies into a wagon and took them into the forest. There we found a few friends who helped us bury them. We were afraid to travel during the day so we laid over to rest and our friends watched for the enemy while we slept. There was not much sleep for me that night, I can tell you."

He shook his head in dismay. "As soon as it was dark, we started out again. We had not gone but a few kilometers when we came upon an encampment of Prussian Soldiers. We had heard them laughing and talking, and had smelled their fire long before we came in sight of them. We were attempting to circle them and get past, when I heard a music box. It had been my mother's and it had a special tune that she would play for us at night. She would wind it up and set it on a chair beside our bed until we went to sleep.

"My first instinct was to rush among them and kill as many as I could, but our landlord prevailed on me to wait and think things out. I was determined I would not leave without taking revenge on those who had killed my family. We returned to the forest where we had spent the day and enlisted four of the best young men. Then we returned to the campsite. There were eight of the soldiers, but all were asleep except one that was standing guard. Our plan was to rush them in their sleep and kill them before they awoke. The plan was going well until one of the men got too excited and let out a loud yell just as we were falling on the sleeping men. The soldiers came out of their blankets in the space of two breaths. We met them with swords, spears and clubs. I ran one through with my sword just as he rolled out of his blanket. I slashed the sword across the throat of another as he rose up to see what all the racket was about. Two of our men bashed in the heads of two more soldiers before they woke up. They never knew what happened. The other three that had been sleeping were fully awake now and hand to hand fighting was raging We had not seen the soldier who had been on guard duty come running up, and before we knew it, he had run his bayonet through the back of the landlord. I turned as I heard my landlord scream. Before the soldier could withdraw his bayonet, I slashed at him with my saber. It caught him on the left side of his neck and severed his vein here," Andraui used his fingers to motion a slash down the side of his throat.

"Up until this point no shot had been fired, but I saw one of the soldiers trying to prime his weapon and I grabbed the rifle of the soldier I had just killed, hoping it was already primed. I aimed it at the other soldier and pulled the trigger. It blew his head half off. I looked around and my men had the other two on the ground and were about to cave in their skulls. I yelled to them to wait. I wanted them alive.

Andraui was now pacing across the floor in short patterns.

"We pulled them to their feet and tied their hands behind them. Then we questioned them until they admitted that they were the ones who had been at my father's home but they said they were only following orders of their sergeant and he was the one I had blown off his head. With him dead, we had only their word. We discussed for several minutes what we should do. With the landlord dead, there was no longer any reason to remain in the area. Besides, if these two lived they would hunt us down and hang us. We decided to hang them, and left a sign around their necks that this was the penalty for killing and raping Polish women.

"We buried the landlord and the men took all the weapons and clothes of the dead soldiers back into the forest with them. They would come in handy, if not to kill other soldiers, then to hunt for meat in the forest."

The angered Cossack cleared his throat, clearly relieved at having expelled his grief.

"Capitan, I was now alone and had the mission to find the landlord's wife in England. I traveled at night and rested during the day until I was on the coast. There I found a good Polish patriot who helped me get to Norway, and from there I got a passage to England. I went to the address I had been given but they had not seen the landlord's wife and daughters. They said they had been notified that some of the Poles that had escaped were being held in Hamburg, Germany. I carefully went back into Hamburg and found a man who would help me try to find the wife and daughter. He was a Jew that had relatives in Poland and he agreed to make some inquiries about them.

"I stayed in hiding for several days while he used his contacts to see what he could find out. On the fifth day, he came to me and said they were all three dead. They were with a group of refugees from several countries who were fleeing the war. At one checkpoint, one of the soldiers began to flirt with the girls and took a special liking to the youngest daughter. When he tried to pull her out of the line with the intention of taking her into the woods, the mother flew at him and began to scratch and hit him with a stick. It made the soldier mad and he hit her with his gun butt. The youngest daughter picked up a sharp stick and rammed it through the soldiers back. The other soldiers put her and her mother against a stone wall and shot them both for killing the soldier. The soldiers then took the oldest girl into the woods. There were six or seven of them and when they returned the girl was not with them. The other refugees figured they raped and killed her."

Another deep sigh left Andraui's body. "The man who had helped me with this information said that now others were suspicious of the Jew, and I would have to leave. If he was caught harboring a Polish soldier, they would all die. I made it to the docks and waited until your ship arrived. I thought it best to get as far away from Germany and Prussia as I could. The new world seemed like the best place for me. There was no longer any reason for me to stay. There was also no one for me to leave the jewels and money with, and so I've kept the belt with me."

Andraui stopped talking. The sun was nearly down and in the twilight, the silence was welcome. "I don't know if I did right or not. It is not my money, but if I had left it in Poland it would be in the hands of the Prussians now. I know of no other members of the landlord's family to whom I might give it to. So what should I do with it?"

Joshua was silent for a few moments. When he finally spoke, he spoke softly and with great feeling. "Andraui, there probably is no one more entitled to that money than you. You made great sacrifices for your country. You lost everything of importance to you, including your family. You made a sincere effort to fulfill the mission given you and at great personal risk. Not many men would have gone back to Germany and taken the risk of being captured. Under the circumstances, I would say that you have earned the right to keep the money and do with it as you wish. You could bring honor to their memories by doing something worthwhile with the money these will bring."

"Thank you Captain. You are an honorable man. I would like you to help me find an honest jeweler and help me obtain a fair price for these jewels. Then I will take enough for supplies and travel expenses and I want to put the rest in a bank until I return. I want to leave this stipulation. If I do not return in 18 months, the next time you are in port here, you are to take the money from the bank and buy the bond of Miss Catherine York. She is to be set free and given one-half of the money to start a new life. You are to keep one-half of the remaining funds for your trouble. Will you do this for me?"

Joshua stared at him. «Are you sure you want to trust me with this kind of money?»

"I saw how you went out of your way to help the slaves and I believe you are an honorable man. I know of no one else that I can turn to for help. Besides, if I return before the 18 months,» he laughed, «you won›t get anything anyway.»

"What am I supposed to do with the rest of the money? You said give half to Miss York, and I'm to keep one- half of what is left. What am I to do with the other 25 percent?"

Andraui smiled, "You may think me crazy, but I would like you to take the rest of the money and buy Witambe and as many of his people as you can. Set them free and tell them to go into the wilderness, as far west as they can go, and set them up a new village or town and see if they can re-build their tribe here in America. Like the people of Poland, they have suffered much, and I think the landlord would look favorably upon the money being used like this."

Captain Wilson was caught without words to express his surprise and approval of Andraui's plan. All he could say was, "I will have to delay my departure an extra day, but yes, by Holy Jesus, I'll do it." "Now, man, let me buy you a drink."

CHAPTER SIX

The captain pulled a bottle of scotch and poured two glasses half full. He insisted that Andraui stay on board ship with him that night and the next day they spent most of the day talking of Andraui's plans and discussing what he would need for his trip.

It was decided that he would need one horse to ride, and another one as a pack animal. He would go as a trader and would take goods along the trail with him. There were still many Indians in the interior, and he would want to pass through their lands without trouble. If they thought he was a trader and not coming to stay, they might allow him free passage.

He would try to find a guide, but he wanted a special type. One that knew the country he would be going into and would travel as a companion, rather than as hired help. The captain admitted that he did not know what kind of supplies would be necessary for the wilderness. Andraui would have to talk with others to find out this information.

Late Sunday afternoon, Andraui bid farewell and returned to his hotel, agreeing to meet with Captain Wilson at eight o'clock the next morning. They wanted to be at the jeweler's store when it opened for business.

Joshua headed off to see English Charlie to find out who the best and most honest dealers were in town. Once at the top of the small hill, he discovered Charlie's tavern was closed, so he went around back to where Charlie lived. A knock on the door brought Charlie's wife to the door. She greeted Joshua with a smile.

"Joshua this is a surprise. I thought you were sailing today."

"I had planned to but something has come up and I want to stay over another day. Is Charlie around?"

"Yes. He is in the back working on something or other. I'll call him."

"Don't bother. I'll just walk back and talk with him."

Joshua stepped through the kitchen and out on the back porch. The house was perhaps 20 feet away from the back of the tavern, and in between, Charlie had built a small workshop. That is where Joshua found him, standing on his one good leg and the peg he used for the lost leg was in his hands.

"Afternoon Charlie. What are you up to now?"

Charlie turned to face him with a smile. "I have decided that if I have to wear this thing, I want it to be dressed up and fancy. I am carving figures and scrolls on it. When I am finished, this will be the fanciest peg-leg in all of the Carolinas. People will come for miles just to see ole Charlie's peg leg." They both laughed at the thought of a wooden leg becoming an attraction.

After a few minutes of polite conversation, the captain told Charlie about part of his conversation with Andraui and ended with, "This is a man that has had his share of trouble. He will need to sell the jewels and convert them into cash. I figured you would know who was honest and would not cheat him in the transaction. Neither of us knows who to go to here. Being a foreigner, a crooked jeweler could rob him and we would not know whether the deal was fair or not."

Charlie asked, "How many jewels does he have, and are they of great value?"

Joshua replied, "I don't know. I saw the belt but he did not show me the jewels. From the size of the belt though, and the way it bulged, I would guess there is a fairly large amount if all of the pockets in the belt are full. He said there were 200 gold pieces as well. I don't know how much of that he has left either."

"There is a Greek by the name of Peter Georgiades who has a reputation of fairness and integrity in business. He is a very shrewd businessman but I believe he would treat you fair. I know him and would trust him more than I would anyone else in town. There is one other thing too. He keeps information confidential and if the amount of money is anything like what it sounds like, everyone doesn't need to know about it. There are those in this town who would slit your throat for $5. If they found out that he might be carrying something valuable on him, they would way-lay him or follow him into the countryside to rob and kill him."

"Good. I think it might be a good idea if you went with us in the morning, to introduce us. And if we should need a witness you could be one. You are well known here, while he and I both are strangers. I would feel much easier, especially in dealing with the bank."

Charlie agreed to come along and they decided to meet Andraui at his hotel at eight the next morning.

Captain Wilson returned to his ship and turned in. He had a restless night and awoke early in anticipation of the morning's events. He dressed, grabbed a cold biscuit out of the ships galley and walked up the hill to Charlie's place.

"Come on in, Joshua. Help yourself to the coffee over there on the stove."

They talked about things, but neither mentioned what was most on their minds. Both were thinking of the momentous event that was to take place that morning, and both were slightly agitated with anticipation.

As soon as Charlie was ready they, walked further up town to Andraui's hotel and sat down in the lobby to wait for him. They didn't have to wait long. At eight o'clock sharp, Andraui descended the stairs and came straight to them. Since Andraui had not met Charlie before, Joshua introduced him.

"Andraui, this is an old friend of mine. I hope you don't mind, but I asked him to point out who the most reliable and honest jeweler was in town. Since you and I are both strangers in Charleston, I also thought it might be best to have a local citizen as a witness when we place the money in a bank. I would not want the money to disappear and when we returned have the bankers declare they had never heard of us before. With a local citizen as a witness, I believe the transaction would be more secure. He owns the tavern where you had your most interesting drink the other afternoon. English Charlie, this is Andraui Vladimir Stanislaski, from Poland."

Andraui spoke to Joshua. "I had been thinking on this same subject. I was wondering if I should place all the money in one bank or put some in different banks. Also, the idea of having a witness with us occurred to me as well, but I did not know of anyone who I could ask.

Andraui turned to Charlie and extended his hand. "It is a pleasure to meet you. Any friend of Captain Wilson's is a friend of mine. I am happy you have agreed to come with us."

The captain noted that Andraui carried a small valise that seemed to be a little heavy. He assumed the gold coins were in the valise.

"Charlie says there is a Greek here by the name of Peter Georgiades that has the reputation of being fair and honest in his dealings. He has suggested we go see him first, but he doesn't open his shop until 9 A. M. So I suggest we go to the little cafe next door and have some coffee."

59

They talked of various things until 15 minutes before 9 o'clock and Charlie mentioned that they should go if they wanted to be there when Georgiades opened his shop, which was about four blocks away.

They arrived at the jewelry store just as the Jeweler arrived in a horse-drawn carriage.

Georgiades noticed the three men approaching him and for just a moment was somewhat startled. Once he realized they would not be attempting to hold him up in broad daylight and in front of the carriage driver too, he relaxed. Then he recognized Charlie. He had not met him before but being a businessman he knew quite a few of the other businessman in Charleston. Seeing he was one of the three men, his fears subsided.

Charlie was the first to speak. "Mr. Georgiades, My name is Charles Windham, I own English Charlie's tavern over on Jefferson Street. This is Captain Joshua Wilson, captain of the sailing ship, Sea Mistress, which is in dock here now. This other gentleman is Andraui Vladimir Stanislaski from Poland. He has some business to discuss with you. We are here merely as his friends. May we go inside?"

Georgiades immediately opened the door and invited them inside. It was a neat shop and held many rings, necklaces and assorted jewelry in cases along the walls. It was unpretentious, but reflected good taste and the jewelry seemed of good quality and excellent workmanship. Georgiades motioned them to a small room to one side of the shop. Both Captain Wilson and Charlie indicated they would wait outside until Andraui had completed his business. They wanted him to have as much privacy as he might want.

Andraui beckoned them to join him. "No. I would like you to sit with us as we discuss the exchange. You are both my friends and I want you to be a part of what I am going to do. If Mr. Georgiades has no objection, we can all sit down together in his office and get down to business."

Georgiades made no objection and they all moved into the room. They took chairs around a table with a glass top. Andraui opened the valise and took out one of the rolls of coins and laid it on the table. As he began to open it, he told Georgiades, "Mr. Georgiades, these coins were given to me in Poland before the Russians and Prussians overran the country. When we could fight no longer, a landed gentleman gave me these and told me to flee the country and take his money with me. He and all his family were killed trying to escape the Prussians. I feel these now belong to me and I need to exchange them for American money. Can you tell me what they are worth here?" With that he unfolded the cloth and showed him the coins.

The jeweler asked "if he wanted the value in the original pounds and shillings which had been used until recently and were still used throughout much of the colonies, or do you want them in the new values, called dollars, which the government recently started using? These have become very popular and usually preferred over the English pound. They come in ten, twenty and hundred dollar gold coins and copper coins of 1, 5, 10 and 25 cent values."

Andraui was not familiar with these coins and turned to Georgiades, "You are more familiar with this type of money than I am which would you recommend that I take out into the territories?"

Georgiades stated "I would recommend the dollars and other smaller valued coins, as that is fast becoming the accepted trade instrument here in the colonies. In your travel outside the regular towns you probably should have some coins in pounds and shillings also to trade with those who are not yet familiar with the dollar."

Andraui turned back to the jeweler and said, "Give me

the value in dollars. I can then exchange some of them at the bank for the pounds and shillings I might need."

The jeweler looked at the coins for a couple more minutes then took out a knife and scraped one of the coins. After examining it carefully he looked at Andraui and said, "The exchange value of these coins is worth roughly one hundred to one hundred and ten American dollars apiece."

Andraui was visibly pleased and mentally calculated the total value of the coins he had. Then his thoughts were interrupted by Georgiades.

"However, Sir, they are really worth much more than that. These are Spanish Doubloons and are more than three hundred years old. They are almost in mint condition as if they were never in circulation. Their real value is as collector items and probably will bring maybe three times their exchange value. I don't know how your gentleman friend came by these, but I would guess they have been handed down from generation to generation. These, because of their excellent condition are quite valuable. How many do you have?"

Andraui, Charlie and Joshua were stunned and they were shocked into silence.

Georgiades brought them back to attention by repeating his question. "How many of these coins do you have?"

Andraui turned the question aside, and instead of answering, asked the jeweler, "Are you saying that each of these coins is worth maybe three hundred American dollars?"

"At least that. If they were delivered to Philadelphia, Boston or New York, they might go as high as $350 or $400 each. I do not specialize in rare coins, but I do have a fair knowledge of their worth."

"Would you buy these from me at say $275 each? That should leave you room for a small profit at the $300 price, and you probably have a way to get them to the bigger cities.

If you can, and can get $400 each, that would increase your profit considerably."

The jeweler said, "Yes. I would buy them at $275, but you can make more if you will wait and let me send them north for you. How many do you have?"

Andraui opened the valise and poured out the bundles on the top of the table. There were five, six or seven coins in each bundle."

Wilson quickly viewed the bundles. There were approximately 30 of them.

Now it was the jeweler's turn to be stunned into silence. He and Andraui began to open the bundles and group the coins in stacks of ten on the table. When they were finished and the count was made, there were 174 coins in all.

Georgiades quickly tabulated the dollar amount, an astonishing amount of $47,850. By this time the jeweler was perspiring and in spite of his professional demeanor and his efforts to remain cool and calm, the excitement of the moment was beginning to affect him as well as the others in the room.

Georgiades raised his head and looked at the three men, then spoke to Andraui. "Do you agree with the total?"

Andraui said, "I do."

"Then if you will give me one hour I will have the funds ready for you. I do not keep that much money in the shop. I will have to go to the bank for enough to cover the purchase. Before I do though, I must ask you once again, are you sure this is what you want to do? Would you rather not wait and let me send the coins north and get you top dollar for them?"

Andraui spoke again, "Sir, I have plans that I want to put into effect immediately and do not want to delay while the coins are sent north to be sold. I am satisfied with the price we have agreed upon and I have no problem with you making any profit you can above what you are paying for the coins. After all, the coins were almost like a gift to me. I have no real investment in them. In my flight from Poland, I have traded them for less than 20 percent of what you have offered me. So I am well satisfied in the deal."

Georgiades excused himself and invited them to wait in the restaurant next door while he went to the bank. He returned in less than one hour and carried a leather bag. He stepped into the restaurant and motioned them to follow him back to the shop.

When inside they all went back into the small room and sat around the table once again. Georgiades opened the bag and began to count out gold coins on the table. He counted out a total of $50,000 dollars and pushed it across the table to Andraui. He said, "I pride myself on being a fair man, and I feel I may yet make a sinful profit at your expense. Therefore, I am paying you a little extra above our agreed price."

Andraui protested that an agreement was an agreement and he did not want one penny more than they had agreed upon. Georgiades was adamant though and in the end, Andraui accepted.

Then Andraui looked at Georgiades and said, "Because of your honesty, I would like to offer you another business transaction."

With that he unbuttoned his shirt, reached underneath and loosened the catches on the belt. He laid it on the table, opened one of the pockets and dumped the jewels in the pocket on the table. All of the men, including the jeweler, gasped when they saw the diamonds, rubies, and emeralds roll out on the table. There were diamonds that shimmered in the light from the window. There were rubies in all shapes, with one being almost the size of a man's thumb. The light showed blood red as it reflected through the stones on the table.

Neither Joshua nor Charlie had ever seen such beautiful stones before, and they were not prepared for such a sight. The air went out of their mouths as if they had been struck a heavy blow in the belly. Sweat popped out on their foreheads and began to trickle down the sides of their bodies. They sat in their chairs as if tied to them. Their eyes were glued to the gems on the table.

Andraui continued to open pocket after pocket and spill the jewels out onto the table. When he had opened 10 pockets he stopped. There were two pockets remaining unopened. There was a pile of jewels unlike anything they had ever seen. Even the jeweler stared in amazement. In all his years in the jewelry business he had never encountered such an array of stones. In addition to the diamonds, rubies and emeralds, there were opals, pearls, and an assortment of other stones. All were exquisitely cut and appeared to be of superb quality.

Georgiades picked up one stone after another and examined it under a magnifying glass. He was silent, but the others could see the interest rising in him. He too, had begun to sweat and his face was flushed with the excitement of the moment.

After several moments of silence during which the jeweler had examined about one tenth of the stones, he raised his head and asked, "Do you intend to sell all of these jewels?"

Andraui responded, "Yes." He reached out onto the table and picked up two stones, one a diamond and the other a ruby. "Except for these two, I have no use for fancy stones. I have a special purpose for these two. I would like you to fashion this diamond into a ladies engagement ring and this ruby into a beautiful necklace. It is to be for someone very special and I would like you to use your best talents in making these two items for me."

"Mr. Stanislaski, I will be glad to design the ring and necklace for you, however, I am not a man of such means that I could buy all these jewels. My first impression is that the value of these stones will run close to a half million dollars. There are only a half dozen firms up north that would be big enough to buy this many jewels. In my whole life as a jeweler, I have never seen such an array of stones of such quality."

Andraui appeared disappointed and seemed to lose much of his enthusiasm. He wanted to be about his business and putting his plans into action. He did not want to have to travel back to Boston or New York. He didn't like those places and he wanted no part of them.

Charlie spoke up, breaking into his thoughts. "Mr. Georgiades, you have access to the jewelry markets and know how to deal in these things. Mr. Stanislaski and we do not. Would you consider acting as a broker for Andraui and selling the stones on a commission basis? You could either sell them in a batch or piecemeal, ever how you thought you might receive the best price. Would you do this for a fee?"

Georgiades answered, "Yes, of course I could do that. Of course it might take me months to move this many stones. I would suggest that they be sold a few at a time rather than all at one time. I would also recommend that we inventory them and sell them in groups. That is how you would get the best price. If Mr. Stanislaski wishes we could draw up a contract to that effect. I would take 10 percent of whatever is received, if that is agreeable."

Andraui, sensing that this would enable him to go on his way and start his plan, said, "That is agreeable to me except for two things. One, as the jewels are sold, I want the funds deposited into a bank account and deposit amounts furnished to Mr. Windham for Captain Wilson. He and I will be out of town much of the time. Secondly, I will insist that you take a fee of fifteen percent for your efforts. I am convinced with our dealings today that you will do your best to obtain the best price on the stones. All of the work will be on your shoulders, so you need to be paid for your troubles."

Georgiades protested, but in the end a deal was struck. Since there was nothing more that Charlie and Joshua could do, they left, agreeing to return at two o'clock to go with them to the bank to establish an account.

Then began the task of weighing and inventorying the stones. Georgiades closed his shop for the day, and he and Andraui remained huddled together, completing the inventory. Each stone was weighed, described in detail and catalogued so that an accurate record could be made.

A few minutes before two o'clock in the afternoon, Charlie and Joshua returned to the jewelry store and met with Andraui and Georgiades. Together, they went to the nearest bank. It wasn't a fancy bank but both Charlie and Georgiades had indicated they liked the people in the bank and considered them to be honest and trustworthy. It was one of the few brick and stone buildings in town and seemed to exhibit a certain degree of permanence that gave Andraui a feeling of confidence.

Georgiades led them into the bank and asked to see a Mr. Miller. The cashier walked to the back of the bank to a door that had the name, Harold Miller, and the title, President, painted on it. The cashier stepped inside and spoke a few words then stepped back as a stout man with a small protruding stomach came out of the office. He was in his mid-50s and had a florid face, bright blue eyes and a receding hairline. In short, he fit the description of a typical banker.

He extended his hand to Georgiades and said, "Peter, I didn't expect to see you again today. What can I do for you?"

Georgiades introduced him to his companions. "Gentlemen, this is Harold Miller, President of the First

Bank of Charleston. Harold, I want you to meet some friends and business acquaintances of mine. This is Andraui Stanislaski from Poland. The other gentleman is Captain Joshua Wilson, captain of the ship Sea Mistress which is in harbor now. And I think you already know Mr. Charles Windham, owner of English Charlie's tavern here in town."

Miller shook hands with all the men and said, "Yes, I have taken a tankard of ale at Mr. Windham's tavern now and then. He also does business with our bank I believe."

Then Georgiades motioned to Andraui and said, "Mr. Stanislaski wants to open an account with your bank. May we step into your office?"

Miller, intrigued by the fact that four men, all appearing to be men of substance, coming into the bank to talk business, had a feeling that something special was in the air. He stepped aside and motioned them toward his office. He had a couple extra chairs brought in and when everyone was seated, he closed the door. Then he took his seat behind a big wooden desk and asked how he could be of service.

Georgiades said, "I will let Mr. Stanislaski explain what he wants to do. We are here merely to assist him in making the arrangements."

Andraui began, "Mr. Miller, I have a rather substantial amount of money that I would like to deposit in your bank. I also expect to have other funds to be deposited from time to time."

Miller listened with rapt attention. Earlier that morning, Georgiades had withdrawn $50,000 from his bank, and he had hated to see that amount leave the bank. Now, he had the feeling that it might be about to flow back into the bank and he was anxious to be of service to this new customer. The mention that there might be even more money coming to the bank didn't pass unnoticed.

Andraui continued. "I have some special requirements, however, and I want these men to bear witness to these terms."

He opened up the same leather bag that Georgiades had brought the money to him in. "In this bag is $50,000. I want to deposit $47,000 with you. The other $3,000 I want in small coins that are easily exchanged in the countryside. I will only need a few large coins to use with the merchants for supplies I wish to purchase here in Charleston. After I leave the town, I suspect it may be more difficult to use the larger coins with the country folk."

"From time to time, Mr. Georgiades will be bringing you other deposits. I suspect that the account will eventually be one of considerable value, possibly exceeding a half million dollars."

With the mention of this vast sum, the banker's eyes shone brightly. Try as he might, he could not keep his excitement from showing. There was no other single account in his bank that could approach even half that amount. If this were true, it would make this man the bank's largest depositor. He could not believe his good fortune. This, with the other assets already in the bank, would make his bank the biggest in the Carolinas; in fact it would rival almost any other bank south of Boston or Philadelphia. He had to force himself to remain calm. He did not want to appear over anxious, but he would definitely make sure that this young man was happy and would personally see to any arrangements he might want.

Andraui was still speaking and Miller pulled himself back to the moment.

"I want a special condition on the withdrawal of these funds. I am going on a journey and although I expect to return, it will be one of considerable peril. I might not return. If I do not return in 18 months, you are to allow

Captain Wilson here to withdraw any or all of the funds at his request. I will leave him written instructions on what he is to do with the money. He cannot withdraw any of it until the 18 months have passed. I expect to return within 12 months, so I have given myself an extra six months in case of some delay or mishap. If I am not back in the 18 months, I probably will not be returning and most likely will be dead. I will sign a release for you so that if I am not back and you release the money to him, you will not be held responsible. These two gentlemen, Mr. Windham and Mr. Georgiades will bear witness to this. Is this arrangement satisfactory with you?"

Miller thought, why not. For this kind of an account he would stand on his head on Main Street. He was afraid he was going to ask him to do something ugly, or perhaps even illegal. Everything he was requesting was perfectly legal and would be easy enough to comply with.

"But of course, Mr. Stanislaski. Your request can be easily accommodated here. I shall have the necessary papers drawn immediately. If you will please wait, it won't take but a few minutes."

As he turned to leave the room, Andraui spoke once more. "There is one more thing. I have left my country behind and have come to a new country. I might as well leave my old name as well. It is too hard for most of the people here to pronounce anyway. Many people look at you strangely and seem to distrust you if you have a strange name. I have decided to take the American or English version of my name. Please enter the account as that of Andrew V. Stanley."

The banker nodded and said, "As you wish," Then he left the room.

The others in the room had been totally silent and now Andraui turned to them with a smile on his face.

"That wasn't so difficult was it?"

They looked at one another and back at Andraui.

Windham was the first one to speak.

"Are you sure you are not some big-time financier? The way you handled that would do justice to any businessman in this country."

Georgiades spoke up also. "Mr. Stanislaski, if you ever want to go into business, I will be glad to take you in as a partner."

Andraui smiled, and then said, "We didn't have much money in my home town and had to bargain over things we exchanged so I learned early on how to bargain for what we needed. First, I am no longer Stanislaski. My name from today forward will be Stanley. Secondly, I look forward to us all having a long and friendly relationship. I would like to forego the Mister and have you call me Andrew. That is the way it is done here in America is it not? Do you not address your friends by their first name?"

They all assured him it was, and each in turn invited him to use their given names as well.

The banker returned shortly and handed Andraui a document to sign. Andraui read it through very carefully then handed it to Captain Wilson and requested he look it over too.

Wilson glanced at it quickly, and then indicated that Georgiades should review it as he was better at legal matters than he. Georgiades took the paper and read it, then handed it back to Andraui with a nod of his head. Andraui took a pen and signed it.

Then Miller turned to Joshua and said, "Sir, since you may be drawing against Mr. Stanley's account at some future date, I will need your signature also."

Joshua signed the document and handed it back to the banker.

Andraui spoke again. "There is one more small detail. The deposits will be brought in by Mr. Georgiades and I would like duplicate receipts made. One for him and one to be given to Mr. Windham the next time he is in the bank to be held for Captain Wilson's return."

Miller replied. "That will not be a problem. I will see to it myself. Here is your deposit receipt for the $47,000 and I will get you the change you asked for. Will you need any bank drafts? These are used for larger purchases, since large amount of coins can be heavy and a burden to carry around. Is there anything else I can do for you?"

"No. I believe that takes care of everything."

"Very well. Mr. Stanley, I welcome you to the First Bank of Charleston. I don't mind telling you sir; it is not every day that I gain a customer such as you. I would like to have you gentlemen and your wives to join me for dinner this evening, to celebrate and seal our new business together. Would 7 P.M. be satisfactory?"

Charlie was the first to speak up. "I'm afraid I will not be able to accept. At that time of the evening I am needed to maintain order in the tavern. Perhaps another time."

Joshua also declined. He indicated that he had delayed sailing to assist Andraui and he would have to take advantage of the outgoing tides during the night.

Andraui said, "I am not married and do not know anyone here, but I am free this evening. If it would not be an imposition, I could come. Besides, I need to talk to someone about getting outfitted for my trip. Who better to discuss this with than a banker?" He smiled at the others in the room.

Miller was delighted. He wanted to get to know more about this man who had so unexpectedly dropped into his bank and brought him such good fortune. He gave him directions to his home and told him to come early if he wished. They would have a drink and talk about his trip before dinner.

With the arrangements made, they left the bank. On the outside, the four new friends shook hands.

Andraui spoke to Peter while holding his hand in his, "Peter, I appreciate what you are doing for me. I hope that you will have good success and we both will profit from our acquaintance. I have placed my trust in you and I'm sure you will do well by me."

Peter returned his firm grip and looked him straight in the eye. "Andrew, long before America was discovered, my family has been businessmen and we have been jewelers for four generations. One thing I learned many years ago from my grandfather was that the good name and reputation of Georgiades must never be tarnished by dishonesty. You need have no worries that I will cheat you or betray your trust."

"I believe that Peter, or I would not have left my jewels in your care. When can I pick-up my ring and necklace?"

"I will begin work on it tonight. By Wednesday noon I will have them ready for you."

"Good. I will plan my departure for Thursday or Friday morning then."

Georgiades left them then and returned to his store. Joshua and Charlie prepared to leave also.

Charlie said, "Gentlemen, this has been one of the strangest and most exciting days of my life. Come down to the tavern. The drinks are on me."

They returned to the tavern and Charlie ordered drinks for them. Wilson took Irish whiskey, Charlie had his Virgin Island rum, and the new Andrew Stanley asked for Vodka. Charlie did not have many people asking for Vodka. It was a clear beverage and had the kick of a mule. Not many men could drink more than three or four drinks and walk out of the place.

Andrew asked for a salt shaker and a fresh lime. When the drinks came, he sliced the lime, sprinkled salt on his hand above his thumb, then raising his glass in salute to the others, tossed the drink down in one big gulp. He licked the salt from his fist and sucked on a slice of the lime.

The others watched in awe. Never had they seen anyone slug down Vodka in that manner. Andrew explained that this was a custom of the Cossacks, their way of toasting, or celebrating, after a battle or some special occasion. The three of them spent the next couple hours talking and drinking and finally, Joshua rose and bade them good-by. It was time for him to return to the ship and make ready for sail. He shook hands with both men and just before leaving he turned to Andrew and the words flowed from deep inside him.

"Andrew, never did I expect when you boarded my ship in Hamburg that I would be standing here tonight, nor that I would be a part of what has occurred today. You are an extraordinary man and I am pleased to have met you and to have you as a friend. Much has happened on this last voyage. I have the feeling that we have not seen the last of each other, and that the future holds a great deal more for you. I believe you will find America a good place to begin a new life and I wish you success with Catherine York. I presume that is who the ring and necklace is for. I hope she accepts them and I wish you much happiness. God bless you and keep you safe on your journey. Maybe He will lead you to the spot you are looking for."

Andrew embraced him in the manner of the Cossacks and wished him a safe voyage also. Then he bade Charlie good-night and walked back to his hotel to change clothes and go to the banker's home for dinner.

CHAPTER SEVEN

A ndrew freshened up and dressed in his finest attire. He wore his best silk shirt, the newest of the black trousers and a coat that was a little snug about the shoulders. Then he added a black string tie. He did not want to appear over dressed, but never having been to dinner at a banker's home before, he wasn't sure how he should dress. He was a bit nervous and thought perhaps he should have refused the invitation. After some delay, he decided to go as he was; after all, he didn't have to impress anyone. He was who he was, and they either accepted him as such, or not.

At fifteen minutes to the hour, he took a carriage and arrived at Miller's home, a couple minutes before seven. The home was situated on a quiet side street in a posh neighborhood; all the houses here spoke of money. Andrew figured this was where the business people of Charleston lived.(He had noticed that the local people no longer called the city Charlestown, but had shortened it to Charleston.) Miller's home was an impressive structure, not because of its design, but rather because of its size and because it was of brick, the same as the bank. He faced the large, two-story home with gabled windows on the upper floor. Andrew guessed it would contain upwards of 6,000 square feet and probably had 6 or more bedrooms. While such a house would be small compared to some of those he had seen in Boston, this was a large house in Charleston. Andrew began to appreciate the taste and choice that Miller had chosen.

He rapped twice on the huge wooden door with the brightly-shined, brass door knocker. It was opened promptly by a black woman dressed in a black and white uniform. When he introduced himself, the woman said, "Masta Harold is expecting you. I will show you into the library."

As they walked down the hall, Andrew was further impressed by the soft elegance of the big house. The floors were of highly polished oak, and the walls were decorated with paintings by names he had read about when he was in classes and knew these must be expensive paintings. The ornate stairway curved in a wide circle around the outside of the largest room, which Andrew assumed would be the living parlor. They passed through this room and into a smaller one, but just as impressive. Bookcases lined the walls on two sides, filled with books, some appearing to be new, but many seemed old with frayed covers indicating long and frequent use. A huge stone fireplace was situated along one wall with a massive board at least four inches thick and twelve inches wide that served as a mantel piece. A small fire crackled in the fireplace, and for the first time, Andrew realized there had been a chill in the air, perhaps due to the damp air blowing in off the sea.

Miller arose from a chair and put down his book. He came forward and extended his hand.

"I thought we might be more comfortable in this room. It is my favorite spot in the whole house. I like to sit here at night when the winds blow outside and read a good book before a warm fire. Do you like to read Mr. Stanley?"

Andrew hesitated a moment. "I used to read, a long time ago before the wars. We have not had much time to read these last few years, and many of the good books that were in our Master's castle were destroyed by first the Russians and then Germans and Prussians. Although I learned to read some, I was never a really good reader. I liked to read, but the books in the Master's castle were not available to us. We were limited in reading materials."

"Well, certainly, if you will be staying in Charleston, I would be happy to place my library at your disposal. You may take any of the books here and read them if you wish."

"Thank you, sir. However, I expect to be leaving for a journey to the west in a day or two; just as soon as I can outfit myself for the trip."

"How long do you anticipate being gone?"

"As I mentioned in your office today, I don't really know. There is much about America that I do not know, but one thing I am sure of, I can never go back to Poland. I must adopt this new country and find another home. I am told that there are many beautiful spots and plenty of land for the taking. I am not much for cities. I prefer the hills and forest lands. My father was a caretaker of a large forest with lots of game. I want to look for such a land here in America. If I find such a place I will try to buy it and make my home there. It may take me awhile, but if there is such a place, I will find it."

Miller said, "Travel outside the areas of settlement can be very dangerous, especially for one who does not know the ways of the savages who inhabit the area. I don't refer just to the Indians either. There are white men who roam the back-woods who are worse than any savages you may meet. They will slit your throat for a dollar and rob you of your clothes, weapons and anything else you have. You should not travel alone. It would be good if you could obtain a guide, someone who is familiar with the trails and the ways of the woods."

Andrew pondered this information.

"I intend to go well armed and I am fairly well versed in combat. Still, I admit to great ignorance when it comes to the ways of this new land. Would you know of someone who I might hire to guide me into these backwoods you refer to?"

"Mr. Stanley, I don't mean to belittle your combat experience, but fighting in the forest that the natives know like the back of their hand, and which will be strange to you, will differ greatly from what I imagine you have been used to. They strike from ambush and you may be dead before you ever see them. They are masters at concealment and the white men I mentioned have adapted well to their type of stalking. If they attack you, you will have no warning and they will be upon you before you can unsheathe your sword."

Miller put his finger to his jaw, lost in thought, and then continued, "I know a couple of men who might agree to escort you, if they take to you. These are very independent men and will not work for anyone they do not like. If you wish, I can contact them. They don't often come to town, but now that I'm thinking of it, one of them has a daughter that lives in Charleston and he sometimes comes to visit her.

"Before you leave this evening, I will give you the daughter's address and you can call on her. She will be able to tell you if he has been to town lately."

At this point, two ladies dressed in silk dresses with large flowing skirts entered the room. The first was a stout woman of perhaps forty years of age. Her hair was dark but there was just a slight hint of grey beginning to appear at the temples. She had dark eyes and a pleasant smile as she entered. Andrew judged she must be Mrs. Miller.

The second woman was in her mid-twenties and she too had dark hair. It was pulled back and tied in a bun at the nape of her neck. She stood about five and a half feet tall, and from what he could tell, seemed very trim. She had an olive complexion as if she might have some ancestor who was either Italian or Spanish. Her skin looked as smooth as the silk dress she wore. The neckline was just low enough to emphasize her large breasts. The dress was cinched in at the waist which Andrew believed he could span with his hands. He couldn't tell about the rest of her because of the fullness of the dress. She was beautiful, but seemed annoyed or uncomfortable about being here.

Miller introduced his wife as Hannah, and the younger woman as his niece, Maria Santiago. Andrew was to learn later that Maria's mother had married a Spanish sailor and was considered the "lost sheep" of the family.

Mrs. Miller greeted Andrew with a strong handshake and a pleasant smile. She welcomed him to their home and was glad he could join them for dinner.

Maria barely took his hand when he extended it and quickly dropped it afterward. She too, smiled, but very briefly and only politely. Andrew sensed that she had probably been pressured to come to dinner in order to round out a foursome. It was pretty evident that she wasn't too excited about the matter.

After a few minutes of light conversation, the servant announced that dinner was ready and they all filed into a big dining room that would have seated forty people comfortably. The four place settings had been placed at one end of the table and, again, Andrew noted the silent expression of wealth. The china was exquisite and the crystal was the finest he had ever seen. The silverware placed at each plate sparkled in its brightness. The display was not ostentatious, just quality done in good taste.

As they sat down, Mrs. Miller said, "Mr. Stanley, we are Protestant and I believe you are Catholic. We always give thanks for the bounty God has bestowed upon us. I hope you will not be offended."

"Not at all, Mrs. Miller. My mother made sure we did the same at our table. We may pray a little differently, but we both worship the same God. And please, call me Andrew. I am not yet used to this new name, and Mr. Stanley sounds too formal to me."

At these words he noticed Maria's head come up and for the first time she seemed to notice him.

Mrs. Miller responded, "Very well, I will call you Andrew if you will call us Harold and Hannah. We are not real formal in this household."

Maria asked, "Mr. Stanley, what did you mean when you said "you were not used to your new name?""

Miller seemed somewhat embarrassed but said nothing. It was impolite to ask such questions of total strangers.

Andrew didn't seem to notice and answered, "My real name is Andraui Vladimir Stanislaski, but I have found this to be difficult for Americans to pronounce so I have taken the English version, Andrew Stanley. I am making a new start for myself here in America and I might as well have a new name."

Miller took up the explanation at this point. "Andrew was in the Polish Army until Poland was over-run by Russia from one side and the Germans and Prussians from the other side. He opened an account in the bank today and will be leaving for the interior in a few days. In a sense he is a refugee, as are many who come to America. Almost all of us are refugees of one sort or another. This is the place where we get another chance, a chance at a new start and a new life."

Andrew wondered how the man knew so much about him. None of his background had been revealed in their conversations earlier in the day. He guessed this man had many sources of information and probably, Peter Georgiades was one of them. Bankers usually made it their business to know what was going on and when new arrivals came to town, they'd want to learn as much as they could about the newcomers.

It was an excellent meal, prepared by a real cook who knew just the right seasonings to use and the right moment to stop the cooking process to serve the item. Not for years had Andrew had such a pleasant meal among such congenial surroundings. He said as much to Hannah.

"It has been many years since I sat at such a table as this and enjoyed such a delicious meal. I had thought I might never have this pleasure again. Your cook should be complimented."

Andrew and the Millers chatted as if they were old friends during the entire meal. Each tried at some point to bring Maria into the conversation, but after several attempts in which her response was abbreviated, although not impolite, they left her alone and talked to each other. It was as if she would rather be someplace else and was not at all interested in their conversation.

As they neared the end of the dinner, Hannah asked, "Do you have a family back in Poland, Andrew?"

They could tell by the grave expression on his face that this was a question that would have been better unasked. He was very quiet and then he answered slowly.

"No I have no one back there. That is why I have decided to stay in America. My father was hanged by the Prussians; my mother was shot trying to defend my sister, who was ravaged by looting soldiers and then bayoneted to death. The master of our lands, one you would probably call the landlord, was killed in the battle when we caught up with the soldiers who killed my family. I tried to locate his wife and daughters, who had fled to England. I later discovered they had not reached England, I returned to Germany and learned that the wife and both daughters had been killed by soldiers also. So there is no one back there, and I cannot return. If I was caught I would either be forced into one of the enemy armies or executed. That is why I have decided to build a new life here in America."

Miller was totally silent and Hannah's mouth gaped open, her face in total shock at the graphic description of these horrible acts. Andrew realized his mistake and attempted to apologize.

"I am sorry. I did not mean to speak so bluntly and at such a pleasant occasion as this. However, the sights are still in my mind and when I think of them I have trouble controlling my anger."

Hannah answered, "You poor man. I apologize to you for bringing up the subject. I had no idea that your life was so tragic. I know that it must be terribly painful for you to talk about these things, but sometimes, talking about them cleanses the soul. Maybe with time, some of the pain will go away. In the meantime, you men retire to the library for a brandy while we girls powder our noses."

Arising from his chair, Andrew caught Maria staring at him. For the first time, she seemed to be interested in what he had said. Her eyes were slightly narrowed and she seemed in deep thought. Entering the library, he wondered what it was that had caught her attention. She was very attractive, and he was drawn to her, but she had seemed indifferent to him all evening. He had decided she just did not like him and he would let the matter end there.

A short time later, the ladies returned and joined them in the library. Maria was almost a different person. She favored him with a smile that began on her lips and ended in her eyes. She now seemed genuinely interested in the conversation between he and Miller. They were discussing his trip into the woods and Maria asked a probing question.

"Mr. Stanley, are you going into the woods to hunt or to look for a homestead? Do you plan to be a farmer?"

"I am not yet sure, Miss Santiago. I farmed some in Poland and I hunted in the forests of our landlord, but whatever I do, I want it to be on my own land. I do not want to work for another man ever again. I have been told that there are great forests and large tracts of land to the west that a man can have almost for the taking."

Hannah joined the conversation.

"That is true, Andrew, however, much of that land is uncivilized and has only the most primitive conditions. Do you think you will be content to live away from people and with the barest of essentials?"

"Madam, right now I think that may be just what I need. I have seen a little too much of civilization. I am still trying to sort out just what kind of future I want and what I want to do with my life. Perhaps this trip will help me find some answers."

They talked on for several more minutes until the big clock on the mantel above the fire-place struck the hour of ten. Andrew apologized for the lateness of the hour and prepared to leave.

Maria said she, too, had to go for she had a busy day tomorrow and it was getting late.

Until this time, Andrew assumed she was a house guest of the Millers. Evidently, this was not the case as she prepared to leave. Miller arose and began putting on his coat.

Maria said, "Uncle Harold it isn't necessary for you to take me home. I can get a carriage and will be home in fifteen minutes."

Harold said, "This is no time of night for a young lady to be out alone. I wouldn't think of letting you go by yourself."

Andrew had wondered if he would have an opportunity to speak to the girl alone. Now he seized the opportunity so conveniently thrown into his lap.

"If Miss Santiago has no objection, I will be happy to

escort her home. I have to go back to my hotel anyway and it will not be any inconvenience."

Maria objects again, but Harold issued an ultimatum. "Either let Andrew see you home or I will go with you. You are not going out on the streets alone at this time of night."

In the end, Maria relented.

After once again expressing his thanks for a wonderful evening, Andrew escorted her out onto the sidewalk and hailed a passing carriage.

During the evening, the fog had crept in off the water and the temperature was slightly chilly. Andrew notice Maria carried only a light shawl around her shoulders, and she shivered as they settled into the seat of the carriage. He moved ever so slightly closer offered his coat for her shoulders. She refused but did allow him to sit closer.

The clopping sound of the horse's hooves echoed in the damp night and their first few moments were shared in silence. Finally, Andrew asked a question that has been on his mind all evening.

"I hope you will not think me forward, but would you mind telling me what it is that you dislike about me?"

She pulled away from him slightly and looked directly at him. Then she smiled, "Did I give you that impression?"

"Yes. You seemed unhappy that I was there tonight and as if I had offended you."

"I'm sorry if I gave you that impression. It was not that I was angry that you were there. I was angry because I was there. It is rather embarrassing, but you see, I am 24 years old and not yet betrothed. My Aunt Hannah and Uncle Harold think this is terrible, and that I will end up an old maid spinster. They mean well, but I do not like to be thrust upon strangers. I will pick my husband; and at the right time, we will get married. If I do not find the right person, then I will stay single and be an old maid. I will not marry someone just for convenience sake. You sir, may not have realized it, but tonight you were a prospective husband."

At that they both had a good laugh. Andrew liked this girl and as she huddled closer for warmth, he could feel the firmness of her shoulder and her body pressing against him. It had been a long time since he had bedded a woman, especially one with the attributes of this lovely creature beside him. He began to feel his male instincts reacting. She was so close he could smell her hair and just a hint of perfume from her neck. Barely realizing it, he had put his arm around her shoulders to help warm her. Instinctively, he rubbed her shoulder and neck with his hand. To his surprise she did not object, and in fact, seemed to enjoy his light caress.

They reached her destination and she turned her face toward him. She looked into his eyes, then, without any warning, she leaned over and kissed him on the lips. He had wanted to kiss her but was afraid she might slap him or make a fuss and was surprised when she kissed him. She opened her moist lips and ran her tongue across his lips and into his mouth. Her arms went around his waist and she pressed against him. Where she had been cool and withdrawn all evening, she was now warm and responsive. The kiss brought on another in which they each explored the other's mouth with their tongues and he pulled her body tightly to him. She came willingly and would have crawled into his lap but for the big bulky dress she wore. His hand pressed against her right breast and she caught her breath and grabbed his hand. He thought he had gone too far. Then she relaxed with a deep sigh and pressed his hand even tighter against the breast.

The carriage came to a stop and the driver stepped down off the carriage to open the door. Andrew helped Maria down to the sidewalk and told the driver to wait until he could see the lady to the door. They went up the steps, and she rummaged in her handbag for a key. They were in the dark doorway and out of sight of the driver. Andrew reached for her again and she came willingly. He kissed her again and held her tight against him and she pressed her body to him.

He whispered into her ear, "Come with me to my hotel. I will only be in town two, three days at the most. I want to be with you this night."

"Me too. You have set my soul afire and I want your body next to mine. Dismiss the driver and come in. I live alone, but we must be very quiet. I would be scandalized if we wake up any of the other tenants and they see a strange man coming into my room."

Andrew stepped to the curb, paid the carriage driver and told him he would not need him after all.

Maria waited at the door.

"Let me go in first. You hold the door open. It will close and lock by itself when you release it. My room is at the head of the stairs and to the left, the second door. I will leave it ajar. But do be very quiet."

With that she slipped through the door and was swallowed in the dim light. He gave her a full two minutes before easing in himself. He felt a little like a robber, but no one was up this time of night. He walked quickly to the stairs and climbed them two at a time. On the first landing he turned left, and at the second door, pushed gently. The door swung open and he stepped inside. It was totally dark as he closed the door behind him.

Hardly knowing what to expect, he waited to give his eyes time to adjust to the dark. Many times during battle he had found himself alone and in strange surroundings. He always remained still until he could make out objects and see well enough before he made a move.

While he stood thus, waiting, he felt her move toward

him and in a second she was in his arms. As he wrapped his arms around her, he discovered she had shed the voluminous dress and was now only in her chemise and under garments. He was surprised at her boldness and her hunger. She was all but ready to devour him. She was tugging at his coat and then the sash around his waist. When she felt the money belt, she stopped and backed away. He removed it and laid it aside. She came back to him then and led him to her bed. There was a little light streaming through the window and as he sat on the edge of the bed, she stood before him. He leaned over and kissed her. With a shiver, she reached behind her to undo the catches that held her chemise. She seemed to have trouble getting them loose, so she turned her back to him and he undid the snaps. As it fell to the floor she wilted backwards onto his lap, totally nude. Her body glistened in the moonlight. Lord, he thought, what a lovely body. He had thought her beautiful before, now she was a goddess.

Andrew could hear her pouring water in a basin and the sloshing of water as she bathed herself. He listened to her other movements as he lay back on the bed to relax and wait her return.

He most have dropped off to sleep, for she was shaking him and told him to get up. She pulled him up and led him to the next room where there was a tub of hot water. Then she motioned him to get in the tub. When he did, she kneeled beside the tub and began to wash his face and neck. Then she moved to his shoulders and began with the rest of his body. He eased down in the tub. He had never been bathed by a woman before, and found that he enjoyed it. When he stepped from the tub she rubbed him down with a thick, soft towel and led him back to the bed. She turned the covers down and crawled in, still naked as the day she was born.

She motioned for him to get in beside her and he did. As she snuggled close into his arms, she seemed almost demure again. She had let her hair down and it cascaded across her shoulders and spilled out on the pillow. She lay with her head on his shoulder and with one hand played with the hair on his chest. After a few minutes she spoke, in a low tone, almost a whisper.

"You must think of me as a strumpet. I have known you less than five hours and here we have made love together and are lying in bed as if we were man and wife. I want you to know that I am not this free with my body to everyone. There is something about you, about the hardships you have endured that attracted me to you. I suppose I must have the hot Spanish blood of my father. My mother always thought of him as the world's greatest lover. She was very jealous of him. But they loved each other very much; so much in fact that she ran away from a good family to be with him. Her family disowned her and she has never been welcome in their house since. Aunt Hannah and mother were very close and they still see each other from time to time, and my grandparents seem to adore me. They have always welcomed me and seemed genuinely happy to see me. I hope that someday they will welcome my mother and father too."

She was silent a moment, then she rose up on her elbow and looked him directly in the face. There was just enough light from the window to outline his features.

"Aunt Hannah sometimes invites me to dinner when they have an important guest and often they are old and fat. I feel like a piece of beef on display to be examined, and offered as a prize. That is why I was rather unpleasant tonight when I first met you. I thought Harold and Hannah were trying to get me married to another one of their business friends in town. As you spoke tonight, and I learned that you were just passing through, and you were not another business acquaintance of Harold's that they perceived to be a "good catch", I began to look at you in a different light. When I did, I found you both interesting and attractive. Single women live a rather lonely life in this town, and in almost any town for that matter. We are constantly watched, and if we dally and talk to a man friend too long, the gossips' tongues begin to wag and a lady's reputation is easily lost. You intrigue me, Andrew Stanley, and the fact that you will be leaving soon, made me realize that we might steal a few moments together without anyone being the wiser. If that shocks you I am sorry."

Andrew had never had such an open and frank discussion with a woman before. He felt strongly attracted to her. He kissed her gently on the forehead and said, "I like a person who is honest with me and it pleases me that you found me attractive for I had feared that I would be shunned because of the scar on my face. Unlike some men, I do not believe that women should be handled like slaves, to be bedded at a man's whim and relegated to the role of breeder of children. Besides, I had heard about the passionate nature of Spanish women, but I have never known one. Now that I have, I doubt I can ever be satisfied again. Of the few women I have known in the past, many were afraid to reveal their true feelings. I find it really pleasing that you can express your innermost feelings and let your desires show without fear. It accents my enjoyment knowing that the feeling is not one sided, that you, too, are experiencing pleasure along with me."

These seemed to be the words she wanted to hear and it raised her passion again and she indicated she was ready for more love-making. Afterward they were both spent and he made a move to get up, she whispered in his ear, "Don't go yet. I want to hold you a little more before we get up."

He lay still and gradually relaxed. He could feel the sweat on both of them.

Shortly, she sighed, gave him a long, soft kiss and gently motioned for him to let her up.

Andraui dressed. When she came to him and asked him to stay the rest of the night, he smiled, kissed her on the forehead and said, "My little spitfire, as much as I would like to, it is almost four in the morning. If I am to get out before your neighbors wake up, I must go now. Besides, there is nothing more I could do tonight. In fact it may take me a month to get my strength back."

Now he took her naked body into his arms and held her close, and spoke very softly and gently to her. "I am so glad that you invited me in tonight Maria. I do not know where our relationship may lead to, but I tell you this. I have never made love with anyone like you before and I have never been so pleased and satisfied. I almost feel guilty in leaving you, as if I may have taken advantage of you."

Now it was Maria's turn to speak.

She pulled away slightly and placed both hands on his arms. "No, Andrew. You are not to feel guilty, nor are you to worry about me. I will be all right." She returned his smile and continued, "You may have been the one who was taken advantage of. After all, it has been many months since you were with a woman and I could tell you, too, were lonely. Nor did you receive all the enjoyment. You are a good lover and I am just as pleased as you are. Let's just call it a pleasant interlude in each of our lives and let it go at that. Although, I must admit that I will miss not seeing you again."

As Andrew stepped out the door, an idea occurred to him. He turned to Maria and said, "Would it be scandalous if you had dinner with me in the hotel dining room this coming evening?"

She hesitated momentarily. "I think it would be best

if we did not. You are under no obligation to me, Andrew. Besides, I don't know if I could keep my hands to myself." And with that, she patted his shoulder and shooed him out into the night.

Feeling fatigued, but strangely, never more content, Andrew walked back to his hotel, oblivious to the fog that shrouded him. His mind was full of Maria and the softness of her body. He wondered if a man could ever find any woman who would better satisfy his physical needs. He doubted it, and the idea began to enter his mind that she just might be the wife he would need to help him build the empire he had in mind.

CHAPTER EIGHT

A ndrew slept a little later than usual the next morning. He was usually up and dressed by six o'clock each day, however, because of the lateness of the hour when he returned to his bed, it was nearing ten o'clock when he awoke.

He climbed out of bed quickly to shave and dress. He had much to do today, and the day was well on its way. He hurried through a quick breakfast and stepped to the boardwalk, motioning for a carriage. He gave the driver the address Harold Miller had given him the night before.

It took the carriage only about twenty minutes to reach their destination. Andrew stepped down in front of a small frame house that was freshly painted and well kept. There were flowers in the yard and a small picket fence around the front. He went through the gate and up onto the porch and knocked. A large woman of about thirty years of age came to the door. She was of German or Dutch descendants and had golden hair tied in a bun at the back of her head. When she spoke, it was with a slight accent that was barely noticeable.

"Mr. Miller at the bank gave me your name and said you might be able to tell me where I might locate Mr. Hans Brinkman."

The lady looked at him for a moment and asked, "What did you want him for?"

Andrew explained. "I am planning to take a trip into the interior and I am unfamiliar with the lands and the local ways. I need both a guide and someone to teach me things I need to learn about America. Mr. Miller thought Mr. Brinkman would be the person to guide me, if I could convince him. Is he in?"

The frosty reception thawed a little, and she favored him with a short smile. "I doubt you will be able to convince him. He seldom works for money and he doesn't like pilgrims, people who are new to this country. He says their lack of experience and understanding will get a man killed in the forest. However, you are in luck. He seldom comes into town, hates being around so many people. He comes about once every two years to see our family and his grandchildren. He dotes on his grandson, small Hans, who we named after him." She pushed a wisp of unruly hair behind her ear and continued, "He is in town now, though, visiting a friend of his who is a gunsmith, Albert Mueller. I think he is planning to leave tomorrow and is stocking up on powder and shot. If you would care to come back later today, I will tell him you were here."

"Could you give me Mr. Mueller's address? I too, must, buy a gun and ammunition. Perhaps I could catch your father at Mr. Mueller's shop."

With the address in hand, Andrew crawled up on the box with the driver. He said, "I hope you don't mind me riding up here. I am not used to being treated like landed gentry and I am more comfortable up here than in the carriage." The driver shrugged, and with that, Andrew provided the driver with the address to his next stop.

The driver was a friendly man and seemed to enjoy someone to talk to. He talked about the weather and things in general.

"I heard you mention that you would be needing guns

for your trip. You are going to one of the best gunsmiths in all the Carolinas. Mueller was born in Virginia but moved to Pennsylvania as a boy. There he apprenticed under Sam Boone, the nephew of Daniel Boone. He helped Boone make the Pennsylvania Rifle, sometimes called the Kentucky Rifle, for the Continental Army before and during the revolution. The Pennsylvania Rifle is the best rifle in the world today, and Mueller is well known for his quality of arms."

Andrew listened intently. "You seem to know a lot about firearms, did you serve in the Army?"

The driver answered, "Yes. All able bodied men fought the British and we have been fighting the Indians since I was a little boy. In this land, a man is the same as being naked if he doesn't have a good gun with him. We Americans are not only allowed to keep guns in our houses and carry them with us, we are encouraged to do so. In fact, General Washington and the Continental Congress decreed that all citizens should be armed. If it were not for us fighting with the regular soldiers, we would never have won our freedom from the Brits. Guns are what has helped us tame this land, what helped us win our freedom and what will help us hold it against any and all who might try to take it from us. And that includes the government. We will never bow down to another king or queen."

Andrew nodded in understanding.

"I have found this same spirit everywhere I have gone since I arrived here and I am deeply impressed by it. As long as a people have this kind of spirit and are well armed any enemy would pay a horrendous price attacking you. If my people had been fully armed my country might be free today. We had the people and the spirit, but we did not have the weapons. The Russians had huge numbers of troops, and the Germans and Prussians had by far the best weapons. Although our men fought bravely, they were no match for the well trained and well-armed troops of the Prussians. We sometimes had to charge lines of enemy soldiers armed with guns similar to the Brown Bess built by the British or the French Charleville Musket. We did not have many guns and we charged them with sword and lances. The enemy fired volley after volley into our ranks. Thousands were killed. Polish blood stains many of the fields in Poland. I can never go back there so I plan to make a new life for myself here in America."

"This is the place where you can do just that. There is no other land in the world that I know of where a man can stand on his own two feet and do as he pleases as long as he does not harm his neighbors. Many have come here for a new life and have done well. But you will need a good gun and plenty of powder to hold any land or wealth you find. There are always those who do not want to work and will try to take what another has earned by the sweat of his brow. I hear tell Mueller has been working on some new ideas for a gun that loads from the breech instead of from the muzzle. You can load and fire it much faster than the old muzzleloader guns. I've been meaning to go by and talk with him but I don't have the money it takes to buy one of those new experimental guns. I took a ball in the leg at the battle of Kings Mountain and am unable to do much more than ride this box now."

The two men rode the rest of the way in silence and soon arrived at the gun shop of Albert Mueller. Andrew dismounted, asked the driver to wait, and went inside.

The shop was not well lit, making it difficult to see many details. As was his custom when he could not see what was in front of him, Andrew stood still just inside the door and waited for his eyes to become accustomed to the dim light.

A small bell on the door had announced a customer,

and now a man of about 40 years of age emerged from the back of the shop and asked if he could be of service.

"Yes, I hope so. I am looking for a man by the name of Hans Brinkman. His daughter mentioned to me he was coming here."

The shop owner acknowledged that Hans was there, in the back of the shop. Then he disappeared behind a doorway hung with a heavy drape, almost like a tapestry.

Directly, a big man, about the same height as Andrew, but with broader shoulders and hands as big as hams, emerged from the back. His age was difficult to determine, it could have been anywhere from 40 to 60, but one could see immediately that he was in excellent physical condition. He moved in a sort of bent-kneed fashion and his movements reminded Andrew of a stalking lion. His hair was turning grey and he had it platted into two braids that hung down either side of his head and in front of his shoulders.

He spoke in a booming voice that could probably have been heard across the street. "I'm Brinkman. What can I do for you?"

"Mr. Brinkman, your daughter said I might find you here. Mr. Miller at the bank recommended I contact you to see if you might be interested in guiding me inland. My name is Andrew Stanley and I have only recently arrived in your country. I intend to stay and make a new life for myself, but I do not want to do it here in town. I was born and reared near large forests and I would like to look for such a place here. Would you consider acting as my Guide? I would be willing to pay you for your troubles."

Brinkman did not hesitate, he answered right off. "Young man, I do not act as a guide nor am I for hire. What money I need I earn by trapping and a little mining now and then. In the woods you do not need much money. But the main reason I do not guide is because most people going into the interior are inexperienced and have no idea of what they are up against. They are unskilled in fighting and the first time they run into Indians or the riffraff that skulk in the woods they wet their pants. This type situation can get a man killed faster than you can snap your fingers. No sir, you will have to find someone else."

Andrew could feel that the man was offended and Andrew was a little put out by his attitude as well.

He said, "Sir, it is true that I probably do not have a fair idea of what I will face traveling in this new land, but I have faced my share of the enemy and I have yet to wet my pants. You were recommended to me and I sought your help. I meant no offense."

"None taken." He turned and reentered the back room.

Andrew turned to the shop keeper. "You are Mr. Mueller?"

"Yes. Is there something I can do for you?"

"Yes, sir. As you just heard, I am planning to go inland and I will need a good rifle and two pistols. I am familiar with the French Model 1763 Charleville Musket, and the British Brown Bess, but I seek something better. I have heard much about the Pennsylvania Rifle, but I have never fired one. I have also heard of the Ferguson breech-loading Rifle. I saw one of these in the battle for Warsaw. A German Jaeger had one and he fired five or six rounds to each one of his companions' shots. He brought down a number of my men before we ran him through with a lance. I tried to grab the rifle, but another soldier had picked it up as he ran. I could never get near enough to examine it closely. Would you have such a rifle in your supply?"

Mueller was somewhat surprised at the knowledge this stranger had about guns. While many knew about Brown Bess's and the Charleville Rifle, not many knew about the Ferguson. It was a new idea in weaponry and Mueller had obtained a number of them after the battle of Kings

Mountain on October 7th, 1780. Ferguson had brought a couple hundred into the battle that the Americans had won. Ferguson had been killed in that battle.

Mueller led Andrew to a rack on the rear wall and took down a long rifle with an octagon barrel with a maple stock and placed it on a table he used as a counter. Then he proceeded to take down a number of other guns and put them on the table also.

Andrew examined each one carefully. He was sure that the first gun was a Pennsylvania rifle. He liked the heft to it and he brought it to his shoulder a couple of times and practiced sighting. Then he went over the others equally as well. He did not realize that Hans Brinkman was standing in the door watching him. There was a Brown Bess, a Charleville Rifle, and two or three others that evidently had been built by American Rifle makers but they did not really impress him.

He spoke to Mueller. "This Pennsylvania Rifle has potential, but it is not quite what I am looking for. Do you have any of the Fergusons?"

Mueller was intrigued with the idea of a breech-loading weapon. He was well aware of the short comings of the muzzle loading rifle and had been making some minor revisions to the Ferguson Rifle over the past couple years. He had added a box to the side of the stock to hold the patches of doeskin and tallow used to grease the barrel. The ball was a fraction of an inch smaller than the rifle barrel bore. The box would hold ten shot and patches. A skilled marksman could load and fire in a quarter of the time that it took to load and fire the conventional musket. He had placed a hinged, spring loaded lid on the box so that it sprang shut as soon as the shooter had removed a shot. This kept the rest of the shot from coming loose and falling out.

Mueller went into the back of the shop and emerged

with two guns. One he stood in the corner, and the other he handed to Andrew. Andrew hefted the weapon, looked at it and noticed that sights had been added just as were on the Pennsylvania Rifles. It had a round barrel instead of the octagon barrel of the Pennsylvania gun. The frizzen and pan were new and the entire gun, though not new was in excellent shape.

Mueller had also made one other variation. He had replaced the frizzen with a metal plate and added a cock with jaws to hold the flint. Thus instead of scrapping the flint along-side the plate to create the spark, the new method allowed the flint to strike the box sharply creating a spark almost every time. One of the troubles with the old type plate and flint was that it did not always strike a spark, thus causing a miss-fire.

Andrew spent several minutes examining the weapon and sighting, hefting and peering inside the barrel. He said, "Mr. Mueller, this is a good weapon, but it is still not quite what I am looking for. This is the first time I have seen a Ferguson up close, I assume this is an original model?"

Mueller indicated it was, and after a momentary hesitation, he picked up the other gun he had brought from the back room. He handed it to Andrew and asked him if he liked that one.

Andrew looked closely. It had the Octagon barrel like the Pennsylvania Rifle with the rifling on the inside spiraling instead of running straight with the barrel. It was about 42 inches long and had adjustable sights at both the front and back. He examined the firing mechanism and the box on the side for carrying shot and patches. The flintlock action was tight and slightly improved over the Pennsylvania models. It was a .45 caliber. There was also an improved trigger guard reinforced with a bronze plate. The stock was not fancy but, was shaped so it fit the shoulder comfortably.

It was of some different kind of wood that Andrew was not familiar with. He asked, "This stock is different from most guns I have seen, what is it made of?"

"It is made of Pecan wood. The pecan is one of the hardest woods I know of. When it dries it is even harder than oak. It will take a blow of considerable force and not break or split. One of the troubles with lots of guns is that the stock breaks or splits with heavy use or when struck at an angle. Then without a stock, the gun is useless. The Pecan wood will take a blow two to three times harder than the Maple usually used for stocks."

"I notice also that the rifling's inside the barrel are spiral. Is there some reason for this?"

"Yes. It is something I am experimenting with. I have not yet had a chance to test it against the Pennsylvania Rifle, but I believe it will cause the bullet to fly truer and hold a straighter trajectory. All rifle shot tend to drop over a distance. It is my belief that the rifling in this gun will keep the shot on a straighter course and the fall will be less. That is why I have shortened the barrel. This rifle should fire the same distance as the longer barreled, Pennsylvania Rifle. I have also strengthened the firing chamber so that a slightly larger powder charge can be added without danger of exploding the chamber. These are just some ideas I am trying."

Andrew pursued with further questions, "This is not like any of the other guns you have shown me, nor like any I have ever seen. These modifications make this really an exceptional gun. Are all of these changes your ideas?"

Mueller was pleased and answered, "Yes. I have taken the best of the Pennsylvania Rifle and the breech-loading process from the Ferguson and put them into this gun. It weighs only 3&1/2 lbs., a full 2 pounds less than the longer barreled Pennsylvania. I enlarged the box on the side of the stock to hold 20 balls and patches. The cock is stronger and the jaws that hold the flint are also larger. It will hold a larger piece of flint, which will mean lesser times you will have to replace the flint, and the plate has a hinged cover to protect the powder from rain or moisture. Then I had the stock specially made from the Pecan wood and as you will notice, I have placed a steel plate at the butt that extends all the way around the stock. If used as a club, or to strike someone with the butt, it will deliver a deadly blow and not splinter or break."

"Is this gun for sale? How much do you want for it?"

Mueller hesitated before answering, "I had not thought to sell it for it is the first of a new gun that I had hoped to build. I do not have another like it. I brought it to show you only because you seem to know guns quite well and I am sort of proud of what I have down with this."

"And well you should be, sir. I believe this will be superior to anything I will find anywhere else. I am willing to pay you double the price of any of these other guns. Could you not make another?"

"Yes, I could make another, but it may take me months. I couldn't take less than $50 for this one."

Andrew replied, "Sir, I will give you $100 for this gun for it is worth every cent of that much, but I have one other requirement. I want two matching pistols, of your best quality, and I want them of a caliber that will match this gun. I do not want to have to carry two calibers of shot. I want them interchangeable with all three guns. Can you provide such pistols?"

Mueller thought a moment and said, ""There is a .45 caliber pistol but the firing mechanism is very unreliable. It is not a popular weapon and we don't sell many of them. The better weapons are of larger caliber, one of .54 calibers and the other .69 caliber. Are you sure you would not like one of the better pistols?"

"Could you take the .45 caliber pistol and modify it as you have this rifle, putting on a better pan and firing cock?"

After a few moments, Mueller replied, "I probably could, but I have never made such modifications on pistols before. It would take several weeks to complete such a task."

Andrew replied, "Mr. Mueller, I leave in two days and may be gone the better part of a year. I would like to have two such pistols to take with me. If you can modify them by Friday morning, I will pay you another $75 each."

"Sir, you should be a trader, you drive a hard bargain. I truly do not know if I can make one such weapon in that period of time, much less two. However, I will try. I am eager to see how they will work. I had never thought to put the same mechanism on pistols as I was using on the rifles. It is an interesting idea."

"Good. I will see you at eight A.M. sharp, Friday morning. I will also need 300 shot, patches and ample powder."

Andrew glanced toward Brinkman, who had come further into the room and was sitting on the corner of one of the tables, and kept talking with Mueller. "I know not what lies in store for me, but I want to be well prepared. I shall return at eight o'clock Friday. I will pay you now, but please hold my rifle for me until then."

Mueller protested that would not be necessary, but Andrew counted out the $100 for the rifle and said he would have the other $150 Friday if the pistols were ready.

With that, Andrew bade the gunsmith good day and departed from the shop. He reentered the carriage and asked the driver to take him to a livery stable. He must arrange transportation.

As they drove to the stable, Andrew pondered the attitude of Brinkman. The man was inscrutable. You could not read him as you could many people. He had turned him down flat without even finding out what the pay was, and yet he seemed very interested in the negotiations over the guns. Strange man!

Andrew asked the driver if he knew much about horses, "I was raised on a farm, remember? And I know work horses, but I don't know a lot about riding stock. I do know that if you are planning to go into the interior you don't want to take full- blooded horses. They don't forage as well as the mustang and they are more high-strung. They can't stand the changes in weather, they are more likely to become sick and if you come in contact with a bear or other wild animal they are apt to run away and leave you stranded. The mustang is hardier and can live off grass if there isn't any feed grain. They don't run as fast as a race horse, but they can hold out longer. They are more sure-footed and are easier to train to stand and be silent when you want them to be.

To this Andrew said, "I am not familiar with this mustang horse you mention. Will you help me select a good horse to ride and one as a pack animal? I want to carry enough rations to last me a long time, and some trade goods as well, to trade with the Indians."

The driver agreed to help.

The livery stable owner was a short man, but had very broad shoulders, and the muscles in his arms bulged. Andrew figured his strength came in handy working with the horses. He did his own shoeing of the animals in his care, as well as repair of wagons and carriages.

Andrew explained what he needed. The stableman took him to a corral in the back of the livery barn and pointed out a couple of animals that looked like they had been treated harshly. Andrew only gave them a glance then turned to the other animals in the corral. He had ridden horses in the Army and he knew a little about them and he did not want any "wind broken" animals.

There were about a dozen horses in the corral. Out of the whole bunch, only two looked half decent. He asked the stableman to catch up those two and let him examine them closer. When he brought them over, he said, "You have an eye for horse flesh. These are the best two I have."

One was a filly and a bit on the wild side as if she had only recently been broken to ride. She was almost coal black with one white stocking on her front leg. She rolled her eyes and snorted. As Andrew reached out to pat her neck, she threw her head back and made as if to bite him on the arm. Andrew pulled the bridle down close, talking very softly and gently to the horse. He judged she must be about four years old. She stood a full fourteen hands and had long legs. He bet she would really run if let loose. He checked her teeth, her fetlocks, and ran his hand down across her sides and back. Then he ran his hand up under her long mane and took a hand full of hair, and without a moment's hesitation, swung up on her back. She snorted again, and began to buck around the corral. Andrew clamped his legs tight around her belly and clung to her. In a few jumps she began to quiet down and he reined her in a figure eight around the corral, in and out between the other horses.

Then he reined in, slid off her and said, "This one is not too bad. She might do if the price is right. Let me look at the other one."

The other horse was a gelding, about seven or eight years old, also about 13 hands high and a little bit on the fat side. Andrew judged that this one might have been lazing here in the corral too long, eating without work or exercise and had put on a few extra pounds. A few days of riding and work would whip him back into good shape. This was a red horse, what he would learn later was referred to as a "strawberry roan."

He turned to the driver and, with a sly wink that the

stableman could not see, said, "These are not very good animals. But they might do until I could pick up something better. What do you think? Should we look at some others before we make a choice? I'd hate to have one of these fall over dead on me after a good day's ride. Are there other livery stables here in Charleston?"

In mock seriousness the driver said, "I agree they are not prime animals, but there aren't many places around you can get a decent riding animal. Most of them are used to pulling plows unless you want to get into the thoroughbred line."

The stableman quickly put in, "If you are going to be traveling, you couldn't do better than the black. She has a good "rocking-chair" gait and will cover more miles in a day than many of your thoroughbreds. When you turn her loose she can run like the wind."

"What do you want for her?"

"I want $50 for her." replied the stableman.

Andrew scoffed, and said, "That horse isn't worth $50. I couldn't pay more than $30. She rides easy enough but she is still a mite on the wild side. She is liable to run off and leave me stranded some place."

After much haggling, a price of $40 was struck and Andrew offered $25 for the roan. Still more haggling and a sale was agreed upon at $30.

"Now show me some riding saddles and pack saddles. I'll also need some packs and other gear."

Finally, when he had everything he thought he would need, he paid the man and told him he would pick up everything Friday morning at daybreak. In the meantime, the carriage driver would be bringing supplies and equipment down to be stored and packed into the packs. He wanted everything safe-guarded and would hold the stableman accountable for his gear.

He prepared to leave and added, "I also want new shoes

put on both horses. Trim their hooves well, but do not cut them too deep. I don't want a crippled animal on my hands. I intend to travel far and fast when I leave here."

The stableman agreed and said they would be ready by Friday morning.

Just as they were leaving the livery, Andrew noticed that the two men he had fought with a few days ago were lounging against the wall of the livery stable. He had not noticed them before, and his first thought was that there would be more trouble with them. He was so engrossed in buying the horses and gear that he had not noticed them before. He wondered how long they had been there and how much they had heard of his plans. All of a sudden he had a premonition of trouble brewing. Just as quickly, he shook it off and decided he was worrying too much. After all, they had made no move toward him; and in fact, acted as if they had not even seen him, although he thought that very unlikely. He walked on to the carriage.

Climbing back on the seat of the carriage, the driver said, "You handled that well. You did not need my help."

"The fact that you drive a horse carriage, and were standing there with me, helped a great deal. He didn't know whether I knew anything about horses or not, but he figured you were there to help point out any poor qualities in the animals. That kept him from trying to cheat me and pawn off one of those poor old, half-dead animals on me."

It was getting on toward sunset now and Andrew asked to be returned to his hotel. He asked the driver if he would pick him up again the next morning at eight o'clock and help him pick out the type gear and supplies he would need on the trip. The driver said he would and dropped Andrew at the hotel.

At the steps of the hotel, a small, black boy about 8 or 9 years old approached and asked if he was "Mr. Andrew Stanley?" When Andrew indicated he was, the boy handed him a note and said he had been told to give it only to him and to wait for a reply.

Andrew opened the small envelope and unfolded a sheet of paper. It had just one sentence, which read, "I have reconsidered, if the offer for dinner is still open." It was unsigned, but Andrew knew who it was from. He gave the boy a penny and said, "Tell the lady I will pick her up at seven o'clock. Don't forget the time now."

The boy nodded his head and took off running down the street.

Andrew entered the hotel and inquired what was on the menu for dinner that evening. The manager gave him a rundown of several dishes that sounded good. Andrew asked if they had any French wine. The manager said he did not but he could get some if the gentleman wanted. Andrew explained he was having a special guest for dinner and he wanted to impress her, that he would like a special table off to one side of the room, with a good linen table cloth, silver and crystal. And he would also like flowers on the table.

The manager smiled and said, "But of course. It seems you have met a special person. We will make sure it is an evening you will be proud of."

Andrew knew this would probably cost him plenty, but he didn't care. Maria already meant a great deal to him, and he had the feeling that before the night was over, she would cement their friendship even more.

He went to his room, stripped and bathed and lay down to rest. It would be a couple hours before he would venture out to go for her.

Drifting off in a light sleep, his mind circled back to the two men again. He wondered why they kept intruding into his mind and if they had actually been following him. He would pay closer attention from now on when he was out and about. Then he dozed off.

CHAPTER NINE

A ndrew awoke with a start. He did not realize he was so tired, but then he had been up almost all of last night, and the memory brought a slight smile to his face. It was 6:15 and he shaved and dressed quickly. He hurried down stairs and hailed a carriage. He looked forward to seeing Maria again and he didn't want to be late.

He arrived at her door about five minutes to seven, just on time. He rang the bell and when an elderly lady came to the door, he stated he was here to see Miss Santiago and would she please announce him. The landlady seemed surprised, but said nothing. She invited him to step inside while she went up the stairs.

Maria must have been ready for she came down the stairs immediately with the elderly lady. She said, "Mrs. Pennshote, this is Mr. Andrew Stanley. He is a friend of Uncle Harold's and Aunt Hannah's. We will be having dinner with them again tonight, so I may be late. Don't wait up for me. If it gets too late, I will stay over at the Millers for the night."

Andrew shook the lady's hand, bowed and escorted Maria to the waiting carriage. When they were inside, she said, "Tongues won't wag so much if they think I am going to the Miller's for the evening. Everyone knows Uncle Harold is a banker and that they have me over frequently." She didn't say anything about the staying overnight bit, but

Andrew had not missed that part. He didn't want to bring it up now, though; it might be embarrassing and he didn't want to spoil the evening before it began.

At the hotel, he paid the carriage driver and dismissed him. Then they entered the dining room through a side door. He did not want it to seem they were going into the hotel, but rather the restaurant part of the building.

The manager greeted them with a hearty welcome and said, "Ah, Mr. Stanley, your table is ready. We are glad to have you and the lady dine with us this evening. I hope everything will be to your satisfaction."

He acted as if Andrew was a guest of long standing, instead of having been here less than a week. It was apparent that the manger was also very impressed with Maria. He was very cordial towards her and kept giving her admiring glances. Andrew felt a twinge of jealousy, and then he put it aside. He instead, basked in the glow of her smile.

The meal was one that would have done one of the more classical restaurants proud. The manager obviously knew where to go for the wine. It was a light rose' and very smooth, with just a slightly sweet taste. They began with a glass and lingered a few minutes before ordering. They both told the manager they would leave the choice up to him, for him to surprise them.

Surprise them he did.

First, he delivered a tray of oysters on the half-shell, baked with a touch of cheese on top. Then a crisp salad with shrimp and crab-meat. This was followed with small fingers of a white fish rolled in cornmeal and deep fried. The main course was roast veal with new potatoes in a cheese sauce, fresh green beans and cream-styled corn.

Andrew could not remember ever having such a delicious meal and told the manager to please share their appreciation of such a fine meal with the cook. This was followed by a bread pudding with raisins and chopped pecans, with a sweet sugar glaze on top. Andrew ordered coffee for both and they sat for a long time, just enjoying each other's company and chatting about one thing and another, but nothing of great importance. They talked at length about the things they liked and what they hoped to do some day. When they finally looked around, the restaurant was empty except for the two of them. They did not realize all the other patrons had come and gone. In truth, they were so engrossed with each other that they could not have said whether there had been anyone else there that night or not.

Andrew paid the bill and left a generous tip. Then they walked toward the door and stepped out on the sidewalk. The hotel manager asked if they wanted a carriage and Maria said no they would walk a bit first, to walk off some of that delightful meal, and then they would get a carriage.

They had gone only a few steps when Andrew said, "I have been trying all evening to think of a way to ask you to stay with me tonight without embarrassing you. But I don't know how to say it except, I want to be with you again tonight. Will you stay with me?"

Maria squeezed his hand and answered, "If you hadn't asked me, I would have asked you. Yes, I'd like to stay with you again tonight, but how can we manage it? I can't be seen going into the hotel with you."

Andrew thought for a moment. "I think I know how we can do it. In the alley behind the hotel there is a stairway that is used in case of fire and other emergencies. It is dark in the alley and we can go up the stairs without being seen."

As they passed the alley, Andrew looked both ways and did not see anyone coming, so they ducked into the alley and made their way to the stairs. He helped her climb the stairs until they reached the top landing. Andrew tried the door and found it locked. He was afraid this was going to ruin their plans and he tried to figure a way to solve the problem. It was Maria who had the answer.

She said, "I will wait here. You go around, enter the front as if you were going to your room. Then when you get upstairs, come open the door from the inside."

They decided to wait a few minutes to give him time to have carried her home before he went down and entered the hotel. While they were waiting, he took her in his arms. It was dark as midnight and he could hardly make out her features, but he could smell the light fragrance of perfume. Being this close, smelling the sweet smell of her he pulled her tightly to him. She came willingly, exhibiting her own hunger. They kissed passionately and probed each other's mouths with their tongues. She wore a long woolen dress that covered her ankles. Her waist was cinched in tight, but the dress flowed loose from her hips down

He kissed her on the neck and her ear lobes. He bent and kissed her again as she pulled him up tight against her.

Andrew ran his hands down her back, onto her buttocks and cupped one cheek in each hand and lifted her up onto the bannister that was behind her. Holding her thus, he pulled her harder against him... Andrew wondered how she remained on the small ledge made by the bannister and still made all the movements she did. For now though, that was not of much importance. He could not believe the sexual prowess of this woman and the passionate nature of her.

After several satisfying moments in sexual embrace, they stood, holding each other close for several more minutes.

Then Andrew broke the silence. "Do you still want to come into the hotel with me or should I take you home?"

Maria answered, "After these last few minutes, I doubt that either of us could make love again this night, but I would love the thrill of sleeping with my head on your shoulder and lying close to you. As much as I would like that, I think it best if I returned home. We might oversleep and if I were seen leaving the hotel after daybreak, my reputation would be ruined. I think you better take me home."

As much as he liked the idea of having her next to him in bed all night, he was afraid he might fail to rise to the situation if she wanted to make love again. He was spent and exhausted. And so, half reluctantly, he agreed.

They made their way back down the stairs and through the alley. Andrew peered around the corner, and seeing no one; they stepped out and walked toward her house. About a block from the hotel they hailed a carriage and rode the rest of the way to her house. On the trip they were both silent, her cuddling to him and he holding her in his arms.

As they neared her house, Andrew spoke for the first time since entering the carriage.

"Maria, day after tomorrow I will be leaving and will probably be gone for a long time, several months at least. It seems strange that so much could happen in two days, but I find you very appealing and enjoy being with you. Do you feel the same?"

She cuddled closer and tightened her arms around him. "Yes! Oh, yes, Andrew. Two days or two years. I could not love you more. Will you take me with you?"

"I cannot take you with me for I fear the trip may be too dangerous. I am not sure how I will fare myself, but I will have a better chance of surviving if I go alone. When I find the place I am looking for, I will come back. Do you want me to come back?"

"Yes. I will wait. But don't be gone too long. I don't know if I can survive without your loving for too long a period of time. Are you sure you will not take me with you? I will wash your clothes, and cook for you and warm your bed every night."

"As much as the thought pleases me, I dare not. If I knew more about the country I am going into and how to deal with the Indians, I might consider it, but under the circumstances, I dare not take you."

They were silent the rest of the trip.

Upon arrival at her boarding house, Andrew asked the carriage driver to wait. He walked her to her door. In the dark they embraced again, once more, pressing their bodies together.

Maria moaned, "Remember this body on those cold nights and know that it is waiting here for you. Hurry back to me."

She kissed him again and let herself in through the door. She stood just inside the door and he put his fingers to his lips and pressed them against the glass of the door. She leaned forward and put her lips to the glass, then turned and walked up the stairs.

Andrew returned to the carriage and rode back to the hotel, in silent bliss. Had he made the right choice? It would be really nice to feel that soft naked body next to him in bed when he awoke. He slapped his knee. The decision had been made and it was too late to change it.

He arose early the next morning, breakfasted quickly; there was much to do this day. He met his carriage driver, and together, they went to the commissary to purchase the items for his trip. Goods included bacon, beans, rice, salt, coffee, and all the things he would need on his journey. He bought blankets, a tarp to spread on the ground to roll out his bedroll at night and another to use as a tent when it rained.

The driver suggested he buy a "poncho." This was an item strange to Andrew. It was sort of like a cloak, but with buttons down one side and with a hole in the middle to slip over the head. The driver showed him how to fit it over his head and draw a string tight around his neck to keep out the rain. Andrew could see how this would be a great asset when he might be exposed to rainy and cold weather. He readily saw how it might be used for a variety of purposes.

When he had everything that he could think of he turned to the driver, "Did I forget anything?"

"There are some other things you may want to take along. If you plan to do any trading, you will want to have some bright cloth, blankets, knives and such to trade with the Indians, or to use as gifts. Then, you will be away from any source of supply for a long time. You may have to make your own shot. I would suggest you get a mold and a couple bars of lead so that you can mold your shots if you begin to run low. If you do not need it before you return you can trade that also with the Indians or other white people who find such things hard to come by once they leave the small towns and go farther away from civilization."

The driver thought a moment longer and continued, "There is one other thing that you should have with you. You need some bandages and antiseptic. Lots of people use whiskey, but I noticed that you were not taking any with you. Such will come in handy for surely you will have cuts, scrapes, or maybe even bullet wounds to treat before you return."

Andrew agreed and he asked the store keeper to put together a small medicine supply for him of those items, and any other medicines he thought he might need on a long journey.

When finished, the total bill came to almost $80, and Andrew was glad to pay it. With the carriage now loaded, his wares almost filled the passenger compartment.

Upon arrival at the livery stable, Andrew noted the tall, thin man he had fought with was sitting on a bale of hay in front of the stable, whittling on a piece of board. He thought it kind of odd that he would be hanging around a livery stable, but Andrew set the thought aside for the moment and concentrated on getting all his supplies inside and packed ready for departure. The stable man and the driver helped him pack. He noted that there was a certain skill in packing the packs. Much of the merchandise, things that would not be needed until later on were put on the bottom of the packs. Those things that would be needed almost daily were placed on the top. Frying pan, coffee pot, and part of the foods were left to go in last. That part of the food that would not be needed until later was also placed down further in the packs.

Andrew also noted that great care was taken to make sure the packs were weighted as evenly as possible so that when placed on the horse's back, they would be evenly balanced He would have to remember that. In the Army they had never used pack animals to any great extent. They usually had wagons and carts to carry most of their supplies and baggage. Andrew realized he had much to learn and wished again that he had someone with experience to guide him.

Finally, Andrew asked the stableman, "Do you know the man sitting outside on the bale of hay?"

The stableman looked up sharply, and quickly, "No, and I don't care to know him. He is not the type who I normally do business with. Occasionally he and his partner will bring their horses here to stable them a day or two, but most often they leave them at the stable across town. It is closer to the docks and they seem to spend most of their time down there."

Andrew probed further. "I noticed him here yesterday as I was leaving, and he is here again today. Are their horses here now?"

"No. He seems to be interested in you. After you left

yesterday he came in and tried to find out about you and what your plans were. He didn't ask outright, he tried to be coy with me, but I'm sure he is curious about what you are going to do. Do you know him?"

"Not really. I had a run-in with him and his partner a few nights ago in a bar down by the docks. I had all but forgotten it until I saw him here yesterday."

"These two are bad medicine. They may be out to jump you again. You sure better watch your back because I suspect they would just as soon shoot you in the back as the front. Are you travelling alone?"

When Andrew admitted he was, the stableman said, "Well, it would be best if you pulled out in the middle of the night and not tell anyone the trail you are taking. You may have forgotten the fight; but my guess is, they haven't. Or they may be just looking for a chance to rob you. You have been spending pretty heavily around town and they probably have you pegged as a rich man."

Andrew was silent a moment, thinking. Should he accost the man now and have it out rather than maybe have to face the two of them on the trail some place. Then he considered, maybe he was just jumpy. The guy may be doing nothing more than passing the time of day. He couldn't jump the man without a reason, and so far he did not have one.

Andrew again put the problem out of his mind for the current moment. But he thought the stableman's advice about leaving in the middle of the night was a good idea. If he left around midnight, he could be five or six hours down the road before they knew he was gone.

"I think your idea of leaving at night is a good one. You might let it drop that I have some business to conclude tomorrow and I plan to leave Saturday morning. Can you have my horse saddled and the pack horse packed by midnight? I will pay you for your trouble."

The stableman said he could, but he would wait until after dark when the man had gone away.

Andrew gave him a ten dollar gold piece and told him to give both horses a good feed of grain tonight. It might be the last they would get for a while.

As he neared the stable door, preparing to leave, he said in a voice loud enough to carry to the man waiting outside, "I believe that takes care of everything. I will want to leave by sunup Saturday morning. Please have the horses saddled and packed for me. I want to get an early start. I have urgent business in Savannah."

Then he and the carriage driver mounted the carriage and drove away. As they moved down the street, Andrew turned and looked back. The tall thin man had got up off the hay and was going into the stable. If the stableman was convincing, maybe he could get a full day's start on them. They may not be looking for him to leave until Saturday. If he left tonight that would give him a good lead. Furthermore, when they discovered he had taken another trail other than the one to Savannah maybe they would consider it too much trouble to try to catch up with him.

If he was going to leave tonight, he had much to do. He told the driver to take him first to Peter Georgiades, the jeweler.

It was almost noon and the jeweler was just getting ready to lock up for lunch, but when Andrew walked up, he reopened the shop and went back inside.

Andrew came right to the point. "Have you been able to finish the ring and necklace?"

Peter went back to the rear of the shop and returned with a small box. He opened it and took out the ring first. Andrew was amazed. It was gorgeous. The diamond was set in a gold band with four claws or clasps to firmly hold it in place. Each of the claws had a small diamond chip mounted on it and the mountings were beautifully set. The smaller diamonds accented the larger stone and reflected the brilliance from one to the other.

Peter then reached into the box and brought out a gold chain. The links were very small and very carefully crafted. The ruby hung like a pendant from the chain, and again, the jeweler had set smaller stones around the main one to add emphasis.

Andrew grabbed the jeweler's hand and shook it vigorously. "Peter, I have never seen such beautiful work. You are a master jeweler. I was afraid that you might not have it ready."

"I worked on the ring most of the night when you first left it with me. Last night, I stayed up until I finished the necklace. My wife kept calling for me to come to bed, but I knew you would be going and would want to take this with you."

"I am so pleased with these Peter. You can't imagine how much I appreciate your efforts. How much do I owe you?"

"Give me $100 for the gold in the ring and the chain. The small stones are a gift from me to your lady friend."

"But I must pay you for your work. You spent many hours on this and it is such fine, artistic work."

"My friend, when I work on something like this and it turns out well and the owner is as pleased as you seem to be, that is payment enough. Besides, you have favored me with a great deal of business. I expect to make lots of money on your jewels when I sell them. Plus, I hope to have your business for many years to come."

"You can rest assured on that point. Speaking of which, I have one more bit of business to transact with you."

With that he opened his shirt and took off the money belt. He opened up the two remaining pockets that he had not opened before and spilled out the contents on the counter.

"I had thought to hold onto these stones in case I lost the others in some manner, but now I think that would be foolish. I want to place these with you, not to sell, but to hold for me. As you can see, these are the best of the entire lot. That one diamond there is the largest of all that I had. What do you suppose it is worth?"

Georgiades took out his magnifying glass and examined it carefully, and then he weighed it on a tiny scale. When he looked up he said, "That stone is almost ten carats and is perfectly formed. I cannot find a flaw in it. It is also what we call a blue diamond. It would probably be worth $50 to $60 thousand dollars. If all of these rubies and emeralds are of equal quality, you probably have over $250,000 to $300,000 in value there."

Andrew was startled. He had thought that they were valuable, but he had no idea they were of such enormous value. He thought what a fool he had been to carry these valuable stones around on his body all this time. If someone had knocked him out and stolen the belt he would have lost it all.

"Peter, I have to go to the bank and to the gunsmith. Will you inventory these and make me a receipt. I will return before four o'clock today. Something has come up and it is important that I leave tonight. There are some men who I think may be following me. I want to leave during the night so they will not know which way I am going. I do not want them on my trail. I certainly don't want these kinds of valuables on my person if they catch me. Should anything happen and I do not return, you are to deliver these stones to Captain Wilson when he returns. I have instructed him what to do with my money. If he chooses to sell and convert them into cash I am sure he will let you handle that for him. Will you do this for me?"

Georgiades seemed troubled by what the younger man

had just told him. He had only met this man a few days ago and for only a short period of time, but he liked him and he was worried about what he had just said.

"If you think these men mean you harm you should seek some help, someone to ride with you. Surely, you do not intend to go out into the backwoods, not having any idea of what it is like, without someone to guide you."

"Mr. Miller had suggested a man by the name of Brinkman, but I must have offended him by offering to pay him, for he turned me down. I had hoped that I might find someone else before I get too far away from civilized communities. Perhaps in one of the towns I will pass through I will find a guide. If not, I will go alone."

"Then do be careful, Andrew. We Greeks do not have many friends and we cannot afford to lose those we have. Besides, you are turning out to be my best customer. How can I make money off you if you are dead somewhere in the woods?"

They both laughed at this and Andrew shrugged, "Do not worry. I plan to keep my head on for a long time yet. If it is God's will I shall return with all my hair before the year is out."

"Then I shall take care of the business for you and shall store the stones in a safe place. They will be here for you when you want them. If there is anything more I can do for you feel free to tell me."

Andrew said there wasn't and that he would be back at four.

Next he went to the gunsmith. Mueller was in the back of his shop. It seemed he spent much of his time in his workshop and very little in the store. When he entered the little bell on the door jingled and Mueller came from the back of the shop.

"Mr. Mueller, I have had to alter my plans. It is important

that I leave tonight rather than wait until tomorrow. There are some men watching me and I would rather they not know when I leave or which way I am going. Have you been able to finish the pistols for me?"

Mueller led him into the back room. "I have been able to complete only one. But before I give it to you, I would like you to look at this other pistol. It is something new I have been working on and I would like your opinion."

With that he handed Andrew a pistol that was unlike anything he had ever seen. The stock and the barrel were the same as most he was familiar with. It was the firing mechanism that caught his attention. It did not have the usual pan to hold the powder that was used to set off the charge which actually propelled the bullet. Instead there was a small plate, about the size of a $5 dollar gold piece. The cock that usually held the flint to strike the pan was different. It did not have any jaws. Instead it was just a flat head, sort of like a small hammer head. Andrew didn't understand how the weapon worked. Mueller seemed to be enjoying his confusion. Finally, he took the pistol and proceeded to show Andrew its' secret.

He loaded the weapon with a ball and poured in a small powder charge. Then he took out of his pocket a small piece of paper and placed it in the pan where the cock would be landing. Then they stepped outside in the back yard of the gun shop and Mueller pointed the gun at a wooden block. He pulled the trigger and a shot rang out. The wooden blocked jumped with the jolt of the bullet. While Andrew was looking at the block to see if the bullet ran true, Mueller had loaded, put another piece of paper in the pan and fired again. Andrew was so surprised he spun and looked for a second weapon. Mueller was standing, holding the pistol.

Andrew said, "How did you do that? How did you fire two shots so close together?"

Mueller smiled and said, "I have tried something new with this pistol. I call it a cap." He took one of the small papers out of his pocket and handed it to Andrew. Andrew examined it and saw that it had a small lump in the middle, which upon closer examination proved to be gun-powder.

Mueller was explaining. "In the regular pistol; and in the rifles too, you have a powder charge that propels the ball, and you either have a flint lock to create a spark to ignite the powder in the chamber; or in larger weapons, such as cannons you have a touch hole where you apply a lighted match. This is something I have been playing with. It is a cap. It has just enough powder in the paper to cause a flash. When the cock hits it, it explodes, setting off the powder in the chamber that actually propels the bullet. It is much faster and much more apt to fire. I believe it will reduce the number of misfires. The problem I have is getting these little paper caps made and keeping them dry."

With this he went back into the shop. Then he handed Andrew another weapon. It was the pistol they had discussed earlier and the firing mechanism was much like the one on the rifle, just as they had discussed. Andrew picked it up and held it in his hand. It had a good balance and although Mueller had not had time to fashion the weapon and smooth off some of the rough edges, Andrew knew the working condition of the weapon would be excellent.

Mueller said, "I only had time to make one of those. I'd like you to take this other one that I showed you as your second pistol. I want it tested in all kind of conditions and weather to see if it will perform as well as the regular flint lock fired weapon. Will you take it and try it out?"

Andrew wasn't sure he wanted to depend on something he wasn't familiar with, but Mueller was so anxious to have it tested, he finally relented and agreed to take it. Mueller gave him a large supply of the small paper caps and showed him how to make others in case he ran out or all of these got wet. He paid Mueller, and tried to pay him for the second gun, but he wouldn't accept payment. He said, "No. This pistol is not for sale. I am loaning it to you to use on your trip. When you return, you will return it to me and give me a full report on how it works."

Mueller put both pistols in leather holsters and then put these in a wooden box. He had already counted out the shot and powder Andrew had ordered earlier and had a smooth leather case for the long rifle Andrew had purchased earlier. As he was leaving, he turned to Mueller and said, "I have often wondered why they never made guns with two barrels. One you could fire, and the other you could hold in reserve if you needed it. Is it possible to build such a gun? It would likely have to have two separate chambers for powder. If both went off at once, the gun would probably blow up in your face."

Mueller looked surprised. "Yes. I think such a gun could be made. I had not given much thought to the idea, but it is something to think about. I will see if I can make such a model and when you return you can test it for me."

Andrew did not want to call more attention to his departure so he did not return to the stable. Instead he went to the bank and asked to speak to Mr. Miller. As soon as he was announced, Miller arose from his desk and came out to meet him. He extended his hand and after shaking hands, escorted Andrew into his office. He offered Andrew a cigar, which he declined. They chatted for a couple minutes and Andrew told him he was going to need another couple hundred dollars and that he had bought more than he had anticipated and he was down to a few hundred dollars. He might need more on the journey. He asked that the coins all be in small denominations. Miller stepped to a station, told the cashier to bring him five hundred dollars in gold and in small coins, and when he brought the money, he had Andrew sign a withdrawal slip.

Andrew thanked him again for the very nice evening he had at his home and although he had not intended to mention Maria, he thought perhaps he should. "I was quite impressed with your niece. She is a lovely young lady and we hit it off nicely together. In fact, she had dinner with me at the hotel restaurant last night. It was a very enjoyable evening. She is not only beautiful, but very intelligent too. A really extraordinary woman! If you have no objections, I would like to call on her again when I return. She tells me she is not promised to anyone."

Miller seemed pleased, maybe at last they had found a husband for Maria, and a wealthy one at that. But with his bankers face, he did not let it show. Instead he said, "Andrew, Maria makes her own decisions. Hannah and I have tried to protect her and watch after her reputation. We have even introduced her to some of the available men in Charleston, but she has not shown any interest in any of them. I am a little surprised that she agreed to have dinner with you for she has turned down the offers of all the other gentlemen we have introduced her to. Perhaps it is because you are closer in age. I have no objection to you calling on her, nor would it make any difference. She decides who she will see and who she will not. It is the same kind of stubborn streak her mother had."

He stopped short, thinking he might have said too much. This young man seemed taken with Maria and she must have liked him to go out with him. He was very wealthy and if Miller was any judge of a person, he would become wealthier still in the years ahead. He would be able to provide her with a good life and he seemed right for her. Maybe he could tame the wild and unruly nature she exhibited at times. He did not want to leave Andrew with the wrong impression. He hastily added, "Maria is a charming lady, and has been trained in the social graces. There are a number of the eligible men in town who seek her favors, but so far none seem to have caught her fancy. If you want my permission to court Maria, you have it."

Andrew said, "I will be gone for a time. If she does not find another by the time I return, I will call on her when I return." He thought to himself, if Miller had any idea of the closeness between the two of them and how intimate they had been, he would probably take a shotgun to him and march him to the alter right now.

"Now I need one more piece of advice. I was unable to secure Mr. Brinkman as my guide. He did not seem to like me. In any case, I had an altercation with a couple of men a few nights ago. I am of the opinion that they may be intending to follow me and do me harm. I am going first to Orangeburg where I understand a man by the name of Charles Heyward has a large plantation. I want to see someone there. From there I intend to go into the western territories of South Carolina and that area that was ceded to Georgia in 1787. Perhaps I may go up into the western territory of North Carolina. If I do not find what I want I may go as far as the River they call the Mississippi. Which route would you suggest? Should I strike out as if going south and then cut back to the west, or should I take the road to Orangeburg and ride fast and try to outdistance them?"

After a moment's thought, Miller replied, "I would spread the word that you are going south toward Savannah, but I would strike out straight for Orangeburg. There is another man there who might be your guide. They call him a mountain man. I have never met him, but they say he is as good as Brinkman, and somewhat more agreeable. His name is David Foster."

"That sounds like good advice. I will look up Mr. Foster when I get to Orangeburg."

With that, he said good-bye and went out to the waiting carriage. It was now approaching four o'clock and neither he nor the driver had eaten since breakfast. He told the driver to take him back to the jewelers and after that they would get something to eat.

Georgiades had the receipt ready and gave it to Andrew. He bade him good-bye once more and wished him a safe journey.

Andrew told the driver to take him anyplace he wanted to go to eat. They went to a small cafe he knew and seemed to be well known there. The waiters all knew him and were pleased he had brought a new customer for the cafe.

Andrew got his first taste of southern country cooking, something he was going to receive much of in the months ahead. He was served collard greens cooked with chunks of ham and a big bone they called a ham-hock. There were barbecued pork ribs, fried chicken, corn bread sticks, fried okra, fresh field peas, sliced tomatoes and corn on the cob. Much of this was new to him, but it seemed the staple fare of the country folk and it was certainly filling enough. When he arose from the table he felt stuffed.

The driver took him to the hotel and Andrew asked him if he would do him one more favor. He asked him if he would meet him in the alley behind the hotel at midnight. When he said he would, Andrew went into the hotel, called the manager to the side and spoke quietly to him.

"I have reasons to leave during the night and I would like to pay you now for my room. I will be gone before day break. I will also need pen and paper and could you have your cook fix up several sandwiches and pack them for me. I don't want to have to stop to prepare a meal tomorrow. I want to get to Savannah as quickly as possible." With that he handed the man a $20 gold piece and told him to keep the change.

Andrew figured if anyone came asking for him, they would say he was going to Savannah. That might throw anyone off his trail for a while at least.

Andrew went to his room and wrote a note to Maria.

Dear Maria:

I had hoped fate would smile on me and I would get to see you again before I leave, but events now dictate that I leave in the middle of the night to avoid being followed. Furthermore, if you were seen with me, the wrath of those who might do me harm might befall you. So it is best that I leave as quickly as possible.

My meeting you has been the best thing that could happen to me and I will carry the moments we have shared in my heart. I can only hope that you feel the same.

My heart was heavy with sadness when I came to Charleston and memories of the past made me bitter. You have erased much of the sadness and made me a whole person again. I shall remember the sweetness of your kiss every day of my journey and long for the softness of your body every night as I go to sleep.

I pray God will watch over you while I am gone.

Love,
Andrew

He returned down stairs and gave the letter to the hotel manager and gave him instructions on delivering it to Maria personally. Then he returned to his room.

It was barely dark when he turned in. He had all of his clothes and gear packed and would be able to dress and depart in a matter of minutes. With that he lay down, and willed himself to sleep. In the days ahead he would need to be rested and wide awake, and even the nights he would not be able to rest completely. He would have to be constantly alert.

It was ironic that instead of thinking of the beautiful woman he had loved so passionately last night, his last thoughts before falling asleep were not of her, but of the two men. He had a strange premonition that they were to play an important part in the days ahead. With this last thought, he fell asleep.

CHAPTER TEN

Andrew awoke and judged it must be close to midnight. He arose and dressed hurriedly and in less than ten minutes, he descended the back stairs where he and Maria had made love the night before. He hesitated a moment savoring the thoughts, then he stealthily descended the stairs. The carriage was not in sight. Andrew thought it was a few minutes before midnight so he settled in the alley to wait.

Within minutes, the carriage pulled into the alley and Andrew stepped from the shadows. He hastily put his belongings and weapons into the carriage and stepped inside. It would be harder for anyone to recognize him inside the carriage, just in case the hotel was being watched.

The driver pulled on through the alley and emerged on the other side of the hotel. He cut straight across town and pulled directly into the open entrance of the livery stable before stopping. Andrew stepped out of the carriage and had reached back inside for his bed roll and luggage when he saw a man from the shadows coming toward him.

He grabbed the pistol that he had left lying on the seat and whirled to meet the man. There was a small lantern that the stableman had left burning. It hung on a post and gave just enough light for Andrew to see the man, who approached at a walk and did not appear menacing. Andrew held the gun at his side in preparation. The nearer he came, the clearer his image and Andrew recognized him as Hans Brinkman. Andrew relaxed a little, although he could not imagine what the man would be doing here at this time and coming towards him.

Brinkman spoke as he came nearer, "Mr. Stanley, it is Hans Brinkman. Do you still need a guide?"

When no quick reply came, Brinkman spoke again. "Mr. Miller came to me tonight and said you might have some trouble in getting to your destination. He asked me to help you get to Orangeburg. I owed him a favor and agreed. That is if you still want me to guide you."

Andrew was so surprised that he was slow to respond and Brinkman took that as a negative reply. He turned to leave.

Andrew came alive and stepped forward to touch his arm. He was surprised at the strength and firmness beneath the shirt. "Wait, Mr. Brinkman. I would very much appreciate your help in seeing me to Orangeburg. It is just that I was so surprised to find you here. Mr. Miller had not mentioned anything to me about contacting you. I had a little fracas with a couple of your town bullies a few nights ago, and I suspect that they may be planning to get even. When I saw you coming out of the shadows I wasn't sure it wasn't one of them. How did you know that I would be here at this hour?"

"I didn't know for sure. But Miller said you were leaving tonight and I knew that this is where you bought your horses. Then I thought what I might do if I were in similar circumstances. So I just came here to wait, figuring you would come sometime between midnight and dawn."

Andrew was elated; not only would he have someone who was familiar with the roads, but if trouble came, there would be two of them.

He extended his hand and said, "Good, Mr. Brinkman. I

am delighted to have you with me. Please call me Andrew. As soon as I can pack these last few items I will be ready." Brinkman spoke up in a louder voice, "O.K. You can come out now."

The stableman emerged from between two stalls farther down the stable, set down a rifle and walked towards them. He said, "How did you know I was there?"

Brinkman said, "I heard you come in and although you walked very quietly, I have trained my hearing to listen for strange sounds in the night. It didn't sound quiet like mice running through the straw."

Andrew understood now. The stableman had been on the watch for anyone who might wait in ambush for him. He was pleased that he had found another friend.

Quickly they packed the rest of Andrew's belongings in the saddle bags and pack saddles. The stableman already had the horse saddled and the packs on the other horse. Andrew flipped the liveryman a gold coin and another to the carriage driver and shook hands with both.

Then he swung into the saddle. The black horse was well fed and rested and didn't particularly like the burden on her back. She tried to buck, but Andrew pulled on the reins hard and jerked her head up. Then he wrapped the lead rope to the pack horse around the saddle horn and urged the black out into the night.

Brinkman was at the door and took the lead. Andrew followed. They walked the horses quietly for several blocks. When Andrew looked back, the carriage was going down the street in the opposite direction, the door to the livery was still open and the lantern still burned in the passageway between the stalls.

He faced forward again and concentrated on following Brinkman in the dark. He could barely see him ahead and he made no noise. Andrew let the black horse have its head and it followed the animal Brinkman was riding.

When they were clear of the town, Brinkman kicked his horse into a slow ground-eating canter. Andrew's horse picked up the pace as if knowing what to do without being told. He was surprised at the easy gait and the smoothness with which she loped. The pack horse seemed another matter however, as he bounced and jostled with every step. Andrew was glad he was not riding him instead of the black. They continued in a steady rhythm, galloping for an hour or so, then walking the horses a half hour to cool them off.

About every three or four hours they stopped at a stream or small lake to water the horses and rest them for a few minutes. Andrew had lots of experience with horses but he allowed Brinkman to set the pace and call the stops. As he observed the man, he could tell he knew about horses. He did not over-tax them and gave them plenty of time to cool down after every gallop. It was a wise man that did not drive his horse to the limit. He saved something always in reserve because you never knew when you might need a little extra burst of speed or a long run to find cover or elude an enemy.

In spite of what some might have thought a slow pace, by daylight, they had covered close to thirty miles and the horses were still in shape for another several hours of riding. Both of Andrew's horses had been standing in a corral for weeks, eating and without any exercise. Now, though they were both lathered heavily, they seemed to be glad to get out of that enclosed circle. The black especially seemed to want to run, but was being held back by the lead rope to the pack horse. Andrew had the feeling that if she were turned loose she would dart ahead like a flash. The time might come when he would need that speed, but right now, what they needed was endurance.

Brinkman had not spoken much at the two earlier stops.

He had seemed inclined to look after his horse and keep his own counsel. On one occasion he checked the cinches on the pack horse and tightened them where they had worked loose. At the second watering, he had pulled his horse back after just a few swallows and told Andrew, "Don't let them drink very much. As hot as they are it may give them a belly ache. When we stop for noon break they can cool down and get a good drink then."

Awhile later, Brinkman raised his head and looked at the position of the sun and said, "It's almost noon. Let's find a shady spot and rest the horses and get a bite to eat."

He led them off the road and into a stand of heavy timber. Andrew wondered why he was going so far off the road.

Brinkman anticipated his question. "When traveling, if you decide to stop, it is better to get way off the road. If anyone is following you, or just passing that might do you harm, let them go on and pass you. Never stop to rest or camp alongside a road. It could be dangerous."

Andrew wondered why he was telling him this. Then it dawned on him. Brinkman in his own way was giving him a lesson in travel safety in this new land. He had not wanted to appear friendly, but in his way, was attempting to patch up the bad beginning earlier. Andrew made a note of this and his impression of the man began to change.

They came to a wooded area where large oak trees provided shade beside a nice, clear stream, with a small meadow of green grass nearby. Brinkman dismounted, uncinched his saddle and took it off his horse. Then he slipped the bit of the bridle out of the horse's mouth and dropped the reins on the ground. Andrew had not wanted to stop for a long rest, but he followed suit and took the saddle off his horse and tied his reins to a tree. Then he turned to the pack horse and removed the packs and then the pack saddle.

Brinkman came forward and said, "I think we better hobble both of these horses. I have trained my horses to stand "ground hitched". That is, as long as the reins are dragging the ground they are not to walk or move. But we don't know if yours will stay or wander off. We don't want to have to go round them up when we are ready to leave."

With that, he quickly tied hobbles around both front legs of the horses. It allowed them to move about and eat, but they had to jump with both front feet to take a step. They wouldn't go far like that.

Brinkman broke out a coffee pot and scooped up a pot of water from the stream.

Andrew had not wanted to stop long enough to cook. He mentioned as much to Brinkman and told him the hotel restaurant had packed several sandwiches for him.

Brinkman sat the pot down on a small bed of rocks and as he began to break twigs and straw to make a fire he said, "The horses need at least two hours rest and to feed a little. We have been riding almost twelve hours ourselves. There is no sign of pursuit and if your plan worked, they will be well down the road to Savannah by this time. However, if they are determined to come after you, you will have to face them sooner or later. The sooner you take care of the problem, the sooner you can concentrate on watching out for other dangers along the trail. For example, did you know that we passed within a few hundred feet of three Indians in the forest about two hours ago?"

Andrew was shocked. "No. I didn't see anything. How did you know we were that close?"

"Well, first I noticed some crows rise up out of some trees ahead of us and to our right. Then I saw where three unshod ponies had crossed the road in front of us. And finally, I smelled them. They often grease themselves with tallow or other fat. When they get hot and start to sweat, you can smell them up to three or four hundred feet if the wind is right. I think they were just watching us and meant no harm. They seldom attack anyone this close to the settlements, but you can never be too careful. Renegades sometimes raid into the small towns to show their contempt for the white man."

Brickman poked at the fire, encouraging larger flames. Then he continued, "Most of the time, though, they will attack isolated farms or ranches. That happens less and less these days. As more and more people move into the country side, the Indians are pushed further and further west. Those that remain in this area are trying to adapt to the white man's ways, but it is hard to give up a lifestyle they have known for centuries."

«You sound almost as if you feel sorry for them. I›ve heard that they are mostly heathens and full of savagery, killing people just for pleasure.»

Brinkman scoffed, "That's the stories told by those who do not know the Indians. I have lived among them and they are an honorable people. They have tribal rules much as we have laws and anyone that violates those rules is severely punished, sometimes even banished from the tribe. For the most part they are not warlike people. Although they have had to fight for their survival for generations; they have certain tribes that are their enemies and they will kill and torture one of the enemy if they capture one. In many tribes, a young man does not become a mature warrior until he has counted coup on an enemy. To count coup, you must strike a live enemy with something other than a weapon, such as a stick or a small branch off a tree. To them, this is bravery, to face an enemy trying to kill you with nothing more than a stick. Of course, once he has done that, then he does everything he can to kill you and take your scalp. That is their badge of courage, their trophy. There are many white men who take scalps because some people pay a bounty for each Indian killed."

Andrew was fascinated with this man. Brinkman was far more complex than he appeared at first glance. He not only knew the woods, but also about the Indians and their customs as well. Andrew hoped to learn a great deal from this man.

When the coffee had boiled, Brinkman took a cup of the cold water from the stream and poured it into the pot, "to settle the grounds," he explained. Then he took two metal cups and poured each a cup of scalding hot coffee. Andrew handed him two of the sandwiches and took a sip of the coffee. It burned his tongue and he set it aside to cool while he ate. He glanced at Brinkman and noticed he drank almost the full cup of hot coffee before he took the first bite of the sandwich.

After they ate, Brinkman got up, walked around the small clearing as if either, listening or smelling, then he came back, leaned against a tree and immediately fell asleep.

Andrew got up and took a handful of grass and began to rub down the black. It was something they had taught him in the Army. Take care of your horse and your horse will take care of you. As he rubbed the animal, he talked to her in soft tones and patted her neck underneath the mane. She responded to him and turned her head to look at him as if she knew what he was saying. When he finished he returned to the shade and sat down next to a tree and closed his eyes to rest. He was unaware that Brinkman had been watching him working with the horse.

He must have dozed, for he awoke with a start. Brinkman had his hand on his arm and was motioning him to be quiet. Andrew was immediately awake and wondered why Brinkman was acting so cautiously.

After a few minutes he arose and said, "We better go.

Four horsemen just went by on the road at a hard run. It may mean nothing, or it may mean that your friends have discovered you didn't go to Savannah after all. Until we know for sure, we better travel quietly."

Andrew noted that Brinkman had already saddled and his horse was standing as though tied. Andrew grabbed his saddle blanket and threw it on the black, then cinched on the saddle. By the time he had finished, Brinkman had the pack horse ready. They mounted and Brinkman took the lead. Andrew noted that he now had his rifle lying across his lap. He didn't know whether there would be trouble or not, but if it came, having the rifle ready might save two or three seconds and that could mean the difference between life and death.

Andrew had strapped one of the pistols around the saddle horn with the butt in easy reach of his hand. It was Mueller's Pistol, the one with the paper caps. Now he pulled it and checked the powder and made sure the paper cap was in place. If he needed it he wanted it to be ready. He also followed Brinkman's example and placed his rifle across his lap.

When they reached the main road, Brinkman held up his hand and slid out of the saddle. He walked to the edge of the road and peered intently at the tracks in the road. Evidently he was satisfied for he mounted and road out heading towards Orangeburg.

Andrew followed him; peering down at the tracks in the road. There were dozens of tracks that had been made within the last few days and Andrew couldn't distinguish one from the other.

Brinkman spoke softly, "I don't feel good about this. Keep your eyes open and if anything happens, dive off into the brush at the side of the road, but be sure and take your gun with you. You may need it."

Andrew noted that Brinkman did not gallop now. Rather he rode at a walk and he was hunched over a little in the saddle.

They had gone about two miles when Brinkman slowed and turned his head to speak to Andrew. "There are two men up ahead sitting in the shade of that big oak. Can you make them out? Are they the ones following you?"

Andrew squinted and although he could see the horses and the two figures they were too far away to make out. He told Brinkman he would have to get closer before he could tell.

Brinkman moved on whispering, "Be careful. Do just as I do, and be ready to act immediately if we have to. There were four men passed and only two are here. Either the other two have gone on or they are in hiding."

They kept the horses at a slow walk as if in no hurry. As they got closer, Andrew whispered to Brinkman, "These are not the men. I do not recognize them."

Brinkman did not relax his caution. He kept his eyes on the two men, yet Andrew was sure, he was also seeing everything else about the surroundings.

As they came closer the two men raised their heads as if seeing them for the first time, but Andrew had the feeling they had been watching them since they first came into sight.

Brinkman nodded as he rode past, not bothering to speak. One of the men raised a hand in greeting and then let it drop. They both appeared to be run-down farmers, but they didn't seem like honest workers just resting alongside the road. They had a furtive look about them and seemed too agitated for some reason.

Andrew felt a cold chill as they passed them. He feared that any minute he might feel a rifle ball hit him in the back. Nevertheless, he did not turn around and they kept walking their horses straight ahead. When they were about a hundred yards past the two men, Brinkman kicked his horse in the sides and he immediately jumped into a hard run. Andrew, who had been very tense, hesitated just a couple seconds and the black horse took the matter into her own control. When she saw the horse she had been following all night and half of the day take off at a hard gallop, she jumped forward to run also. That leap forward saved Andrew's life.

The horse jumped and began her run. Andrew first tilted backward, then in an effort to regain his balance he leaned forward across the saddle horn. Just as he did, he heard the rifle fire and the bullet passed by so close that he could feel the wind of it.

The sound of the shot startled him so that he let loose the reins of the pack animal and freed from the pull on the saddle. It was at that moment that the black horse shot forward in a dead run. In less than a second she was pounding down the road after Brinkman's horse.

In the span of two breaths Andrew heard another weapon fire and felt the tug of a bullet through the side of his jacket. It was so close that it burned his flesh like fire. At first he thought he had been hit, but he leaned forward over the neck of his horse and let her run. Just as he turned a sharp bend in the road he saw Brinkman motioning for him to follow him into the woods. He cut sharp and went into the brush behind Brinkman. There was a lot of shouting back behind them and they could not make out what was being said.

Brinkman had not gone but about a hundred yards before he slid off his horse, dropped the reins and headed back towards the road with his gun. He motioned Andrew to tie his horse and follow him. Pointing to the rifle he whispered, "Are you any good with that thing?"

Andrew said, "I can usually hit what I shoot at."

"Good, then follow me and be ready to use it."

Brinkman ran through the woods, back down the way

they had come. Travelling parallel to the road, they knew when they had passed the first two, the ones who had evidently done the shooting.

Brinkman kept going. Andrew was amazed how fast the man travelled and how little sound he made. Try as he might, Andrew had trouble keeping up with him, and certainly knew he made far too much racket. He was sure he would give away their positions.

They must have run at least a quarter, and perhaps a half mile, before Brinkman slowed and waited for Andrew to catch up. Andrew was out of breath, but Brinkman scarcely seemed to be breathing heavy. He motioned Andrew to follow and silently slipped through the woods. They had not gone but a short distance before they heard the two men beneath the Oak tree talking. They moved on quietly and soon they could make out what was being said.

"I don't know what happened. Why don't you run up there and find out?"

"Not on your life. Johnson said wait here and not let them come back past us. That's what we better do!"

"But I heard shots several minutes ago. Maybe they killed both of them and are getting away with our share of the loot."

"Then you ride up and see what happened. It sounded to me like they missed them because I heard Winslow cussing way back here."

Just as they finished that sentence, a voice in the edge of the woods said, "Stand pat and don't move a hair on your head or you are both dead men." This statement was punctuated by the cocking of a rifle. It was enough to convince the men they should heed the warning.

Brinkman emerged from the woods closely followed by Andrew.

One of the men blurted out, "By gawd, where did you come from? We just saw you go up the road."

Brinkman said, "You can't always believe what you see. Sometimes your eyes lie to you."

He quickly disarmed them and motioned for Andrew to tie them up.

Andrew took their belts and lashed their hands together behind their backs, then taking some pigging strings from their saddles, he tied their feet securely.

Brinkman said, "I'm only going to ask you this question one time. I expect an honest and direct answer. If I don't get it, I will hamstring you so you will never walk right again." To emphasize this he drew a skinning knife and stuck it in the sand next to one man's boot.

"Is this the man you were after? Did you plan to rob him?"

The men hesitated and Brinkman pulled the knife out of the dirt and raised the man's pants leg. That was all it took. Both men began to talk at once.

"Yes. We were told he was carrying a lot of money and we are to get 20 percent of whatever he had on him. It was Johnson's idea."

"Did you intend to kill him or just leave him in the woods a foot?"

"All we wanted was just his money and goods. I don't know about the others. They are pretty mad at him. Says he jumped them and hit them with a chair when they weren't looking."

In spite of the tenseness of the situation, Andrew had to smile. Bullies always needed a cover story to explain how they got the worst end of a fight they started.

Brinkman said, "Who are the other two men?"

"The tall, thin one is Brad Johnson, and the other one is Bill Winslow. They are mean ones. Don't leave us here tied up like this. If they find we have let you escape they'd just as soon cut our throats and leave us here."

Brinkman stood up and holstered his knife. He said, "I wouldn't worry about them too much if I were you. You better worry about what we might do to you when we come back."

With that he motioned for Andrew to follow him and again he slipped into the woods. He was as silent as a snake and if Andrew was not so close to him he would not have known he was even there.

They retraced their steps through the woods until they were at the approximate place where the shots were fired. Then Brinkman slowed and moved a little more cautiously. Andrew saw the pack horse standing beside the road and thought it strange that the two bandits had not caught it up. He started to move towards it when Brinkman caught his arm and motioned him to remain still and stay where he was. Then he was gone. He just seemed to disappear. Andrew peered through the woods and could see no sign of him or that he had even been there. He waited another few minutes and then he heard a light conversation.

"They ain't coming back. Let's take the horse and get outta here. Maybe the money is in the packs."

"Keep quiet! I don't think they are running away and leaving all that gear on the horse. They will be back for him as soon as they think we are gone. Keep quiet and wait. They'll be back."

Andrew was startled to find Brinkman at his elbow. He had not heard him return.

Brinkman said, "Come on. They have tied their horses back in the brush. I've got a plan."

Andrew followed him as quietly as he could but he was sure they must have heard him.

They reached the horses, and Brinkman said, "Here's what let's do. We'll take their horses and get ours. Then give me a couple minutes to get behind them. You take all four horses and go charging down the road and as you pass the pack horse, you grab its reins and take him with you. They can't take a shot at you squatting down. They will have to stand up to get a shot, and when they do, I will nail the boogers."

With four horses gathered up, and Andrew mounted, Brinkman said quietly, "Give me about four or five minutes. I know exactly where they are."

Andrew did not have a watch so he counted to 300 slowly while he was inching his way back to the road. He walked the horses a short distance and then tied the reins of the other horses together and slapped them on the rump. As they began to run, he bent low in the saddle and let the black horse run with them. He was coming up now on the pack horse and he pulled the black down to give him a chance to grab the reins. Then he noticed that they had tied the reins to a small tree and it would take him a couple of seconds to untie the knot. Just as he was deciding whether to stop and untie the horse or go on without it, he heard a rifle bark and a scream of pain. Immediately in front of him, hidden in the brush, he saw the tall thin man, the one they called Brad Johnson, rise up and turn toward him.

Johnson had his rifle in his hands but hesitated, trying to decide whether to fire at Andrews or head back into the woods. He could see Andrew on the horse and he couldn't see anyone in the woods. He turned and began to raise the gun to his shoulder.

All the pent up stress and anger came to a boil in Andrew. These two had tried to bully him in the bar and he had been forced to either fight or tuck his tail and run. Now they were lying in wait for him, intending to ambush him and rob him and probably kill him. It was enough to make a person really mad. And now, here one of them was raising a gun to kill him.

Andrew snatched the pistol hanging on the saddle horn, swung it in line and fired point blank at the man. Johnson pulled the trigger on the rifle just as the bullet took him square in the chest. It knocked him back and the gun jerked upwards, the bullet going harmlessly into the air.

Andrew slid off his horse and taking his rifle in hand stepped beside a large tree just as Brinkman materialized out of the brush with his knife in his hand. He bent over the tall man ready to strike, but one look told him there was no need. The man was dead. He died the minute the bullet hit him. It went straight through his heart.

Brinkman had seen the whole thing. He had shot the short man but knew he could not reload fast enough to get the tall one so he was going after him with his knife. When the man turned to fire at Andrew, he was too far away and he was afraid that the man would kill Andrew. He had not seen a weapon in Andrew's hand and he appeared to be concentrating on getting the pack horse untied. The quickness with which Andrew had drawn the pistol and fired escaped him. He didn't know how he could have done it. Andrew must have been holding the pistol in his hand with the reins. That is the only way he could see it happening.

"He's done for. So is the other one." He stepped back into the woods to retrieve his rifle and came dragging the body of the short one called Winslow out to the side of the road.

"Go get the other two and bring them up here."

Andrew mounted the black and walked down the road. Reaction was setting in now as it always did after he had to kill someone. He shook as though he had chills and felt sick at his stomach. While the killing was justified, as it had been all the times before in the war, the taking of another's life was a frightening thing and he did not think he would ever get where it would be an easy thing to do. At least he hoped he would never get to that stage.

He rode down the road and picked up the horses of the two men that had just been killed. Then he returned to the two men they had tied up. He cut the thongs holding their feet and told them to walk up the road to where the pack horse was. As they moved along he gathered up the reins of their horses and followed them.

When they came to the pack animals, Brinkman had dragged both bodies out to the road and had them lying side by side.

The two bandits gaped at the dead men and their faces turned ashen. The looked at one another, probably thinking, that could be us laying there. They were very quiet, but very much afraid as to what their fate might be.

Andrew dismounted and tied the horses to tree branches.

Brinkman noticed that Andrew avoided looking at the dead men. The man could do what needed doing, but he had no stomach for killing. He was not like those who gloated over killing someone and bragged about it as if the killing was no more important than the taking of a deer. His respect for Andrew grew a little more. In fact, he might just get to like this man. He had remained cool during the first shoot-out and had followed his instructions right down the line. He had not questioned who was the more experienced in this situation and when the going was tight, he stood his ground and returned fire.

He spoke now. "What shall we do with these bodies and the two live ones?" Just to throw a scare into the other two he added, "Or shall we make it four bodies and leave them for the buzzards?"

All three men turned to face him and though he had been joking he kept a straight face. The two bandits were frightened and their faces were chalk-white. They fell down on their knees and begged for mercy.

"Please don't kill us. We didn't mean to do you any harm. We are poor people and a couple hundred dollars would mean a great deal to us. We intended to rob you but we didn't intend to hurt you."

Brinkman said nothing, leaving it up to Andrew. "I am puzzled. How did you pick up our trail so fast? We told everyone that we were going to Savannah."

The younger of the two couldn't find his voice, he was so scared. The older one spoke, "Johnson had eased into the corral the day after you bought your pack horse, after it had been shoed, and filed a big X on the bottom of the front shoe. When we discovered you had gone all we had to do was look on the road to Savannah and when we didn't find the print we knew you had not gone that way. We just kept checking the roads out of town until we found the print. Then we came on as fast as we could. When the sign played out we figured you had turned off to rest and would be on sooner or later. Johnson and Winslow knew you would recognize them so they hid in the brush. We were supposed to block your retreat in case you tried to turn back."

When Andrew spoke his voice shook with anger.

"You sniveling dogs. You would have robbed me and left me here afoot, and I doubt you would have raised objections to these two torturing or killing me. It is just that your luck was bad." Turning to Brinkman, he asks, "How far are we from Orangeburg? Do they have a sheriff or some law enforcement officer there?"

Brinkman said, "We are about two hours from Orangeburg and while they may have a marshal there I doubt that they will have a jail for these two. If you want to press charges you will probably have to return to Charleston with them."

Andrew shook his head in disgust. Taking his knife, he slashed the belts that held their hands behind them. Then he ordered them to lift the bodies of their erstwhile friends and tie them on the backs of the horses. When this is done he turned to the two men.

"Today you attempted to rob me and take what was not yours. You wanted something for nothing, something you did not work for and earn. Your greed almost cost you your life. I am going to turn you loose and let you go back to Charleston or wherever it is you came from. But the next time you may not be so lucky. You should ask yourselves if the risk of a couple hundred dollars is worth your life. You will have plenty of time to think about this question as you walk back to Charleston. We are keeping your horses. Even though they were wicked, evil men, your friends deserve to be buried decently. Your horses will pay for that burial. If I ever have another run in with you I will not be so easy on you. I will hang you from the nearest tree. Now, get yourselves down the road. You had better give my advice some serious consideration. The next time, you may not be so lucky."

It was a long walk back to Charleston and unless someone came along and gave them a ride, it would take at least two days to get back, maybe longer. For men who were used to riding, such a long walk would be pure torture. Brinkman thought, Andrew was right, these men would have plenty of time to think about their wicked ways, and it would either make them meaner or turn them into honest men. He was pleased again by Andrew's decision.

They rode on into Orangeburg and arrived there at sunset. They went directly to the town hall and asked to see whoever was in charge. A crowd began to gather around and everyone wanted to know what happened and who the two men were. Brinkman stood in the background and let Andrew do the talking. He told everyone to wait until the law arrived and he would tell everything.

Shortly, a middle aged man, a bit on the portly side, hurried up while pinning on a badge. He seemed angry that he was taken away from his supper and he didn't like having to handle cases involving dead people.

When he stepped forward, Andrew asked, "Are you the law here?"

The man answered rather curtly, "I am. I'm the town constable. Who are you and what happened to these men?"

"My name is Andrew Stanley. My companion and I were on the way to Orangeburg when we were attacked by these two men and two others. I had a run in with them several nights ago and they evidently followed me intending to rob, maybe kill me. At least they shot at me from an ambush." Andrew pulled up his jacket to show where the bullet had passed through and for the first time noticed that the shot had come closer than he thought. It had passed through the skin of his side and blood was oozing out slowly. "We managed to get into the woods and came around and surprised their two accomplices. We tied them up and then eased up on these two. When we attempted to reclaim our pack animal which they had caught and tied to a tree, they tried to shoot us again. My companion shot one and I shot the other."

The Constable wanted to know if there had been any witnesses and why had they been brought to him. He was a little too officious to suit Andrew and he let some of the pressure inside exit.

"You were the closest town to where the incident occurred and we felt the matter should be reported to some official. No there were no other witnesses except the two men walking back to Charleston. If you hurry you can probably catch them about four hours ride down the road. They won't be travelling too fast I don't imagine. These are their horses and they are to pay for a decent burial for these men. Is there anything else you want to know?"

The Constable was a bit flustered but he wasn't finished yet. "You will have to stay in town until I talk this over with the town council."

Now Andrew was put out and he exploded. "Sir, I plan to be here a day or two because I have business here. However, I will leave when my business is completed whether you or your town council like it or not. We were set upon by these bandits and we defended ourselves. We brought the bodies in to inform the proper authorities. If you do not want to file the report we will take them up on the hill and bury them ourselves but we will not stay in your town longer than we plan to, while you put your heads together to try to figure out what you should do."

As he finished a mumble of agreement went up from the crowd and one man said, "He brought in the bodies, would he have done that if there was any foul deed here? Thank him for a job well done. That is two less rogues skulking in the woods for us to have to worry about."

Brinkman stepped forward and spoke for the first time. "It is just as the man said. I was the other party with him and he told it just the way things happened. These two men had been following Stanley for a couple days trying to find out which way he was going. We left in the middle of last night and rode all night trying to outdistance them, but they caught up with us. One of them had cut and X in the hoof of the pack animal so they could follow Stanley. We did nothing more than defend ourselves."

Brinkman was well known throughout most of the Carolinas, Georgia, and Tennessee and Kentucky. Several people in the crowd recognized him and when he was finished, one said, "If Hans Brinkman says that it is so, it is so. Let the matter end."

The Constable took the reins of the horses and led them over to the undertaker's parlor and had nothing more to say.

149

Andrew and Brinkman led their horses down the street to the livery stable and walked in under the big double doors. They left the animals and ordered them fed and rubbed down.

There was only one small hotel in Orangeburg, and they headed for it. After checking in and going to their rooms to clean up, they met again and went across the street to eat. It had been a trying day for Andrew and he was very silent while they ate. After the meal they lingered a few minutes over coffee. It was Brinkman who spoke first.

"You seem quiet tonight. Was that your first killing today?"

"No I have had to kill men before. Some with guns, some with swords and lances; one or two in hand to hand combat with knives. But I never learned to like it. It always leaves me sick at my stomach and I wonder what God must think of someone who kills another human being."

Brinkman went silent a moment, studying this man who was a contradiction to so many things he had assumed when he first met him.

Shortly, he spoke, "I don't know how God may look upon the taking of a life, but for my part, it depends on whether the killing is done out of wantonness and with criminal intent, or whether it is done in self-defense. Maybe Christ could turn the other cheek, and maybe he was sent here to be sacrificed for other men's sins, but I don't think men in general have that capacity, to let themselves be slaughtered out of piety. If we did not fight back and defend ourselves against bandits, robbers, kings and dictators, we would all be slaves; or worse yet, be killed at their whim. I can›t accept that type of life, nor will I let another abuse me, my family or friends without taking a hand.»

"I suppose you are right," nodded Andrew. "We were not meant to immolate Christ. I know that sometimes it is necessary to fight and even to kill to defend ourselves and your property, but I still regret it when I am the one doing the killing."

"You would probably regret it more if you were the one being killed." At which they both smiled and agreed.

Then Andrew knew it was time to speak his mind. "Mr. Brinkman, I appreciate you coming with me to Orangeburg. Without you I probably would have walked into that trap today. I do not wish to insult you, but I would like to pay you for a day's guiding if you will accept."

"Well, I didn't have anything to do and I was getting lazy and rusty lying around Charleston. I can only stand so much of city life and then I want to get back into the woods. Where was it you said you were going?"

"I don't really have a destination in mind. I want to travel some of your back country, get away from civilization for a while and try to forget some of the ugly things I have witnessed. I also am looking for a place to settle down. I want to start a family, but I want it to be on my own land. I don't yet know where it is, but I will know it when I see it. I intend to go west of what they call the Smokey Mountains, into what is referred to as the territories of Georgia, the western parts of the Carolinas and maybe up into the new area they refer to as Tennessee. I wish it were so that you could take me into the back country. Mr. Miller said you and David Foster, here in Orangeburg are two of the best guides. He said you both have spent time in Indian country and know their ways pretty well."

Brinkman leaned forward in his chair, unable to hide the excitement in his voice. "Lord, there is pretty country out there. Just thinking about it makes me want to pack up and go. Once a person has travelled the backwoods, he is never content to live in civilization again. I'm rotting away back there in town. Might be I could go a ways with you, unless of course you would rather have Dave Foster. I know him and he is a good man. Don't talk much, but he knows his injuns."

Andrew was delighted. "Mr. Brinkman, I would be glad if you would accompany me. Besides, we've already had our first action and your lessons on the trail were a big help."

Brinkman laughed. "You caught that did you? I just thought it might be helpful for you to know a few things I could show you on the trip. It might save you some grief as you got further away from civilization. What are your plans?"

"I want to find a man by the name of Charles Heyward. He is supposed to have a plantation near here someplace. There is a lady at the plantation that I met on the ship while coming to America. I want to talk with her before I leave. I don't expect to be here more than two, perhaps three days. Then we will leave. I may go as far as the big river you call the Mississippi."

Brinkman raised his eyebrows and said, "Whoosh! That is a long journey. It will take the rest of this year, until at least Christmas to go that far. Man, what a trip though. I may never get to go that far again in my life. To make it one more time would be like giving me a birthday wish. I'm your man, Hoss. One thing though, you got to quit calling me Mr. Brinkman. My name is Hans to all my friends, and if we are going to be together for this long a time, we better be friends."

Hans didn't want to discuss pay for something he enjoyed doing, but finally agreed to accept three hundred dollars when the trip was over and if anything happened to him, it was to be given to his daughter. Andrew insisted that he would pay for all supplies and expenses of the trip.

They shook hands on the deal and returned to the hotel. It had been a long and hectic day. A good night's sleep and a couple days' rest would do them good.

When he was in his room, Andrew stripped off his shirt and washed the wound in his side. He decided it was not serious but would probably be sore for a few days. After applying some antiseptic and a bandage, he turned in for the night.

CHAPTER ELEVEN

A ndrew awoke early, washed, shaved, dressed and went downstairs to have breakfast. As early as he had arisen, he looked out the window and saw Brinkman riding out of town on his horse. He didn't know where he was going and decided it wasn't any of his business. He was sure he would be back when Andrew was ready to leave.

After breakfast he asked directions to the plantation of Charles Heyward. Then he went to the livery stable, saddled his horse and rode out. The people at the restaurant told him the plantation was about an hour's ride from town, so he put the horse into a trot. The black had rested well and been fed a good meal of corn and oats and wanted some exercise. Andrew let her gallop along at her own pace.

This was pretty country they were passing through. A little too flat to suit him, but pretty just the same. There were lots of fields with corn, cotton and other crops in them. The harvest was still a month or two away. Several of the fields had slaves working in them, hoeing and clearing out weeds.

There were several pastures with cattle grazing in them. The grass was green and lush. In a couple of months the pastures would be planted in oats or rye so the cows would have pasture during the winter.

This was good farm country. The soil was rich and land had been cleared almost as far as the eye could see in all directions with just a clump of trees standing here and there. A number of huge oaks spread their branches and provided shade for the cattle from the summer heat.

It was nigh onto 10 o'clock when Andrew came in sight of the Heyward plantation. From the road a long lane led up towards the main house that was set on a small hill. There were majestic oak trees lining both sides of the lane. The house must have been at least a quarter mile from the main road. There were numerous barns and sheds and a long row of cabins that would be the slave quarters. There were two smaller houses in the back of the house. One set part way between the big house and the slave quarters. Andrew figured that would be a foreman or overseer's house.

The other was on the opposite side of the main house and probably was a guest house or something like that.

Andrew turned his attention to the main house. It was huge, as big in its way as the castle was on the farm back in Poland. It sort of reminded him of the owners he had worked for before the war, although it was constructed differently. There were six tall pillars in the front that extended up to a roof that was two stories high. Andrew had noticed that lots of the plantations here in the Carolinas were built like this, all a little different, but resembling the others in the front appearance.

He rode up to a hitching rail in front of the house and stepped down. He tied his horse to a ring in the rail and walked up to the door. There he raised a large bronze door knocker and rapped it twice on the huge wooden door. He stepped back and waited. In a couple minutes a black woman opened the door and asked what he wanted.

Andrew said, "Is this the home of Mr. Charles Heyward?"

The woman indicated it was but he was in the fields right now. She expected him back by noon. She invited him in or he could sit on the veranda and she would bring him something to drink. He took a seat in a big rocking chair on the porch and gazed out across the land. It sure was pretty, but it had started to warm up and he was glad to be on the porch in the shade.

Shortly, a man rode up on a well-groomed, richly colored, roan horse that pranced and stepped sideways as the man held him in check. He went to a barn nearest the house and stepped out of the saddle. A black man came out of the barn and took the reins. The man spoke to him then turned and walked towards the house. He had evidently seen the horse tied in front for he came directly to the porch. As he came up the steps, Andrew rose and went to meet him.

He extended his hand and said, "Good day sir. I am Andrew Stanley and you must be Mr. Heyward."

The man acknowledged that indeed he was Heyward and shook Andrew's hand.

Andrew felt a little awkward and didn't know how to broach the subject he wanted to talk about. Finally he said, "Mr. Heyward, I recently arrived by ship in Charleston. I had to leave my country of Poland or face death so I have come to America to find a new life. I am leaving to go inland for a fairly long journey which may take me up to a year. On board the ship I met a lady who was indentured to you. Her name was Catherine York. She is one of the few people I know in America. Would it be possible to see her before I leave?"

Heyward watched Andrew carefully. The man was nervous and somewhat ill at ease. He guessed this was something new to him and he did not know how to proceed. He motioned Andrew to sit back down and stuck his head inside the door telling the maid to bring them some lemonade. Then he came and took a chair next to Andrew.

"How long have you been in America, Mr. Stanley?"

Andrew answered, "Just a little over two weeks now. It took me that long to settle some business and obtain supplies for my trip. I was raised on a farm and near a forest. I don't like staying around towns too much."

"And where is it you plan to travel?"

"I'm not sure just where I will end up. I have heard that there is much land available for the taking further west. I will go until I find the right piece of land, something that reminds me of my homeland, and I will buy it or homestead it. I may have to go all the way to the big river you call the Mississippi. I am prepared to go even beyond that if I must."

"But surely sir, having just come to this country, and being unfamiliar with the natives and customs of this area, you do not intend to go alone do you?"

Andrew smiled, "No sir. I admit my shortcomings. I have hired a guide and someone who has great knowledge of the terrain and the ways of the Indians. His name is Hans Brinkman."

"Ah yes. I have heard of Brinkman. They say he is one of the best in the area. From what I hear he has lived among the Indians and fought them for thirty or more years. I would say he is a good choice and you are lucky you found someone with such experience."

"He was recommended to me by Mr. Miller at the bank in Charleston. At first he didn't want to accompany me, but Miller asked him to do so as a favor to him."

At the mention of Miller's name, Heyward began to pay closer attention. This man must be of some importance. Miller was a kind man but he would not have used his influence to get Brinkman to accompany this man unless it was in his best interests.

"Mr. Stanley, I have no objection to you calling on Catherine. She may be indentured to me for a period of time, but she still is entitled to have friends and a life of her own. She was brought here as a school teacher and she teaches in the house that you see off there. She also has quarters in the back room of the school. I believe that all children should learn to read and write and all of the children on this plantation attend that school, both white and black. Many of my neighbors say I am crazy for wasting time trying to teach the blacks to read and write, but I find it an advantage. If they can read, and I am not going to be around, I can leave a message of what I want them to do. Or if I need supplies from town, I can write a list and send them to town to get what I need without me having to make the trip. Furthermore, my slaves do not run away."

Andrew was surprised. He did not think the white owners would allow the blacks any form of education. Again, it was somewhat like the owner of the farm where Andrew grew up. He said, "Sir, I think that is admirable of you and I am sure you will not be disappointed. I grew up on a farm like this in Poland. My parents were serfs who worked the land for the landlord. He too thought the young ones should be able to read and write so he let us go to school. When the wars came we became soldiers and because I was better educated than some of the other soldiers conscripted into the army, I was made an officer. Had it not been for the education our landlord allowed us, I might well be dead today."

"Mr. Stanley, you may go down to the school house and see Catherine if you wish. School lets out here at noon so she will have some time free this afternoon. Have you had anything to eat?"

"No. I left town fairly early but I had a large breakfast."

"Then do come in and have a bite with us. I don't know what we will be having, but I'm sure there will be plenty. Besides, I'd like to hear more about your travels."

Andrew thought it might be rude to say no, and although he was anxious to see Catherine, he went inside.

The house had looked large from the outside, but inside it

was enormous. There was an open entrance way that led into a huge living room with a vaulted ceiling that extended all the way to the roof of the house. There was a spiral staircase that began on the left side of the entrance, run half-way around the room and ended on the second floor. He could see numerous doors opening off the stair way and landing on the second floor. To the right was another big room, which was pretty dark, but Andrew could see bookshelves all along one wall and they were all filled with books.

Heyward led him through the living room, then through a very large dining room with a table that would probably seat 30 people. Then they entered a small alcove just off the kitchen that had a smaller table and six chairs. The table was loaded with perhaps a dozen different dishes of food. Andrew thought this was food fit for a king.

Heyward led him to a wash stand on the back porch and bade him wash up, and he proceeded to do likewise.

While they ate, Heyward asked lots of questions about Andrew's past, about Poland and about his plans. All in all, it was a very pleasant meal and when it was over, they both felt as if they knew a great deal about each other. Then Heyward told Andrew to go on down and see Catherine.

He walked to the little school house and began to have second thoughts. He wasn't sure how she would greet him or even if she would be glad to see him.

He knocked on the door and waited. In a couple of minutes the door opened and he could not believe his eyes. Catherine had been lovely in her rags, tangled hair and haggard appearance. Now she stood before him, as beautiful as anything he could have imagined. She was clean, her hair combed and curled, and she had on a gingham dress that accented everything about her. His mouth must have dropped open for he couldn't speak.

Catherine recognized him right away and grabbed his

hand, "Andraui, what are you doing here? I never expected to see you again."

Andrew found his voice and smiled, "I kept thinking of you every day since we left the ship and I had to come see you before I go away."

"Where are you going? Aren't you staying in the Carolinas?" Then she led him to some benches under a big tree and they sat down to talk.

Andrew explained what he had decided to do and how long he might be away. Then he asked her if she was happy here.

Catherine said, "Yes. The Heyward's are nice people and they do not treat me like a servant. They have set up this small school and I teach the white children of the area in the mornings and three afternoons during the week I teach the black children. Many of the parents don't want their children taught in with the blacks and some of the white children are very cruel to the blacks so we decided to teach them at different times. I have a certain amount of freedom. I can go to church, into town and almost anywhere I want to. Most of the town's people do not even know that I am indentured. Mr. Heyward hasn't told them. He thought the parents and the children would show me more respect if they thought I was someone hired to teach them. It probably will work out better that way."

Andrew asked, "Assume for just a minute that you were not indentured, that you were free to do anything you wanted to, what would you do?"

Catherine was caught by surprise. "I don't really know. I had not even given it any thought and I don't want to think about it much because the time when I will be free seems so far away. Why do you ask?"

Andrew continued, "Please think about it for a minute.

It is important to me. What would you do if right now you could walk out of here and go wherever you wanted to go?" She looked at him curiously, and spent several minutes thinking. Then she said, "I guess I would stay right here for a time. I don't know anyone else in this country. I wouldn't know where to go or who to turn to. Here I am fairly safe. The Heyward's are my protectors. No one would bother me while I am under his protection. Besides, I have no money. How would I live without them? Perhaps in time I would find employment elsewhere, or" she added, with a giggle, "I might find a husband."

Andrew asked, "What would you want in a husband?"

She laughed and said, "How did we get into this conversation. I don't really know what I want in a husband. He must be honest, upstanding, willing to work, kind and considerate of others. He must consider me as a person and not as a chattel or as a broodmare to raise a house full of children for him. Don't misunderstand. I love children, and I would like two or three of my own, but I do not want to be treated like I have no feelings, nor do I want to be a man's plaything, taken any time it suits him." She ended this with a little blush. It was something she was not used to talking about, especially with someone she knew only so slightly as she knew Andraui.

They talked of other things for a few minutes and Andrew explained that he had officially taken the name Andrew Stanley and that he hoped to find a place for himself in the West, a place he could settle down on and call his own, where he too could have a family. He wanted to build a new life for himself and he did not want to do it in the cities.

Finally he asked her, "Had you ever considered going west? Would you feel comfortable away from the city life that passes for civilization?"

"Well, again I don't know. I had never considered going

anyplace because I didn't think it would be possible. I was afraid to make any kind of plans because I am bound for such a long time. As for city life, I have been very happy here in the country. I thought I might miss London but I have not. In fact, I find this life very exhilarating. I am even thinking of learning to ride a horse. It seems like it would be such good fun."

Andrew drank in every feature, every word she uttered, and every movement she made. He was totally fascinated with her. He had remembered her as an exciting person, now he wanted to reach out and take her in his arms. Just sitting this close to her made him want her all the more. Her hair was like nothing he had ever seen. It was platted part way down her back then and tied with a bow. The last eight or ten inches hung loose and flowed around her when she turned her head or the wind caught it. With the sun shining on it the reflection was as if the red sunset had been caught and forever held by her hair.

Andrew took up her hand again, and cautiously asked, "Catherine, we have known each other for such a short time, but I would like to know how you feel about me. I am very fond of you. It may seem silly to you and certainly you have not given me any indication that you have any feeling for me. I will only be here for a couple days and I must leave. But before I go, I would like to know if you have any feelings for me and if you do, would you consider me as a husband? Do not say anything right now. I realize this is so unusual, but we are under unusual circumstances and time is against both of us. I have admired you since we first talked on board the ship. Will you think of this and let me come again tomorrow and talk with you again?"

Catherine hardly knew what to say. She stared at him in disbelief, and he thought he had made a serious mistake in being so blunt. He was still holding her hand and she withdrew it and kept staring into his eyes. She could see the seriousness there and she knew he meant everything he said.

Then she took his hand again and said, "Andrew, I truthfully cannot say. I had not thought of you in this way. In fact, I had not dared think about any man or a life of my own until after my indenture is over. I know so little about you and you know so little about me. We both may have violent tempers? I don't know if we have anything in common and we may like totally different things? You are an attractive man and I think you have a kind heart, but that is not enough. You, like me, are new in this country and you do not have a job. We would need to get to know one another better before I could answer your question. But this is all foolishness. I must serve Mr. Heyward for four years. In that time you will fall in love a dozen times and I will probably end up an old maid. Would you wait that long for me?"

"I think I would wait forever if you told me you loved me and would be mine someday. But I want you to think of me for a few minutes and think along these lines, if you were free today, your indenture ended, would you consider marriage?"

"Andrew this is silly. My indenture is not ended. It has only just begun. Besides, are you sure that you would want me as a wife? You don't know anything about me. I may not be able to cook or mend, and I may be a regular shrew to live with. This is all so sudden. I don't know why we are even talking about it."

She saw the pain in his eyes and she felt her heart going out to him, but she stopped. If she is to have any kind of relationship with him, it cannot be based on pity. Thoughts raced through her mind and she tried to imagine a life with this man she barely knows. He seemed kind and gentle, but is he really? They have never kissed, and just barely touched hands; and here he is talking marriage. He must be out of his mind.

Andrew reached inside his tunic and brought out the little jewelry box. He opened it and took out the necklace. Catherine watched him and gasped with amazement. She had never seen such a beautiful necklace, not even in the house of the rich woman in London. The large ruby must be worth a fortune, not to mention the other stones around it.

He held it out to her. "Catherine this is for you. It as a gift from me, you can keep it as a remembrance of our friendship or you can use it to buy your freedom with it. This will more than pay for the four years' indenture you are under."

She could not believe this was happening to her. She was speechless, totally unable to talk. She just sat there and stared at the necklace. It was as if she was in a dream and she was unable to wake up. Tears began to run down her cheeks and she could not speak. She lifted her eyes to his and only then did she see the concern and longing in his eyes. They were all but begging her to accept the necklace and say she felt something for him. Still she could not speak. She laid the necklace down on the bench and got up and went inside. She returned a few minutes later with a picture of tea and two glasses. Neither spoke while she poured them something to drink.

After she had taken a deep drink and gotten control of her wits she asked, "Andrew where did you get such a beautiful necklace? I have never seen anything so beautiful. You did not steal it did you?"

He laughed. "No it is not stolen. You have been on my mind since you left the ship. I had this made especially for you. Will you accept it as a sign of the deep affection I feel for you?"

"You are really serious aren't you? Do you really care for me that much? Aren't you a little worried that I may take the necklace and buy my freedom and move away while you are gone?"

Andrew answered, "If that is what you want to do. It is yours with no strings attached; no obligation. I had it made for you. It would never look right on anyone else. Besides, if you are going to flee from me, it is better you do it now than later; for the more I am around you, the more I will learn to care for you. It will hurt me if you turn me down now, but after I have fallen totally and madly in love with you, should you leave me then, it would break my heart."

Catherine said, "I consider marriage a lifetime matter and once we were into it, there would be no turning back. For better or worse."

Andrew added, "In sickness and in health." Then they both smiled and held hands.

They sat thus for some time and the daylight was fading. Catherine looked at him, peering into his eyes as if looking into his soul.

"Andrew I will not give you an answer now, for there are some things I must figure out. First I must analyze my feelings about you. Except for a few brief conversations on the ship and this afternoon, that is all that we have talked to each other. Another consideration is whether I can get free of my indenture. I don't think I would want a husband that would have to take second place in my life.

"Also, I must think a little on what a life with you might be like. I believe you to be a good man, but I do not know much of you. And finally, I must think about this trip and the life you plan to live. Will I be happy and be a good wife to you in the circumstances and surroundings you are planning? When are you leaving?"

"I had planned to leave Monday. I want to go west as soon as I can. I want to find some land for us and I fear it may be all taken if I delay."

"Let me think of this tonight. Take the necklace with you. I will not accept it if I am not going to marry you. You come back tomorrow and if I have decided to accept your proposal we will talk with Mr. Heyward. You do not propose that we marry before you leave, do you?"

"I do not believe that we could make the arrangements that quickly. We will have to wait until I return. I would like it if we were engaged before I leave so that I know I have someone to come back to when my journey is over. If you accept, I will make arrangements for you while I am gone."

"If I decide, could I not go with you? After all, if we are going to live in the wilds, we might as well go now as a year from now."

"It is not that simple. I don't know exactly where we are going and it may be very dangerous on the trail. I would not want to take a chance on you getting hurt or killed."

"If it is going to be that dangerous, we had better wait until your return. I would hate to become a widow before I have ever been really married. Come back tomorrow. It is Sunday and I will have the day off. I will fix us a picnic basket and we can go down along the stream and spend some time together and get to know one another better."

Andrew was delighted. He had been afraid that she might turn him down. At least she was going to think about it. That was more than he had expected.

He leaned over, took her hand and raised it to his lips. He kissed the open palm and it sent a shudder through Catherine. Her lips compressed and her eyes shone a bit brighter.

He released here hand, said good-bye and walked back around the house to where his horse stood. He mounted and rode away.

Catherine stood still in the shade where they had been these last few hours. Her mind was a jumble of a thousand thoughts all flying around in her head. She still didn't know if she could accept all this as happening to her or not. Andrew was real. The necklace was real. And his proposal of marriage was real. Her thoughts kept jumping to the idea of being free from the indenture, but she would not marry him just to get free of her debt. That would be too much like selling herself for the payment of her debt. She would feel like a prostitute if she did that.

Again and again she came to the question of how did she feel about him? She was flattered that he cared so much for her and she was fairly sure he would be good to her, but did she love him? She had vowed to remain an old maid if she could not find the right person. She wanted to marry for love, not wealth.

That was something else that bothered her. Where had Andrew obtained such a fabulous necklace? It was worth a fortune. He did not seem to have money before when he was on the ship. Had he come into great wealth in this short time he had been ashore? It was said that great fortunes could be made in America, but was it possible in just a couple weeks?

These and many other questions were rolling around in her head when she finally turned down her bed that night and prepared to go to sleep. Then the final question came, how would she feel about getting into bed with someone she hardly knew? She had never had a man and she had been frightened by the tales some women told of how horrible their wedding night had been. Would Andrew be kind and gentle? Would she respond to him and would he be satisfied with her love making? She was woefully inexperienced in this regard and she knew it. She frowned, worried that she might be a disappointment to any man. As she lay in bed and thought of these things, she became hot and sweaty and kicked the cover down off her. She wore just a loose fitting cotton nightgown and it was plastered to her body.

Then she remembered the touch of his lips on her palm. That had sent a chill through her body and she was startled by it. Shocked, and also thrilled by it. She didn't know why hot and cold flashes ran through her at the same time. With this thought and Andrew on her mind, she fell asleep.

CHAPTER TWELVE

A ndrew arrived about 10 o'clock Sunday morning and Catherine was waiting for him. She had a picnic basket packed, and he tied his horse in the shade and slipped the bridle so she could crop the brown grass. Then they walked a short distance to a small creek that flowed through a pasture about a quarter mile from the house. There was an abundance of pine, hickory and oak and a number of other trees that Andrew wasn't familiar with. They came to a little grassy knoll under the limbs of a big magnolia tree. Catherine stopped and said this was the place she had found one afternoon while walking after class. She sat down, took off her shoes and stockings and indicated she was going wading in the creek. Andrew followed suit. After taking off his shoes he rolled up the legs on his trousers and stepped into the water. It was cold and she shivered.

He turned to give her a hand so that she wouldn't fall on the slippery stones and he was shocked to see that she had tucked the end of her skirts up under her bloomers and her legs were bare all the way to just above her knees. While he was shocked, the sight of those shapely legs was a pleasure to behold. She took his hand and waded into the water and they walked along the edge of the stream for a couple hundred feet. Then the water began to get deeper and they turned around and walked back. All the time her dress wanted to come loose and drop into the water. She tugged at it and finally pulled the ends of the skirt up behind her and tied them like a diaper, exposing even more of her legs.

Andrew could hardly keep his eyes off her. Each time he saw her she was more beautiful and desirable than the time before. As they left the water he reached to give her a hand. As she came out of the water, he pulled her to him and put his arms round her. She looked up at him and he leaned forward and kissed her. To his delight, she returned the kiss and did not pull away from him as he feared she might. He kissed her long and gently and she responded. She leaned into him and he pulled her closer again.

When they stopped kissing, she leaned back against his arms and looked into his face. She knew he was getting excited for she could see the excitement in his eyes and the tightness of his mouth. She was a little frightened by it. Strangely she also felt flushed.

Andrew noted her skin's reaction; and her eyes sparkled like stars. He was tempted to kiss her again, but thought better of it. He disengaged himself and moved over to the shade tree and sat down on the blanket. He did not want to move too fast or do anything that might discourage her from accepting his proposal.

Catherine misinterpreted his movements, thinking she had failed to please him. She had never kissed that much and she considered their first contact to be a disappointment to him. She moved over and sat on the blanket beside him and began to wipe the water off her legs with her hands preparing to put her stockings back on.

Andrew picked up a cloth and said, "Let me do that for you."

She was a little shocked because a lady never allowed a man to put his hands on her legs, but having disappointed him with her kiss, she didn't want to discourage him completely. As he rubbed her legs, he never came above the knee and was as gentle as if he was handling a baby. The mere touch of his hands on her skin began to excite her again and she was embarrassed. How could the mere touch of a man make you feel that way she wondered? She also wondered if he knew or could tell. She let him finish then she pulled on her stockings and fastened them just above her knee. Andrew watched unabashedly.

Then he said, "When you were on the boat, the dress you wore was torn down one leg and I used to marvel at how beautiful your legs were. I don't mean to embarrass you but watching you now putting on your hose confirms what I saw before. Your legs are perfect."

This embarrassed her, but pleased her at the same time. She dropped the hem of her dress and proceeded to spread out the lunch she had brought. During the meal they talked about everything except themselves.

Andrew did not want to be the one to bring it up for fear she had decided to turn him down. If that was to be, he wanted to put it off as long as he could. He wanted to stay here close to her and bask in her beauty.

They finished eating and everything was placed back in the basket.

Catherine said, "I don't know much about being a wife or a lover. I have never been either. I am sorry that you were disappointed in my kissing a while ago. It is just that I don't have much experience in that area."

Andrew couldn't believe what he heard. Where had she got the idea he didn't like her kissing? He went over to her and took her by both arms and held her at arms' length so she had to look into his face.

"Catherine, you were not a disappointment to me. The fact of the matter is that your kisses excited me so much that if I had not turned you lose I would have tried to seduce you there on the creek bank. That's why I went over there and sat down. Just touching you arouses me and I want to make love to you, but I'm afraid to touch you for fear I will offend you. You can't imagine how much I wanted you and when I was drying your legs, I could hardly control my emotions. There is a physical attraction about you that brings out the worst in me. I want to ravish you every time I am around you. No, you are far from being a disappointment to me."

Catherine's spirits rebounded and she was pleased that he liked her so much. She could understand his desire, for she felt some of the same things, but she just didn't know what it meant. Then with a coy little smile and said, "Do you think I would be enough of a lover to please you?"

"Do I! I want you so badly that I am tense as a spring. But I want everything to be right between us. I do not want to do something that might make you dislike me. That is why I am trying to maintain control of my emotions."

She smiled and leaned into his arms. "Let's try that kissing some more. I kind of liked that." She put her arms around his waist and raised her lips to his. Without realizing what she was doing, her lips opened slightly.

Andrew could hardly believe how soft and responsive her mouth was. He slipped his tongue into her mouth, and she pulled back a little. He understood that is the first time she had ever been kissed that way.

Then she responded back to him and opened her mouth again, inviting him to kiss her again. He felt her trembling and beginning to squirm. At first she held her body away from him so that she didn't touch him, but then as they continue to kiss and hold each other tight, she pressed her body to him. He understood that they were both losing control.

Andrew pulled back gently, and gently brought her at arms' length from him. He sighed, letting out a deep breath. "We better stop right now. If we do not, I will not be responsible for what happens."

Catherine felt a little embarrassed and shocked at her wantonness. She didn't understand what made her act that way. She returned to sit on the blanket, and removed the pins out of her hair and it fell down her back.

As she started to comb it, Andrew asked if he could do it for her. She handed him the comb and turned her back to him. He stroked her hair and she began to relax.

She leaned against him. It was such a comforting feeling to have him close and touching him. "Andrew, do you still think you want to marry me?"

Andrew replied, "Yes, very much. I believe I have loved you since the first day I saw you on the ship. You may not love me now, but I will be good to you and maybe you will grow to love me."

"I care for you Andrew. I am not sure yet if I love you for I have never been in love and do not know exactly how it feels. I know that I was happy to see you and could hardly wait for you to come this morning. It seemed the day wouldn't pass fast enough. I don't think I would ever consider marrying someone I did not love.

"It is too early yet for we hardly know anything about each other. I think we need time to get to know each other. I don't know how good a wife I would be but if I accept I will try awfully hard to please you. I do not want to say yes right now and I know you will be leaving tomorrow. Will you accept a maybe and give us some time when you get back to get to know one another?"

Andrew answered, "Yes, As long as you will promise not to fall for someone else and run away with him while I am gone."

Catherine laughed. "That is not very likely. You have set my soul on fire and I will be dreaming of you until you return. Besides, if you buy my indenture from Mr. Heyward, I will be bound to you legally."

He said, "No. I would not want you to feel beholden to me. If you agree to be my wife, I want it to be because you love me and want to be with me, not because you are obligated to me. If Heyward sells your indenture, I will set you free and you will be your own woman while I am away."

"If we can work it out with Mr. Heyward, I will promise you that I will wait until you return and if our feelings remain strong as they are now I will marry you when you return."

Andrew was ecstatic. He half turned her and tilted her head back so that he could see her face. She looked a little pale, as if frightened by her decision. He leaned forward and gently kissed her again. She turned and rose up on her knees in front of him. She hugged him and he put his hands through her hair and pulled her close to him. He could feel her breasts rising and falling with her heavy breathing as they pressed against his chest. He wanted her so badly and he felt she was ready too, but this was not the way to start off a marriage. He would wait until they were legally wed.

He got up, pulled her to her feet, kissed her once more and said, "Let's go talk to Mr. Heyward."

Heyward was in his library when they came to the house and he invited them in. This was only the second time that Catherine had been in the house and she was awed by the size of it and the magnificence. Andrew came right to the point. "Mr. Heyward, Catherine and I are close friends and someday we hope to be married. I would like to buy her indenture and obtain her release from her obligation to you. Will you sell her indenture, sir?"

Heyward was totally surprised. He had not expected this and he did not want to lose the school teacher. She was very good with the children and did not mind teaching the black children. Some teachers did.

Then he said "Mr. Stanley, I have several thousand dollars invested in this young lady and if I let her go, I will have a hard time finding someone to teach classes here. I am not real anxious to sell her indenture."

Andrew said, "Sir, I will pay you double for what you have invested in Catherine's fines and transportation here. We do not plan to wed right now. I will be gone for several months and we will only wed when I return. She will stay here and teach in your school while I am gone at no cost to you. I will provide for her keep if you will allow her to live in the school house as before. When I return, if she accepts my proposal of marriage, I will then take her with me. If for some reason I do not return she will be free to pursue her own life. That will give you the better part of a year to find another teacher. Will you take that deal?"

Heyward thought for a few moments. He would receive a good return on his investment and have a teacher for a year free of charge. He could see these two young people were in love and he did not want to stand in their way. Besides, if this young man had this kind of money, it might be good to stay on his good side. He looked at them and said, "How do you plan to pay for her indenture?"

Andrew said, "I have certain funds in Mr. Miller's bank. You tell me how much and I will send a rider to Charleston to bring back either paper or gold. I figure a rider can go and come back in a day or so enroute. Do we have a deal?"

Heyward stood and extended his hand. "We have a deal. However, it will not be necessary for you to send for the money. I will accept a draft on your funds at the bank and the next time I go into Charleston I will have the funds transferred to my account. I will have the papers drawn terminating the indenture. When do you plan to leave?"

"I plan to leave tomorrow morning. I am anxious to begin my journey to find land. I want to make certain arrangements for Catherine in case she needs anything while I am away."

"You do not need to worry about Catherine. While she is here we will see that she does not go without anything she may need."

He told Andrew the sum he had invested in Catherine's indenture and transport expenses was roughly $35,000. Andrew asked him if he would come into town early the next morning and they could sign the draft before he departed. With that agreed, Andrew walked Catherine back to her house. Then he kissed her again and asked if she was sure of her decision. When she answered yes, he folded her into his arms and held her close. She disengaged herself and turned towards the kitchen and said, "I was just kidding about not being able to cook. I will fix us some supper."

As they entered the kitchen Andrew took the little box out of his vest pocket and began to open it.

As he did so, he spoke. "Catherine, ours has been a strange court-ship and many things are not as they should be. However, when you do decide you will need an engagement ring. I have had one made for you and I dare not take it with me on my journey. Will you take it and safeguard it until you reach your decision? When I return, if you accept me, I will place this on your finger for good."

With that he opened the box and moved the huge diamond ring across the table to her.

Catherine gasped. She had never seen anything so large and so beautiful. She could not believe her eyes. Her mouth hung open and her face was as white as a sheet.

It was several seconds before she caught her breathe and then she began to cry. She literally burst into tears. She sat down at the table with the box and the ring extended out in front of her full length as if she could see it better from a distance. Andrew couldn't understand. He had thought she would be happy and smiling, instead here she was bawling her eyes out.

Finally she raised her eyes to meet Andrew's and spoke, "Andrew it is beautiful. I have never seen a more magnificent ring. It must have cost you a fortune. I never dreamed I would have such a beautiful engagement ring. In fact for the past several months I wondered if I would ever have a future, anyone to love me, a family or any kind of future. You cannot possibly know what these last two days have meant to me. I still think I am dreaming. I can't really believe it is all happening to me."

With that she walked into his arms. They embraced and kissed for a long minute.

Andrew then took out the necklace and said, "Remember, this is yours also. I had it made especially for you and I want you to wear it tonight. It is yours and it will only look its best when you are wearing it. It is yours whether or not you agree to marry me. It is worth a great deal of money so you should keep it in a safe place. Perhaps Mr. Heyward will allow you to place it in his safe."

Catherine turned around and raised the hair off her neck so that he could place the necklace around her neck and lock it. He allowed the ruby to glide down onto her chest and fastened the clasp behind. Her skin, so white, reminded him of milk and cream. When she turned back around, the blood-red reflection of the ruby, lying between her breasts, flashed as she moved. The other diamonds and stones picked up and reflected the light from all angles.

She raised it off her neck and exclaimed what a beautiful stone and such lovely work in the chain and settings for the jewels. She turned to Andrew, "This is fabulous! Where did you find such beautiful stones?"

"I brought the jewel from Europe, but the necklace

was made by a jeweler in Charleston. His name is Peter Georgiades. The style and everything is his own design."

While Catherine cooked supper they chatted about dozens of things, what they liked and didn't like, what foods they like. Andrew saw that she looked so natural in this house and doing womanly things. She is a natural jewel, he thought to himself, and smiled.

Finally, after the meal they rose and went into the large room she used as a classroom. The kitchen was hot from the cook stove and Catherine said it would be cooler in the class room. "I wish you wouldn't go Andrew. If you could stay, it would not take us long to get to know each other and perhaps we could be married soon. I would like for us to build a home and have a real marriage. I will be lonely until you return. Please do not be gone too long."

Andrew replied, "I will return as quickly as I can. You can rest assured of that."

She kissed him again, "I understand and I would not want to interfere with your plans. It is only now that we have found each other; I do not want you to go. I am afraid I might lose you."

"As long as I live," he said, "I promise I shall return to you. Do not fear for me. I love you and I hope that by the time I return you will have come to love me too."

Catherine looked him in the eye, "Oh Andrew, I think I do love you, but I want to be sure. Marriage is forever as far as I am concerned and I want to be sure I am the wife you will be satisfied with for the rest of your life. I will keep the ring safe and when you return, we will talk about it further. Please be careful and return to me safely. You are so good and kind to me, I do not want to lose you."

Andrew kissed her once more with assurances again that he will come back to her. Then he mounted up and rode back to town. His mind is filled with thoughts of what marriage will mean to him. Marriage to this beautiful woman will be all any man could ask for. He knew by her kisses that she had a deeply passionate nature. Had he pressed his advantage, he could have made love to her tonight. But he wanted it to be a good marriage and he did not want to start it off wrong.

CHAPTER THIRTEEN

It was a restless night for Andrew and he awoke early. He packed his belongings, including his bedroll and went down stairs for breakfast. To his surprise, Hans was already seated at a table having coffee.

Andrew strode over and clapped Hans on the shoulder. "I will be ready to leave in about an hour. I have to do a little business at the courthouse as soon as it opens. Then we will be on our way. Is everything ready?"

"Yes. I went to see Dave Foster and we had a long chat. I told him about our trip and he would like to ride along with us. He said staying cooped up here in town is about to drive him crazy. He also told me that there have been some recent raids, a little farther to the west, by Indians from up north. It might be a good thing to have another rifle along. Dave is a good man to ride the river with. What do you think?"

"Sounds good to me, and I don't mind having another person along. If it will help save my hair, he's welcome. Can you get word to him?"

"I thought you'd see it that way, so I told him to meet us at the livery stable."

"Hans. I feel I am a pretty good judge of people. I have placed my life in your hands. You have already saved my life once, and may have to do it again in the weeks ahead.

We will have to rely on one another and work together. I consider us friends and I have complete trust in you. If you say Foster is alright, he is O.K. in my book too."

Hans looked at him a few seconds and then lowered his eyes. It was as strong a declaration of confidence as anyone had ever spoken to him and he knew that from this day forward he had a friend and companion he could rely upon. Such trust and personal talk embarrassed him for he didn't like to discuss himself and his personal thoughts. He did not reply. Nothing more was said. Nothing needed saying.

The two men ate a hearty breakfast and Andrew told him of all that had taken place and that the woman he hoped to marry would be coming into town any time now.

Hans said, "I am anxious to see what kind of woman would have anything to do with a no-good like you."

They both laughed and walked towards the livery.

At about 8:30 the buckboard with Mr. & Mrs. Heyward came into town and went directly to the courthouse. Catherine had come with them. Andrew walked across the street to meet them.

Andrew greeted Mrs. Heyward, shook hands with Heyward and helped Catherine down from the carriage. He embarrassed her by holding her and kissing her right there in front of the courthouse. When she objected, he told her, "I want to be the envy of every man in town. I also want them to know you are spoken for and to keep away."

They entered the courthouse and asked the clerk to write out the draft for the amount Andrew had agreed to pay Heyward. Andrew paused a moment and asked the clerk to add another $500 to it. Andrew turned to Heyward, "I intend to leave sufficient funds with Catherine to see to her needs for the immediate future, but I do not have enough funds with me to take care of all her needs. When the extra $500 comes will you please give it to her? I would also ask that in case some emergency arises or she runs out of money before I return, if you will see to her welfare I will reimburse you when I return."

Heyward agreed to look after Catherine as if she were his own daughter.

When the business with Heyward was completed and he had formally recorded the release of indenture for Catherine, Andrew asked them to please wait a few minutes before returning to the plantation. He wanted to talk to Catherine alone. He walked Catherine to the back of the courthouse and stepped into a hallway that led out to the rear of the building.

When they were alone, he turned to her and said, "Miss York, you are a free woman. How does it feel?"

She leaned close to him and said, "It feels great to be out from under the bond, but I fear I will never be a free woman again. I think I will be bound to you forever and that is the way I want it to be. Andrew, I was lonely for you last night, and I am sorry that you are leaving. If I thought I could keep you from going I would say yes right now."

Andrew took her in his arms and kissed her and was aware her lips parted to invite his tongue. He was slightly surprised and wondered if the others might be watching and could tell of the passion they felt for each other.

He reached into his pocket and took out several hundred dollars in gold coins and handed them to her. He said, "Take these and use them for whatever you need. Heyward will give you another five hundred dollars when he cashes the draft I have signed. He also indicated that he will pay you a monthly salary as a school teacher. That should be sufficient to take care of you until I can get back. I will return as quickly as I can."

He returned to shake hands with Heyward, and Mrs. Heyward came forward and gave him a big hug. They both wished him a safe journey and told him to return soon. Mrs. Heyward could not say enough about the beautiful necklace Catherine was wearing. Heyward too was impressed. He knew that the necklace was worth many thousands of dollars. His first impression of the man was correct. He had great wealth and was likely to be a man of great substance in the future.

Andrew saw Hans and Dave Foster standing near the door of the courthouse. He led Catherine over to them, for she had not yet met them.

"Catherine I want you to meet the two men I will be traveling with. This is Hans Brinkman. He has already saved my live once on this journey. This other gentleman is David Foster. He is from here in town and will be traveling with us from now on."

Both men kissed Catherine on the check and wished the couple well. It was Hans who won Catherine's heart when he said, "Man, I didn't know they still made such pretty girls. I understand now why you fought like a bear back there on the road. I would have too had I had something like this waiting for me. Are you sure you want to go out into the back country and leave this pretty gal here for all the local men to moon over?"

She said, "Mr. Brinkman, you sure know how to flatter a woman. Please watch over this foolish man and bring him back safely to me."

"You can count on it miss."

Then the two men mounted their horses and Brinkman and Foster led out with the pack horse.

Andrew escorted Catherine to the buckboard and helped her up. Then he turned once again to Heyward and thanked him for releasing Catherine from her indenture.

Andrew lingered for a few minutes more, looking into Catherine's face. He could see that she wanted him there beside her, and he hesitated for a second thinking he was foolish to be leaving such a beautiful woman. But then he knew that if he was to fulfill his vision of a new life, he would have to go and find the place for them. He took her hand and kissed the palm. She folded her hand as if to keep his kiss there until his return. Both of them knew it would be months before they would see each other again.

Without another word, Andrew mounted the black horse and rode out after the other two. He rode with mixed emotions. He was sad to be leaving her, but he was exhilarated to be on the way to his future and what destiny may have in store for him.

* * * * *

The first few days of the journey, the three men adjusted into a routine. They arose at daybreak; one fixed a hasty meal of fried fat back and a hoe-cake. Sometimes they would have a little sorghum syrup with their bread.

Another saw to the horses, checking them over, taking them to water for a drink and making sure there were no saddle sores, scratches or bites that might get infected.

The third rolled their bedrolls and fastened the packs, so that after they had eaten, they could be on the road in minutes.

Foster was the best cook, and he usually took on that chore although all of them took turns. Brinkman saw to the horses and Andrew handled the packs. It was a routine they learned well and in a few days they could be on the road within 30 minutes from the time they left their blankets.

They headed almost due west, aiming for the town of Augusta on the Savannah River. They would skirt the foothills of the Great Smoky Mountains. Andrew was anxious to get as far as he could before real cold weather set in. It was now late September, and while it was still warm farther South, as they climbed out of the coastal areas, it became a bit cooler. The days were still warm enough, but the nights were turning colder and Hans knew that it wouldn't be long before snow would start falling more to the north and at the higher elevations.

Although they travelled at a fairly rapid pace, Andrew stopped every so often to look at the country they were passing through. This was rolling hill country and the further inland they went, the fewer farms they saw. Here and there, a big plantation would be found, but they were usually within twenty or so miles of one of the larger towns. As you moved out farther, the farms became smaller and the homes often nothing more than clapboard-sided houses of two or three rooms. There were even a few frameworks with sod roofing. These were the poor farmers, the ones who lived from crop to crop, and often had to supplement their food with hunting and working part time, either in town or helping on the bigger plantations.

Most often, as they approached one of these farms, they would see only women and children. As they came nearer, the children scampered closer to the house so that they could run inside if they were attacked. Something else Andrew noticed, all the men and most of the women carried a rifle or had one always near at hand.

Hans explained to Andrew, "These folk have fought the Indians for this land and although most of the local tribes are at peace, they never know when a lone Indian or small war party of young bucks will attack and butcher a whole family. Then too, the Huron's from up in Pennsylvania, New York and Ohio often raid during the fall before the snows come. They don't often come this far south but they are blood thirsty savages and kill everyone in a family when they are moving south. Sometimes when they head back north they will keep any young girls or women, take them back to their tribe and make slaves of them. The rest they rape and butcher. So they don't take any chances. They know their lives depend upon them always being cautious. Their children are raised from birth with the knowledge that if they aren't always on the alert they will die."

Dave Foster was a quiet man and sparse with words, but now he joined in. "It isn't only the Indians that the settlers have to worry about. They are just as cautious with strangers passing by. Since law enforcement is not close at hand, protection against a criminal element is often what a man can do for himself. A large number of thieves and robbers have sprung up in the border areas. Some have formed gangs and operate over a wide area. They are about as vicious as the Indians. They won't hesitate to rob and kill for a few dollars. Now-a-days the farmers watch for them more than for the Indians."

Andrew absorbed all of this and asked, "Why do these people stay out here where it is so dangerous. Why does a man expose his wife and children to such danger?"

It was Hans who answered. "It is the spirit of individualism that, once freed, will not again be subjected to rulers and kings. Many of these people fought against British rule and were part of the revolt against unjust taxation and unfair representation. They feel they have earned the right to live their lives as they choose and as long as they do not harm their fellow man, they want to be left alone. They want a place to raise their families as free men and they don't cotton to laws very much. They know that owning land is something few people in the world are permitted, especially from where they have come. This is their chance to have something of their own and they will defend it with the last drop of their blood.

"Then too, they help one another. If one is attacked, the

rest will take up their arms and in a few minutes they are a formidable force to reckon with. While a farmer battens down to defend his farm and family, he may send one of his older children racing through the woods to warn other families. The attacks come sudden and often without warning, but there are a few Indians in the area that will warn the white families if they see sign of strange Indians. They are in the woods all the time and once they pick up a strange trail they will alert their own tribe for they don't know whether their people may be the object of attack, or the white people. There have even been some cases where the Indians have helped white families fend off an attack from the northern Indians. They are not liked very well by either the white people or the Indians of this area."

Andrew nodded in understanding. "I notice that these folks don't have any slaves and they are working their own ground."

"These people are poor and can't afford slaves, but even if they could they probably wouldn't have one. Some, having come from lives in European countries, where their lives were very close to slavery, they don't believe in it. They want to be free and they are not about to put chains on anyone else. Most are content to work their own land and believe that if left alone and not taxed to death, they can make a good life for themselves and their families. They all have dreams of getting more land and having bigger and better farms, but they see it as something they are building with their own hands and the sweat of their brow. These are good solid people and if you come in peace they will welcome you and share what they have with you. But if you come to make trouble, you better be quick about it and be gone, for justice is swift. If you do a crime, you may pay dearly for it. They don't have jails and prisons nor believe in paying over their hard earned money to house the criminals.

Give him a swift trial and if he is guilty, hang him and let's get back to work."

Andrew thought about this as they continued to ride. These people were facing dangers as great as or greater than any he had known and yet they seemed a happy people for the most part. Like Hans had said, they were friendly but cautious and you could see the determination in their faces. They would not be the first to do you wrong, and you better not do wrong to them.

Along their journey, he saw a number of homes burned to the ground and just a few logs remaining of what had been a homestead. Fields had been burned or were growing up in weeds. In many yards you would see crosses marking graves of the owners who had fell defending their property. The general idea seemed to be that if one died defending his property he should be buried there where he fell. It was his land and he should remain there even in death.

In some cases homes had been burned and now, children, barely old enough to be on their own, returned to re-build and take over the farm, sort of carrying on the dream their parents had begun.

Andrew imagined how, sometimes, other families would move in and rebuild and take up where the others had left off. He could see how this spirit, this thirst for freedom was sweeping the land. It would continue until it either pushed the Indians off their land or they adopted the ways of the white man. But the wave of white people coming from Europe could not be stopped and more and more would come. That was something he would keep in mind. Much of the lands they were passing through were already claimed by someone. It would be thus no matter where he went. He would need to get a parcel as big as he wanted to start with and hold onto it as the new families came in.

These people, many like himself, had caught this

American dream, the dream of being a free man and owning his own land. They were a hardy bunch. Many had died and many more probably would die before this land was tamed, but tamed it would be. It was a chance for a new life, something that existed no place else that he knew of. They would have this dream, this new life, or die in the trying.

On the fifth day, they came to the Savannah River and could see buildings on the opposite bank. That would be Augusta. They forded the river and led their horses to a livery stable. They instructed the liveryman to grain the horses and guard their pack. Then they walked to a restaurant for something to eat and a night's' sleep in a bed. The further west they went the less chance they would have of these luxuries.

They had a hardy meal of steak, fresh potatoes, beans, squash (something Andrew was not used to), tomatoes and hot corn-bread. They topped this off with a big slab of fresh apple pie and several mugs of steaming coffee. Coffee was something else new to Andrew. Tea and wine were more common in Europe, but here, these Americans drank coffee by the buckets full, steaming hot and black as smut. At first he didn't care much for it, but he found it stimulated him and kept him alert. Finally, it began to grow on him, sort of like the spirit of the country.

After they ate, Hans suggested they retire to the bar and see what they could learn about the roads west. Dave Foster seconded that, said he hadn't had a drink in a week and was as dry as a gourd.

It was just getting dark when they walked toward the bar. About half-way across the street, they were almost run down by four men racing into town on horses. They slid to a stop in front of the bar and flipped the reins of their horses over the hitching rail and pounded across the wooden sidewalk and went through the swinging doors.

Dave had been in the lead and the men had almost run him down and never even looked around. He was red in the face and he spoke through tight lips. "Damn fools. Somebody needs to teach them some manners."

They followed the four men into the bar and saw them standing up at the bar. They were loud and profane and where sloshing their drinks down one after the other.

Andrew led his men to a vacant table in the back of the room. Hans asked for a bottle of bourbon and three glasses. Then he took the bottle and joined the other two at the table.

Hans poured a round and held his glass up, "Here's to pretty women and better days."

They clinked their glasses and downed the liquor. Andrew tasted this fiery drink these people poured down their throats. They seemed to drink it with such gusto. It was strong and he guessed it would have a kick to it, so he just sipped on his drink. Brinkman and Foster both had sloshed the half full glass down in one swallow and were now pouring a second.

There were not too many men in the bar as it was a bit early for most of the working people. Andrew surmised it would be another hour or so before the bulk of the crowd would come in.

After the second drink Brinkman said, "Let's see if we can get any information about the trail ahead." He looked around the room. Most of the patrons seemed to be local folks except for the four men at the bar and one young man of about Andrew's age sitting at another table by himself. Hans stood up and walked to his table.

He said, "Friend, we are traveling west toward the place they call Atlanta. Would you know anything about how things lie along that route?"

The man had been a little tense and he seemed to be

watching the four men at the bar. Now he shifted his gaze from them to Brinkman and after looking him over briefly, he said, "Yes I have just come from there and everything seemed pretty quiet along the trail. You shouldn't have any trouble."

Brinkman thanked him and offered to buy him a drink. The man said, "Thanks, perhaps another time." Brinkman noticed that he shifted his gaze back to the four men and he suspected there was no love lost between them. He returned to the table where Andrew and Dave were sitting and told him what he had learned. He also told them that, unless he was wrong, there was going to be some trouble between the four men and the fellow at the table.

They drank in silence and watched the four men. They seemed to be riling themselves up for some reason. After a couple more drinks, the biggest one of the bunch, who appeared to be the leader, wiped his mouth, poured himself another drink and walked over to the table where the young man was sitting.

He said, "Harris, I thought you got our message before. Maybe you need another lesson. You are not welcome in this town. Are we going to have to horse-whip you before you understand that there is nothing in this town for you?"

The young man shifted slightly and Brinkman could see the pistol lying on his lap but the big man standing in front of him could not. Brinkman and Foster both eased up out of their chairs and moved as quietly as cats to the back wall, with their backs to the wall and their rifles in their hands. Andrew thought it might be best if he followed their lead.

Now the young man, the one called Harris, spoke. "Knudsen, you and your bullies whipped me one time. But you will not catch me by surprise again and you will not lay your hands on me. If you do I will kill you. Now go back to your crooked bunch and leave me alone."

Knudsen's face turned red and it looked as if he would explode. It was clear that he wasn't used to being talked to this way, especially in front of his friends. He was about to say something, when one of his men said, "Joe, look-out! He's got a gun under the table."

Knudsen then looked closer and saw Harris's hand under the table and noticed for the first time how he was slumped a little to his right side. He was so sure that no one would oppose him that he had gotten careless and now he was faced with a man who already had his gun drawn and aimed directly at him. He got control of himself pretty quick and you could almost see his mind thinking. He could throw the drink in Harris's face and dive to one side, but that was taking too big a chance. It could get him shot. On the other hand he couldn't crawl away like a yellow-belly. That would make him the laughing stock with his friends. He had to do something.

He stood undecided for several seconds while his mind raced to come up with an idea. He couldn't think of anything except to bluff his way out.

He leaned on the table and said, "Harris, you will never leave this town alive. And don't think for a minute that you are taking anyone with you. We'll be watching her house and if you come near it we will bury you there."

"Knudsen you don't own her and you don't own me. If you've got the guts to meet me one on one, we will settle this. You pick the weapon, either guns or knives. Or are you too yellow to fight me man to man?"

There it was. Knudsen knew now that he couldn't back down and stay in this town. He stood straight up, and said, "Put that pistol down and come out back with me and we will see who the better man is."

Harris said, "And have your men shoot me in the back?

No. I will pick the time and place when you don't have your bully boys to back you up."

You could almost see the relief in Knudsen. He might squirm out of this yet. But he just couldn't let well enough alone. He had to get the last word in and he did not know how costly those words would be.

He drank the drink he had in his hand and smiled back at his men. "See even with his gun on me he won't fight. He's chicken shit to the core."

Brinkman stepped forward and said, "Mister, if you want to sink your spurs into this rooster, go right ahead. We will see that you aren't disturbed. These boys are having too good a time. They wouldn't think of leaving the bar. We want to have a drink with them and we would consider it terribly unsociable if they refused."

The three men at the bar had been watching their leader so intently that they were not aware that the two men in buckskin had moved up behind them and had their guns pointed right at their guts.

Knudsen spun to see who had spoken. He was mad and he was scared. This was a bad combination. He lashed out at Brinkman, "Fella you are taking a hand into something that doesn't concern you. You don't know what you are getting into."

Hans answered, sort of matter-of-factly, "Well now, you may be right, but it sort of goes against the grain when one man is being pushed around by a big bully that has three others to back him up. Besides, you almost ran my friend down when you came roaring into town. I don't think I like you or your kind very much. You need a lesson in manners. Do you want to settle your score with this man, one on one, or do you want to teach me a lesson?"

Harris came forward, "Knudsen. This is as good a time as any. If these men will keep your thugs off me, we will settle this right now. Take off your gun and lay it on the bar and I will do the same with mine. We will settle this with knives."

Knudsen now faced his moment of truth. He wasn't near as brave without his men behind him and he didn't know whether Harris was good with a knife or nor. He thought he might not be a match for him, even though he outweighed him by fifty pounds. His bluster was gone and he began to sweat. He had thought he and his men would give Harris another beating and run him out of town for good. Now he was standing here and knew if he faced Harris alone he might get killed. There was only one thing he could do, and he did it.

"Harris we have had our disagreements but there ain't no need for us to go out there and cut each other up. Why don't we just go our own ways and let by-gones be by-gones?"

"Knudsen, I owe you a whipping and by God, you will get it, either now or later. If you are too yellow to fight me in a fair fight, I won't strike the first blow. But I am warning you here and now, stay out of my way. The next time you or any of your men come at me someone is going to get hurt real bad. I have a long memory and I will remember the beating you four laid on me. This is the last time I will tell you. Stay out of my way!" "Now get out of here so white men can drink without holding their noses."

Knudsen had never taken such a tongue lashing and his pride was hurt beyond anything that had ever happened to him before. He bowed his head and bit his lip. As he headed toward the door he motioned his men to follow. They all left the bar together.

Dave Foster spoke first. He let his breath out in a long "wheeew". "I thought that last remark was going to make him come unhinged. That child will be a bad enemy. He has had his feelings hurt in front of his friends. You better watch your back trail."

Harris said, "He's nothing but a coward and won't face a man face to face. He has got to have those pug-uglies to help him out. Forget them and let me buy you a drink now. I appreciate you pulling the stinger out of his men to give me an even break. Four to one makes me a little nervous."

Hans invited Harris over to sit with them and poured a round. Now all were sipping their drinks. The excitement was enough to take the edge off their thirst. After the introductions, Andrew spoke to Harris. "Who is this Knudsen? Is he from around here?"

Harris sensed that they wanted to know what the ruckus was about but were too polite to ask a point blank question. Instead they were going about it in a round-about way. He guessed that since they had befriended him and maybe kept him from getting killed or badly mauled again, they deserved an explanation.

"Knudsen has a pretty large farm out about ten miles. He keeps pretty much to himself. No one knows how he gets his money because they don't seem to grow much on his place. He swings a pretty wide loop and when he is in town he rubs a lot of people wrong. Not many like him or his men. He is pushy and a real bully as long as he has his men behind him." Harris paused and took a drink, and the others remained silent. They felt there was more to come.

He resumed, "I had always avoided him until one day I was coming into town and stopped at the dry-goods store. Just as I was dismounting, a pretty girl, one of the farm girls, came out of the store with several packages in her hands. Knudsen blocked her path and tried to take her packages and help her into the buckboard. She was about twenty and as cute as a button. This went on for several seconds, with her trying to get around him and him blocking her way. There were several men there but all were afraid of him. Finally, the girl was getting frightened and looked to someone for help. I was the nearest so I walked down the sidewalk and bumped into him so hard that I knocked him off the sidewalk. I immediately apologized and helped him back up onto the walk. In the confusion, the girl had acted quickly and climbed into the buckboard and slapped the horses with the reins and rode out. Knudsen was livid with rage, and although he ranted and raved, his men were not along and he didn't do anything.

"He went into the dry-goods store and I got back on my horse and went after the girl. I thought it might be wise to see her home, and besides, she was the purtiest thing I had ever seen and I wanted to know where she lived. When I caught up with her she was really frightened and I explained I meant her no harm and if she did not object I would see her home. When we arrived at the farm her father met us with a shot-gun and looked at me pretty hard. She explained what had happened and I was kind enough to see her home. The old man relaxed, reached up and shook my hand and invited me to stay for supper. I couldn't resist the opportunity to get to know her better. Well, to make a long story short, we began to see one another and I brought her into town one night for a dance. Knudsen and his men cornered me and the four of them gave me a good beating, put me on a horse and told me to get out and not come back. I thought I would die, but I made it to Atlanta and there I stayed until I got well. Now I have come back to see if the girl will marry me and come to live in Atlanta. I had stopped off here to get my courage up to go see her and pop the question, when they walked in. You know the rest."

Brinkman said, "I thought it might be something like that. Those type people get under my skin. Where does this little lady of yours live?"

About two miles north of here. Her father's farm is on some real rich land. If it wasn't that I have a small business in Atlanta, I would stay here and take up farming. But I have to go back tomorrow and if she won't go with me, I'll have to leave her here. I'm going to see her right now." With that he got up and prepared to leave.

Andrew spoke again, "You watch out for yourself and don't let them catch you alone. If you want you can ride along with us. We will be leaving at day-break. Meet us at the livery stable."

Harris shook hands, thanked them again and went out the back door. Brinkman looked at Foster and nodded. This Harris was nobody's fool. He figured that Knudsen may be waiting out front so he slipped out the back. In a few minutes they heard horses' hoofs pounding out of town.

Andrew finished his drink. "I have had enough excitement for one night. If you gentlemen will excuse me, I'm going to turn in. See you at the livery in the morning." With that he went up to bed. Hans and Dave followed shortly.

They were just finishing breakfast and had headed towards the livery stable when Harris and a pretty young blond girl rode up. Their horses were lathered as if they had been rode hard. As Andrew and the rest left the restaurant, Harris met them and explained. "Fellas, I'd like to introduce you to my fiancé, Miss Martha Simpson. She has consented to be my wife and we are to be wed in Atlanta. But we may have a little trouble getting there. Evidently Knudsen knew where I was going last night and he followed me. This morning, as Martha and I were leaving her father's farm, Knudsen and five of his men jumped us. Before we realized it, they had us surrounded and he knocked me off my horse and grabbed the reins to Martha's horse. Just as they were closing in to beat me up again, her pa and two older brothers came out of the brush with scatter guns aimed at Knudsen and his men. You know the damage one of those things can do. Well, he released us and let us go, but he said we'd never make it to Atlanta. Her pa is holding them to give us a head start. If that invitation is still open, we'd like to ride with you."

Andrew said it was, but they better get moving. They would need to put as much distance between them and Augusta as they could. They went directly to the livery stable and in ten minutes were on their way out of town. Dave Foster took the lead and Brinkman brought up the rear. Harris and Andrew stayed close to the girl.

They rode hard all that day, stopping only long enough to water and rest the horses. It would be almost five days to get to Atlanta and Knudsen could hit them anywhere along the way. Andrew figured it would be close to his home territory though. His anger wouldn't let him wait and there was no use riding two or three days away when the roads along here were deserted enough for them to do whatever they planned to do. This kind of complicated things for Andrew. He had not wanted this extra responsibility, but he couldn't turn his back on these two people who wanted to get away from this bully and get married.

Nothing happened the first day, and as was their pattern, they left the main road before dark and sought out a stand of oak near a small creek for their night camp. The night passed without trouble and they were up and moving shortly after day-light the next morning. This time, Brinkman was in the lead and Dave was behind. Andrew noted that Hans held his rifle at the ready and walked his horse along the edge of the road. Every once in a while he would cut off into the timber and ride a few yards. Then come back to the road again.

It was during one of these side trips into the woods that he let out a light whistle and motioned the others into the woods also. They looked around and Dave had disappeared. When they caught up with Hans he said, "I don't like the feel of things. Just a little bit ago I noticed where several horses had turned around and around in the road and just now, a bunch of crows flew out of that big clump of trees up ahead. I figure something scared them."

Andrew looked for Dave again. Hans, seeing his concern said, "Don't worry about him. We talked it over and if anything looked suspicious, he was to fade into the woods on one side of the road and us on the other. He is out there some place now looking things over. You stay here and hold the horses. I'm going to go ahead on foot and see what I can see." With that he was away.

Just as Andrew began to get nervous and was almost ready to do something on his own, Hans came back. One minute he was gone, the next he was there as if he had materialized from nowhere. He made no sound and didn't seem to disturb a leaf. Andrew was impressed, the rest were surprised.

"There are five of them waiting in the woods ahead. I figure they plan to way-lay us and shoot us out of the saddles before we know they are there. We can either go around them or go through them. I'm for going through them. I don't want them dogging us all the way to Atlanta. What do you say?"

Andrew thought a minute then said, "This is a violent country. In less than a week we have been way-laid twice and have had to kill two men. I do not like having to fight all the time and I do not like going into battle with a lady present. I will leave it to you Harris; it is your bride and your fight."

Before he could speak, Martha spoke up. "Mr., Stanley, do not be concerned for my safety. I can handle a gun as well as most men and we have fought off such as these since I was a little girl. They are evil people, just as bad as the savages who have killed and butchered many of my friends and relatives. They are little more than scavengers. I personally do not want to have to live my life in fear that these men will keep coming after us. Do what you must. God will decide my fate."

"Do you feel the same Harris?"

"Yes. I don't want them on our trail all the way to Atlanta. If they can't find the opportunity to take us on the trail, they will haunt us down in Atlanta. Let's do what we have to here and now."

Andrew turned to Hans and said, "How do you want to do it?"

Hans looks at Harris and asks, "Have you done any injuning?"

Harris answers, "I can slip through the woods without waking up the whole town."

"Good. Harris and I will ease off into the woods and come up on them from the rear. You and the young miss give us about fifteen minutes to get around behind them. I figure Dave is already in position on the other side. Then, I want you two to bring the horses and walk them until you get to that big oak with the branches that hang over the road. When you get even with that, hit your horses into a hard run. They are just around the bend. If they think you are going to get past them they will come out of hiding and when they rise up, we'll be ready. Don't stop until you are a quarter mile past that spot. Then pull off the road and wait for us. We'll be along shortly." He motioned to Harris and disappeared into the forest again.

Andrew looked at Martha. Her face was white and she had fear in her eyes, but there was no panic. She would keep her wits about her and do what she needed to do when it was time.

He tied all the saddle horse's reins together and gave them to her. The pack horse was slower, so he took it and fastened the reins to his saddle horn. Then he checked his rifle and pistols. He asked the girl if she knew how to use a pistol. When she said she could, he handed one to her and told her to keep it under her skirt. Then they lead the horses out and mounted.

They walked them to the big oak Hans had mentioned and looked at each other. Andrew took a deep breath and hit her horse across the rump. Then he did the same to the other two horses and dug his heels into the black he was on. In a split second all the horses were in a dead run and they rounded a sharp turn in the road. Just as they passed a dead tree on the side of the road two men raised up with rifles in their hands. They never got them leveled. There were two shots from back in the woods and both men slumped across the dead tree they had been hiding behind.

There was another shot from the other side and several shouts. Andrew heard one say, "Look out. They are behind us. They just got Shorty. He's dead."

Andrew grew angry and was tempted to turn and give battle. He hated cowards who would not face you but would try to shoot you in the back. He almost slowed the black, and then he remembered Martha. He could see her racing on ahead of him and he knew he must see to her safety. That was his part of the plan. So he raced ahead and caught up with her just as she pulled the horses to a stop. He stepped down, tied the black and reached up to help her down. She came off the horse and collapsed in his arms. Her legs wouldn't hold her up. He could feel her soft body through her thin clothing and she was shaking. Then he eased her down to the ground and sat beside her. Now that it was all over, she began to cry. He put his arm around her and patted her shoulder. She only cried for a moment then she raised her head, wiped the tears from her eyes and looked at Andrew.

"Please don't tell Clifford (this was the first time he had heard Harris's first name) that I was such a cry-baby. He might think I couldn't stand up under pressure and he might not want me for his wife then. But I was so scared."

Andrew patted her on the shoulder again and said, "I was scared too. Anyone who said he wasn't would be lying. And don't worry about him not wanting you for his wife. He would go through fire for you. I can see the love he has for you in his eyes. Don't be afraid to let him know you are human. He will want to take care of you all the more and he will love you for being honest with him."

They waited almost an hour before the others joined them. Andrew was starting to worry when Dave rode up. He had blood on one sleeve of his jacket. Andrew went to him and asked how bad it was. Dave just said, "It's only a scratch. One of those bustards got off a shot at me. After I shot, I got up to reload and he took a shot at me. Hit my arm but just went thru the skin."

Andrew peeled back the shirt sleeve and saw that the ball had taken a slice of skin and some flesh, but it would heal. It would be sore a few weeks, but he would live. He took out some bandages and poured antiseptic into the wound, which brought a cuss word out of Foster. Then he bandaged the arm and turned when he heard a noise. It was Harris coming out of the woods. He looked haggard but his eyes were bright as stars on a clear night.

He went immediately to Martha and asked how she was. She smiled and said she was fine, but she felt lots more comfortable when he put his arm around her.

He turned to Andrew and said, "Brinkman should be along in a bit. He took after Knudsen on foot. He and one man got away. We got all the rest. Brinkman wanted to make sure Knudsen didn't come back. He is too much of a coward to come back now that his men are gone. He will go back and get another bunch of cut-throats before he attacks again. But I do think he would return. He has been beaten and his ego hurt too bad to let it go now. He will never be satisfied until he kills me, or I kill him."

Hans returned shortly and they mounted and rode away, leaving the bodies were they lay. It would be clear to anyone finding them exactly what happened. There wouldn't be much sympathy for them.

The rest of the journey to Atlanta was without event, and they pulled in there five days later. Harris and Martha bade them farewell and invited them to come see them anytime they were in Atlanta. Andrew and his men were tired. They ate and went to bed. They would strike out again tomorrow and after leaving Atlanta, they would soon be into the wilderness. There was only one other town of much size, that was a mining town called Birmingham. Iron ore had been found there and they were starting to mine it as they did up in Pennsylvania. They would need a few more supplies before they left the next day.

Andrew had been so busy and so preoccupied with events he had hardly had time to think about Catherine. But now as he lay in bed, he wondered what she would be doing and how nice it would be to have her there beside him. With that thought he went to sleep, but it was a dark-haired girl with olive skin and Spanish eyes who haunted his dreams.

CHAPTER FOURTEEN

When Andrew arose the next morning, he went downstairs to the restaurant and wasn't surprised to find Hans and Dave both there. They had already eaten and were lingering over coffee, although dawn was just breaking.

Hans looked at Dave over his coffee mug and said, "Lordy, these city folk do sleep late don't they? I guess it's just their nature to lolly-gag in bed most all day."

Andrew knew this was just good-natured bantering so he shot back with, "Well, that's one of the advantages us young people have over the older folks. When you get old you can't sleep much because you have to get up every hour to go take a leak."

Andrew ate a good breakfast and they went to one of the local mercantile stores to replenish their supplies. Then they went directly to the livery stables. The sun was just starting to peek over the horizon as they mounted and rode out. They took the road due west towards Birmingham.

As soon as they were away from the major settlements, Hans pressed onward and they made good time. Travel was hazardous and travelers had to move carefully. In addition to the natural dangers of wild animals, river crossings and such, there were the human dangers caused by marauding whites and Indians. More than once they had to slow their pace and move off the road to check out danger signs. The burned homes and the scattered bones along the side of the road gave ample evidence that this was a harsh country and those who got careless did not live long.

The journey to Birmingham passed without incident and the three decided to stay over an extra day and give the horses a rest. They had now been on the move almost eight weeks and the horses needed rest. So did the men. Andrew longed for a good hot water bath. They had been bathing in cold streams and as they got into the higher altitudes and later in the year, the waters were getting cold. A quick dip was about all one could stand and that left your lips blue and a body full of goose bumps. A tub of hot water would feel good on saddle weary bones.

After the stopover, they were on the move again, headed northwest into territory that was claimed by North Carolina. During their stopover in Birmingham they had heard a number of stories about Indians being restless and the Iroquois tribes from up in western Pennsylvania and Ohio raiding down through Kentucky and Tennessee. No one had heard of any strikes down this far, but everyone was pretty jumpy.

Indian raids were usually made during the fall of the year and in the spring. The fall raids usually were to raid and pillage to get whatever they could to take back to their camp for the winter. Anything of value that they could trade or might have value would be taken, but only if it could be moved in a hurry. The raiders knew that they must strike and move fast to get back to their own territory for war parties from the raided villages or towns would soon be after them for revenge.

Often the braves would capture young women and take them back to their camps. Either they would be treated as slaves, or one of the braves would take them as one of his wives. Those who were not looked on with favor by the men were often treated with unbelievable cruelty. During the winter months they would be left out in the cold, thrown scraps of food that they had to fight the dogs for and often beaten by the Indian women who resented them. They were treated barbarously in an effort to break them. Quiet often the captured women would be turned over to an old woman to help her maintain her lodge. The captive would be kept tied hand and foot at night, and beaten with sharp sticks during the day. All foreign women were badly treated, but white women were treated the worst. Unless one was picked to be the wife of a brave, she led a life of ceaseless toil and drudgery.

Andrew and his companions now travelled through territory generally claimed by the Creek and Muskogean Indian tribes. As they got a little farther west they would be going into the Chickasaw lands to the north and if they cut south they would be in the Choctaw lands. These last two were near the Mississippi River basin. They were all part of the Cherokee Nation as were several smaller bands, and most were basically friendly.

The Shawnee were further north; less friendly and often raided the white settlements. They had helped the French during the French and Indian wars and during the Revolutionary War General Washington had sent an expedition against them and killed many of them. He had burned their villages and fields and the survivors suffered a winter of cold and hunger. Of all the Cherokee Nation tribes, the Chickasaws were the most war-like and often raided not only the white farms but were known to pounce on other Indians from the Cherokee Federation if they came on them by surprise. It would be several days before they reached the Chickasaw lands, and both Hans and Dave indicated they should stay south of those if they could.

The spring raids were somewhat different. Most of the time these raids were to give the young bucks a chance to prove their manhood. Few prisoners were taken during these raids. Men, older women and children were often slaughtered and their bodies either thrown into burning buildings are used for target practice. The younger women were raped repeatedly and then mutilated. These were hit and run raiding parties and excess baggage or prisoners could not be allowed to slow down the parties.

Travel went much slower now because they were getting farther away from the more populated towns and there were frequent sightings of small groups of Indians. Andrew had learned quickly, that those you could see were not the ones you had to worry about. It was those that did not want you to see them that you had to be concerned with. They were masters at concealment and from what Hans and Dave both said, they could travel through the grass without bending a blade. Unless you were very careful, they would be on you before you even knew they were anywhere around.

Andrew and his party had been on the road again for almost two weeks when they had their first brush with any of the Indians.

It happened by accident for neither party was prepared for the encounter. Hans had been scouting ahead and was some quarter of a mile in the lead. There had been lots of sign from unshod ponies all morning and he had decided to ride on ahead and scout the area before Andrew and Dave arrived. He had been following a wash and had not seen the two braves on the high ground looking down on him. His horse was picking its' way around boulders strewn across the bed of the wash and he was reading sign on the ground. His first inclination that he might be in trouble was when his horse raised its head and snorted.

Hans pulled it to an immediate stop and looked up. Blocking his path were three braves. They had known he was coming and had waited at a narrow part of the wash for him. He had walked right up on them. They were not more than 200 feet from him. He immediately looked around and what he saw made the sweat run down his back. The sides of the wash here were steep and no horse could climb out of either side. Then he raised his eyes and saw the other two braves on the bank above him and he knew he was boxed in.

They had not made any overt move towards him and he guessed that they had not been out looking for trouble, but be that as it may, five Indians and only one white man made him uneasy. Under these circumstances the Indians might figure they had an easy victim and, friendly or not, they might feel inclined to add his hair to their coup stick. Hans mind was racing and he knew that if this wasn't handled right, it could become messy, and he might be the mess.

There was another consideration too. Dave and Andrew would be following his tracks and they also might wander into the trap he found himself in. He could attempt to turn and race back up the wash, but the two on the bank could shoot down at him at almost any point.

He could slide off his horse and use it as a shield, but that would most surely mean a dead horse if they meant to do him harm.

At this point they were watching him like a pack of cats watching a mouse they are about to pounce on. They had given no indication that they were unfriendly or that they meant to hang his hide out to dry. Hans quickly decided on a plan. He would bluff this out and warn Dave and Andrew.

He raised his hand in a gesture of friendship and slid off his horse on the side facing the three in the wash. He raised his gun towards the sky and pulled the trigger. If it came to a battle, he would have only one shot anyway and the other four would cut him down. By firing his gun, that would be a warning to Dave and Andrew, and at the same time it would show that he had no intent to do them harm.

It was a sign that the Indians understood, but they still were cautious. The white man had two pistols in his belt and a large knife in a sheath, and he looked as if he could use it. Even though he was alone and they outnumbered him five to one, he could still kill two of them perhaps before they could bring him down.

Hans continued to hold his hand up in the sign of friendship and walked towards the three in front of him, all but ignoring the two on the bank. However, he was acutely aware that they walked their ponies along the bank as he moved towards their three companions in the wash. It made the hair on the back of his neck stand up.

He was within about 100 feet of the three in the wash and continued to walk towards them. The closer he got the better chance he would have to use the pistols if it came to a fight. He was watching them very closely and at the same time trying to figure out which tribe they were from. As he got closer he recognized their manner of dress as being Creeks. He had seen a number of the Creek Indians in his earlier travels and knew some of their language. He spoke to them now using the few Creek phrases he knew, but he must have pronounced them wrong or something because it seemed to infuriate the younger of the three. He seemed to be about 20 and was naked to the waist. The others wore buckskins and Hans judged they were a hunting party and he had just blundered into them. They weren't necessarily looking for a fight, but the young buck was ready and was very agitated. Hans thought he had bought the farm and he stopped, lowered his hand and put it on one of his pistols. He heard one of the two above him cock his rifle and he was expecting a bullet in the back any minute.

Hans raised his hand again in the sign of friendship and looked toward the older of the three men, but at the same time, he kept one eye on the younger man. He wanted to count coup and he moved his horse forward as if to make a run at the man on the ground. The older man barked a few sharp words and the younger man turned his horse around and moved back beside the older Indian. Hans couldn't quite decide whether they meant to harm him or not. Indians were very inscrutable. They were masters at hiding their feelings. A strange thought crossed his mind; they would make good poker players.

The older man spoke now and although Hans had trouble following his remarks, it seemed he was asking what a white man was doing traveling the woods alone. Hans decided to try to bluff it out. Using sign language and a few Indian phrases he knew, he explained that he was admiring the beautiful country and had strayed off the main roads. That he was on his way to the Big Muddy and intended to go west into the big mountains before snow fell. He might spend the winter trapping and trading with the Indians west of Big Muddy.

As the white man became more numerous, the Indians were being forced off their lands and they had fought the encroachment of these white skinned ones with the pale eyes. But the more they killed, the more seemed to come. Many of the elders were talking about changing their ways and adopting the ways of these white skinned ones. The younger people didn't want to give up their old ways and certainly didn't want to give up their land to these strange people. Many, like the young buck, were itching for a fight. They felt invincible and bragged they would run the white eyes back into the sea. The older ones were more cautious. They had seen some of the destruction that these white men could deliver with their sticks that spouted fire. Although their braves had been acquiring guns for more than 50 years now, they still had not learned how to use them with the accuracy of the white man. Those who stuck with the old ways and used spears and bows and arrows, these were no match for the white man's fire power. Some of the chiefs were beginning to see that if they did not change and adopt the ways of the whites their people and their culture would be destroyed forever. While they preached peace the younger men wanted to wage war.

Hans was glad that the older man seemed to be one who believed in coexistence. He appeared willing to let Hans pass and go on his way. The young Indian shouted something and waved his lance in the air. One of the younger ones on top of the bluff answered with a shout and Hans began to sweat. They wanted his blood and he was afraid that his time was up. Just as he reached for one of his pistols, their attention was distracted by three horses coming running down the wash. As they reached Hans horse, recognizing another animal they knew, they came to a stop.

This distraction startled the Indians and they immediately turned their attention to the horses. It was obvious that two were saddle horses, which meant that there were at least two other men with this one. He wasn't alone after all and they didn't know where his two companions were. The Indians on the bluff began to mill their horses around, looking in all directions for the other two men. They were uneasy that they might be in the sights of two of the long rifles at that very moment. It also had a quieting effect on the three in the wash. The older man appeared very apprehensive and while they still outnumbered the one they faced, he knew the precision with which these men could shoot and how fast they could reload. At the very least, three and perhaps all of them might die. Very quickly he decided that this did not look like a good day to die.

Perhaps he was also thinking that some white men would kill any Indian who happened to cross their paths. Now he began to figure how best he might get his men out of this confrontation without a fight.

He shifted his gun to his left hand and raised his right hand in the peace sign. He spoke to the younger Indian, turned his pony and made the sign to go in peace. He spoke out loud to the two men on top of the bluff and then rode away. The younger man looked at Hans. He had bitter hatred in his eyes and Hans knew that if it had been left to him, there would have been a bloody fight that day. Then he turned his horse and rode away, but he had the look in his eyes that said someday he would kill as many white men as he could. Hans hoped he would not be one of them.

The sound of galloping horses disappeared in the distance. Hans looked up and saw that the Indians above had also gone. The horses coming on the scene so abruptly had disconcerted them. They did not like to attack when they were not sure of what lay in wait for them. It wasn't that they were not brave; it was just a matter of being cautious. The one leading them was a smart man. They might have handled the situation differently if all their enemies were facing them or they knew where they were, but the idea of not knowing just where the enemy was decided the issue. Their surprise of the lone white man had turned into a surprise against them and they would pick another day to count coup.

A few minutes later Andrew came walking around a bend in the wash and Dave slid down the bank from the top. Hans breathed a sigh of relief and quickly loaded his rifle. He didn't expect the Indians to come back, but if they did he would be ready.

Dave walked towards him and said, "That's what happens when you get old. You get careless."

Hans shot back, "Oh, shut up. It took you long enough to get here. What's the matter? Your arthritis acting up on you?"

Andrew knew this was just idle banter to relieve the tension they had all been under. He had seen it in troops before and after battle. Now he took charge.

"If you two will stop passing compliments around, I think we better get out of here and put some miles behind us."

Hans said, "I'll say Amen to that."

They mounted up and rode single file down the draw, the same way the Indians went, but as soon as they came to a side where they could climb out of the wash, they climbed out to high ground. The Indians had gone on down the wash. Andrew and his party headed west again.

Riding on, Andrew was thankful that no fighting had come out of the encounter. This land was big enough for all if they would learn to live with one another and respect each other's rights and customs. But the few short weeks he had been in America lead him to believe that there were many who coveted the Indian lands and many thought there was great wealth in the land and was being hidden by the Indians. They would kill whole tribes to get this wealth if they had to. He was afraid future encounters might not be resolved so peacefully, and he was right.

There were many Indians who resented the encroachment of the white man and would fight to hold onto their lands. There were many tribal disputes and many of the Indian tribes fought among themselves. If they could have pulled their forces together, they would have stood a good chance of holding onto much of their lands, but with the inter-tribal jealousies and old wounds, it was not likely that they could mount a combined force against the white invasion.

Andrew and his party moved westward and slightly to

the south. They crossed many rivers and streams and were getting nearer to the Big Muddy, the Mississippi River. It was now mid-December and the weather had been fairly dry, with only an occasional thunderstorm. They had made good time even though they had taken a few detours to the side to look at the terrain and richness of the soils. Nothing so far had really matched what Andrew was looking for.

By now the men had formed a rough style of camaraderie and though they would be the last to admit it, a deep level of affection and respect had grown with this journey. Dave and Hans were both skilled woodsmen and each respected the others abilities. Along the way they had instructed Andrew on how to move through the forests quietly, how to look for and read signs, how to listen to the sounds in the woods, the noise of birds when disturbed and how to take game without firing a rifle. When traveling in Indian country it was important not to attract attention to yourself. You passed through their lands as quietly and as quickly as you could.

The Indian bow and arrow was an effective weapon, and quiet. Game was plentiful and Dave was as good with a bow as any Indian. As they moved farther from the settlements, it became his task to keep them supplied with fresh meat. Now they hoarded the little bit of bacon they had left, having it for breakfast only once or twice a week. Deer, wild boar, squirrels, turkey, wild hens and a wide variety of game were plentiful. Andrew was amazed at the many types of animals and fowl that flourished in this wild land. In his native Poland, only a few species lived. The poor people had killed off many of the wild things for food. Only in the big forests owned by the lords and king were game so abundant as here. But here, everywhere they went it was the same. It was a hunter's paradise. He could well see how these men, and many like them, loved the raw untamed land. It was taking a hold on him too. The more he traveled over the land, the deeper his feelings became. He knew he would find the home he was looking for and he would be a part of this great land. He would be happy here, and although he would always hold a special place in his heart for Poland, from now on, this would be his homeland.

It was two days before Christmas when they arrived at the big river they called Big Muddy, the Mississippi River. They had known they must be getting close. A few days earlier they had run into a couple of Frenchmen who were hunting. Dave had spied them from a distance coming towards them and had waited in the woods for them. When they were a couple hundred feet from them Hans stepped into the open and "hallowed" them. The Frenchmen were instantly alert and stopped to observe the three men. The English and French had not always gotten along and there was bad blood between some of them. Dave was busy building a fire and had a coffee pot setting next to the fire and the other two were standing with their arms folded across the top of their grounded rifles.

The Frenchmen decided they were friendly and came forward. After brief introductions, they shared a cup of coffee and Andrew talked with the Frenchmen. His journeys in Poland had enabled him to pick up some French, never realizing that he might have use of it in this new country. The Frenchmen were pleased that he could speak their language and spoke freely with him. They informed him that they were from a small community called Kilmichael and the big river was about a day and a half farther west. They said that as far as they knew the Indians were quiet and there had not been any recent incidents in that area. That if they struck a little more to the north they would come to Roseville and they could cross the river there or follow a road on the east side north into Memphis. Both parties were eager to get on their way, so they extinguished the fire and bade each other farewell and God speed.

They arrived in Roseville and decided to stay over for a few days. There were no hotels so they dropped their gear in one of the livery stalls and that would be their sleeping accommodations while they were in town. Their horses were gaunt; they needed a rest and some grain. The men rubbed the animals down and poured a peck of oats and corn into their feed bags.

Then they went out into the short street. There were perhaps a total of ten buildings in this little town. Two of the biggest were the commissary building were you could buy almost anything you needed. The other was a combination bar, restaurant and bath-house. Dave and Hans wanted to head to the bar first while Andrew wanted to go to the bathhouse. They finally convinced him and the three of them walked into the bar. It was only three in the afternoon and they were the only ones in the bar. A big man with a florid face came out of the restaurant and walked behind the bar. Hans and Dave ordered straight whiskey; Andrew asked if he had Vodka. He had not yet acquired a taste for this American whiskey. It burned the throat like fire and had the kick of a mule. When the bartender said he only had two kinds of whiskey; that brought in from Tennessee and the local brew called "white lightening." Hans told Andrew he ought to try some of the local white lightening. It would put hair on his chest. One swallow and he thought his insides were on fire. He coughed and took a glass of water for a chaser. Both Dave and Hans were laughing at him. Dave said, "These foreign boys just can't handle our dainty American brews, can they?"

Andrew asked the bartender about a bath. He turned towards the kitchen and yelled, "Helen. Put some water on to heat. We got a man wants a bath."

Andrew walked back to the livery stable and took out clean clothes and went back to the bar. The barman directed him into a room behind the bar where he could undress and his bath water would be ready in a few minutes. Andrew had taken off his boots and shirt and was standing in his underwear and pants when a pretty young girl came into the room carrying two kettles of steaming water. She poured them into a big wooden tub and told Andrew to ladle out as much cold water as he needed from a big tub that sat nearby. There was a bar of brown soap and clean towels. As she left the room he undressed and put his foot into the hot water. He immediately withdrew it and poured several big dippers full of the cold water into the wooden tub. When he had it down to where he thought he could stand it he stepped into the tub and lowered himself down into the tub. He took the soap and lathered himself real good and then sort of slid down into the tub until just his head was above water and he leaned back and rested his head on the edge of the tub. He must have fallen asleep, and he awoke with a start. The young girl was standing beside the tub with another kettle of hot water. He was a little embarrassed that she had caught him naked in the tub, but she didn't seem to pay any attention.

She said, "Monsieur, I have brought more hot water for you to rinse off with. I will set it on this stool here where you can reach it. Will there be anything else?" Andrew first said no, and then he quickly added, "Yes, there might be. We have been on the trail for several weeks and our clothes are filthy. Is there someone here who could wash them for us?"

"Yes. I could do it but it would have to be tomorrow. I work in the restaurant in the afternoons and nights, but my mornings are free. If you will bring them to my house early tomorrow I will wash them for you. Come into the restaurant when you are finished and I will tell you how to get to my house."

Andrew was impressed with her calm and easy manner under these unusual circumstances. She must be in her late twenties and yet she had the maturity of a much older, more experienced woman. She had long dark hair and her eyes were a deep brown. She was slim but had very ample hips. She wore a plain linen dress that clung to her body and from the close way it fitted, he judged she had only the bindings around her breasts and pantaloons on underneath for no slip or other sign of garment showed. Though she was clean and unruffled, she had perspiration on her forehead and he guessed she was the cook for the restaurant. He asked her as much. When she answered that she was, he asked what they would be having for supper.

"Fresh vegetables from the garden, turnips, fried potatoes, chicken and dumplings, fried pork chops and corn bread. Dessert will be cherry cobbler."

"I can hardly wait. After what we have been eating that sounds like a meal for a king."

"Have you been on the road long?" she asked.

"Yes. Almost four months. We have come from Charleston in the Carolinas and are headed either up the river or will cross it and go on west from here. Do you and your husband run the bar and restaurant alone?"

She laughed and Andrew caught a pleasant lilt to her laughter.

She said, "No. Winslow and I are not married. He has a wife. I just work here. I became stranded here and he gave me a job until I can save enough money to get back to Memphis. When you get out of the tub, come into the restaurant and you can test the cobbler for me to see if I've got enough cherries in it."

Andrew wondered what she had meant when she said she had been stranded in Roseville, but then he returned to his bath. He poured some more hot water into the tub and

218

eased back down. He just wanted to soak for a week to get the sweat and dirt off him.

When he finished his bath and had washed his hair, he dressed in his clean clothes and rolled the dirty ones up in a bundle. Then he walked over into the restaurant. The restaurant was empty so Andrew pulled a chair out from a table close to the kitchen. Helen saw him and brought out a dish of cherry cobbler and a cup of coffee. It must have just come from the oven for steam was still spiraling upward.

Andrew said, "Boy, does that look good. I can hardly wait until it cools."

Helen pulled up a chair a sat down. "I've got a few minutes until I have to get back in the kitchen."

Andrew welcomed the chance to talk to her. She was a pleasant girl and he had been alone with two men these past four months. It was nice to talk to someone different. They discussed the weather, the people in this area, and the lands on farther west.

Helen said, "As you know once you cross the Mississippi you will be out of the United States. That is French territory across there. Although the French helped the United States in its war with the British, they have become increasingly belligerent these past few years. There have been too many Americans crossing over and settling in their territory. Now you have to swear allegiance to France in order to settle land in their territory."

This caught Andrew by surprise. He had assumed that all the land westward was part of the United States. Now he learned that for all intent and purposes, America ended at this river. France was ruled by a king, much the same as England and Poland. He did not want to go back to that kind of life.

Helen went back to the kitchen and Andrew finished his cobbler. He thanked her, took his hat and rifle and walked down to the river. He sat on a bluff watching the brown water swirling past on its way to the Gulf of Mexico. He had intended to go on farther west, but now he would have to look for land this side of the river, either north, south, or back the way he had come. He had not paid a lot of attention to the lands they had crossed for he had plans to go on west. Now he would have to look at them with a more critical eye. When he thought on it though, he decided that maybe this was too far west already. They had travelled over roads that were hardly more than game trails and had gone two or three days without seeing another white person. The people who were blazing a path into the wilderness had to cluster their houses close together. Anyone bold enough to move off by themselves often lost their hair and the whole family was killed.

He asked himself, if he wanted to subject Catherine to this type of danger. Someday, hopefully, he would have children and he could not guarantee their safety in this wilderness. Reluctantly, he decided they must go back to the areas more civilized and with more people. The time might come when that area would become too settled and too many people. If it did he would have to pick up and move again, but for now, that seemed the only alternative.

It was almost full dark when he arose and walked back to the restaurant. He was very solemn, and Hans and Dave suspected there was something bothering him. They did not ask, figuring he would tell them when he was ready.

They finished their meal. He walked out onto the veranda and sat down. His two friends followed him outside and lit up their pipes. They sat smoking in silence for several minutes and finally, Andrew spoke.

"Did you know that the United States ends here? That all the land across the river belongs to France?"

Hans answered. "Ya, but this land is so wild most people

don't know where the boundaries begin and end. I have travelled across that river and gone all the way to the dry lands to the west. I was almost to the Pacific Ocean one time. Nobody has ever bothered me but the Indians."

He blew a bit of smoke and continued, "It is different though if you are crossing the land than if you intend to settle down and live there. To stay, I would have to swear allegiance to the king of France and I will not do that. I will stay in America where men have a say in their government. I will never again live under a king. We will stay here until after Christmas. Then we will decide whether to go north, south or back the way we came. Rest and enjoy yourselves. We will leave the day after Christmas."

Andrew rose and turned back into the restaurant just in time to see a loud, obnoxious man grab Helen's dress and try to pull her back to him. He had been drinking, but was not drunk. He was just being smart in front of two other men sitting at the table with him. They were all laughing at Helen's embarrassment, but they didn't see the steely look in her eyes.

She spoke to the man holding her skirt, "Turn me loose!" There were only two other men in the place and they did not seem inclined to help Helen. Evidently this was the bully of the town and no one wanted to stand up to him.

The man laughed and said in a booming voice, "Aw come on honey. Give me a kiss and we'll leave this place and go have some fun." He tried to pull her towards him again, but that was his mistake.

Helen had been going around to the tables refilling coffee cups and she had a big gallon coffee pot in her hand. She turned towards him and poured it directly into his lap.

With a roar, he came up out of his chair and knocked the table over. The plates with the balance of the food, the freshly filled coffee cups and the cherry cobbler spilled into the laps of his friends. It was a sight to see and Andrew couldn't help but smile.

They were all mad, but the big man was livid with rage. "You scalded me with that coffee." He reached for her but she eluded him and darted around the vacant tables. Andrew sensed that Hans and Dave were coming back off the porch. He moved to intercept the man and ran directly into him. He pretended it was an accident and apologized.

For the moment the big man turned his anger onto Andrew. He was almost out of control but something in the smile on the man's face told him to go slow. He made to push past Andrew and go after the girl, but Andrew stood his ground. The man couldn't get past him as long as he stood there.

Finally, the man bellowed, "Get out of my way. I'll teach that little bitch a thing or two."

The smile left Andrew's face and he took hold of the man's shoulder. "Mister, where I come from we don't treat women the way you just did. You got what you deserved. Now you apologize for what you just called this lady and get on out of here and there won't be any more trouble. Otherwise, me and you have got a few things to settle."

«Apologize. Never! She almost scalded me. This ain›t any of your business. Get out of my way.»

Again, he raised his arm as if to move Andrew. Andrew caught the arm, twisted it behind the man and shoved him out the front door. He stumbled across the porch and fell in the street.

The big man looked startled. It had happened so fast, he didn't know how the stranger had done it. One thing was for sure, he had been humiliated in front of his friends and the townspeople. He couldn't let it go. If he did, he would never be able to show his face in town again.

The man was standing on the steps and he could see

222

his friends behind the stranger. Once the fight started, they would grab the stranger and hold him while he beat the tar out of him.

What he didn't see was that Hans and Dave had moved up beside his two friends and had effectively blocked their paths so that they could not get to Andrew. Everyone in the restaurant and in the bar had surged out onto the porch. There was nothing they liked better than a good fight, if they were not part of it.

Andrew tried once more to reason with the man. "My friend, there is no need for us to fight this out here in the street. Just be a gentleman and apologize to the lady and we'll forget the whole thing."

"Like hell I will." He lowered his head and charged with his arms spread wide to encircle this smart aleck. But as he reached the steps, there was no one there. He raised his head to see where the man had gone and felt a sledgehammer blow strike him on the side of the jaw. It brought stars to his eyes and he slumped to his knees. He shook his head and tried to focus his eyes. The man was standing leaning against the hitching rail and appeared to be resting.

The big man climbed to his feet, determined to be a little more cautious this time. He moved towards the stranger and took a tentative jab at him. Andrew just weaved backwards slightly and stood his ground. The big man thought he was making fun of him for he hadn't even brought his fists up into fighting position yet. He took a round-house swing at Andrew and missed. Again, he wasn't where he was supposed to be, but before the big man could straighten up again, he received two hard blows to the body. One into the rib cage, and the other to the kidney area.

This knocked the wind from him and he whirled, thinking his opponent would jump him now that he was hurt. But to his surprise, the other man just stood off to the side and watched him. This infuriated him even more and he reached to his back and drew a long knife. To his surprise the other man did not draw his knife although he had one at his belt, nor did he back away. He lunged at Andrew with a cutting swath, but to his surprise, the man wasn't there again. The man moved like a cat, and before he could realize it, he felt two strong hands grab his knife arm and bring it down hard across the man's knee.

Everyone on the porch could hear the bone break and saw the knife drop to the ground. The big man screamed with pain and sat down in the road, holding his arm and rocking back and forth. He was cussing and swearing that Andrew was a dead man, that he would follow him to the ends of the earth to get even.

Andrew bent over and picked up the man's knife and put the point directly under his chin.

"Mister, you got just what you deserved. You had your chance to apologize like a gentleman, but you wanted to show what a big man you are around these parts. Now let me tell you something. I better not see you on my back trail or ever run into you again; if I do it will be more than your arm that gets broken."

Then Andrew turned to the two men standing on the porch, "Get him out of here and fix that arm. While you are at it you may teach him some manners and how to treat women. Real men don't bully women or swear at them. I'll just keep this little pig-sticker for a souvenir."

The two men gathered up their friend and moved off into the shadows.

Andrew walked back into the restaurant. Everyone had gone outside and Helen was standing at the door. Her face was white and she was frightened. To relieve the tension, he said, "Is it too late to get another cup of coffee, or do you still have any left that someone isn't taking a bath in?"

She smiled and went into the kitchen to get him a cup. When she returned she was a little calmer and she thanked him for helping her. She said he had been after her for weeks and when she wouldn't give him the time of day, he got abusive. She ended by saying, "You have made yourself a bad enemy. He and his men have killed two or three white men and they brag about killing dozens of Indians. You will have to be very careful when you leave here."

"That is my problem. Don't you worry about it. Finish up here and I will walk you to your house to make sure that they won't bother you anymore." Now that the fight was over, the adrenalin was easing out and as always, Andrew felt let down and began to shake. Although he had not seen Hans or Dave, he knew they were out there and would come if he needed them.

CHAPTER FIFTEEN

At a little past 9 o'clock, Helen finished cleaning the kitchen and locked up the restaurant. Andrew had waited for her, and as they stepped off the porch, a large man arose from the steps where he had been seated and moved toward them.

Helen was a little apprehensive, but Andrew steadied her with his hand and said. "Don't be alarmed. This is a friend of mine."

Then he spoke to the man. "Everything quiet?"

Hans answered, "Ya. Dave followed our friends to make sure they didn't double back. They have a camp a short distance from town. With all the caterwauling the big guy is doing, I don't think they will be back in town tonight. The other two are getting him drunk so they can set his arm."

"Good. I am going to walk the lady to her cabin. I'll see you back at the livery stable."

Now as they walked through the dark night Andrew could feel the girl shiver. It didn't seem that cold to him and he wondered if the thought of the bully and his friends coming back worried her. To break the silence he offered her his coat, but she refused.

"It isn't the cold I was thinking about. This thing tonight isn't over. He will be back as soon as his arm gets well and he will be meaner than ever. There isn't anyone in town brave enough to stand up to them. They have the whole town buffaloed. I'll have to make my move quickly now. I wasn't quite ready, but I'll have to go anyway."

"Maybe I better have another talk with him before I leave town."

"No. You are in enough trouble now. He will hate you and if he gets the chance, he will kill you."

"Don't worry about that. Better men than him have tried to do that. I'm still here."

They arrived at her cabin. She said "Well, this is home sweet home. Would you like to come in for a few minutes? I think I have something to make a drink out of if you'd like one." He said he would and they stepped up the steps and into the cabin. There was no porch.

It was hardly a cabin, much less a house. Just some rough boards tacked onto some posts in the ground. There were large cracks that had rags stuffed in them to keep out the wind, it would be a cold place in the winter. Andrew was sure that the roof leaked and although there was a wood floor, there were large cracks between the boards also. It was only two rooms. The front served as a kitchen/sitting room and the back, which was hardly more than a lean-to, was the sleeping area. In the front was a fireplace with two iron pot holders on either side. There were two kettles and Helen asked him if he would fill them for her from a barrel just outside the back door. While he did that she busied herself starting a fire in the fireplace. When he returned she had the fire going and she hung the two kettles on the iron pot holders and pushed them into the chimney above the fire.

A lit candle sat in the center of the table on a broken piece of plate. Beside the table were three chairs, one with a broken leg. A cupboard along the wall held a few bags and tins that probably contained foodstuff, a few tin plates and some coffee mugs. She took down one of the mugs, reached down in the corner of the cupboard and withdrew a jug of wine that was about half full. She poured him a cup and said "This is some local home brew that old man Douglas makes. It is not as good as commercial stuff, but it isn't as bad as some of the rot-gut that some make."

Andrew pulled out one of the chairs for her and another for himself and sat down at the table. He asked, "Aren't you going to have a drink?"

She answered, "No, not right now. Probably before I go to bed. But I want to get a bath as soon as that water gets hot. I've got the smell of that kitchen on me and I feel almost as greasy as those pork chops we had tonight."

They talked about this and that for several minutes and he learned why she had been stranded here. She was from a French family named LaBelle that had moved up river from New Orleans on the coast when she was about fourteen years old. Shortly after they arrived in Memphis, everyone was talking about the money that could be made trapping. Her father couldn't wait to try his hand. He just knew that he would make a fortune trapping for furs. For a couple years he had tried to run a trap line by just staying out a few days or weeks at a time. Then her dad, angry because there was not enough game close in to make trapping profitable, decided to go on a winter trip with two other trappers. He had gone off on this trapping trip and left her, her mother, one older sister and a brother to fend for themselves. Times were awfully hard for them and her mother, partly because she was lonely, and partly for the money, began to see other men. Her father returned from one of his trapping trips and discovered her mother with another man. He killed the man and cut his wife's throat. Then he took off into the wilderness and none of the family ever heard from him again.

By then she was nineteen, her sister twenty-two, and her brother was seventeen. They took whatever jobs they could find. The girls doing house cleaning, washing, looking after sick people, anything they could. The brother worked in stables, doing a little carpentry and eventually became a fairly decent cabinet maker. In fact, one of the heaviest demands for his work before she left home was for caskets. It was sort of strange to her that if people died on the road or out in the wilderness, they just rolled you in a blanket and put you in a hole, but if you lived in town, everyone wanted to be buried in a wooden box. Her brother got two or three dollars for a casket, and only a little more for a set of cabinets. So he began specializing in caskets and by the time he was twenty-five, people for miles and miles came to get him to make their casket. He had built a fairly good business out of people dying.

The older sister had taken a number of jobs and when things got really desperate, she went into prostitution for a while. Then she got a job for one of the wealthiest families as a house-keeper. The wife had died of the fever and left the man with two small children. He owned the mercantile store and because of the hours at the store, couldn't spend much time with the children. The sister, Elaina, took over their care and in a short time they became so attached to her that they would cry when she left to go home. After almost two years, the father came home from the store one night and asked Elaina if she would marry him. At first she refused, telling him he didn't know about her and the things she had done. He stopped her in mid-sentence.

Helen was still spilling out her story. "The man said, 'Elaina, don't you know that there are no secrets in a little town like this. I have known about what you have done since I first asked you to work for me. There are certain busy-bodies that made sure I knew everything they knew about you. But I also know about how hard your life was after your mother's death and how you worked to keep your family together. You did what you had to do at the time. I have also watched you with the children. They love you and you love them. I have grown to love you also, although I have never told you so, partly because I wanted to wait a decent interval after my wife's death, and partly because I was afraid I might lose you if I made advances to you. You may not love me, but I will treat you kindly and perhaps in time you may come to love me too. I have the respectability also to stop the vicious rumors about you that still surface from time to time. No one in this town would dare talk about the wife of the owner of the only store in town. I'm not asking you to have a tawdry affair, I'm asking you to be my wife and a mother to my children. Will you accept?'

"And so," Helen continued, "Elaina went home that night and cried most of the night. She had developed a strong liking for the man, but had not thought that of anything beyond a friendship, an employer and employee relationship was impossible. She accepted and a couple weeks later they were married. That was almost three years ago and today they are one of the happiest and most respected couples in Memphis."

Helen got up to check the water and said it was hot enough for a bath. Andrew indicated he would leave, but she said it would not be necessary. She would set two chairs up on the table and hang a sheet over them. He could turn his back and stay if he would like. He was enjoying his conversation with this young woman who was out-going and he still wanted to know more about her.

He helped her bring in a wooden tub and half fill it with water from the barrel outside. Then she poured one of the steaming kettles into the tub, and tested it, and poured part of the other kettle in also. Then she took a sheet and placed it on the back of the two chairs and Andrew sat down in the other and sipped his wine. He could see her silhouette with the fire behind her and although a little embarrassed at being a peeping tom, he watched as she un-buttoned the dress and stepped out of it. The reflection through the sheet was almost as if he were looking directly at her. She undid the cloth that bound her breasts and stepped out of her pantaloons. Then she stepped into the tub and began to lather her body.

To break the awkward silence, Andrew began to talk again. "So how did you get to Rosedale?"

"Well, I married a wood-cutter back about five years ago. We got along pretty good for about a year, then he began to come home drunk and wanted to show me what a big man he was. At first, he just slapped me around some and I thought that was normal in most marriages, for my dad had beaten up my mother from time to time. He spent all his money on booze and then got mad because I didn't have decent meals for him. I was taking in washing and ironing to earn enough to keep the house going. One night he came in roaring drunk and started in on me. I was in the kitchen cutting up a chicken and he came at me. When he pulled back his arm to hit me, I cut him pretty bad. It took almost two dozen stitches to put him back together. My brother heard about it and came over to the house. When I told him about the beatings I had taken, he went looking for my husband. He took a wooden maul with him and when he found him, he gave him a tongue lashing you wouldn't believe. He also told him to get out of town and if he ever saw him again he would bash in his brains with that maul. My husband must have believed him for he disappeared the next day and I've never seen him since.

"After my sister married I stayed with her awhile and although her husband treated me nice, I felt I was in the way. I moved back to stay with my brother, but he soon found a girl and wanted her to come live with him. The house just wasn't big enough for both of us. I moved back into the cabin I had shared with the wood-cutter and lived by myself. Jobs were hard to find and men began to come by the house, just for a visit you understand. It is amazing how easily it is to become a prostitute. I was lonely and flattered by the attention. The first time was mutual desire and sort of fun. Then before you know it the word gets around and more and more men come to see you. First they bring little gifts, baskets of food, etc., then they drop the pretense of being friends and start offering you money. When you are hard up and need money to live on, you decide, what the heck, I might as well get paid for what I've been giving away."

She looked away for a moment before continuing, "I became an embarrassment to my brother and to my sister and when I would go to visit them they were very cool towards me. You see, nobody wants a sister who is the town whore. So finally I stopped going to see them. About three months ago a trader came to town on his way to New Orleans. He was going to set up a trading route among the French settlers and the friendly Indians. He asked me to go with him and I decided it might be best for my brother and sister if I made a life someplace else. New Orleans seemed like it might be a good place to begin again. I told Robert and Elaina that we were going to be married as soon as we got to New Orleans, but the trader never asked me to marry him. We got this far and he went out to trade with the Indians and didn't come back. I don't know if they killed him or if he changed his mind and went on to New Orleans without me. Either way, I ended up in Rosedale with one small suit case and nothing else. I was able to get the job in the restaurant and this cabin was empty so I have been living here trying to get enough money to either go on or go back to Memphis. One thing I don't want to go back to and that is being a whore. I've avoided it here although I have had several offers, and then this jug-headed bully comes along to make life more difficult."

Now she rose up out of the tub and her silhouette showed against the sheet. Tried as he might, Andrew couldn't help but look. He was still staring when she stepped from behind the sheet. She has pulled a robe around her body and she smiled. Realizing he was watching her.

"You cheated. You were supposed to have your back turned."

Andrew, embarrassed, stammered, "Well, your outline was on the sheet and it has been almost four months since I had seen a woman. The temptation was too great to resist. Besides, you have a beautiful body. I could tell even in your dress, without the dress it was worth getting caught peeping."

A warm look came into her eyes as he paid her the compliment and she smiled a coquettish smile. It had been three months since she had been with a man and here was someone who was a gentleman, seemed kind and gentle. He certainly was strong and handsome. Without a moment's hesitation, she made her decision.

"Would you like to get a better look?" as she spoke, she opened the robe and revealed everything beneath it. There was nothing but pure woman, from head to foot. She must have stood five feet and five or six inches, yet she would not have gone over 110 to 115 pounds. There were still a few drops of water clinging to her skin. What caught Andrew's attention most was the large firm breasts. The dress had not done them justice. Now, without the bindings, they stood out as firm and straight as an eighteen or nineteen year old in the bloom of youth. He sat with his mouth open and a look of wonder in his eyes. The mere excitement in his gaze seemed to ignite a similar fire in her. She dropped the robe and turned slowly for him to enjoy the view from all sides.

As she turned, he noticed the arched curve of her back and how it flowed outward to firm rounded buttocks that were as white as driven snow. As she turned her back to him, he reached his hand out, putting his palm in the middle of her back and moving it downward across her hips ever so gently. The minute his hand touched her, it was if the fire inside her began to glow more brightly and she turned and walked into his arms.

Now she began to undress him and her fingers furiously tugged at the buttons on his shirt and trousers. She bent down and unlaced his boots and pulled them off. Soon they were both naked. She took him by the hand and led him toward the bed. "Come, I think it has been too long for both of us. I will show you what it is like to love a French girl."

When they had satisfied their passion and were lying beside one another, Helen said, "You are a good lover Andrew Stanley. What are you going to do tomorrow?"

"I have no plans. We plan to rest up another day and will be leaving day after tomorrow."

"Good. I do not have to work Christmas day. Why don't you spend the day with me tomorrow and I will fix us a Christmas dinner."

"I am with two friends. Could they share dinner with us?"

She hesitated a moment, then replied, "Yes, although I don't know if I have enough food for three hungry men. I can get some things from the kitchen at the restaurant, but I don't know what all there is."

Andrew answered, "You don't worry about the food. If you will cook it I will go into town the first thing in the morning and see what all I can find."

With that settled, she snuggled closer to him and began to rub his chest. He felt the warmth of her touching him and he again became excited. Her smooth hands caressed his body, and started the blood racing through his body again. She sensed his excitement and raised up on an elbow so that she could look at him. "You have been out in the woods too long."

Andrew could just barely see her from the candlelight glowing from the next room. She had a provocative smile and gently teased his body into action. Helen proved to be a skilled companion, and after their love-making, Andrew was so weak he was all but trembling.

Helen slipped into a tub for a quick bath. When she returned to the bed, he was asleep. She eased in beside him and snuggled close, trying not to disturb him.

Tonight, she was a fulfilled woman in the arms of a man she would love forever, who, no matter where he was, she would long for his embrace. But she knew when this brief interlude was over she would probably never see him again. She knew without a doubt, although neither had spoken of it, that he had a wife or another woman somewhere, that she would not have his love for long. But for now, he was here and she would make the most of the moment she had with him. With tears on her cheeks she fell asleep.

CHAPTER SIXTEEN

A ndrew awakened to see the sun shining through the cracks in the walls and turned to find the bed next to him empty. He sat up on the side of the bed and looked into the kitchen. Helen was in her gown and leaning over the fireplace. His clothes had been folded and placed at the foot of the bed. He began to dress and hearing him; she turned in his direction. "Breakfast will be ready in a few minutes. You can wash up out back if you want."

Finished dressing, he made his way to the outhouse and relieved himself. Returning to the house he saw a little shelf by the back door with a bucket and pan, soap and a towel. After washing his face and hands he went inside to find Helen putting breakfast on the table. She was a good cook and had done an outstanding job this morning. There were fried eggs, potatoes, a big steak, hot biscuits and a steaming pot of coffee. He was impressed by how much she was able to do over and open fire in the hearth.

He pulled a chair up to the table and sat down. Helen turned to him, hugged his head to her breast and said, "For today, you are my man and I figure you need a good steak and eggs to restore your vigor. You seem a little peeked this morning. Did something tire you out last night?"

"You know what tired me out. I got caught up in a whirlwind and couldn't get loose."

"That's strange. I was in that same whirlwind and it didn't seem to me you were trying to get out very hard. In fact, the last I saw of you before the candle went out, there wasn't anything hard about you."

Andrew blushed and shot back, "Hush your mouth girl and eat your breakfast. You're going to make me think I was a disappointment to you."

"No sir-re-bob. Just the opposite kind, sir. I knew you were a strong man when you handled that bully the way you did, but I didn't expect you to have the stamina you did. There isn't a man I have ever met that could perform the way you did last night. Though I loved every second of it, I am so sore this morning I can hardly sit down. You, sir, drive a hard bargain. I probably won't be able to touch myself for a week after all the action we had last night."

This line of talk was embarrassing Andrew and he sought to change the subject. This woman was very open and said what she felt. There was no toying around, no games, no being a coquette. She said just what she felt and to many men, like Andrew, it was something he was not used to. While it was good to let your partner know that the pleasure was mutually agreeable, it was rare from Andrew's experience, that men and women talked so freely. She was not being vulgar; she just was caring on light banter while they ate. Now she sensed his embarrassment and they talked of other things.

Andrew asked, "You said you would fix Christmas dinner, while I am out getting some groceries, I will let my traveling companions know that we will be having Christmas dinner with you."

Helen replied, "Yes, ask them to come and I will impress them with what a good cook I am. Maybe one of them needs a wife."

"If either of them knew what I know about you, they

would kill to get you, and never mind whether you could boil water or not. You do the cooking and I'll get the fixins."

As he finished, he pushed back his chair, got up, kissed her on the cheek and left to walk up town. As he went out the door, she called to him to bring back his clothes and she would wash them while the meal was cooking.

He found Hans and Dave at the livery and told them they were having Christmas dinner together and that they would be leaving at daybreak the next day. They should make sure everything was in order; the horses were in good shape and ready to go. He asked Hans to go with him to the mercantile store for the few extra things they might need to finish out their food stuffs for the next leg of their journey.

Then he took off to make the rounds. Even on Christmas, the Mercantile was open for a couple of hours and he and Hans went there first. First he bought the things they would need for the journey and gave them to Hans. He also instructed him to take any clothes he and Dave needed washing to Helen's house. Hans told him they had already taken care of that chore while he had been otherwise occupied. Then he loaded up a big basket of food and bought a ham and asked where he might get a turkey this late. He was told to go along the creek until he found a lean-to open towards the river, with a large chicken pen. It was unlikely he could get a turkey, but old man Brown had some chickens. Maybe he would sell him a baking hen. The store keeper had a cake and two pies that one of the local women had made and brought in to trade for some items. Andrew took all three. If he knew Hans and Dave's appetite, one pie would not be enough to satisfy them.

He walked a short distance down the river as he had been told and shortly came to a shack. It could not be called a house or cabin. It was a shack and hardly habitable. An old man with a scraggly beard and an unwashed look came out to meet him. There was no greeting, just a steady stare as if asking, "What do you want?"

Andrew spoke first. "The man at the mercantile said you might sell me a chicken or two. Do you have any you want to sell?"

The old man waited a minute or two then said, "Maybe so. I get ten cents each for the pullets and fifteen cents for the hens." He was sullen and Andrew figured he didn't have a whole lot of visitors, and few if any friends.

"Sir, that is more than most men charge, but this is Christmas and I am not prone to bargain. I will give you fifty cents for two hens and a young rooster that is frying size. What do you say?"

The old man's greedy eyes brightened and what passed for a smile appeared on his face. "Sir, you are a gentleman and have made a trade. You can even pick out the ones you want. Come with me to the chicken pen and I will catch the ones you select."

They walked around the corner of the shack and there were three or four kinds of chickens. Andrew pointed to a big Rhode Island Red hen, then a spotted Dominecker hen and finally a black rooster that was strutting around amongst the hens. The old man caught the chickens, tied their feet with small pieces of rawhide string and laid them on the ground. His attitude seemed to have brightened considerably. Andrew judged that the fifty cents he was paying him was probably more hard money than he had seen in months. On the frontier like they were here, most everything was barter with little money changing hands.

This was Christmas and Andrew was feeling happy. On the spur of the moment he dug out an extra quarter and handed it to the old man. He said, "It is Christmas and I want you to have this extra coin. Maybe there is someone you want to get a gift for, or something in town that you would like. This is the season when we celebrate the birth of our Lord and Savior. Thank you for selling me the chickens and I wish you a merry Christmas."

Andrew saw the surprise on his face and turned to leave. The old man caught his arm and asked, "Why are you giving me this extra money? You never saw me before."

Andrew answered, "You are right sir. But you seem like a very unhappy man. I do not see signs of any family and a man needs family and friends, especially at this time of year. Please accept the extra coin as a gift from me to you on this joyous season. Use it to buy something you would like, something to make your life less barren."

The old man stared at him for a moment and Andrew turned to leave. He spoke again now. "You knew I charged you too much for those chickens didn't you?"

"Yes. But you have chickens and need money. I have money but no chickens. I cannot eat money and money is only good for what it will buy. I know people who hoard away every penny they earn, living in poverty because they love money. They are unhappy and live like beggars because they do not want to part with money. They will go to their graves hiding their money and will have missed the joys and pleasures it could have bought them. I do not choose to live that kind of life. Life is too short and when you are gone, someone else will have the pleasure of spending your money. I prefer to spend it now and it gives me pleasure if I can help another as I pass through this life."

As he spoke the old man stared hard at him and tears began to appear in his eyes. By the time Andrew had finished, tears were streaming down both cheeks. His face was so dirty the tears were cutting little muddy channels on his cheeks. He sat down on a bench by the door and buried his face in his hands. He wept as a child would weep after a whipping.

Andrew was embarrassed and wanted to leave, but something held him to that spot. He couldn't walk away and leave this man so distraught. He lived alone, like a hermit, with little or nothing to call his own. His house was not worth calling a home, and there was nothing of value in it. Everything seemed to have been something discarded by others.

Finally the old man raised his head, wiped his eyes and his nose on his sleeve and looked at Andrew. "I beg your pardon sir. I have lived like this for almost ten years. No one ever comes and when someone comes to buy chickens, I treat them badly. But you, a total stranger, have shown me friendship and have talked to me as a human. I see now that to have friends, you must be a friend. I was hurt very badly one time and I have shut myself away from every one, and let no man be a friend. It has been a lonely life and not one I would recommend to another. What you said about the money is right. For many years I have hoarded every penny, never spending a cent and it has not brought me any happiness. There will be no one to bury me when I die, and no one will mourn me when I am gone for I have left nothing but sadness and sorrow with those I have come in contact with. This day, you have opened my eyes and shown me how foolish I have been." "Will you share a drink with me?"

Andrew did not want to drink anything this dirty old man might have, nor drink from any container he might own, but he could not refuse in good conscience. He hesitated a moment, then agreed. The old man turned and rushed into his shack, rummaged around and came out a few minutes later with a bottle of wine and a cloth bag. He set the bottle down and opened the bag. He took out something wrapped in paper and in soft cloth. Meticulously he unwrapped the package. To Andrew's surprise, it was a beautiful goblet of cut glass. It had blue triangles with red lines around each triangle. It was as beautiful as anything you would find on a fancy dinner table in one of the rich homes. He poured it half full of wine and offered it to Andrew.

"For you sir. For opening my eyes to the fool I have been. No one has drunk from that goblet in more than ten years. I was once a man of some possessions. My wife ran away with another man and took our son and all of our money. I had to sell my farm and everything I owned to pay my debts. But I kept this goblet as a reminder of what I had lost. I used it to refresh my hate and it has almost destroyed me. If not for you this day, I probably would have died a hermit, no one knowing or caring. I swear to you that from this moment forward, I will change my life. I will burn these rags I wear, find me a better place to live and share my life with anyone who will accept my friendship. Because you have done this for me, I want you to have the first drink from this goblet."

Andrew thought that was probably the most the old man had spoken in the last ten years. He was moved, and he raised the goblet, and said, "Mr. Brown, I toast you. The fact you have decided to cast aside this poor life you lead makes me happy that I came here today. I think that your life will be much different from this day forward. I wish you much happiness, sir."

He raised the goblet and drank the wine. It was somewhat soured and tasted tart, but he never let it show. As he finished, he handed the goblet to Mr. Brown and said, "I must go for I have several people waiting to prepare Christmas dinner. Good day to you sir, and may God be with you."

"And with you kind sir. But before you go, please tell me your name."

"I am Andraui Stanislaski, recently from Poland. Here in America I have adopted the name Andrew Stanley. Merry Christmas, Sir." With this last remark, he walked back up the river.

For some reason the day seemed much brighter and the air fresher than when he came down river. There was also lightness in his step that had not been there before. He thought to himself, Isn't it a beautiful day?

At Helen's cabin he found Hans and Dave waiting and handed them the three chickens and told them he had done the getting and their job was getting them ready for the pots. He set the other packages on the table and Helen was surprised at all the food he had brought. She commented, "Which army is coming to dinner?"

Andrew pointed to the two men out back and said, "That army. You have not seen those two eat before."

It was a very pleasant day, a great meal and everyone sat out in the yard after dinner, rubbing their stomachs and complimenting Helen on what a fabulous cook she was. Dave and Hans both had figured out that she and Andrew had spent last night together and there was a certain intimacy between them that gave them away also. Shortly before dark, she fed them again and they left to go back to the livery. She said she would pack a lunch for them to take with them the next day.

After they had gone, Andrew and Helen continued to sit outside and watch the night stars come out. It was a clear night and although it had been fairly warm during the day, it was now turning cool and Helen moved closer to him and he put his arm around her. A little later they got up and went inside and prepared for bed. She had heated water at the fireplace and poured fresh water into the tub. They each took a bath, washing each other and drying each other, hardly talking at all. Their hands and the soft strokes each gave the other conveyed all the message they needed.

When they were finished, they walked hand in hand back to the bedroom. They lay down and pulled the sheet up over them. Helen snuggled close to Andrew with his arm around her and her head resting on his shoulder. They knew they would make love again tonight, but there was no urgency, no wildness as they had experienced before. This was a calm, easy, deeply moving kind of love. The kind of love few men and women ever learn to share. Each knew that they would probably never see each other again after tonight, and each wanted it to be something special.

They lay for some time, just enjoying the closeness of the other. Andrew had his arm encircling her body. She lay beside him, savoring the man scent of him and using her fingers to run back and forth through the hair on his chest. The time would soon come when their instincts would take over and the urge for physical love making would propel them into another cataclysmic union. But for the moment, this was sweet love, a deep feeling of loving, caring and sharing just the presence of the other.

They talked of various things, but it was Helen who finally brought up the subject that had been on her mind. She had not meant to say anything, but her love for this man forced her to ask him. "Do you think you will ever come back here again, Andrew?"

He thought in silence. "No, I doubt it. I had planned to go on farther west, but I will not go into French Territory. The French still live under the rule of a king. They do not have the freedom of the Americans. I will find me a place in America, east of here. I will probably settle somewhere here in the territories of either Georgia, Carolina or maybe up in Tennessee."

"Then it is unlikely we will ever see each other again after tonight."

"That is very possible. I must tell you Helen that I plan to marry a woman in the Carolinas. We are not yet engaged but I intend to return and if she will have me, we will be married. I hope you do not feel that I have misled you or shared your bed under false pretenses."

"No. I knew we were two strangers who had met in passing and would probably never see each other again. I knew what I was doing. I was lonely and wanted someone to love. You came along and I am glad you did. I have no regrets and you should feel no guilt when you leave tomorrow. I have enjoyed these hours with you, and I will remember them always. I have no regrets, and neither should you."

"Helen you are a beautiful woman and a fantastic lover. You were right, I never loved anyone so furiously and so many ways as you have shown me. I will never forget you. Who knows, fate has caused our paths to cross once, they may cross again someday, although we do not see how now."

"I hope so Andrew. No one has ever had the capacity to fulfill me and satisfy me the way you have. I fear I shall never find another like you."

He pulled her closer, wanting to feel of her naked body up against him. "Then let us enjoy each other one more time before we part. All this talk of making love has put me in the mood again."

She replied, "So it has. Let me see if I can take that swelling down for you."

Afterward, she laughed gently, "You have given me all the love I can stand. I will let you sleep now." She rose on one elbow and kissed him on the mouth. "Good night, my darling." Then she turned her back to him and they both drifted off to sleep.

Andrew slept like a log and he awakened about an hour before dawn. During the night, Helen has turned and cuddled next to him and they were now lying, facing each other, in each other's arms. When he moved slightly, she slowly came awake. She realized he is ready to get up and will be leaving her for good. She felt his naked body close to her and although he does not appear to be aroused, she moved her hand down to touch him and began stroking him gently. Almost immediately, this has the desired effect and before he is ready she pulled him over on top of her.

He said, "I thought you said you had enough last night."

"That was last night. Besides, I lied. Make love to me one more time, Andrew. Then I will let you go."

He was not sure he had anything left in him, but he bent his head and kissed her. She opened her mouth, inviting his tongue into her mouth. She sucked on his tongue and gently bit his lips. This has the desired effect and once again they joined in a loving embrace. She had a deep need and a strong hunger to be fed and Andrew did his best to meet that need.

They now lay all but exhausted.

"That was the best of all, Andrew. I want to lay here and hold this pleasure as long as I can."

After a few more minutes, he got dressed and rolled up his clothes. He is almost ready to leave when she appeared out of the bedroom in her robe and busied herself with fixing a package of food from the left-overs from the day before.

As she handed it to Andrew, he kissed her long and hard and said, "Helen, I have more money than I can use, and I want you to have this to make your trip to New Orleans on and help you get set up there. I have been trying to figure how to give this to you without you misunderstanding. It is not for the time we have shared. That was too good and sweet to be tarnished by payment. This is because I care about you and I want to help you get a new start. It is $200. Will you take it and not be insulted?"

She was flabbergasted and could not speak for several

seconds. Then she said, "Andrew, I cannot take money from you. It would cheapen what we have enjoyed."

"Only if you thought of it as payment for our love-making. If you did, I would be insulted. I would never offer you money for what we have shared. This is not for that at all. I have plenty of money and have more waiting back in Carolina for me. If you won't accept it as a gift, will you accept it as a loan?"

She thought for a minute and studied his face. He was serious and he was not trying to pay her as if she were a common prostitute. He really wanted her to have the money to help her get started. With this she could make a new start, get some decent clothes and find a place to live. She would not have to go back on the streets. She began to cry and went into his arms.

"Oh Andrew, I was going to be so brave and not show any emotion about you leaving. I have only known you a couple days, but I love you so. Why did I not find you before the other woman? I could make you happy and you make me so happy. You are such a good man, in so many ways."

Then she pulled back, brushed the tears from her eyes and kissed him long and passionately. Although they had just made love a few minutes ago, she was telling him she would be ready again if he wanted to. He hugged her close, kissed her again, then reached down and picked up his belongings and the sack of food.

"I must go Helen. I will always remember you and these days together here. If I ever get to New Orleans, I will look you up. Good-bye and thank you for the most exciting two days and nights of my life. I hope life is good to you."

With that, he turned and walked toward the door. He heard her start to sob again. He stepped outside and closed the door. He hated to go. He has not yet found his destiny, but he does not believe it was meant to be with her. He took a deep breath and walked toward the livery stable. When he arrived, Hans and Dave had the pack mule ready and the horses saddled. They mounted up and rode out of town without saying a word. The two see the set of Andrew's jaw and the sad expression on his face and decide to wait until later to tell him about the Indians.

CHAPTER SEVENTEEN

They rode in silence. Andrew was deep in thought and neither Hans nor Dave wanted to disturb his thinking. It was not until they had cleared the small town and well into the woods that Andrew noticed that Dave had led out and was walking his horse several hundred yards in front. Normally they would be riding bunched closer together. Hans was lagging back with him and Dave was too far out front.

This observation jerked him back to their situation. He had all but forgotten the dangers that lurked in the woods, and men who rode along, day-dreaming, often ended up without their hair. He became instantly alert and sensed that something was wrong.

He noticed his companions were far more wary than they had been a few days ago.

Hans' eyes and head were always in motion. He watched everywhere at the same time. He did not intend to be caught again the way he had in the gully.

The mere fact that Hans was acting so cautiously made Andrew suspect something. Automatically, his hand tightened on his rifle and he sub-consciously checked his pistols. He had loaded them and primed them that morning, but now he checked them again. If his men were expecting trouble, he did not want to be caught with a gun that would not fire because it was improperly loaded or improperly primed.

They were travelling north, parallel to the river and were five miles or so above the town. The road was hardly more than a trail where they often had to go single file. It was a well-used trail, probably used by the various tribes of Indians who had lived here in the ages past, and now, by both Indians and white men. Raiding parties went north and south using these trails. Someday, if the white man stayed, he would probably clear the trails and widen them so that a wagon could pass. The Indians never used wagons, preferring travois instead and the trails were wide enough that they could go single file.

Dave stopped and they walked up to him. He spoke, mostly to Hans, but now that Andrew was "awake" he spoke loud enough for him to hear also.

"It's like the kid said. There are lots of pony tracks. I can't tell whether they are made from the same groups going back and forth searching for the raiders, or if they are even from the same tribe. It may be raiders going south and returning. Either way, I'm nervous. There has been too much traffic on these paths to suit me. I am surprised we have not run into someone already. If we run into the Shawnee, and there are as many as the boy said, we wouldn't stand a chance. They would ride right over us. If we run into the Cherokee, the Chickasaw or the Creek, they may not be in any mood to let us pass friendly either. They have been bloodied and right now they might just as soon take it out on us as the Shawnee."

"You are right," agreed Hans. "I think I would be a little more comfortable back off the river a few miles even though the trails might not be as well defined."

Andrew asked, "What are you two talking about? Has there been trouble? You mentioned Shawnee, that's not a local tribe is it?"

"No. The Shawnee are from up in the forests to the

North, around the Allegheny and Monongahela River areas. That's in western Pennsylvania and Ohio territory. I don't suppose you noticed that the corral was filled to capacity with horses and mules. Several people brought in animals late yesterday. And along about dark, a young boy came in leading two horses and a mule. He had a young girl about four years old on the back of the mule. He said small parties of Indians who he thought were Shawnee had attacked his home and killed both his ma and pa. The little girl had been down along the creek picking flowers and got scared when she heard the Indians screaming. She hid in the bushes and that's where the boy found her. He had hid also, like his pa had told him too. When the raid was over, he followed the party and saw them join up with a larger group. He said there were almost a hundred altogether. Of course he could have been exaggerating."

Hans spat on the ground and continued, his eyes still scanning, "The boy then returned, went looking for his sister and brought her into town. Afterward, went back to bury his parents before the animals got them. The townspeople had advised him to wait until some of the town people could go with him but he was determined. He had an old beat-up rifle, but looked as if he could use it. Maybe he made it. It's not likely that the same party would come back to the same place, but there seems to be a number of smaller parties moving around. Another one could have come by and caught him. If they did he is probably a goner."

Dave took over now. "There isn't any love lost between the Shawnee and the Cherokee. Another rumor buzzing around is that one group of the Shawnee attacked a group of Creeks, about 15, including women and children, and butchered every last one. They didn't even take the women prisoners. This indicates they are not through raiding yet and are moving fast. If they were headed back north they would have probably taken the younger women and real young boys prisoners. They would raise the boys as tribal warriors and taken the women as wives or concubines. But the forest is a bee-hive of activity. The Choctaws and Chickasaws have joined the Creeks now and they are hunting the Shawnee. They'll be a real to do if they meet up. The Shawnee are fierce fighters and are bigger in build than the Southern Indians, but the Chickasaws are real mean and Creeks are not cowards. They will outnumber the Shawnee. If they can catch them, there will be a blood-bath. That's why I think we need to go farther inland. We don't want to get caught by either one of these groups."

Andrew took it all in. If he had not been so engrossed in enjoying himself with Helen, he might have learned of this himself and made other plans. Now it was too late. He did not want to turn back, but they certainly would have to move carefully. Now was no time to let his mind wander. Quickly, they made plans. They would move a few miles inland and find a little used path. They would keep inching their way north and come back to the river as they neared Memphis in the Tennessee Territory.

They moved out, every sense now alert and watching for any sound or noise that might either give them away, or alert an enemy that they were coming. Dave slid off his horse and tied it to the pack saddle and then took off on foot. He could travel almost as fast afoot as he could on horse, and a whole lot quieter. Andrew continued leading the pack horse with Dave's horse following. Hans brought up the rear. They traveled this way for the rest of the day and as dark approached, Dave reappeared as if out of the ground. He motioned them forward and when they were close, he whispered, "There is a heavy thicket ahead with a small stream running through it. It is real thick and I don't think anyone could get to us without us hearing him.

I suggest we get off the trail, back track a little and come at that thicket from the other side." They all agreed and turned back for a few hundred feet, then moved off through the pines and oaks. Dave led the way now and they began to move into a really heavy growth of underbrush, briers, low shrubs and thick hardwoods.

They reached a spot that they thought would be safe. They quietly off-loaded the pack mule and loosened the cinches on their saddles, but did not take them off. It might be necessary to move quickly and it might take too long to saddle. They watered the horses and rubbed them down although at the pace they had moved today, the animals had hardly worked up a sweat.

They finished off the rest of the food Helen had packed for them. They figured it might be too dangerous to have a fire so they made a cold camp. At breakfast they might heat some coffee, because they would be gone before smoke drifted too far. But if they had a fire tonight, an Indian would be able to follow that smoke directly to them.

Hans agreed to stand the first watch, Andrew would take the second, and Dave would take the last, morning watch. They checked their weapons once more, wrapped themselves in a blanket and sat down with their backs to a tree and were immediately asleep.

At about 11:00 0'clock, Hans woke Andrew and said everything seemed quiet. There was nothing untoward during his shift and he woke Dave around 3 in the morning. There was a slight mist, or fog, rising from the ground. It made everything feel damp and it was getting a little colder.

Andrew wished he had a roaring fire to back up to and warm himself. It also crossed his mind that it would be nice and warm in bed next to Helen also, but he put that thought out of his mind. He had to keep his mind on where he was and what was happening or they may not get out of here.

He wrapped himself in his blanket and sat down, resting his back against a big Bay tree.

It seemed like just a moment, but he later discovered that it was nearly five o'clock when Dave touched his shoulder and motioned him to be quiet. He did the same to Hans, and then motioned them to get the horses. They eased over to where they had hobbled the horses and after checking their guns, proceeded to hold the horses' nostrils to keep them from smelling any other animals. A stud horse, or a mare in heat, would sometimes whinny if they smelled another horse. That would give them away and might be the end of them.

Andrew still had not heard anything and was beginning to wonder if Dave might be mistaken, but he had a high regard for the old man's abilities. He was seldom wrong about Indians. That was why he was still carrying his hair.

Almost fifteen minutes passed before Andrew caught the first sound of movement.

There were low guttural sounds of Indians talking. They were moving slowly, as if looking for something. Then it dawned on him. It was them the Indians were looking for. They must have picked up their trail and lost it again in the dark. They milled around and moved on up the ridge from them.

Andrew thought they were going in the same direction he was traveling and wondered if he should plan to change direction. Just as he prepared to let go of his horse's nose, he heard them coming back.

It seemed there were two, no more than three, of them. Chances are there would be others within shouting distance; certainly within range they could hear a rifle shot. If it came to a fight, they would not dare use the rifles; the sound carried too far. The black mare made as if to snort and Andrew pinched her nose. She jerked her head up and he patted her on the neck. He had to keep her quiet.

The minutes dragged by and although it had been cold a few minutes ago, sweat now ran down his back and from his armpits. It seemed an eternity before the Indians gave up and moved back the way they had come. They had totally lost the trail and would go back further south and pick it up again when it got light. Dave turned loose his horse and disappeared into the woods. As soon as he was out of sight, he noticed Hans tightening the cinches on his saddle and he followed suit. Hans quickly moved to load the pack horse and when Dave returned, they were ready. Dave moved out on foot again and they followed, leading his horse.

All morning they moved rapidly, setting a fast pace, wanting to put as much distance between them and the Indians as possible.

Andrew judged it was near two o'clock when they stopped and Dave set to building a fire. At first Andrew thought to object, but he knew Dave would not be taking a chance unless he thought it was safe. They had not seen any fresh tracks, or any sign of Indians, in the last two hours. They had not stopped to eat all day and Dave got real cranky if he didn't get his coffee. The fire he built was of oak limbs and gave off almost no smoke. It was a small fire, but a hot one. He brewed a pot of coffee and Hans handed around some dried jerky. This would have to do them for now.

The stop only lasted perhaps 30 minutes and they were on their way again. Dave had led them toward a high ridge, sort of a hump-back hill. Now as they approached it, the steep hill rose up, sort of like a small mountain, heavily wooded with pine and oak.

About an hour before dark, they were still headed directly toward the steep hillside, looking for a place to camp. They crossed a small creek, no more than a foot wide. They stopped to allow the horses to drink, and then moved on. Dave came back with a grin on his face.

"I thought there ought to be a cave or a cut-bank along that hill. There is a high ridge about a quarter mile ahead. There is a small wash with grass along the side for the horses. It empties out into a big gully. We can tie a rope across the mouth and keep the horses penned in for the night. Just above, looking down on this valley is a dead-fall where lightening must have hit one of those big pines and as it fell, it brought down four or five more. We can camp under it and have a good view of the valley without anyone seeing us."

As soon as they arrived at the dead-fall they penned the horses and unsaddled. They would not be seen from the trail.

Hans took the coffee pot and walked back to the little stream, filled it and came back. They all busied themselves getting something to eat before dark set in. A flickering camp fire could be seen a long way off on a clear night. In less than a half hour they had a meal of hot beans, fat back and sourdough bread. It wasn't fancy, but it was filling and with the hot coffee, it would do for tonight.

Before it got full dark, they threw sand on the hot coals and unrolled their blankets underneath the downed trees. They set up the same watch schedule as the night before and shortly Dave and Andrew were asleep.

Shortly after midnight, a horrible scream brought them bolt upright with their rifles in their hands. Each looked at each other and around, trying to decide where that soul wrenching sound came from. Hans eased over beside them and Andrew asked, "What in the world was that? And where did it come from?"

Hans said, "I think it came from that camp fire there across the creek. I have been watching it since you went to sleep. There is lots of movement around the fire, but it is too far away to get an accurate count. Whatever is going on, someone is in mortal pain. It must be a white-man being tortured because Indians rarely let pain show. They will suffer unbearably and never let out a whimper."

Andrew was on his feet now. He checked all his weapons and the other two men, knowing what he had in mind, were doing likewise. They could not stand here and allow one of their own to be tortured. The Indians were masters at prolonging death. They would cut and torture just enough to inflict the greatest pain, yet stop short of causing death. They could keep someone alive for days if they chose to do so. Andrew figured some helpless farmer had got caught and they were having sport with him now.

In less than three minutes after the first scream, they were moving towards the fire. Just as they came to the small stream they had crossed earlier, there was another piercing scream, a sound of pure agony. They moved ahead rapidly, but cautiously. They had no idea yet what they would do. It was useless to try to formulate a plan until you knew what the situation was.

Dave, who was in the lead, held up his hand and motioned them to remain still while he went ahead and checked things out. It seemed an hour, but he returned in less than five minutes and spoke to them in a whisper.

There were seven or eight Shawnee and it appeared they had captured four Cherokees. Three were tied to trees with their hands tied behind the trees. One, it appeared perhaps to be the young boy, was spread-eagled on the ground on his back. The Shawnee were torturing him by putting red coals on his stomach and chest. He had strained at his bounds until blood now soaked the ground. The wounds seemed fairly deep and Andrew surmised he would likely sever a vein before much longer. The other three prisoners had to watch, and knew their time was coming.

Andrew surmised the Shawnee planned to keep the

young one alive as long as they could, then would work on the others, either with the same process or with knives. It seemed to give them sheer delight with each scream. They danced around the fire and laughed, intoxicated on the pain they were inflicting."

Andrew's survival instincts kicked in. There were too many to attack openly. But they could not stand by and see even an Indian treated so barbarically. He turned to Dave and asked, "Is there any chance we can get the other three free without the Shawnee knowing it?"

Dave shook his head, "I don't know. They are sort of back in the shadows and I could not see any guards. They were all watching the torture. There is a small chance that we could injun up from behind and cut them loose. It's risky though."

"We can't just stand here and let them torture that boy to death, and kill the others without a chance. How do you feel Hans? Shall we help them?"

"Why not? What the hell, I don't want to get to be as old as Dave here."

"Dave?"

"Might as well. Can't let this child here show me up. My blood is as red as his."

"O.K. Here's what we try to do. We will each take one tree. Snake up from the outside and cut the Indian loose. When we do, put your knife in his hand. Then back off about ten feet and fire point blank at the Shawnee that is nearest to you. Even with the other Indians free, we will still be out-numbered. If they don't act quickly, we may wish we had stayed out of this. Agreed?"

Both nodded agreement and Dave turned and led the way. As they neared the fire, the boy let out another scream. That was the fourth time, and he was beginning to sound weak and hoarse.

Dave stopped and motioned with his hand, the three Cherokee were on this side of the fire and in the edge of the shadows. Andrew counted nine Shawnee, instead of eight. He could tell they felt secure and were all staring towards the fire and the boy withering on the ground.

Quickly, and quietly the three travelers picked their men and eased down on their bellies and quietly moved forward.

The Shawnee danced around, hooting and shouting, doing their war dance. Fortunately, they were not paying any attention to their prisoners.

Andrew reached his tree and with one slash of his knife, cut the rawhide bindings on the hands of his Indian. The Indian froze, and then he looked at his companions and saw the surprise and uncertainty on their faces. He shook his head to indicate they should remain still until the right time, whenever that might be. He felt the knife pressed into his palm and must have figured some of his people had come to rescue them. As Andrew moved back to where he had left his rifle lying, he could see the Indian flexing and moving his hands to get circulation back in them. They wouldn't wait long before they made their move, and so much depended on Andrew and his men getting a clear shot before the frenzy began.

Andrew picked up his gun and pulled back the cock. He saw Dave and Hans in the shadows doing the same. Just then, one of the Indians bent and rolled another red coal out of the fire and picked it up with two sticks. He turned around twice, held up the coal, sort of whipped it in the wind to make it glow even more. He took two steps toward the boy and out of the corner of his eye he saw one of the Indians come to his knees and start to move.

At that moment, Andrew fired and blew a hole in the middle of the Indians chest and he collapsed where he was standing. The sound of two more shots rang out and two more Indians fell. Andrew drew one of his pistols and fired, bringing down a forth one.

By now, the three Cherokees were in the battle. The biggest of the three brought his target down with a savage lunge that sank the knife to the hilt in the Shawnee's side. The other two had not been so lucky to get a quick kill. They had been startled by the shots, and had hesitated just a second before making their move. This gave the two Shawnees time to raise their weapons to fire. But in the time it took them to cock their rifles, the Cherokees seized the opportunity of the brief pause and thrust their knives into the two Shawnees.

One of the Shawnee received a massive gash across his forearm and down one side, but he was far from being out of the fight. He was badly wounded but, he still had enough fight in him that the Cherokee had his hands full.

The third Cherokee met a swinging gun butt and received the blow on the side of his head. It dropped him, and the Shawnee raised his rifle to finish him when a roar like a mountain lion distracted him. He turned to see a black form rushing at him from the dark. He was partially blinded from the flames of the campfire. He swung his gun to shoot at the wild animal charging toward him but it was too late. The charging animal struck him with the jolt of a bull. Dave rolled to his feet and as he did he scooped up the knife and turned to face the Indian. Now recognition dawned on the Indian's face and he realized they were being attacked by white men. If there was anyone he hated more than Cherokees it was white men. He drew his knife and began circling Dave.

Andrew saw Hans wade into another Indian who had fired once and missed and was trying to reload. Hans hit him on the run and bowled him over. The Indian dropped his gun and the two rolled on the ground. The Indian had a wooden club attached to his belt and tried to get it free.

Andrew had almost completed reloading his rifle when he glanced up and saw two more Shawnee coming from out of the darkness. They had been minding the horses and had not previously been seen.

This was not good. That meant there were six Shawnee left, with one wounded badly from the earlier knife fight. There were the three of them and the three Cherokees, one of which was out cold on the ground.

Andrew yelled at Hans, "There are two more coming from the horses." Then he pulled the other pistol and fired on one of the two Indians coming out of the dark. One went down, but the other raised his rifle and Andrew saw the fire spurt toward him. Something hit him in the side like a tree limb. That was the last he remembered as darkness came over him.

The fight raged on. The first Cherokee Indian that had killed his man turned just as the rifle carried by the Shawnee went off. With a wide swing, he cut the Indian's throat, almost severing his head from his shoulders. Without waiting for the Shawnee to drop, he charged toward the last standing enemy that was not engaged in hand to hand combat.

The angered Shawnee swung his lance, attempting to plunge it into Hans' back. The Indian had turned slightly aside and didn't see the Cherokee coming until it was too late. He forgot Hans and instead tried to bring the lance between him and the charging Indian. When he saw he would not be able to do so, he dropped the lance and reached for an ax he carried on his belt. He was just a second too late at that also. Before he could get it clear, the Cherokee was on him, and although the Shawnee had raised a hide shield to protect himself, the ferocity of the charge knocked him over. Both fell toward the ground. As he was falling, the Cherokee brought the knife in front of him with the blade pointed toward the Shawnee. When he landed, he let the full weight of his body slam onto the handle of the knife. It plunged through the shield and into the Shawnee's body beneath him. The breath left the Shawnee in a wheeze. The knife had gone through a lung and red froth bubbled out of his mouth. The Cherokee withdrew the knife and slashed it across the dying Indian's throat.

The Cherokee rolled free and came to his knees taking in the scene through the haze of dust now rising from all the fighting. He glanced to his friend and saw him go in under the arm of the man he was fighting. His friend slashed the assailant across the belly, then watched as the man stood, transfixed as his intestines rolled out of his stomach. The wounded savage lowered his hands to catch his spilling gut, as the Cherokee's knife plunged deep into his neck just above the collar bone.

Hans had broken the neck of his Shawnee opponent, and was lowering the limp body to the ground.

The struggle between Dave and the other Indian was still going on. Both were bloody, but Hans couldn't tell whose blood it was. He picked up one of the rifles that had fallen to the ground and checked it. It had not been fired. He quickly checked the pan and pulled back the cock, intending to shoot the remaining Indian and put a stop to it. Just as he raised the rifle, the Indian swung at Dave. But Dave ducked under the blow, causing the Indian to swing through and go off balance. Before he could recover, Dave plunged the knife into the exposed stomach and yanked upward, splitting him from gut to the middle of his chest. The Indian collapsed against him. Dave put his foot against him and pulled on the knife. It had been embedded in bone and there was a scraping sound as it tore loose.

As quickly as it began, it was over. The entire skirmish lasted less than three minutes. The two Cherokee that were in the fight stared at their rescuers, showing surprise to find them white. The biggest Indian went to the one tied down and cut him loose. He helped him stand and supported him. The other moved over to his friend on the ground; this one hadn't moved since he was hit with the rifle.

Hans looked around and realized Andrew wasn't nearby. Then he saw him crumpled on the ground. He yelled to Dave and they both raced to Andrew's side. They saw where the bullet had hit, looked at each other, and their faces went grim. Hans ripped the shirt open to reveal a gaping hole with blood seeping out. He probed with his finger and pushed his hand behind him.

Hans looked at Dave and said, "The bullet went on through but left a hell of a hole. He is losing blood fast. It didn't get his heart. If it didn't get a lung, he might make it. He is still breathing."

The three Indians and the boy came over and looked down at the white man on the ground. Hans was busy pushing cloth into the hole to stop the bleeding. The big Indian said something to the second Indian who turned and disappeared into the dark. He returned in a couple minutes with a double hand full of a dark moss. He handed it to Hans and motioned for him to use that to plug the hole.

The big Indian supporting the boy moved him to a log and helped him sit. The big one spoke quietly to the other two. They disappeared into the woods again and returned in a few minutes with two long poles. They laid them on the ground and spread two of the dead Shawnee's blankets over the poles and tied the ends together; they had improvised a sled. Then they picked up Andrew's feet while Hans raised his torso, and eased him onto the blanket-wrapped poles.

Dave used his small vocabulary of Cherokee and he explained that their camp was only about a quarter mile from here across a little stream. He invited the Cherokee to come to the camp if they wished. The Indians looked at each other and nodded their heads. Dave and Hans quickly gathered up all the guns, putting theirs in the stretcher with Andrew, while the Indians wrapped all the weapons of the Shawnee in two other blankets. They each carried a blanket of arms while the big Indian all but carried the boy. The boy was almost delirious from pain and babbled.

It was a rough journey, and they feared the bouncing and bumping might kill Andrew before they reached camp. After what seemed like hours, they crossed the little stream and climbed the hill. The deadfall loomed in the darkness. They were relieved to reach camp; Andrew weighed a thousand pounds.

Hans rolled up some straw and spread Andrew's blankets, Dave kindled a fire. It was still dangerous to have a fire, but right now they needed hot water and light to see by; they could not wait until daylight. If there was any chance of saving Andrew, what could be done would have to be done quickly. Otherwise, he would likely bleed to death by morning.

Dave handed one of the Indians the bucket and indicated he wanted it filled. The Cherokee nodded in understanding and raced toward the creek. By the time he returned, the fire was well underway. Dave set the bucket on the fire, dipped out enough to fill the coffee pot and poured coffee in. He reached into one of the packs and withdrew a box of salve. He handed it to the big Indian and motioned for him to rub it on the burns of the boy. The burns are not likely to kill him, but if infection set in, that might.

There were livid sores where the hot coals had burned the young boy. Five spots covered almost his entire belly, from his chest down to his navel. They were wicked burns and Dave knew he was in excruciating pain. Burns are more painful than cuts or rifle wounds. The big Indian tenderly smeared the salve on the boy. There was a slight resemblance and Dave gathered that the older Indian was perhaps an older brother.

With the water now heated, Dave brought a small pan to Andrew's pallet. Hans had cut Andrew's shirt free and they saw the blood still oozing around the moss. Two of the Indians disappeared toward the creek and returned in a few minutes with large gobs of moss dripping wet. Dave took a piece of the shirt and washed away as much of the blood and any dirt that he could. They turned Andrew slightly and washed his back also. While they had him tilted up, Dave stuffed more moss into the back and pulled a cloth underneath him. Then he placed more moss on the hole in Andrew's chest and tied the cloth tightly around him to hold the moss in place.

He looked at Hans, "That is all I know to do. If he lives till morning, we will see what else we might do."

They all moved over to the fire and Dave pulled out extra mugs and poured everyone a cup of coffee.

The Indians watched as the white men took a swig of the steaming liquid before touching it to their own lips. All three jerked the cups away. It was apparent these white men could stand much pain, else how could they drink this fiery liquid? Once it cooled, they sipped and drank. It was not the first time they'd had coffee, but it was the first time they'd had white man's coffee. It tasted rather good.

After a few sips, Dave attempted to introduce himself and Hans to the Indians. Afterward, he motioned to where Andrew was lying and said, "Our chief, Andrew."

They grunted their acknowledgment and understanding. Then the big Cherokee Indian stood and said in a proud voice, "I am Night Hawk, oldest son of Great Eagle, a sub chief of the Cherokee Nation. This is my younger brother Howling Wolf." He pointed to the other two Indians. "These are two of my cousins of the Natchez tribe. They are warriors from the Wolf Dog Society. They are Black Bear and Runs Long."

Dave asked, "How did the Shawnee get you?"

Night Hawk looked embarrassed, but pulled himself up proudly and said, "We had been hunting all day and when evening came, we went to bathe in the lake. We had no warning that anyone was near. While we bathed, these dogs stole our clothes and our weapons. Then as we came out of the water, they surrounded us with drawn weapons. We had no chance to fight. They were cruel and enjoyed inflicting pain. My brother has not yet earned his warrior's title. They knew he would be the easiest to break, and they knew that by torturing him, they would hurt us most, for any of us would have traded places with him. We have you to thank for our lives."

Dave waved the thanks away, and asked another question. "How far is your village from here, and in which direction?"

"We are perhaps a half day's journey from our village. They tied ropes around our necks and made us run behind their horses until we almost dropped. They dragged us some, but they did not want to choke us to death. That would have spoiled their games. Our village is northeast of here; near the territory you call North Carolina at the foot of the mountains."

When the conversation lulled, Night Hawk said, "Can I leave my brother with you? He is not able to travel. We will go back and get the horses, our clothes and other things. The Shawnee will have no use of them now." When Dave signed O.K., the three rose and disappeared into the night.

He and Hans went to check on Andrew again and judged the time must be close to three in the morning. It seemed forever since they had heard that first scream, but it had been only less than two hours.

There was nothing more they could do for Andrew or for the boy, so they decided to get some rest. They rolled in their blankets, and when the Indians returned, they turned the Indian ponies into the enclosure where the other horses were. Just before the Shawnee had captured them, they had killed a large stag and they had carried this back with them. Then, they too, rolled into their blankets.

Except Night Hawk.

He took a rifle and climbed up on the trunk of one of the large trees in the deadfall and sat hunched under his blanket. He would not again be taken by surprise. Except for these white men, they would all be dead now. As the night wore on, he tried to figure why they had come to help them. While the white-man and the Indian were not at war, there was little friendship between them. The Indians distrusted the white-man, and the white-man hated the Indian. Neither understood the other's ways. Their help may have cost them the life of their chief. Yet neither of the other two seemed bitter or angry that he may have died defending an Indian. Strange.

When the daylight came it was a brilliant, sunshiny day, but a cold wind had begun and Night Hawk knew that by night fall snow would probably be falling. If the white man was still alive, it would be important to get him inside out of the cold. His brother also needed more attention than he could give.

Before going to sleep they had placed a large chunk of the meet near the fire and it looked as if it was cooked now, if not, by the time they got water heated for coffee, it would be done enough to eat.

He descended to the ground and motioned to the two warriors. They talked briefly and then went to where Dave and Hans were kneeling beside their chief. He asked, "How is he?"

Dave responded, "There doesn't seem to be any change.

We need a doctor, but there probably isn't one in a thousand miles."

"There is a doctor in my cousin's village. She is an old and wise woman. She could help save his life. The wind from the north sends a message that Mother Winter is on her way. It may turn the ground white by tonight. We will be leaving shortly to go to our village for our families will be worried that we have not returned. These are troubling times and they will send out search parties for us. We would consider it an honor if you would come to our village and allow us to help care for your chief."

"We are afraid to move him. He cannot ride and we have no wagon to carry him in. Yet we know that we cannot stay long here. As you say, winter is here. If he gets chilled he will surly die."

Dave turned to Hans, "It is closer to their village than it is back to Rosedale or to Memphis. What do you think?"

Hans replied, "I don't think we have any choice. Maybe they have some medicine or something that will help him. At least he would be out of the cold. It will probably kill him to stay here, and it may kill him to try to move him, but I guess we need to try."

Sensing that they had reached agreement, Night Hawk spoke quickly to Black Bear and Runs Long. They took hatchets and walked into the forest. Shortly they returned with four long slender poles. Quickly, they saddled two of the horses and then ran the butt end of the poles along the sides of the horses and tied them in place. Next, they took several rawhide thongs and wove them back and forth across the poles behind the horses. They took smaller branches and wove them in and out between the rawhide and over this they put a piece of hide. Then they laid two blankets down on top of the hide and motioned for Hans and Dave to help them lay Andrew on the blankets.

The five of them lifted him gently and placed him on the blankets. Night Hawk wrapped another blanket around him and tied him in place with more rawhide. When he was finished, Andrew looked like a papoose in a blanket. Now Andrew could be dragged along behind the horses and not jolted as he would have been if he were riding. The branches sprung up and down, cushioning the shock of any bumps.

Both Hans and Dave had seen the Indians use this method before to carry their belongings, small children and old people. It was an excellent way to travel. They called it a travois. This increased Andrew's chances of surviving the trip.

The Indians quickly made a second travois for the boy and wrapped him in it. He was barely conscious. During the night he had lapsed into a sort of stupor. It was as if the shock and the pain were too much for him. Like Andrew, they had to get him to where better care could be provided for him.

Hans loaded the pack mule, and they tied Andrew's horse and the extra horses on lead lines. It was almost 10 in the morning by the time they started out. They made good time, but by noon, the wind had increased and a few small snowflakes began to fall. Night Hawk instructed Runs Long to ride on to the village and bring back some help. They were still three or four hours away at the pace they were going, and it was getting colder. Struggling with the horses, and trying to pick the easiest route to follow, was costing them time. Runs Long was off like a shot. Night Hawk knew he would ride that horse to death if he had to.

In just over two hours Runs Long was back with five other Indians. They took charge of the horses and one got on the back of each of the two horses pulling the travois. With them guiding the horses and urging them on they begin to make better time. In another hour they came in sight of the village.

As they rode down the path into the village, Dave and Hans noted that the Natchez did not live in tepees like other Indians they had visited. They had rounded huts made of thatch and grass, coated on the outside with mud. The doors of the huts were covered with two leather hides, one on the outside and another inside the door. The Indians came out to stand in front of their huts. They were wrapped in blankets, for now, the cold wind was whistling and snow was falling fast.

Night Hawk stopped in front of a hut and slid off his horse. He untied the thongs that held Andrew in place and said, "This is Black Bear's lodge. He and his wife will stay with Runs Long. You and your friend can stay here. They are taking my brother on to my uncle's lodge. Let's get your friend into bed and I will go get the doctor to take a look at him."

They lifted Andrew off the travois and carried him inside. There was a small fire in the center of the lodge and robes had been thrown across a bed of pine needles. It was the closest thing to a bed you would find out here. While Hans brought all their gear in off the pack horse and the saddle bags, Dave checked the wound. The moss was soaked and the back wound had opened. The one in the front had clotted and surprisingly had not reopened. When he finished, he spread a tanned doeskin over Andrew and then covered him with a big bearskin rug. Andrew had begun to run a fever and that could mean his wound had become infected.

Just as Dave finished, the flap of the hut raised, and an old woman came inside followed by Night Hawk. He introduced her as the village medicine woman. She looked to be nearly 90 years old, yet she moved with the ease of a younger person. Her skin was crinkled and looked like tanned leather. She walked with a cane and was slightly stooped, but it was her eyes that caught Dave's attention. They were a light blue. Most Indians eyes were brown or black. This was the first one he had ever seen with blue eyes, and a light blue at that.

Night Hawk told him her name, and he knew how she had come by the name. She was Sky Eyes. She moved quickly to the side of the bed and folded the skins back so she could see the wound. She placed two fingers beside the hole in his chest and pressed downward slightly, then did the same against the rib cage. When one of the ribs moved, she grunted. Then she asked Night Hawk to help her turn him up so she could examine the back. She did the same around the wound there. Then she reached into a bag she had brought and took out a square of tanned doeskin about five inches square. She spread a black looking ointment on the doeskin and placed the doeskin over the wound in his back and pressed it gently. Then she took another patch and placed it on top of the first. When that was done she laid him back down on his back. His weight kept the patch in place. She rearranged the bed so that his head was elevated at about a 15-degree angle. She removed the moss from the wound in front and placed another patch with ointment over the hole.

Next, she took out some herbs and placed them in a pot of boiling water that was setting near the fire. In just a couple of minutes a strange, pungent smell began to permeate the lodge. She took the pot off and poured up a cup of the brew. It looked a little like tea, but didn't smell like any tea either of them had ever smelled before. She took a spoon made out of a bone and scooped up a spoonful, opened his mouth and dribbled it into his mouth. She watched to see what reaction there would be. She repeated this process four or five times, hesitating a few seconds after each one and examining the injured area. After about six or seven spoonful's, she turned to Night Hawk and spoke in a dialect Dave did not understand.

Night Hawk looked at Dave and attempted to translate. "Sky Eyes said that the bullet broke one of his ribs where it went in but she does not believe it punctured his lung or he would have died before now. Because he has lived this long, if we can control the fever and infection, he may live. The most danger is the wound in the back. It is still seeping and she wants to keep it open so that any blood inside the body can drain out. That will reduce the chances of infection. The front is already starting to heal. What condition the rib will be in is hard to say. It may grow back together and it may always give him trouble. If it doesn't grow back together the pieces may pose a serious problem to him later. They will not be firm and braced like the other ribs. If he were to receive a hard blow at just the right spot, it could drive one of the broken pieces into his lung, which would kill him.

"He must have liquids put into him. This tonic she has made must be given to him every two hours to keep his fever under control. My aunt and my sister will bring you food and will stay to help you if you wish them to. Do not give him much water at one time, but make sure that he gets about a cupful every hour, a few spoons full at a time. She will come back tomorrow to see how he is doing. Rest and time are the things he needs most right now."

When Night Hawk finished, they went out and closed the flap.

Hans picked up the cup and spoon and began to spoon the liquid into Andrew's mouth, a little at a time. He took a taste of it and spit it out. He looked at Dave and smiled. "She may be a smart old lady, but she sure makes a bad cup of tea. It's a good thing Andrew is unconscious. He couldn't stand this otherwise."

They didn't say as much, but they had come to love and respect this man they worked for, and they were very worried about him at this moment.

Within an hour, the flap of the lodge raised and an Indian woman of about 40 entered. She was not near as fat as most Indian women her age and she had a pretty smile. They figured this must be Night Hawk's aunt. She was followed in by two young girls. The first wasn't over 15 but she was a younger version of the mother and had already begun to fill out her doeskin dress. She was very shy and stayed behind her mother.

The other girl was more mature, probably in her early or mid-20s. There was hardly any resemblance between her and the older woman. Hans guessed this must be Night Hawk's sister. She was a pretty girl, not strikingly beautiful, but pretty in a calm, self-assured way. There was little shyness about her. She came forward, setting bowls and cups in front of them. Then her aunt handed her a large pot and she spooned out a stew into the bowls. There were large chunks of meat, potatoes and onions and a green vegetable that was strange to them. Then she placed a pone of bread beside the bowls. She poured what looked like tea into the cups and bade them to eat.

The two men watched her in silence.

Her hands were long and slender and the skin of her arms was brown below the sleeve of her dress, but was surprisingly light underneath the sleeve. She had nice firm breasts that pushed at the tunic she had on and as she kneeled in front of them they could see slim tanned legs to well above the knee. She had well rounded hips and a flat belly. This was one Indian that had not let herself go to pot.

When she finished, she arose and stood looking squarely at them as if sensing their thoughts.

They were so engrossed in watching her that they had not taken a bite. She had to tell them again to eat.

The glances they had given her were not lost on the aunt, and she shot a look at the older girl that was a warning. But the girl did not seem concerned. She moved over and kneeled beside Andrew. She picked up the cup and spoon and spooned several spoons full of the tea into him. She ran her hand underneath the skin and turned to the men.

"You have not taken his pants off and he has wet them. Give me a hand." She removed the skin, unbuckled his pants and motioned for Hans to pull them off over his feet. Then she did the same for his drawers, leaving him stark naked. She moved him slightly and the mother slid a dry skin under him. Then she put the cover back over him and got up to leave.

Hans thanked her and the mother for the food and the women left.

Andrew slept fitfully that night. They took turns spooning the tea into him. Twice more, he wet himself and they dried him off as best they could. When the mother and the younger girl brought them food in the morning, the two men were very tired. They had been up almost 48 hours now.

Sky Eyes came about 8 o'clock and checked him again. She made another pot of tea for him and left. Night Hawk stopped by and they asked how his brother was doing. He said he was awake and he would live, but he would have very bad scars on his stomach all his life. He said that Sky Eyes had told him that the next 24 hours would be critical for Andrew. He was running a small fever but that it might go up very high later that day and night. That they should bring in snow and rub it over his body if it got too high. If he survived the next night and day, he would probably live. Under no circumstances should they let him get cold or his body get chilled. He needed all his energy to fight the infection and none could be wasted fighting off the cold.

The weather continued to turn colder and colder. The winds whistled outside and each time someone entered, snow blew in through the flap. Hans went to check on the livestock and came back with ice cycles on his eyebrows. He said the Indians had moved them back into a canyon to keep them from drifting with the wind.

In the morning part of the day, Andrew seemed to rest comfortably, but as the afternoon came, his fever began to rise. They rubbed him with snow and continued to spoon the tea into him. By dark, his fever was high and he was delirious, talking in his sleep, calling first Helen then Catherine. Then he thought he was talking with his dad. Finally, Hans went to Night Hawk's lodge and asked if he would speak once more to Sky Eyes. The Indian girl heard him speaking and she came forward with a blanket around her and said she would go and help take care of him. Hans walked back to the hut with her and she could see the concerned look spread across both Hans and Dave. They loved this man and would do anything for him, but they did not know what to do and they were near exhaustion.

Night Hawk came and said Sky Eyes would not come out in this weather, that she would pray to the Great Spirit for his help, but the decision was his now.

Dave had learned the girl's name was Bright Day and he thought that fit her well. She was certainly a bright spot in someone's life. She came in now and went directly to the pallet and pulled the covers off Andrew. He has wet and he had sweated until everything was wet. She removed the skins and blankets and put new ones down then covered him back again. She spooned more tea into him and scooped up several hands full of snow and washed his face and arms with it. Then the fever seemed to break and he began to rest easy. It was almost midnight, when he began to shiver and shake. She was sitting beside him holding his hand when he began to shake almost uncontrollably. She rose and rubbed his body to increase the circulation and they could tell she was worried. Up to this point she had remained calm as if she had everything under control. Now she was disturbed.

She said to them, "We have to stop this chill. He is shaking so bad he will open all the wounds inside him and start bleeding again. His body is losing heat."

Dave spoke to her, "We have piled more blankets on him but it doesn't seem to help."

Then she seemed to reach a decision. She said, "We must bring his body heat back up. If he stays chilled he will die before morning. There is only one thing left to do. Turn your heads to the wall."

They did as she bade them do, but Dave, wondering what she had in mind, turned back to glance toward the bed and saw her untie the strap over her shoulder and let the doeskin dress drop to the floor. The fire flickered and he could see her naked body in all its glory. She was one perfect woman from head to foot. She stepped over Andrew's body, next to the wall, raised the skin and blankets and crawled in next to him. She pressed against him and hugged him close to her as she would a small child. She placed one leg over his and Dave could all but imagine her skin and the hair between her thighs pushing against his body. She was sharing her body heat with him. He thought, "Too bad, Andrew won't remember any of this when he wakes up." Then he turned back to face the wall.

Dave and Hans both dozed off. About four in the morning, they heard her moving around and turned just as she dropped her dress over her head. She punched up the fire and said, "The fever has broken. I think he will be alright now. I will go home."

Dave thanked her and she left the hut.

CHAPTER EIGHTEEN

For the next six days, Andrew remained unconscious and Bright Day spent most of every day and part of the nights with him. She patiently spooned broth into him and cleaned him when needed. It was as if she had taken over the nursing all by herself. The aunt and younger girl came in to help her change his bed and clean him up, but she would spend the rest of the time alone with him.

Finally, his fever broke. Bright Day came in early one morning and hurried Hans and Dave out of the hut. She said Night Hawk and some of the braves were going on a hunt and they should go along. She would stay and take care of Andrew. The men had been cooped up in the hut for most of a week, except for brief trips to check on their animals, and they were anxious to get out.

It was Dave who first noted that a fairly large number of braves were going along, more than would have been expected on an ordinary hunt. He mentioned it to Hans.

Hans looked around and said, "Yes, and do you note that they are taking their war-bows and have their war-paint on? I suspect this hunt will be for more than wild game."

As they were saddling up their ponies, Night Hawk came to them. "I told my sister and my uncle that we were going on one big hunt before I leave to return to my people. But I have a different hunt in mind. Black Bear and Runs

Long have gathered almost fifty braves who are anxious to find the Shawnee if they are still in our territory. We have had several scouts out since the snow stopped and we think there are some still in the area.

"The Choctaws to the South are looking for them and the Chickasaws to the North are also out scouting for them. Normally they do not stay this long. They will raid a village or the white farmers, rape and destroy and then head back. Most of them seem to have already left. But there is one group that has raided all the way down to the salt water and we think they are on their way back north."

Night Hawk looked at each of them, and with determination in his voice, he continued, "We plan to catch them if we can and repay them for the harm they did to my brother. We intend to teach them a lesson about raiding in our villages and in our lands. You are welcome to come along if you wish, but this is not your fight."

Dave looked at Hans. After a brief pause Hans spoke, "Night Hawk, we will ride along with you because we have been cramped up and need to stretch our legs. If we are attacked we will fight with you, but we do not like killing just for killing sake. It is not our way. We did what we did when we came to help you because you were being tortured and would have been killed. We knew there was no reasoning with the Shawnee. We killed eleven of them, and only received two wounded. To our way of thinking, the score is settled. We will hunt with you, and if we are set upon, we will fight. But we do not want to go searching for a fight. I hope you understand. To us, all life is sacred. Our God teaches that we should not kill. We kill only in self-defense. We do not even kill animals unnecessarily, only for food. It leaves a scar upon our soul every time we have to kill another human, no matter if he is white or Indian."

Night Hawk looked at him for a long time, then he said,

"I do not understand your ways, and I do not understand your God, but I respect you for your thoughts. I had never thought about it the way you just explained to me. To an Indian, if he is harmed, or one of his tribe is hurt or killed, we feel we are honor bound to seek revenge. If they kill one of us, we must kill five of them. But I have been on these raids before, and it does not erase the pain for the ones we have lost. And often, in the need to get revenge, we lose other friends and warriors. When you have an enemy and are mad at him, it is hard to think that he too is some mother's son and if we kill him, his friends will come seeking revenge against us. Thus the war goes on and never ends. Perhaps your God sees the wisdom of fighting only to defend yourself. It is something I will think upon."

Everyone mounted up and rode out into the forest. They headed westward, toward the big river. Most of the Indian trails run parallel to the river and the scouts are observed as they study each path to see if there are any Shawnee that have not returned yet. In the meantime, they engaged in hunting, but only with bows, arrows and spears. Gunshots carry too far and they wanted to remain as quiet as possible.

Dave and Hans joined the hunters. Dave was almost as good with a bow as the Indians, but Hans, not as much. He preferred to use the spear and successfully killed a couple of wild hogs. By night fall, the band had taken five deer, several wild hogs, some wild turkeys and sage hens. The game was gutted and loaded on horses. Several of the warriors and three of the youngest boys were detailed to go back to the village with the meat. Dave and Hans agree to accompany them.

A couple of miles from the village, a horse pounded up behind them. Their first inclination was to take cover and be ready to fight, but the manner in which the horse was being ridden indicated it was not an attack. One of the Natchez from the main band skidded to a halt and jabbered to the Indians with the meat. Everyone became very excited and orders were given for the three younger boys to take the meat on to the village. The warriors originally accompanying the meat haul turned their horses and joined the messenger, and they all took off to rejoin the main group.

When they had gone, Dave asked the younger boys what happened. The Indians told them that they had located a band of about twenty Shawnee returning from the coast and were tracking them now, waiting for the right moment to attack. The older warriors had gone back to join in the fight. The younger ones were disappointed they couldn't go also.

Dave kicked his horse into motion and Hans followed suit. It was their job to get the meat to the village. The others would take care of themselves; at least they hoped they would.

Shortly after dark they arrived at the village and left the meat to be distributed according to tribal custom. They took a foreleg of one of the deer and hacked off the hind quarter of one of the hogs and left the rest for the Indians. They wanted to get to the hut to see how Andrew was.

As they entered the hut, they noticed that the room had been cleaned and new pine boughs had been brought in to improve the scent of the room. Bright Day was sitting on a low stool near Andrew's bed. They moved over to her and she could see the question in their eyes. Before they spoke she said, "No he has not yet awakened but he is doing well. His breathing seems stronger today and he has had lots of good warm soup. I believe he is going to be alright."

"How long do you think it will be before he awakens?"

"No one knows, except the Great Spirit, and He won't tell. But I do not think you need to worry. He is better each day now."

This satisfied them and they went about their business of getting something to eat.

Just a little past mid-day the next day, the braves returned. They raided the Shawnee and killed fifteen of them. Their hair is hanging from lances and from their belts. Blood is still dripping from the scalps. Most of the braves are jubilant, but Hans noticed that there are three bodies across saddles and Night Hawk was very solemn. Their progression into the village slowly resulted in first one, then another and finally several women wailing. The wives, mothers and sisters of those killed wailed to show their sadness for the loss of their loved ones.

Night Hawk stopped in front of the hut where Andrew was being cared for and said to Hans, "You are right to not seek revenge. We have blooded the enemy and he will think twice about coming into our territory again, but we have paid a heavy price. There will be much weeping in our village tonight and in the village of the Shawnee. Only three of their number escaped. We have captured all of their stuff taken in the raids. But it is a very hollow victory and next year, we will have to watch very closely for their brothers and friends will be seeking revenge against us. It has been this way for all time. I think I might learn more about this God of yours. He seems very wise."

Then he added, "We have regained five women that the Shawnee had taken captive. One is a white woman. Will you speak with her? She is afraid of all of us."

Hans said he would and Night Hawk led him to where the women were standing. The white woman was close to thirty. She had been beaten and her clothes were in tatters. She had been so mistreated that she was almost in a trance. Hans walked to her and spoke to her in English. "Miss, my name is Hans and you are safe now. These Indians are friends of ours and they will not harm you. What is your name?"

The woman looked up, and when she saw him, some reason seemed to return to her. She mumbled something that he could not hear. He asked her to repeat her name again. This time she found her voice and said, "My name is Magdalene Harper."

Hans turned to Night Hawk and asked if he could take her to his hut and help dress her wounds. He agreed.

The other four women were somewhat younger than the white woman. They were all Choctaws and the Natchez women were already administering to them. Night Hawk indicated that they would send a messenger to the nearest Choctaw village and inform them that they could come get their women. Hans led the woman to their hut and asked her to enter. At first she hesitated and Hans spoke to her again telling her she had nothing to worry about. They meant her no harm. She bowed and went into the hut. When she saw Bright Day and the injured white man she seemed a little less apprehensive.

Bright Day came forward and offered her water and a basin to wash in. Dave brought her a bowl of food which she wolfed down as soon as she had washed up. She had not said a word until she finished eating, then she looked at the two men and spoke for the first time. "Am I free from those savages?"

Hans answered. "Yes. You are free. You don't have to be afraid anymore. As soon as we can we will return you to your people."

Then she began to cry. Huge tears ran down her cheeks and her body shook with the sobbing. Hans put his arms around her and held her close to him, trying to reassure her and to soothe her fears.

Bright Day sat beside Andrew's bed and watched. She seemed to share the woman's sorrow. Friends of hers had been captured in the past by unfriendly Indians and she knew the stories of how cruel they could be and she also could imagine the indignities this white woman had to endure. Indian men seemed to prefer the white women and she imagined the degradation and pain this woman had suffered. Noting the woman's clothes were hardly enough to cover her private parts, Bright Day left the hut, and returned with a dress and jacket made of a fine doeskin.

When the woman's sobbing subsided, Hans indicated that he and Dave would step out of the hut so she could finish cleansing herself and change clothes. Bright Day said she would help her and she went to get more water.

The two men stood just outside the hut smoking their pipes and were silent. Dave could tell that Hans was deeply moved by the woman's plight and waited for Hans to start the conversation.

Finally, Hans spoke. "If I had known they were taking white women prisoners I would have gone looking for them myself. I wonder how many people died at their hands."

Dave was silent a moment longer, then he answered, "There is no telling. They have been raiding for almost two weeks now. They hit several villages and homesteads each day. I'm surprised they stayed down here this long. They must have been crazy for they knew that these Indians would mount a campaign to find them."

Hans spoke again. "They must have been having so much fun with the women and the food and drink they captured that they lost sight of where they were and the danger of remaining down here so long. Miss Harper is in a bad way. They must have treated her very badly. I'm glad that Night Hawk's band found them. I wish I had gone with them now."

"Ole Hoss, this is not the first white woman captured and ravaged by the Indians. It won't be the last. It is fortunate that she was rescued by Night Hawk and we were here.

Otherwise, she might have been traded to another band, sold or taken as a wife by one of the local braves. You know how these things are done. There are probably many white women and white children in the Indian camps out in these woods. They have been raiding and stealing women and children for the last hundred years. There are a lot of half-breed children roaming these woods who have been brought up believing they are full Indian."

"I know, but this is the first time in all my travels that I have been this close to one of them. I am going to ask Night Hawk to release her to me and I intend to return her to her people."

Dave didn't say anything, but he looked at his old friend and wondered why this particular woman had become of such interest to him all at once.

Bright Day indicated they could come back into the hut and they reentered. The woman had washed off most of the dirt and had put on the clean clothes that Bright Day had brought her. She had thrown her old dress in the fire. The men both noticed that in addition to being badly torn it had blood on it in a number of places.

If you looked beyond the scratches and bruises on her face and arms, she was an attractive woman. Not beautiful in the classic sense, but attractive never-the-less. Her face was sort of rounded and she had blue eyes. Dave figured she was of either German or Danish ancestry. Perhaps that is what had taken hold of Hans so much, because he was German and he felt a kindred spirit with this woman. Her hair was a sandy blond and hung almost to her waist. She was a full bodied woman, with large breasts and amply rounded hips. If she had children it had not ruined her figure. She was solidly built and seemed strong. She probably had worked in the fields with her man and that had kept her body firm and relatively trim. The callouses on her hands bore this out, for her hands were rough, like a man's. Dave judged her age at between 30 and 35. She was roughly 5 feet and 9 or 10 inches tall. Fairly tall for a woman, yet she probably would not have topped more than 125 lbs. on the scales. It was apparent that she had been badly used by the Indians.

Hans went over and sat down near her. He began talking to her. "Ma'am, my name is Hans Brinkman and this is my friend Dave Foster. We are travelling with this man over here as his guide. He has been injured in a fight with the Indians but this is a friendly tribe and they are helping us take care of him until he gets well. You are safe here with us and no one will harm you. I swear to that. Do you feel like talking? Can you tell me who you are and where you came from?"

At first she was hesitant, and then she began to tell her story.

"My name is Magdalene Harper. Me and my husband and two children lived down near the coast in what is known as the Florida territory. We had moved west about two years ago and had taken up a homestead. We built a small cabin first and last year we had just a garden with enough to feed us through the winter. This year we cleared about twenty acres and put in corn, potatoes and other vegetables for us and about fifteen acres of cotton. My husband figured we could sell that in Mobile or in the small town of Pensacola and get enough money to improve the cabin and perhaps clear another twenty acres this winter."

She let out a deep sigh. "The Indians came upon us without warning. We were both working in the field when we heard the children scream. We looked up and saw the Indians circling my little girl and son. The girl was only four years old and the boy was nine. We had left our guns at the edge of the field and had worked our way about two hundred yards down the row, planting. We made a dash for the guns, but before we could get to them, more Indians rode out of the woods. One of them ran a long lance through my husband and he died there in the field."

She broke down and cried again. Hans held her hand and waited. His face was bleak and his jaw was set.

After a few moments, she continued her story.

"The sight of blood seemed to whip them into frenzy. One of the Indians circling the children grabbed up my son and began to ride away with him. Another drew back a club and hit my little girl in the head. I heard her skull crush all the way into the field."

Now, sobs wracked her body as she remembered the horrible scene.

"Three of the Indians jumped off their horses and grabbed me. I fought them with the hoe that I had in my hands and they laughed, a woman with a hoe against three armed Indians. As they came near and tried to grab me, I swung at one and barely scraped his arm, but it cut enough to bring blood. He became enraged and wanted to kill me. But when I swung again, the other two grabbed me from behind and they prevented the other one from killing me. I wish they had let me die on the spot.

"They tied my hands and feet and put me across one of the horses they had taken out of our corral. We rode for about two hours and as it was getting dark they met another band. All total, it seemed now about fifty warriors. They had several prisoners; three French women, about a dozen Indian girls and five or six young boys, all under 10 years old, including my son. That night, they made sport of the women, taking us time and time again until we were hurt and bleeding. One of the French girls took her life and two of the younger Indian girls were killed. I don't know if they were killed by the braves or died from the abuse they received.

"The next morning we were dazed and could hardly move around. They wouldn't let us out of their sight. We had to relieve ourselves, and doctor our private parts as best we could in front of them. They joked and laughed at our injuries and our attempts to hide ourselves from their view. We were given a little food that morning and let go to a spring nearby to drink. As we passed where the boys were huddled in fear, I saw my son and called to him, mainly to let him know I was O.K. He jumped up and ran towards me and I went to meet him. The Indian that was taking us to the spring hit me and knocked me down. My son picked up a sharp pole lying on the ground and rammed it into the back of the guard who had struck me. One of the other Indians ran him through with a spear and left him lying there on the ground. I got up to go to him and another Indian hit me in the head. When I came to several hours later I was tied on a horse and we were miles from where we had camped. There was nothing I could do."

"That night was a repeat of the previous night, and the next day the band split up. I think the larger group went directly north along the river. They took the two remaining French girls and most of the Indian girls with them. This group swung eastward and headed north. It was that afternoon that your Indian friends found us."

Bright Day had listened to all of the woman's explanation and although she did not understand everything that was said, she understood most of it and her heart went out to the white woman. She could almost feel the pain she suffered. She had lost a husband, a daughter and a son and had been repeatedly ravaged by the Indian braves.

Hans held her close to him as she cried. She was exhausted and he prepared a place for her to lie down and told her to get some sleep. He would be nearby and no one would bother her while she slept.

It was just a few days after the Indian raid that Andrew became conscious. The weather was warm that day and Bright Day had thrown back the flap to the hut. She sat beside his bed, bending his arms and legs, like she had done most days. She massaged his muscles, rubbing them with an ointment that she brought with her. On this day as she was rubbing one of his arms and was about to bend his wrist, she felt a tug and the arm moved by itself. The hand closed around her hand and held it tight. It happened so suddenly that it caught her off-guard and almost caused her to pull away. Even in his weakened condition though he had a firm grip. She looked at his face and his eyes were staring directly at her. She couldn't tell if he was frightened to find her there, or just curious.

He tried to speak but his voice wouldn't come. She spoke to him now and told him he was alright, he was safe and that she had been taking care of him. If he would turn her loose she would go get his friends. He held onto her for another moment and then relaxed his grip. She rose and went out the door.

In just a few minutes Hans and Dave came rushing through the door and dropped to their knees beside his bed. Andrew could see the relief on their faces. It was Hans who spoke first.

"Man are we glad to see you awake. You sure had us scared. We thought you might die and we wouldn't get paid for this vacation we been on." It was meant to be funny, and to help break the ice, but Andrew could see behind the levity. These men were his friends and they had been caring for him. Still he didn't remember why he was lying down and felt so weak. He started to sit up and felt the searing pain as if a hot poker was sticking in his side. He lay back and sweat broke out on his forehead.

Dave was quick to caution him to lay still. "Lay still ole

hoss. You took a bullet through your side and have been laid up here for a couple weeks. It tore a pretty good hole in you and you have been out cold ever since."

Andrew tried again to speak but his voice only croaked. He swallowed and tried again. This time, he was barely able to make himself understood. "What happened?"

They explained everything, about the battle with the Shawnee, the ride to the village, where they were, and everything. Then he asked who was the angel with the dark hair that had been leaning over him when he came to.

Hans laughed, "That is Bright Day. She is the sister of the boy that was being burned. He and his older brother, Night Hawk, were on a hunting trip with two of their cousins when the Shawnee caught them. His sister and her aunt have been helping us nurse you back to health. She has practically lived here since you got here. She has taken your clothes off, bathed you, changed your bed when you wet it and fed you almost every drop of water and broth you have received this past two weeks. The part you will regret missing is the night you were having chills and we couldn't get you to stop shaking. She took off her clothes and crawled in beside you, naked as a jay-bird. It did the job though. You stopped shaking."

Andrew was about to ask more when a tall Indian entered followed by a woman he would guess was about 40. The Indian came over to the side of the bed to see for himself that the white-man was awake. He grunted with satisfaction, patted Dave and Hans on the shoulder, said something to them that he could not understand and moved back toward the entrance. Dave translated.

"That is Night Hawk. This is his aunt. They are all glad that you are awake and he said we shouldn't tire you out too much. She has brought food for you and he wants you to eat just a little at first. They will stay here and help you eat every hour or so until you can start taking a full meal. We will go outside and leave you to them now. Your stomach has been empty so long; do not try to eat too much at first. It may make you throw up."

For three more days Andrew stayed in bed, fed by the older woman and the young girl. He did not see the older girl again and he wondered why she didn't come back. The fourth night he asked Hans why she hadn't been back.

Hans said, "Well I don't know for sure, but I think it has to do with one of two things. Either she is afraid you will be embarrassed to see her now that you are awake and know that she has seen you naked and washed your whole body. Or it has something to do with the fact she is a young woman and as long as you were sick, it was totally proper for her to care for you. But now that you are awake, it may be improper for her to be alone with you. I really don't know. I have not seen her since she came and told us you were awake."

Andrew dropped the subject and asked what he and Dave had been doing while he was laid up. Hans told him that he and Dave both had been practicing to speak the Indian language. That Night Hawk was Cherokee and the village was Natchez. The Natchez had been a big nation at one time, several hundred years ago, but now there were not that many of them. Night Hawk's mother's sister had married one of the Natchez men and come to live in this village. Night Hawk, his brother and sister had come for a winter visit and would be leaving soon to return to their village which was back east in the mountains. They had also been practicing with their Indian weapons, and although Hans would probably never be as good as Dave, he was getting pretty darn good with the bow and with the throwing axe.

Then Hans told him about the Indian raid on the Shawnee and the capture of the white woman, that she was getting over the shock and was recovering, but other than the first night when she told them about what happened, she wouldn't talk very much. Bright Day attempted to be friendly with her, but Magdalene seemed afraid of all Indians and rebuffed Bright Day's attempts to friendship. He and Dave had been talking about whether to try to take her back to New Orleans or back to one of the settlements where she could make her way back to Pennsylvania where she had relatives. She wouldn't say what she wanted to do.

The next day Andrew struggled to get out of bed. He was too weak to get dressed so he just wrapped a blanket around himself and walked outside. The sun was warm and he sat down with the blanket around him and relaxed for several minutes. No one came by and spoke to him, but he could see lots of people looking out of the huts and glance at him as they passed. He wondered if any of them were Bright Day.

A couple more days passed, and Dave helped him get dressed and held his arm as he went out and walked around the village for a bit. Each day thereafter, he would walk farther and farther. The hole in his side and back had completely scabbed over now and except for a little seepage out of his back, he was healing nicely. His side remained tender and Dave told him about the broken rib. He felt of it often and could feel a lump where the bone had broken. It seemed to be knitting back together though and he was glad of that. Sky Eyes had been in once since he woke up, and probed his side, feeling the bone. When she was finished she said it was too early to tell yet, but she thought it might be healing properly.

It was now four weeks into February and Night Hawk had indicated they would be leaving to return to their village in a few more days. He had been coming by every afternoon and at first Dave would translate for him, but after a few days, he was pleased to see that Andrew was picking up a lot of Cherokee words. Andrew had a good ear for sounds and he had learned to speak French. German and English in addition to his native Polish. After the fifth or sixth day, Dave decided he wasn't needed so he left the two of them alone.

The day before Night Hawk was to leave; Black Bear came to the hut with Dave and Hans. They were very serious and Black Bear launched into what sounded like a speech. Andrew caught most of it, but he asked Dave if he would translate for him. Dave asked Black Bear to repeat it one phrase at a time.

"My cousin, Night Hawk, eldest son of the great chief of the Cherokee Nation, Great Eagle, says he owes you not only his life, but the life of his brother, Howling Wolf. It is a debt that weighs heavily upon his heart. He has talked with you and thinks you are a good man with a great heart. He does not have a life to give you, but he said you would do him great honor if you would become a blood-brother and be one of his family. He leaves tomorrow to return to his village. He would perform the ceremony tonight if you agree."

Andrew didn't know what to say. He sensed that this was a great honor and that to refuse might be taken as an insult. He looked at Hans, and then turned to Dave with a question. "What does this becoming a blood brother entail? How does it work and how am I obligated?"

"This is a special honor. I have only ever heard of it happening a few times and most of those times it has been when a person goes to live in an Indian camp and does some very heroic deed. As I understand it, it is one of the highest honors the Indian can bestow upon you. You actually become as his brother and he will share everything he has with you and fight to defend you as if you were truly one of his family. It is not to be taken lightly."

Andrew hesitates only a minute, and then he turns to

Black Bear and speaks in Cherokee. "Tell Night Hawk I would consider it an honor to be a brother of such a great warrior. That my fight with the Shawnee was but a brief moment in both of our lives and I feel unworthy of such great honor he has offered me. That the care his people have given me helped give me back my life and any debt has been repaid. If he truly considers me worthy of the honor, I will accept and become his brother." Black Bear seemed surprised that Andrew had learned to speak their language so quickly. He was also pleased that Andrew was accepting the offer made by Night Hawk. The life of Night Hawk had been saved by this man and his companions. Night Hawk was already a heroic warrior, and he would probably be a great chief one day. It was indeed an honor for the white-man. He too, would remain a friend of these men.

There was a huge fire built in the middle of the village and it seemed that everyone was assembled there. Night Hawk's aunt brought Andrew a new suit of clothes. They were made of the finest doeskin and tanned until they felt as soft as silk. The shirt was beaded with porcupine quills and painted dozens of colors. They were interwoven across the shoulders and down both sides of the front. The pants had a row of painted quills down the side of each leg. To his surprise, they were a perfect fit. He wondered how they had gotten his exact measurements, and then his face reddened a bit when he remembered they had seen him naked for several days and perhaps had taken his measurements at that time.

Dave and Hans helped him dress and he was to stay in the hut until all was ready. He had not trimmed his hair since leaving Charleston and by now it was long and hung past his shoulders.

About an hour past dark, four Indian braves came to the hut. They were dressed in their finest outfits and their faces and chests were painted several different colors. Andrew was to learn later that these colors all had meaning and others could often identify an Indian's family by the colors of paint he wore. He came out and walked in the midst of the four braves. He sensed this was some kind of honor guard to escort him to the fire where everyone was assembled. Dave and Hans brought up the rear.

The Indians had been beating on drums and dancing around the fire. They also had rattles made out of dried gourds and it seemed the whole village was there. Now as he entered the circle of Indians, the music stopped and everyone became silent. There were two rows of Indians with huge headdresses sitting directly across the fire from the way he had come. These must be the chiefs of the village. There were three in the first row and five in the second row. Andrew could tell this was a very important occasion for them.

The four braves walked with him around the fire and stopped directly in front of the chiefs. They then spread out and made a line behind him between him and the fire. It sort of reminded him of a trial. Were these an honor guard, or guards to keep him from running away? It was sort of amusing.

But then he turned his attention to the chiefs. The one on the end was getting up and coming forward. Indians, contrary to what many believed, were not people of few words. Indians loved oratory and on special occasions could make very flowery speeches. Now Andrew was to be treated to an event few white-men would ever see.

The chiefs, one at a time came forward, put both hands on his shoulders and spoke two or three minutes each. Each was telling of the great exploits of Night Hawk, of the Cherokee history and the pride they and their cousins, the

Natchez, felt in their kindred-ship. They recounted great events in their history and what great people they were, and how the Great Spirit had smiled upon them. Andrew was pleasantly surprised that he was able to comprehend almost everything they said.

When all the chiefs had spoken, Night Hawk arose from behind where the chiefs had been sitting and came forward. He came beside Andrew and walked all the way around him. Then he turned to the chiefs, bowed slightly and began to speak.

"Oh great chiefs of the Natchez, cousins of the Cherokee Nation, your son, Night Hawk comes before you tonight to take this man as his blood-brother. Before I do, I want to tell you of the great exploits of this man, a chief of his own people, a man loved and honored by those who follow him. This man and his companions were traveling through our land and could have ignored the screams of pain they heard on that recent night. When they heard our screams they could have rode away. Instead they came to investigate and discovered we were tied to trees and my brother being tortured. They could have rode away. They are not Indians. They are white-men. We have heard and seen many bad things that white-men do. But just as all Indians are not thieves and murderers neither are all white-men killers and rapers of women. In spite of the fact that there were nine Shawnee holding us captive, this man and his companions ignored the danger they faced. They crept up to the camp and freed us, gave us knives to fight with and helped us kill the nine Shawnee."

He hesitated and a deep grunt of approval came from around the circle of seated Indians. Night Hawk should have been an actor. He was playing to the crowd and he was making Andrew seem like a knight in shining armor.

He continued, "As we watched my brother being burned,

I was filled with despair. Me and my cousins knew that we would be next. We could not get free no matter how hard we tried. I prayed to the Great Spirit to make our deaths quick and to give us the strength to withstand the torture without the loss of our pride as warriors.

"The Great Spirit answered my prayer by not letting us die, but by sending someone to save us. He said, 'My children, it is not yet time for you to pass over into the lands of mist. You have not yet fulfilled the purpose I have set for you in this life' "

"It was as if He had set us free and placed the knives in our hands. I, Night Hawk, my brother Howling Wolf, and my cousins, Black Bear and Runs Long, are alive today because this man came to help us. In the helping, he took a serious injury that almost took his life. He is not yet fully recovered, but I must leave tomorrow to return to my village. Before I go, I want all of the Natchez to know what great deeds this man has done and what great courage he has shown. In front of you oh great chiefs, and in the presence of my cousins, the Natchez, I want to become one with this brave man."

Night Hawk drew his knife and sliced it across his palm. He took Andrew's hand and did the same. Then he clasps the hands together.

In a loud voice he said, "Oh Great Spirit, you have sent this man, whose skin is paler than mine to save my life. Perhaps there is a greater message you also intended for me. Before you and my family I hereby take this man as my blood-brother and from this time forward our blood and our bodies shall be as one. I will share all that you have given me with him and his family. I will care for him, fight for him and do all things one does for his brother. To all my cousins among the Cherokee, the Choctaw, the Chickasaw, the Creek, the Natchez, the Muskogean and other of my kin,

I say to you, this is my brother. You are to treat him as you would me or one of my family. You shall give him shelter and food and help him if he needs help; the same as you would do for me, for this is my brother and I owe him my life."

With the end of the speech, Night Hawk embraced Andrew and a great whoop swelled up from the Indians. Night Hawk took a leather thong from around his neck and placed it over Andrew's head. It held a round medallion with a piece of green jade mounted in the center.

Night Hawk spoke. "Wear this, my brother, and everywhere you go, my kin will help you. When you are well I want you to come and visit my village. My mother and father will want to meet their new son. But wherever you are, if you need me, send this amulet and I will come."

All the chiefs approached Andrew now and he is invited to smoke with them. After lighting the pipe and blowing smoke to the four winds, it is next offered to Andrew as the guest of honor. He took a puff and almost coughed, it is so strong. But he held back the cough, sensing that it would be a breach of etiquette to cough or to refuse to smoke with the chiefs.

Now it was time to feast. The food had been cooking all afternoon. They seated Andrew to the left of the chiefs, and Night Hawk brought his brother and sister over. This is the first time Andrew had seen the boy since the night of the fight. The young boy's stomach was still scabbed but it was healing. Where the hot coals had burned him so badly, the skin was puckered and pulled together, but it was healing. Andrew tried not to think about the scars that would remain.

As they are introduced, the boy was embarrassed and in an attempt to make him feel at ease, Andrew addressed him in Cherokee. "Howling Wolf, I did not expect you to live. With the burns on your belly I was afraid we had got there too late to save you. That burned belly will be with you all your life, but you will have a life after all."

The boy looked at him and then turned to Night Hawk. "When I have earned my manhood name, I would like it to be Burned Belly. It is the name my new brother has given me and I like it."

Night Hawk looked at him and said, "Little brother, after the pain you have suffered I think you have earned your manhood. From this time forward you shall be known as Burned Belly."

Andrew turns now and looked at the girl, Night Hawk's sister, now his sister. He spoke to her, "Not only have I gained two brothers tonight, but I have a new sister also. I have been told that you know me a lot better. I hope I have not been a real problem."

"No. Not at all. In fact, you didn't give me any back talk and I like that. We women get lots of back talk from our men and you never said a word, even when I took all your clothes off."

Andrew was embarrassed to think this beautiful girl had seen him totally naked. He also sensed she was teasing him about it.

He said, "Well, you had me at a disadvantage. The next time it won't be so easy. I'm not used to pretty girls taking my clothes off."

They chatted during the time they were eating. She and Night Hawk seemed to be well liked for many of the men and women came by to wish them a safe journey and to return soon. After the meal, he wanted to talk to her more and get to know her, but she excused herself and left the gathering. He was somewhat disappointed.

A short time later, he was growing weak and he asked Dave to help him back to the hut. The white woman had come to the ceremony with Hans and he had not left her side all evening. She seemed ill at ease around the Indians.

As he was getting ready to leave, Andrew went to Night Hawk and took his hand. "Night Hawk, I have never had a brother. I had a sister but she was killed in a great war way across the big salt water. Now I have two brothers and a sister. You have done me a great honor and made me very happy. I will see you as we go back to Carolina. Before I go though, I am worried. I fear I may have offended our sister for she left without saying good-by."

Night Hawk smiled, "Brother, do not be concerned. You have not offended her. It is just that she is unhappy about you being her brother."

This surprised Andrew. "Why is she unhappy? Did she not want me as a brother?"

"No. She did not want you as a brother. She tried to talk me out of making you our brother." When he saw the look of confusion on Andrew's face he went on. "It is not that she dislikes you. It is just the opposite. You see brother, while you were sick; she tended you and took care of your every need. She felt needed and she fell in love with you. She had mentioned that she might move into your lodge and be your woman if you wanted her. Now she cannot do that with her brother. Although you are not blood of her blood, the tribe would never let her live with you now as your wife. That is forbidden."

It was a shock to Andrew and he turned and walked to his hut. Perhaps this way was best. He had already betrayed Catherine with Helen. His dalliance with Maria was before he committed to Catherine and he did not consider that a betrayal of her. Bright Day was very attractive and had an animal magnetism about her. His strength was returning and as he sat beside her tonight, he felt the attraction she had for him. The idea of taking her to his bed had occurred to him. Now he found that is what she wanted, and because he was her brother, it could never happen. That sort of took some of the excitement about the brother ceremony away. But he guessed it was probably best. He didn't dare get involved with another woman. Helen was one thing. She didn't expect anything and was willing to let him go on his way. Bright Day would probably be a different story.

CHAPTER NINETEEN

Night Hawk, Bright Day and Burned Belly left the next morning. Hans, Dave and Andrew rose early to say good-by and Andrew had a chance to speak alone with Bright Day.

"Bright Day, Night Hawk told me you were unhappy having me for your brother. I understand how you feel for I have a strong heart for you also. Can we not care for one another as brother and sister?"

"Brother, I will love you as a brother, but I would have rather been your woman. The night I lay beside you when you were chilled, I knew then that I would come to you if you wanted me. In the days that you were asleep and I cared for you, I thought of all the things I would do to make you happy and stay in our village. I should have known that couldn't be for we are too different. But wherever you go, my soul will go with you. I love you not only as a brother, but as a woman loves a man. I will pray that the Great Spirit watches over you and that your wound heals quickly."

She mounted her horse and turned away without another word. All has been said that can be said. They must never talk of this again.

A few days after their departure, a cold blizzard descended upon the village and winds whipped the snow into deep drifts. It was unusual for this area to have heavy snow but winter seemed to hit with a vengeance. Everyone was confined to their huts for almost a week. It was during this time that the three men and Magdalene discussed her future.

Hans brought up the subject one night while they were eating.

"Andrew, Magdalene and I have been talking and she doesn't want to go back to her homestead down south. It has too many sad memories for her. She had not wanted to come out here in the first place, but her husband thought they could homestead a place and get a new start. It might have worked out if the Indians had left them alone. She said she can't go back there. The only folks she has are in Pennsylvania and she has set her mind to go back there. She is a strong-minded woman and I can't leave her here. As I see it, I have only two alternatives. Either take her with us or she and I strike out alone. As soon as I can get her to Augusta or Charleston so she can get transportation to her people, I can come back and catch up with you. Dave is a good guide and knows the woods better than I do. He could see you to wherever you want to go."

After a couple minutes Andrew spoke. "Hans, I don't like the idea of splitting our party. It would increase the danger for all of us. If you two struck out on your own and something happened to you, she would be at the mercy of the forest and might fall into the hands of Indians again. It is dangerous for a woman to travel the forest the way we will be going, but it would be more dangerous for you two travelling alone. I think we should stick together and if Magdalene doesn't mind travelling with us, we will take her with us when I am able to travel. What do you think Dave?"

"I agree with that plan. It will be really rough on Magdalene but no rougher that what she has been though. It would take a mighty strong woman with lots of guts to withstand what she has and not go out of her mind. I think she can make it with us easier than she could with just the two of you alone."

Magdalene had been offered lodging with some of the other women but she had declined and wanted to stay close to Hans. Somehow, she felt he would protect her, and she had been staying in the same hut with the three men. Up to now, she had not entered the conversation, but now she came forward and spoke.

"I do not want to split up your party and I agree that it is much safer travelling together. If you do not mind, I will go with you and I will hold up my end of the work. I will do my best not to be a burden for you. I cannot go back to our homestead. I feel certain that the people down there found my husband and children and have given them a decent burial. The thought of going back there with all the horror is more than I could stand. It is all still so vivid in my mind that I will have nightmares about it for a long time. But to go back would just make it worse. As soon as we reach any civilized town I will hitch a ride with someone and make my way back to Pennsylvania. I have a brother and a sister there. My father died before I left, and I think my mother may be dead although I don't know.

"By the way, they call me Maggie, rather than Magdalene."

The men looked at each other and when no one spoke, Andrew said, "O.K. Then it is settled. Maggie goes with us. I will speak to Black Bear and Runs Long. Perhaps they will let us have one of the ponies the Shawnee were riding. There is one thing though, Maggie. We will be crossing the paths of many Indians; and in fact, we may stop at the village of Night Hawk and Bright Day on the way back. Will that make you uneasy? After what you have been through, can you put up with the Indians you meet in the future?"

"I think I will always be uneasy around Indians, but I

have had to fight off white savages since I was a little girl. I was raped when I was caught in a corn field one time by two white men. One of them was the real father of my son. My husband knew about the rape, and when he learned I was pregnant, he married me to protect my honor. He loved me and tried in his way to protect me. That is why I came west with him although I did not want to. I will live this last episode down but I will always be worried around Indians that it might happen again. If I am ever caught again, I will kill myself before I let another man, white or Indian, abuse me."

The men felt a deep anger at what had happened to this woman. She had been abused by both white men and Indians, yet she had maintained her composure. She seethed with anger, but she was able to control it and it only heightened her determination to overcome the trouble she had seen.

Andrew looked at Hans, whose face was red and his jaw was set in a determined fashion. Hans either felt great sorrow for this woman, or he had fallen in love with her. In either case, he was determined to protect her from any further harm.

Andrew was at once glad for him and sad for him at the same time. It was good to find someone to love, but he feared that Maggie did not feel the same for Hans and that could mean a broken heart when she left to go on her way. Hans was a grown man, and old enough to make his own decisions. Andrew would keep quiet unless he was asked for his opinion.

Finally, the weather broke and the sun returned to warm the ground. The melting snow turned the ground into a quagmire. Mud clung to boots and clothes and everything was damp and musty. In a couple days snow had melted and the ground began to dry up. The Indians were hanging blankets and bedding out to dry in the sun. Hans and Dave followed their lead.

Andrew, his men and Maggie, continued to live in the village through February and part of March, although they moved into another hut and let Black Bear and his family return to their lodge. Andrew's wounds healed slowly and his ribs continued to give him considerable pain. He walked a lot to regain his strength, but when he tried to lift something or to ride a horse, it was too painful. One day he went to see Sky Eyes and asked her if she thought the rib was healing properly.

Sky Eyes looked at one side then the other. She put two fingers on either side of the rib and measured the rib cage on the opposite side. Then she pushed gently against the rib, and at the point where the rib attached to the breast bone. Afterward she nodded to him and said, "You are a lucky young man. It seems that the bone is growing back together. If you do not get a blow there or hurt it again, I think you will be alright in another moon. You must be very careful though that you do not take a blow on that side for another two or three weeks."

The first week of March Andrew felt good enough that he had Hans saddle his horse and rode her a bit to take the wildness out of her. Then Andrew mounted up and walked the black around the village. He repeated this every day for another week, then began to gallop a little. By the end of the second week he was able to ride at a full run. He decided it was time for them to be on the road again.

Hans and Dave both agreed. They had been cooped up for almost three months and are anxious to get moving as well. Maggie had not said a word. She had been patient too, knowing that Andrew was not yet able to travel. But she, too, is anxious to be on the road and away from the Indians. Although she made friends with a couple of the Indian women, she always became silent and returned to her hut when any of the men came around.

Andrew spoke to Night Hawk's uncle and thanked him for the care and the hospitality of his village. He presented the uncle with a new knife and leather scabbard. And to the uncle's wife and daughter, he gave a bright bolt of cloth that would make them each a blouse. With the bright colors, they will be the pride of the village.

Next, he visited Black Bear and Runs Long and paid his respects to them. They gladly let him pick the best pony out of those that they had taken from the Shawnee. They hated to see the white men leave. It had been nice to have them on the hunting trips. They had learned much of the white man's ways and it is as if they were losing a fellow warrior. It was Black Bear who put their feelings into words.

He put his hand on Andrew's shoulder and said, "Night Hawk is our cousin. As his blood brother, you are also our cousin. We have you to thank for our lives. You are a good man and you will always be welcome in the village of the Natchez. We hope you will come back some day. If you will permit, we will ride with you for a few days. Your friends have been teaching us to speak the white man's tongue and we would learn a little more."

Andrew thought this was probably an excuse to ride with them and help if they ran into trouble. He accepted their offer, and the two braves seemed delighted.

It was now the last of March and the trees were budding and flowers were blooming. Spring was a beautiful time of year.

They moved eastward and made good headway. Runs Long knew the best trails and where the easiest river crossings were. The first day tired Andrew, but in a few days, he was holding his own. Black Bear and Runs Long stayed with them for three days and then turned back to their village. The last day before they left, they had encountered a Creek hunting party and Black Bear and Runs Long had made it a point to introduce Andrew and his party and to inform them that these were good friends of theirs and that Andrew was a blood brother of Night Hawk of the Cherokee. Black Bear told them to spread the word to all their relatives that the white men were returning to their village on the coast and that they were to have safe passage through their lands. Andrew and Dave listened as Black Bear spoke and the other Indians nodded in understanding. It should make their journey a lot less hazardous, he hoped.

They had given him directions on how to reach Night Hawk's village and Andrew thought that they would stop on the way back.

They travelled in a zig zag pattern. Andrew was paying close attention to the land and during the second week after leaving the Natchez village, they came into an open plain that had rich black soil. In the distance they could see the beginning of mountains rising in the back ground. To the north, there were heavy stands of oak and poplar trees. On the sides of the mountains, he noted evergreens that looked like aspen. To the south were great stands of huge pines and along the river bank, oak, gum and cypress.

They camped here for several days and Andrew rode back and forth across the land. Hans and Dave took turns riding with Andrew, keeping watch while he looked at the surroundings. The other stayed with Maggie or hunted nearby and usually had a meal cooked by the time they returned. Andrew followed a pattern each day. He would head out for three or four hours, turn either to the right or left, ride a couple more hours, then head back to camp.

After the second day, Andrew grew more excited and Hans and Dave noted his interest in the land. They also paid closer attention to their surroundings. They were in a broad valley, approximately five miles across and as best they could tell, about twenty miles long. They were still west of the Smoky Mountains and somewhere north of the line separating the South Carolina territory and the North Carolina territory. They figured they were about three days journey northwest of Birmingham.

There was a small river that ran the length of the valley and several small springs that seemed to flow from the foothills and the mountains to the east.

Several times during the day's riding, Andrew would dismount and with a sharp stick dig into the soil 8 to 12 inches deep. He rode along the stream beds to see how high the water had risen during rainy weather and to see if the water was clean and pure. He would cup his hand and drink from almost every stream and spring.

The third night as they gathered around the fire, Andrew announced, "Hans, I think this is the place I have been looking for. This valley has rich soil and will grow almost any kind of crop. The streams provide a plentiful supply of clean, sweet water and there doesn't appear to be a tendency of the land to flood. The only place I found signs of flooding was along the banks of the big river. The banks are fairly steep and if we stay back a short distance it is not likely to be a problem. This is where I want to settle down and make my home. What do you think of it?"

Hans said, "It is pretty alright. There is plenty of game and there are also plenty of trees to build a home and buildings. The biggest draw-back is you are right in the middle of Indian country and about two weeks from the major towns along the coast. Your nearest supply point will probably be Birmingham and it is just a small mining community. You would have to haul in everything that you needed on mules or horseback. There are no trails that a wagon could get through. Do you think Catherine would want to live like this?"

"I don't know, but this is a lot like my home in Poland. I want this to be my home."

Dave spoke up now. "There is one thing you are forgetting. This is Indian lands and although the Carolina governments and that of Georgia claim these lands as their territories, it really belongs to the Indians. We don't know exactly where to file a claim. But before I did anything, I would talk with the Indians and see if they are going to give you any fuss before I cut the first tree."

"Yes, you are right Dave." He turned to Hans, "Do you think we are in the land of the Creeks or Cherokees?"

"I would guess we are about half-way between them. The Creeks are to the south and the Cherokees are to the north. If this is correct, that might work as an advantage for you. You might sell this to both tribes as being the dividing line between their lands and this could become a marker identifying where each land begins and ends. If you plan to build a trading post, both tribes could easily reach your post without crossing the others' lands."

"Good idea. Tomorrow I will go to see if I can find Night Hawk's village and ask him to come here with me. He can help us define where we are and if there is a dividing line between him and the Creeks."

With that they turned in.

Andrew was excited and could hardly sleep. He was up before day-break and Dave, who had stood night watch, began stirring up the fire and getting the coffee brewing.

They decided that Night Hawk's village shouldn't be more than a day or two away and Andrew and Dave would ride for it. Hans and Maggie agreed to wait and watch the camp. The two of them could ride faster if they didn't have to wait on the pack horse. Hans assured Andrew that they would be alright. They had not encountered any trouble since they had met up with the Creek hunting party. All the Indians they had met merely watched them and then went on their way.

They had an extra rifle and plenty of shot so they left it with Hans. Maggie said she knew how to use a rifle as good as most men and she wasn't afraid to stay with Hans.

By good light, Dave and Andrew were on their way. They rode hard and stopped to rest only when the horses began to lather and tire. They rode until dark and made camp in a clump of tall trees beside a spring with sweet smelling honey-suckles in the trees.

They had finished supper, hobbled the horses and were getting ready to turn in when Dave looked up and saw the Indian standing within 20 feet of them. His first inclination was to reach for his gun. Instead he remained still and spoke quietly to Andrew.

"Don't move rapidly, but we have company."

Andrew didn't act as if he had heard, but Dave noted that he put down his blanket and moved close to where his two pistols were laying on his slicker.

Dave held his hand up in the sign of peace and motioned for the Indian to come on into the fire. When he moved forward, Dave noted that there were two more behind him. He motioned them to come in also. He indicated the fire and coffee and picked up two mugs and poured out coffee for them. They had not made any overt move towards them, but they had guns and they held them cradled in their arms, ready for use.

When they were near, Dave handed the first two the mugs of coffee and spoke to them in broken dialect that he had learned from Night Hawk and the Natchez. Although it was not pure language, the Indians, never-the-less, were somewhat surprised that a white man had learned that much of their language. The one in the lead spoke now in Cherokee.

"You speak some of our language, but it is not Cherokee. Where do you come from and where are you going?"

Andrew told him he had learned much of the language

of the Cherokee from Night Hawk. "We have been among the Natchez tribe near the big river and are headed for the village of Great Eagle, chief of the brave Cherokee. You are welcome to share our camp and our food."

The Indian was surprised again. Here were two white men and both spoke as Indians, this last one as though he were a Cherokee.

"Why do you seek the village of Great Eagle?"

"Because he is my father and we go to visit him and my mother."

This really surprised the Indian and there was an audible grunt from the two Indians in the rear. The one up front turned and looked at them, then turned back to Andrew. "You are not Cherokee. How could you be the son of Great Eagle?"

"Almost four moons ago we were travelling in the woods and heard a great scream in the night. We went to investigate and found four braves captured and tied to trees by Shawnee. The youngest had been staked to the ground and the Shawnee were making sport of him by putting burning coals on his stomach. We cut the captives free and gave them knives. Then we attacked the Shawnee and killed eleven of the braves.

"The Indians we freed were the two sons of Great Eagle, Night Hawk and Burned Belly. The other two were their cousins in the Natchez tribe, Black Bear and Runs Long." Andrew let that sink in for a moment and continued, "I am the blood-brother of Night Hawk and I am on the way to his village to meet my new family." With this he took the medallion out of his shirt so the Indians could see it.

It had a great effect on the Indians. They immediately set down their weapons and came forward to place their hands on Andrew's shoulder.

The lead Indian spoke, "Hoopa. It is good. Night Hawk has told us of you and said we should watch for you. But he said there would be three of you and maybe a woman too. I am Running Fox and these are my friends, Spotted Owl and Wind Walker. We are of Great Eagle's village and will take you there tomorrow. You are only a half day's journey away."

Andrew was pleased and invited them to have supper with him. They had not eaten, but one of them went back into the woods and brought out their horses. They had killed a buck that afternoon and they cut off a leg and spitted it over the fire to cook. Dave mixed up a batch of bread and set it in the coals so that when the meat was ready they would have hot bread. While the meat cooked, Andrew began to question Running Fox about where they were and how far the Cherokee lands went.

Running Fox stated that there were not clear markings, but that it would take a full day's hard riding to take them to the area claimed by the Creeks which were their cousins. This sort of matched what Hans and Dave had thought.

Then Andrew asked him how they had found them.

"We crossed your trail about two hours ago and followed it to here. We are always on the lookout for strangers in our lands. We knew you were white men because your horses wear the steel shoes. We are very suspicious of white men travelling through our lands for many times they are out to kill our men and rape our women. You travelled in the open, not trying to hide your trail and we were curious as to what you were doing. We left our horses in the woods and walked into your camp. We watched you finish your meal and get ready to sleep. You were careless not to have a guard. Had we meant to kill you, your scalps would be on our shields now."

"We met some Creeks a few days ago and told them who we were and that we wanted to pass through their lands without trouble and that we were coming to see Night Hawk. We felt we would be safe in the land of the Cherokee.

They are not sneak thieves who murder people in their sleep."

"That is true, however, all the Indians that travel these forests are not Cherokee. You will do well to remember that."

Their meat was partially cooked and they did not want to wait longer so they ate the outer portions and left the rest over the fire. It would make a good breakfast. Then they all rolled into their blankets and slept. Running Fox and his two men took turns standing guard. Andrew felt a lot better having them as friends.

CHAPTER TWENTY

W ith the break of dawn, the party was on the move. Now that Running Fox and his party were with them they relaxed their caution and moved rapidly towards Night Hawk's village to the East. The Cherokee village was in the foothills of the mountains, not high up enough to be terribly cold, but sheltered by the hills to block some of the north winds. The little valley they were in opened towards the south so that the winter sun would shine full on them without interference. There were close to 80 lodges and judging from the number of people that had been in the lodges of the Natchez, Andrew guessed there would be close to 200 people here. That was a pretty good size village. Running Fox told him that this was only half of the tribe. About this many more lived about a mile farther. They had divided the tribe in order not to deplete the graze for the animals during the winter and to make it easier to hunt for game. One group would hunt to the west and north, the other to the east and south. If trouble arose, help was just a few minutes away and the braves from each camp stayed in close touch and kept each other informed of any signs of danger.

As they rode into the village, Spotted Owl rode ahead and shouted the good news; Night Hawk's brother had arrived.

The party had hardly entered the edge of the village when Indians began to run out of the tepees and jump on their horses. They came riding at full tilt to meet the new arrivals, shouting and waving their bows and lances in the air. By the time they reached the center of the village, almost every brave in the area was there with them.

Night Hawk came striding out of one of the larger tepees and waited for Andrew to come to him. When he stood in front of him he dismounted and they placed their right hand on the other's shoulder and then clasp hands.

Night Hawk spoke first. "It is good to see you, brother. We have been waiting for your arrival. My mother grows restless that it has taken you so long to recover. How is the wound?"

"It heals nicely Night Hawk. The rib is still a bit tender but it gets stronger each day. Even after three months it still causes pain when I bend over or something bumps me. How is Great Eagle and the rest of our family?"

"Burned Belly has gone to the neighboring village. He will return later today. Our sister wants to greet you alone after we have spoken to mother and father. Come let us go to see Great Eagle now."

Andrew was a bit nervous for he was about to meet a great chief and one he would be calling father. He did not know how Night Hawk's family would receive him. He should not have worried. It was almost as if he was really their son and had only been away on a journey.

Great Eagle sat on a large mat with a number of furs and skins spread over what seemed like a stump of a tree about 6 or 8 inches high. Andrew didn't realize it until he had entered and Great Eagle invited him to sit, but the stump or log placed him about 8 to 10 inches higher than anyone else sitting on the floor. Andrew thought to himself, very smart. The height elevates him slightly above anyone else and makes it easier to dominate them if you are above someone. He was dressed in fine doeskins and had a large headdress on. The head band must have had a hundred feathers stuck in it, and it trailed down his back almost to the floor.

Great Eagle bade him and Night Hawk to sit across from him. Then he spoke. "Welcome my son. Night Hawk has told me of your actions and how you were wounded saving his life and that of our youngest, Burned Belly. We thank you for your sacrifice and are pleased that you have come to visit us. Tonight we shall feast and I shall introduce you to the rest of our tribe. I will send a messenger to the other camp and ask them to join us also. You are welcome my son, but now you must be tired from your travels. You can share the lodge of Night Hawk and Burned Belly. When you are rested we will talk more. Go now!"

Andrew had not yet met Night Hawk's mother, nor had he seen anything of Bright Day. He did not have to wait long. Night Hawk took him next door to a smaller lodge. What he did not know at first was that the bigger lodge was a ceremonial lodge where meetings were held and visitors were greeted. It was not where Great Eagle's family lived. As they entered the smaller lodge, Andrew was greeted by a short woman, probably no more than five feet and one or two inches tall. She was small in size, weighing probably no more than 100 lbs. Andrew wondered how such large children as Night Hawk and Bright Day were descended from such a small bodied person.

Night Hawk introduced him.

"Mother this is my new brother and your new son, he is called Andrew. Andrew this is our mother, Little Turtle."

She was all smiles and she came forward and put her arms around him and hugged him. She was much stronger than she seemed. This was the first time anyone had hugged him. He judged that was permitted by a mother to show she loved him. She was chattering so fast that Andrew could not follow her and he looked at Night Hawk for help.

Instead help came from the back of the tepee. Bright Day stood up and came forward. He had not seen her there before. Now she scolded her mother. "You must slow down Mother. Although your son knows some Cherokee, he is not able to follow so much at one time. How was your journey brother?"

"It was good. We have made good time and I feel much better each day. I will be completely healed by summer time. How have you been?"

"Well. Burned Belly will be sorry he was not here to greet you. He all but worships you. He has the foolish idea to get you to stay with us, or to let him go back to the white man's town with you. You will have to tell him how foolish that idea is. Where is the one you call Hans? I did not see him with you."

Andrew explained about the closeness that has developed between him and the white woman that was rescued in the raid by Night Hawk. He also shared that they were taking Maggie back to the town so that she can travel north to rejoin her family, and for now she and Hans were waiting back in the valley for him to return. They would turn south and go back to the Carolina coast.

Andrew decided this was not a good time to tell them that he wanted to stay on their land.

Little Turtle left to get firewood so that she could fix a meal for Andrew.

Bright Day asked Night Hawk if he would leave them alone for she wanted to visit with Andrew. When they are alone, she asked him, "Do you plan to stay with us long?"

Andrew said, "Not more than a day or two this time, for we must get back to Hans and Maggie. I don't want to leave them alone too long. Besides, I want to get back to the white town for I have important things to do there."

She sidled closer and touched his arm. "I have thought of you much since I left the Natchez village. I find myself dreaming of you at night and I am restless. Why did you agree to become my brother? I wanted it otherwise."

"I think I would have liked it better if I were not your brother too, Bright Day. But the ceremony has been performed, and it is too late for us to think of each other except as brother and sister now."

"Yes. I know. My head tells me you are right, but my heart will not listen. I have not been happy since I left you."

At this point Little Turtle returned, and the two moved away from each other, pretending they were engaged in idle talk. Then Andrew excused himself with the pretext that he must go and take care of his horse and unload the pack horse. Little Turtle indicated that he and Dave are to eat with them that night.

With that, he took his exit, glad to be away from Bright Day. Just being near her was a temptation. He would have to be very careful, for he did not think of her as a sister, but as a beautiful woman who had told him she longed for him too.

The rest of the day passed rapidly for Andrew and Dave. They busied themselves off-loading the horses and moving the gear into Night Hawk's lodge. Andrew unpacked some of the gifts he brought for his new family. He intended to present them later, after they have eaten.

Andrew expressed concern for Hans and Maggie. He feared for them being alone. Night Hawk said he would send a messenger to the villages nearest where they are with the word that they are friends and are to be left alone.

"There are both Cherokee and Creeks in that area. They will watch out for them and warn them if any strange Indians come into the area. But it is the season for the spring raids and there could be dangers."

Andrew remained nervous and concerned. He decided that he would not stay here long.

By late afternoon, the village is beginning to fill up

with arrivals from the other camp. A festive atmosphere prevailed and preparations were made for a big fire in the center of the village. Smaller fires were already burning around the village as meats, vegetables and a wide variety of foods, were prepared.

Just before dark, Great Eagle and the other chiefs emerged from the ceremonial lodge and they declared the celebration to begin. A great deal of shouting and whooping emerged from the crowd, and beating drums started with a strange cadence. Almost immediately, young braves and young women danced around the fire in two separate groups. The men whooped and thrust their lances at imaginary enemies as they danced back and forth, round and round. The women were quieter and danced in a flat-footed shuffle that wove in and out, sort of in a snaking pattern.

After close to an hour of dancing, the men put aside their lances and formed a circle inside, near the fire, facing out. The women broke their circle and crated a new one on the outside of the circle of men, facing toward the men. The dance began again, but slightly different this time. The men moved in one direction, the women in the opposite. They moved away from each other, and then back toward each other. Then they faced in the same direction and danced side by side. There was considerable movement and changing of places in both of the lines. Andrew later learned that it was the young men lining up beside the maidens they were courting, and when the dance ended, the girl and boy next to each other would spend the evening together, under the watchful eyes of the elders, of course. This was one of the ways a young couple picked each other's company and announced to the rest of the village that they were considering the other as a possible mate.

Night Hawk continued to explain the courting process to Andrew as they watched the young people. "The rules of courtship are pretty rigid and there is very little touching between a young man and woman during this stage."

Andrew was surprised to learn that there is a strong degree of discipline and order in the Indian's life. They were not the ignorant savages he had been led to believe they were. True, their customs were different, but he saw the purpose behind them and the reasoning was good. In fact, his own people could learn much from the Indian's ways if they would just try and see them as a people.

After the dancing was finished, it was time to eat.

Little Turtle and Bright Day had gone to lots of trouble to prepare a special meal. There was fresh venison, sage hen and several vegetables that had been cooked in the big pots. Andrew was invited to sit with Great Eagle and the rest of the chiefs. All the chiefs ate together, the women feeding them first, then the children and themselves last.

It was a meal to be proud of. Some of the things Andrew ate he did not know what they were, but he saw others eating them and decided it wouldn't hurt him. To his surprise, most of them were good and he thought, maybe it is best I don't know what they are.

After the feasting, came the story telling. Several of the chiefs stood and told a story. Some were humorous; some were of things from the distant past, history of the tribes or of the Cherokee Nation. Others were just boasts and brags of some adventure the individual had participated in. Finally, when it came Night Hawk's turn he rose and spoke to the assembled crowd.

"Night Hawk has told of his adventures in the past and he has no new stories to tell. But I have a new brother that has come from a place far away that we may never see. I ask my brother now to tell his Cherokee friends of the things he has done and the land he comes from." With that he sat down and motioned over to Andrew. There is a chorus of "Hoopa's" then the crowd grew silent.

Andrew stood and spoke slowly. He first apologized that he did not speak the Cherokee language as well as the others, and he must speak slowly to choose the right words.

Then he said, "My home lies in a land very much like your land here. There were great forests, and lots of game in the forests. There were beautiful rivers and lakes with lots of fish in them. But there the sameness ends. In my land, there were huge buildings that covered areas as big as your entire village."

With this, a great mumble arose from the Indians. It was impossible for them to conceive such large buildings.

Andrew continued. "Great chiefs lived in these buildings that we called castles. The chiefs who lived in these castles were chiefs of great numbers of people, perhaps as many as all the Indian tribes from the mountains to the north where the ice never melts to the salt sea in the south, and from the great river called big Muddy in the west to the salt sea in the east. As many as three or four hundred villages all combined and under the control of just one chief."

Again the Indians whispered and grunted although the impact escaped them.

These chiefs owned much land and the boundaries were marked so that the chiefs in other castles would know where the land of one began and ended. They were not allowed to enter the lands of another without that chief's permission. They could not take game from his land or food or anything that grew on his lands. Among the Cherokee you do not feel you own the land, but you do have certain areas that you hunt and other tribes do not come onto your lands without your permission. When they do, there is often fighting."

Andrew continued, "It was the same in my country. My homeland was a place called Poland. It was almost as big as the lands of the Creeks, the Choctaws, the Chickasaws and the Cherokees all put together. We were called Polish or Poles. There were other great tribes on all sides of us. These were Germans, Russians, Hungarians and Prussians. They also had braves numbering into the thousands. These were very war-like people and they wanted the lands of the Poles. They were very greedy and although they had plenty for their own people, they wanted what our people had and they went to war. It was a war that is hard to describe. They had as many braves as there are trees in the forest and they all had the fire-sticks you call rifles. We were few in number and we only had a few fire-sticks. Most of our braves fought with lances like you have and long knives that were two feet long. We call them swords. The Polish braves fought bravely, for more than twenty seasons we fought, first one tribe and then another to drive them back off our land. Then during the moon of heavy rains, while our braves were away fighting the enemy on one side of our land, another enemy attacked us from the opposite border and took the main village of our land. We called it our capital because it was the largest village in our lands and our great chief held council there. We returned and although we were outnumbered, we drove the enemy out of our capital, counting coup on many of their braves. But over half of our warriors were killed. Thousands upon thousands died on both sides and their blood turned the ground red. There was much weeping and wailing in the houses of our people all across the land."

Andrew stopped and bowed his head.

The Indians saw the tears on his face and they remained silent, waiting for him to continue. For a brave man such as had saved the life of Night Hawk to shed a tear meant his heart was very heavy; and their hearts went out to him and a deeper bond of friendship was born, for most had lost a son, brother or husband in war with the enemies of the Cherokee. They too could feel his pain.

Finally, Andrew brought his head up and continued his story.

"By then, we were weak and our enemies attacked from three sides. We beat the Hungarians back, but the Germans and Russians had too many warriors that were fresh and had not been tired by all the fighting. They over-ran all of our lands and when they had finished there was no more Poland. They divided our lands between them and those of us who still lived were hunted down to be killed. I and a few of my warriors escaped and took a big boat to come to your land. The boat brought me across the salt water for more than 30 suns. This great salt lake, which we call a sea, is so vast that when you are in the middle of it, you may not see land for many suns. Great storms roll across the waters and sometimes wreck the boats and carry all aboard to the Great Hunting Ground. It is a long way and I cannot go back, for if I do those who control my land will kill me. They have already killed my father, my mother and my sister. Until Night Hawk made me his brother, I had no remaining family. Now, once more, I have a mother, a father, two brothers and a sister. It is a great day for me." Abruptly he ended and sat down.

There was total silence for several minutes and Night Hawk rose again.

"My brother, your story has touched the heart of the Cherokee. They understand the loss of a loved one. They understand the need to defend one's home. Just as your land was violated by those you mentioned, so is our land violated by such as the Shawnee who captured us. You are a brave man and you have travelled far to escape your enemies. Here, you are among friends. You are welcome to stay with us. We Cherokee are a proud people and we will fight when we are attacked, but we do not make war on our neighbors. You now have a new family, that of Great Eagle, and we hope you will stay with us."

With that, a great shout of approval went up from the braves in the crowd. Night Hawk and Burned Belly had told them of how Andrew and his men had saved them and in each telling, the number of Shawnee grew. The Cherokee braves were voicing their approval. He knew now he would be welcome and safe in the Cherokee territory.

Andrew's story ended the story telling. No one could top the tale he had just told. The Indians broke off into smaller groups now and went on with the celebration. Andrew and Night Hawk were invited to sit and smoke with the chiefs.

After the pipe was lit and passed to everyone the talking began and touched on many things, but none of great importance. Andrew wondered if now was the time to bring up his idea of buying land for his own. As the conversation lagged, he decided to go ahead now while all the chiefs were present and while the mood of welcome still prevailed.

When it seemed that no one else had anything to say, he spoke up.

"Oh great chiefs, on my journey to your village I came to a place that is much like my homeland. It is a beautiful valley and has tall trees like those in the forests near my home. There is a stream running through the land and it has soil that is black as night. I stopped and camped there for three days, just remembering how my home was before everyone was killed. I do not know if it is the lands of the Cherokee or of the Creek. I am not familiar with where your lands begin and end. I had planned to leave and go back to the white man's town, but now, you have made me feel as if I am a part of the Cherokee Nation, and have invited me to live among you."

He waited a minute for this to sink in.

"If I am truly welcome as a Cherokee, I would buy this land from the Cherokee and make my home there. Would you sell me this valley?"

The Indians did not understand selling land. They voiced their opinions that no one owned the land. It was put there by the Great Spirit for everyone to use.

Andrew understood, but he persisted, "Just as there were boundaries between the Cherokee and the Creek, he wanted a land that he could call his own, a place that he might define the boundaries and if he did not want strangers coming there to hunt and take his crops, he could make them leave. They understood this, but how would they define such boundaries. He described how they might take a fine piece of doeskin and draw the diagram of the valley on there and place his name on it. Then each of the chiefs would place his symbol on the doeskin to signify his agreement. There was some hesitation and Andrew again reminded them of the battle he had fought for his home and that he would never feel safe and secure until he had something that he could say was his. He hastened to add that in exchange for giving him his own land, he would pay by bringing all of them gifts.

This sweetened the pot and the discussion of what type of gifts began. He first offered one pony for each brave in both camps. Indians were great traders and they haggled for the better part of two hours, first one idea and then another. In the end it was agreed that since the land belonged to all the Cherokees, he would provide one horse and two new wool blankets to every lodge in both camps. Every brave would be given a new knife of the shiny steel, and every lodge would get a bolt of cloth for the women to make dresses out of. In exchange Andrew was to receive the valley from where the river flowed over the rapids to where it pinched into a gorge at the lower end, which was approximately 20 miles long and all the land back from the river as far as the foot hills to the east (which Andrew estimated was some five miles). By rough calculation, Andrew figured he was asking for a tract of land 20 miles long and some 5 miles wide. This would be between 65,000 and 70,000 acres. He did not expect to receive all of this, but he figured to start big and negotiate for something smaller. (The Indians did not understand miles or acres so Andrews explained by time it would take to ride the distances up and across the area.)

This was a mere drop in the bucket. The Cherokees had millions of acres and would not miss a small parcel like this. Andrew would own one side of the valley and could keep people off his land, but the part west of the river would still be Cherokee land and the Indians could travel that side of the river when going through the valley.

The chiefs nodded in agreement. They felt they had made a good bargain. The only thing that worried them was how would Andrew get all the horses, blankets knives and cloth, and how would he get them here to the village. There were 160 lodges and 230 braves in the two camps. Therefore he would have to get 160 horses, 320 blankets, 230 knives and 160 bolts of cloth.

Andrew explained that he would have to go to the white-man's largest village and it would take him almost six cycles of the moon to get that much together and return. They thought this was fair so they had the design of the valley drawn on the doeskin and Andrew wrote his name at the top, and the names of each of the chiefs. Then he affixed their names at the bottom and had each make his mark. Some used a thumb print, some made little emblems and one used the foot of a bird. He dipped it in the ink and pressed it upon the doeskin beside where Andrew had printed his name.

When it was all done, they smoked the pipe once again as if to cement the deal. Then Andrew excused himself because it was getting late and said he would turn in. He decided he would rest tomorrow and visit with Night Hawk and Great Eagle one last day, then leave the following day to go back and get his friends. They would then go on to Charleston along the coast and start gathering the stuff that he had promised. He had asked for, and received permission, to deliver it all to Night Hawk who would see that it was distributed as it should be. It was now near the middle of April. He promised he would be back by the sixth full moon. That would give him until late October.

When Andrew turned in that night he couldn't believe his good fortune. He had hoped to get perhaps 20 percent of what he had received, but he had asked for more thinking they would cut down any amount he asked for. But they didn't. They had given him all that he had asked for. They considered him one of them and what good was land anyway. They had plenty of it. He would remember how they had taken him at face value and trusted him. He vowed he would never betray them and would champion their cause as other white men moved into the territories, and they would come, as sure as the sun rose and the moon set.

CHAPTER TWENTY ONE

O n the second day, Andrew and Dave left to go back to the valley. Night Hawk and two of the other braves decided to ride with them. They knew the trails, and with them leading the way, the trip went much faster. By nightfall they were in sight of the camp. Dave fired his rifle into the air and when Hans looked up, he waved. They came on at a hard run and pulled to a stop in front of the cook fire. Maggie was a little apprehensive, but when she saw that it was the Indian who had rescued her from the Shawnee, she relaxed.

Hans stoked up the fire and put extra food on for them. Andrew asked him if everything was okay and had they had any trouble?

Hans said that he had seen Indians in the distance two or three times but that they had not come near. And there had been someone skulking around their camp during the previous night, he didn't see anyone.

Andrew could hardly wait to tell him of the trade he had made with the Cherokees. When he explained that he now owned all of the east side of this valley, from the river to the mountains, they couldn't believe it. This was the first Dave knew of the deal for he had not been at the meeting with the Chiefs and Andrew had not told him anything before now.

Hans said, "Why man, this makes you one of the biggest land owners in America. How did you do it?"

Andrew gave them all the details. Then he said, "Now the big job begins, getting all the goods together and getting them back here by the end of October. I figure it will take at least ten wagons, perhaps more, to haul all of the goods I have promised them, plus what I will need to build a house here and supply us for the winter. Will you two help me get it together, buy the horses, wagons and hire the men I will need to transport it here?"

Dave spoke up right away. "You dang tootin! I knew when I signed on with you two yahoos that this was going to be an adventure, and it ain't over yet. But man do you have any idea what trouble you will have getting ten wagons through these woods? There aren't any roads and most of the trails are not anywhere near wide enough to let a wagon pass. You will have to cut a road for much of the way. It would take a crew of twenty or thirty men just to clear the underbrush and help get the wagons across rivers and creeks. Some are deep and swift."

"I know. I figure to use mules and it will take at least two men to the wagon; probably six or eight more to herd the horses, probably 90 to 100 people in all. It will be a sizable group. Can we get that many men that are reliable who would take the risk of going into Indian country? Of course, the risk should be much less once we get into Creek or Cherokee country. We would probably have clear passage. What do you think?"

Dave slapped his knee and said, "Man I wouldn't miss it. Sure there are a number of mule-skinners and farmers who need some hard money that would hire on to make the trip. You might have trouble lining up that many wagons. I know a few horse traders but none of them will have that many riding animals and you don't want to take a plow horse to those Indians. You have gotten off to a good start with them, but don't try to pawn off a bunch of broken down nags on them or you will have trouble. They will fight over the good ones and the ones who get the poor animals will hate you. Where will you get that many blankets, knives, and stuff? You'll clean out all the mercantile stores in Charleston and Savannah and probably still won't have enough."

Dave and Andrew had been so excited about the trip and bringing back what they would need that they had not noticed that Hans had been quiet and hadn't said anything.

Hans had remained silent since his first comment. Now he spoke up.

"When we arrive back in Charleston I will help you round up some people to help you but I won't be coming back with you. Maggie wants to go on to see her folks and I have been thinking of going with her to see that nothing happens to her on the trip."

Andrew looked at him and saw the hang-dog look in his eyes. "Are you thinking of staying in Pennsylvania with her Hans?"

"Well, I had thought about it, but I don't know if I could handle living in a civilized town like they have up there. I am real taken with her and am going to ask her to marry me. Of course, I am almost 15 years older than she is and she will probably turn me down. But I am going to ask her anyway, just as soon as I get up the courage. She doesn't have any family except the sister in Pennsylvania, and I don't have anyone except my daughter and grandson back in Charleston. My wife has been dead almost fifteen years and I never figured to marry again, but Maggie is good company and I like being around her. Maybe I could help her get over the loss she has suffered."

Andrew put his hand on Hans' shoulder. "Hans, you have been a good guide and a fine friend. I will miss you and I had hoped that you and Dave would take a homestead here so we could all be together. However, a man must do what he must do. A man was not meant to live alone and if Maggie will have you, I wish you the best of everything. I only have one piece of advice and you can take it or disregard it, whichever you wish. You are a woodsman, what some call a pioneer. You like the wide open spaces, the forests and the wild. You yourself told me that being cooped up in town was about to drive you crazy. Do you think you can adjust to living in a big city with all the noise and people? I fear that although you love Maggie, you may be miserable with that type of life. Please think about that before you make your decision."

"I have been wondering if I could make the adjustment. That is what has kept me from asking her to marry me up to now. I don't know if I'll be happy without her, or if I would be happy living in her world."

Dave spoke up, "Ole Hoss, me and you are birds of a feather. We have heard the owl hoot. We have lived the life of the free, where we answered to no man, where the law was what we carried in our rifles or on our hip. You will never be happy living in civilization, but if that is what you decide to do, I want to be your best man."

The three of them embraced and sought out Night Hawk. Andrew spoke to him.

"Night Hawk, will you and your braves ride the river and the boundaries of the land I am buying from the Cherokee and blaze the side of trees so that we will know where my land begins and where it ends? Also, will you go with me to the south end of the valley and tell me if you consider that Cherokee land or if it is part of the Creek lands. I understand the boundary between the two lies somewhere close to here." Night Hawk agreed and the next day they rode south.

Near the end of the valley, the hills pinched in and the valley narrowed. The river ran faster and narrower also. It poured through a gap in the hills and then spread out in another valley to the south. They climbed the trail up out of the valley to the top of a high knoll. When they reached the top of the knoll, Night Hawk stopped his horse and pointed to a jagged scar in the side of the mountain. It seemed like a giant landslide from maybe a century before and the slide had taken all the trees and soil off the side of the mountain and left the bare rock showing.

Andrew judged it was a half mile further south. Night Hawk indicated that was the end of the Cherokee lands and the beginning of the Creeks. It was a marker that has been accepted for a long time.

Andrew said, "If you are in agreement, I will call that the south boundary of my land and it will be a buffer between you and the Creeks, at least on this side of the river. Will you ride farther with me and see if we can find some of the Creeks to tell them I will be coming here to live and have the permission of the Cherokee?"

Night Hawk agreed and they rode down into the next valley. They had ridden for perhaps an hour and a half or maybe two hours when they saw the first Indians. Night Hawk hailed them and they rode to meet them. After speaking to them, the Creeks led them toward their village. It is an Indian custom that when you enter another's village, you go to the lodge or tent of the chief and speak with him first. The Creek braves led Night Hawk and the white-man to the lodge of their chief, Bear Claw, and remained sitting on their horses. Night Hawk and Andrew dismounted and handed the reins of their horses to the braves. It was a warm day and the chief emerged from his tent. Night Hawk spoke first.

"Oh great chief of the Creek Nation, I am Night Hawk, eldest son of the Cherokee chief, Great Eagle. I have come to you to introduce you to my blood-brother, Andrew Stanley. My brother saved the lives of myself, my younger brother,

Burned Belly and two of my cousins in the Natchez Nation when we were captured by the hated Shawnee. He is a brave warrior and I am proud to call him brother. Although he is white, he thinks like an Indian and he is an honorable man. The Cherokee have sold him the land east of the river that runs through the valley above the scar in the mountain. He will be returning there with his family to live before the snows of winter come."

Night Hawk stopped to give this time to sink in.

Indians did not understand about selling land and they weren't sure what he meant. They did understand that there would be a white man and his family living near them and they didn't know what to make of this. There were those who hated the white man and the Creeks that had contact with the whites perhaps more than some of the other Indians. These contacts had not all been friendly. They had been attacked by some of the renegade whites, and although they did not admit it, they had done their share of raiding the white farms also. There was much bad blood between them and the whites.

Out of courtesy for Night Hawk, Bear Claw did not want to bring that up at this point. Bear Claw indicated they should smoke the pipe and talk. He moved over to a big oak tree and sat in the shade. When the pipe was lighted and smoke blown to the four winds, it was passed to Night Hawk as the guest of honor. He in turn passed it to Andrew to show that his brother was to be accorded the highest honor.

Andrew pulled on the pipe and blew the smoke toward the sky, and then he passed it to Bear Claw who did the same and back to Night Hawk.

When the formalities were over, Bear Claw spoke.

"We have fought many battles with the white men who come over the mountains and steal our furs and horses; ravage our women and kill our people. Not all are honorable men and we have not had any friends among them. There are many of the young braves who have lost brothers and other relatives to the white man's fire sticks. There are many lodges that are empty of men because the father and husbands have been killed. I do not know if I can control all of the young braves who thirst for revenge."

Night Hawk spoke again now, "Oh great chief, I have much respect for you and the Creek people. I know that our relationship with the whites has not been good. But I ask that you consider this man as my brother and treat him as you would another Indian. This white man has given back four lives to the Cherokee and Natchez people. He is not like those who come to destroy and kill. He will only kill to defend himself and his family. He will take nothing that is not his and he wants to be friends of the Creeks. Let him speak now for himself."

Bear Claw grunted approval and bade Andrew to speak.

Andrew had planned just what he would say.

"Chief Bear Claw, we have traveled all the way to the big river and there we made friends. The only time I have raised my hand against any man was to protect myself or to save the lives of Night Hawk and his party. The Great Spirit put all of us here on earth for a purpose. I believe he meant us to live in harmony."

"I come from a land far away, across the great salt lake. I once had a land there. We called it a country. There were war-like people on three sides of our country and they attacked us, killed my family and many of our warriors. For many years we fought to defend our land. They did not come and ask us to live on our land. They did not offer to buy land by trading gifts of horses and other things we could use. They sought to take the land by force and make slaves of my people. That is not my way. I come offering to buy the land of the Cherokee with gifts and things they can use. If it had been the land of the Creek, I would have come to you. I have had enough of war and killing. I have seen the blood of my friends run like a river. I will fight to defend myself and my family, but I prefer to live in peace with the Indian. There is much I would like to learn about your ways, your language and your customs. Perhaps there are some things I could teach you about the ways of the white man. All of our customs are not bad. I come to you as a neighbor, offering only friendship. I hope you will accept me as a friend. Perhaps the time may come when you will need a friend to go among the white men and speak to them. I will be your spokesman if you wish it."

Bear Claw listens intently to Andrew, and when he finished speaking, Bear Claw asked, "Will there be other white men coming to your valley?"

Andrew noted the implied acceptance in the way Bear Claw had said 'your valley.'

"I have two others who are my friends and who have traveled with me for many moons. I would like them to stay if they will, but I do not know if they will remain or not. I also expect to bring a group of black men and their families to live and help me work the land. You see, the white man likes to see things grow, so we will be planting corn, potatoes, cotton, and many kinds of trees that bear sweet fruits. I cannot do all of this by myself. But the land I have obtained from the Cherokee is plenty for all that will join me. We will not encroach on the lands of the Creek. On this you have my word."

Bear Claw had raised his head at the mention of blacks. Now he asks the question, "I have been told that the white man keeps black men in shackles and treats them badly. Do you plan to keep slaves on your land?"

"No, Great Chief. When I was little, my father and mother were treated little better than slaves and when I grew up I, too, would have been a slave if I had not become a warrior. I do not believe in slavery. On the boat that brought me to this land, there was a black chief. He had been captured in his homeland and was sold into slavery with some twenty of his men, a few of his women and children. All the rest of his tribe, including his wife and children were killed. He was sold as a slave when we landed. I intend to try to buy his freedom from the white man who purchased him in the slave market. I want to set him and his people free. I will ask them to come and live on my land and work for me, but I will pay them in food and goods so that their families can stay together and they can see their children grow. That is my way and why I have purchased as much land from the Cherokee as I did. It is not all for myself. These people, though their skin is not the color of mine, like me, were put here by the Great Spirit. Like me, they have had their families killed and their lands stolen from them. I want to begin a new life, and I want to help these people begin a new life also."

Bear Claw looked long at Andrew and puffed several times on his pipe. Finally he spoke.

"You are a strange man, not like the other white men who have come onto our lands. You have a true heart, the heart of an Indian. I can see why a chief like Night Hawk would take you as a brother. You should have an Indian name. With Night Hawk's permission I will call you "One Who Sees Far". It is not just with the eyes that one should see, but with the mind and heart as well.

"As long as you keep the promises you have made this day in front of your brother and the other chiefs of the Creeks, you shall be safe in the lands you hold. These lands are in the area claimed by our cousins the Cherokee, and we will honor their agreement with you."

Andrew, greatly relieved, replied, "Oh great chief I thank

you. I hope that when I have returned with my family, you will come to visit me and we will feast to celebrate our friendship. There is one more thing I would ask. I will need many things to build my home and plow the earth. We will need to bring these things in on big wagons and we will need to cross the lands of the Creek. We will not stop or build anything on your lands. All I ask is passage for my wagons through your lands. I also will set up a trading post near my home. There I will have blankets, knives and goods that the Creeks must travel long distances to get. I would like to trade with both the Creek and the Cherokee and any other tribes who may come to the trading post. In order to get the goods my wagons will need to travel back and forth through your land. I would negotiate a route for this purpose and I will be willing to pay for the route. It would have to be wide enough for wagons to pass. Would you allow such a route across your land?"

Bear Claw hesitated again, deep in thought. He believed this white man and the thought of a trading post near-by would be a boon to his people. Now they had to travel many days to take their skins and trade items to the white men's settlements. Many of the traders there were dishonest and only gave his people a fraction of what their goods were worth. But could he trust this man to be any different. He spoke his thoughts now.

"It would be good to have a trading post close so that our people did not have to go into the white man's villages. But too often, the white traders cheat the Indian out of his furs and charge double for the blankets and cloth that they sell the Indian. How do I know that you will not do the same?"

Andrew sensed that much hinged upon his answer and he did not hesitate. "Bear Claw, often in trading, one may feel that he is not getting true value, or he may be trying to trick the other into paying more than an item is worth, but

I will make you this promise. I will have to make a profit to be able to buy more goods and transport them here, but I will keep my prices down as low as I can and I will give as high a trade value as I can for the goods your people bring to me. If they do not agree, we will not trade. If a dispute arises, we will come to you to settle it and I will abide by your decision. Is that not fair?"

"It is and I accept. What will you pay for this passage route you seek, and where do you want it to be?"

"I do not know exactly where it should be for I am not that familiar with your land, but I would ask that it be as direct a route as we could get to the nearest white town, which I think is the white man's town called Birmingham. We would need to find where it is best and easiest to cross the rivers and streams. The big wagons that will be bringing my goods will bog down in wet areas so we will need to stay on high ground as much as possible and just descend when we are ready to cross the river. If you agree I will have one of my men come and you can send two or three of your braves with him and together they could mark out the road we would travel. As for payment, I am prepared to offer you two methods of payment. I will either pay you a one-time amount; or I will pay you another amount for each trip that we make across your land. I would prefer the amount for each trip so that every time we cross your land your people will receive some goods. If I pay everything over now and it is all used up in a year, perhaps your people will begin to resent me and try to prevent me coming across your land in the years ahead."

"I think you are right Sees Far. The payment for each trip would be better. What is your offer?"

"Each time that my wagon train passes through your lands, whether it be one or ten wagons, I will give you 10 new blankets, 10 pounds of coffee, 10 pounds of sugar and 10 pounds of salt. Is that agreeable?"

Andrew knew that was low and did not expect that Bear Claw would accept. Indians liked to bargain.

Bear Claw shook his head and sort of scoffed. "Sees Far needs to look again at the distance he must travel through the lands of the Creek. To the white man's village that you speak of is a journey of almost three suns by horseback and by wagon it will take close to seven suns or more. It means the white wagons will be on Creek lands for several days. Also, once the road is open, there is the danger that other white men will want to cross Creek land also. How are we to keep them from following your road and spilling into our lands?"

Andrew conceded that may be a problem, and one he hated to think about. He answered, "You are right. There is that danger however, it will provide an easy means of travel for your people also when they head south to the coastal areas."

He continued, "If it gets to where there are many coming across your land, you will have to charge them the way you charge me. The white man calls it a toll. If they do not pay, make them turn back and go another direction. There should not be that many for there will not be any way for them to go beyond my land. The roads will end at my property and I will not allow them to stay there. That is why I bought the land from the Cherokee. With title to it I can make anyone stay off my land that I do not want there."

Bear Claw said, "Uh. That is good. It is yours the same as this land belongs to the Creek. Now I can see why you wanted to say it is yours. But it will still be a problem. I believe 25 blankets and 25 pounds of the other items would be a fairer bargain."

"If my wagons were many I could perhaps pay that much, but suppose I just had one wagon passing, it would be too much to pay. I could not afford to give so much for one wagon."

After much discussion, it was agreed that the "toll" would be 5 blankets and 5 pounds of coffee, sugar and salt for each wagon in each train. It appeared that an agreement was close and Andrew decided to sweeten it a bit.

As Bear Claw hesitated over the latest offer, Andrew said, "Because I want Chief Bear Claw to believe I am a true friend, during the Harvest Moon each year I will bring to his village 50 blankets, and the years that the harvest is good, I will share a wagon load of food that we have grown on the land in the valley. I wish to share what Mother Earth provides for me with my Indian friends."

Bear Claw said, "Agreed. We have reached a fair agreement. You shall have your road and I will pick two braves to go with your friend to mark the route." They shook hands and passed the pipe around again. The deal was made.

They left the village and Andrew felt good. He had obtained safe passage for his wagons and cemented a working agreement that would provide him continued access. The "toll" agreed to was not that much and would not be a big burden for him. If everything went well at the trading post, he would make it back out of each shipment. But whether he made a profit or not, it was essential that he have free access to his valley without having to fight Indians all the time.

Night Hawk had remained silent and now he spoke. "My brother is an honorable man. The deal you made with Bear Claw is a fair one and one that will help all of his people. The continuing supply of blankets and salt are things the Indians have trouble getting. It will be a big help to them. I suspect that they will also become good trading partners for many of the places they go to trade, they are cheated. They are good people. If you treat them fairly, they will also come to your aid if you are attacked by any other bands of Indians. You have made a good start in your new land my brother. I am proud of you. You deal fairly with the Indian and I believe you will become a big chief in this land."

That night, Andrew outlined his plan to Hans and Dave. Dave was to go to the Indian village and with the two Creek braves they would blaze a route to the town of Birmingham. Then Dave would come on to Charleston to meet Andrew. He and Hans would take Maggie and go on to Charleston and to Savannah if necessary to start lining up supplies and wagons. When he finished issuing instructions he walked over to the fire and poured him another mug of coffee. Then he returned and sat down with the two men and Maggie. She had been sitting quietly listening to what he was saying.

Hans spoke now for the first time. "I will go to Charleston and help you arrange for the wagons and buy the horses you need. Maggie has agreed to marry me and we will be going on to Pennsylvania as soon as you can get a replacement for me."

Andrew clapped him on the shoulder and said, "Hans I am happy for you. Maggie, you have a good man here. He will treat you good. I hope you will be very happy. I will hate to lose you Hans. I had hoped that you and Dave would take some of the land I have bought and live here with me. This is a rich valley and it will make good farm land. There is plenty of timber to build homes and I believe I have made peace with the Indians. I think we can live in peace here. We could have a good life together."

Hans was somewhat down cast. "Maggie would not be at ease here after what has happened to her. Every time an Indian appears she is frightened. She has nightmares about the brutal killing of her husband and children. It will probably be with her always; so I am going to take her back to civilization where she will feel safe."

Andrew and Dave both said they understood and congratulated them again. They would not speak of the matter again.

Andrew asked Night Hawk and his braves to traverse the valley and blaze a symbol on trees as they went to indicate where the line would run that would indicate his boundary; a symbol that the other Indians would recognize. He particularly wanted this done on the south end of the valley near the slide in the side of the mountain, and in the north end of the valley. It was pretty much established that the river would be the western boundary and the foot-hills of the mountains would be the eastern boundary. But the north and south were not so well defined and Andrew left the marking to Night Hawk. If he marked the boundaries there should never be a dispute with the Cherokee and with as much land as he had, a few hundred feet one way or another would not make much difference.

He spent the next day picking out a site for his house. He rode to a high knoll that was at the foot of one of the smaller outcroppings from the mountain. It was a high ridge that ran from the mountain part way down the valley toward the river. This site would provide a back drop for the house on the south side of the hill, out of the winter winds and facing into the winter sun. It was a beautiful location and provided a clear view of most of the valley. You would not be able to see all the way to the north because of the hill behind the house, but you would see a lot of it anyway, up to the tree line some three miles or so. There was a small spring just above where the house would set that could provide clean water to the house. To the south, though, was the most fantastic view anyone could ask for. It was an open meadow almost to the river. There was a row of trees along the river and at some places along the way you could see the water glistening between the trees. Hans said it was filled with trout and other fish and there was plenty of game that came into the valley to eat the lush grass.

Andrew sat for over an hour just gazing out across the land. He could hardly believe all of this was his. Had he really been successful in acquiring title to so much land, and such beautiful land at that? This was more than his landlord back in Poland had owned, and not even in Poland was it as beautiful. He had truly come to a great land; this new world would be a new beginning. He began to think of a name. At first he thought of Black Valley, because the soil was so dark. Then, deciding that Black carried a connotation of something evil, he changed his mind and finally decided on Bright Valley. When Night Hawk returned that evening, he told him of his decision and asked him to tell Bright Day that he had named the valley for her.

Night Hawk smiled and said, "She will be pleased, my brother. The last thing she told me before we left my village was to "take care of you, not take care of myself, but to look after you. I fear she still has a strong heart for you Looks Far."

This was the first time Night Hawk had used his new Indian name and it came as a surprise. Little did he know that in the months and years ahead this name would become well known throughout the Indian tribes in the Carolinas, Georgia and Tennessee territories.

CHAPTER TWENTY TWO

Night Hawk and the braves prepared to leave the next morning.

Andrew bid Night Hawk farewell and told him that if all went well he would be back in four months, but that it might take longer to get the wagons through the forest, so no longer than 6 months.

Andrew knew they were going to have to cut a road for most of the distance. He instructed Dave to try to follow as many open valleys as he could to reduce the amount of cutting they would have to do. Then he, Hans and Maggie, took the pack horse and headed due east. The trip was without incident and they arrived in the little town of Augusta in late May.

They stayed over one day to give them a chance to get a hot bath, some clean clothes and to sleep in a regular bed. They next day, Andrew contacted the livery stable owner and began to discuss horses with him. When Andrew asked him how many good riding horses would he be able to get if he set his mind to it, he thought for a few minutes and said perhaps twenty. He said it would probably cost at least $15 a head. Andrew told him to buy them and to make arrangements for pasture for at least 100 more. That he would be back with them in twenty days and he would need a pasture to hold them for three or four days while they grazed. He would also be checking on the status of the wagons he required. The livery man thought Andrew was crazy until he began to count out $3,000 to him.

Feeling much better, but being urged on by the excitement, they left the next morning and rode straight for Charleston. Andrew did not want to miss seeing Catherine, but time was pushing him now, and he must start arranging for wagons and things he would need. Besides, Orangeburg was about a day's journey out of his way. He would go to get her when he went to Sumterville to talk with Thomas Sumter.

Back in Charleston, Andrew stopped in at English Charlie's tavern. He entered dressed in buck-skins and his long hair braided like an Indian's. He walked to the bar, laid his rifle on the bar and asked for Vodka. The wind and the sun of the past eight months had turned him as brown as an Indian. Only his eyes and his speech reveal him as a white man.

The bartender hesitated, unsure whether it is a white man or an Indian. As the bartender serves him he asks for English Charlie.

The bartender retreats into the back, and in a moment, English Charlie appeared. He didn't recognize Andrew.

"I am English Charlie. What can I do for you?"

Andrew decided to play a joke on him. He said, "I am looking for a low-down shiftless skunk named Joshua Wilson. They tell me you are a friend of his and can tell me where I can locate him."

"Indeed he is a friend of mine and no man will drink in my bar that calls him names. He is a good man and if he were here he would wipe the floor up with you."

By the time he had finished Andrew was laughing. "Charlie, it is me. Don't you recognize me?"

Now Charlie looked closer and stared into his eyes.

"Stanley? Andrew Stanley. Is it really you? My God

man how you have changed! You don't look anything like yourself. Where in the world have you been?" He grabbed his hand and pumped it up and down, not turning it loose.

Andrew clasped his fist with the other hand. "Man stop shaking my hand like you are pumping water and I'll tell you a story you won't believe. Bartender gives us another round."

Charlie motioned to the bartender that he is not to sell this Indian any whiskey, but he is to give him anything he wants. His money is no good in that bar.

They retired to a table and Andrew briefly told him the highlights of the past nine months. Charlie stared in disbelief, thinking, nothing this man does is normal. First he comes to town with a fortune in jewels and turns them over to a stranger. Then he puts his money in a bank and authorizes the banker to give it to someone else if he doesn't return. Now he has come back the blood brother of a Cherokee Chief and the owner of almost 70,000 acres of land in Indian country.

When Andrew stopped talking to take a sip of his drink, Charlie continued to stare at him. Finally, he said, "Andrew, it was a terrible tragedy that happened to you in Poland. But it seems God is trying to make it up to you. You are a very fortunate man. When do you plan to return?"

"Just as soon as I can buy wagons and supplies that I will need. It is probably going to be difficult for me to get wagons, horses, blankets and things I need to take back with me. But I want to be on the road by mid-July. I'm going to the bank this afternoon and first thing in the morning I will start rounding up all the things I must buy."

He said good-by and caught a carriage to the bank. When he entered in his buckskins, the bank teller was a bit unnerved. It was unusual to see people in Charleston in buckskin, but his regular clothes had long ago worn out, and the buckskin suit that Bright Day and her Aunt had made for him was still in good shape. He asked for Mr. Miller and the teller went to get him.

Miller did not recognize him either. He did not realize he had changed so much. He spoke to Miller.

"Mr. Miller, I am Andrew Stanley. I have returned from my journey into the wilderness. I have not had a chance to get new clothes yet. I wanted to touch base with you first. Can you tell me how much there is in my account now?"

Like English Charlie, Miller was startled at his appearance, but upon recognizing him, there seemed to be a slight frown cross his brow. Andrew did not know why this was so for the man had been friendly to him before. Miller motioned for the teller to come forward and he told him to check the account of Mr. Andrew Stanley and give him the balance in the account. Andrew was further surprised that he did not invite him into his office.

Shortly the teller returned and indicated that the ledger showed that Stanley had around $300,000. Andrew was shocked. Peter Georgiades had been busy. He told Miller that he would need 10 or 12 drafts so that he could draw on the account. There were a number of large purchases he would be making. When Miller did not unbend and act more friendly, he left the bank.

His first stop was the mercantile store where he had bought his supplies earlier. He asked to speak to the owner and when he came out of the back office, Andrew introduced himself and said, "Sir I have several large orders I want to place and I cannot stress the importance of time. How many woolen blankets do you have in the store?"

The merchant said, "There are probably 35 or 40 if you count all of them."

"How many good knives, skinning knives and other types?"

"Perhaps 50."

"How many days would it take you to get 400 blankets here, 200 hundred bolts of cloth and 300 knives of good quality steel?"

The merchant's mouth dropped open and he began to moisten his lips and try to regain his voice. Finally, he said, I could have them in two weeks, if they have them in Savannah. I might get as much as another 50 or 60 blankets from the other merchants in town. Maybe some of the knives as well."

"Good. I want you to personally take charge of rounding up the items on this list. How much are the blankets and knives?"

"The blankets are $2 each and the knives, the good ones, are $2.50. Bolts of cloth will run $3.50 to as much as $4.00 for some kinds of cloth. How do you plan to pay for all this stuff and what do you plan to do with it?"

"As for what I plan to do with it, you wouldn't believe me if I told you, but I don't intend to go into business against you. As to how I will pay for it, if you will give me a figure, I will pay you in advance 75 percent of the order. When the goods are here and stored in a warehouse I will rent, we will total the amount and I will settle the balance then. Is that satisfactory?"

The merchant hastened to agree and hurried to his office to run up the totals. He couldn't believe his good fortune. This was more than he had sold during the last six months all together. He had never had such a big order to fill before.

When he returned he told Andrew that he had used $4 a bolt for the cloth because he might have to pay more for it in Savannah. The total was $2350. Andrew wrote him a draft for $5,000 and told him he would have many other items in a day or so. That he had to see how many wagons he could buy. The merchant gave him directions to a warehouse he might be able to rent, and also to a freight line where he might be able to get wagons. As Andrew was departing he said, "If you have everything I request of you here in 14 days, I will pay you an extra $200. I want to be able to leave here in no less than 20 days and I have much to do. Please make sure these items are here by then."

He went to the warehouse first and was able to obtain a portion of the warehouse for his use. He told the owner he wanted a guard on the merchandise that would be delivered there and he wanted it 24 hours a day. He would pay for the guard, but if one item turned up missing, he would cut his fingers off. Looking at Andrew's appearance, he believed him and said it would be done.

Then he returned to the mercantile and told the owner where he could deliver the goods, but that he was to keep a tight tally on everything he delivered there.

It was getting dark so he went to the same hotel he had stayed in before when he was in Charleston. He had picked up a new suit of clothes and wanted a bath. He figured it might take two to get the dirt and grime off him.

Finally when he was cleaned and dressed, he went to the barber to have his hair trimmed and his beard shaved off. At first, he was going to have his hair cut back like it had been when he arrived in Charlestown, and then he decided to have it trimmed only and to leave it long and platted like the Indians had taught him. People stared at him but he didn't care. Already he was thinking of them as strangers, foreigners and he knew then he would not be happy in towns like this again. He was already thinking of getting back into the woods. Now he began to understand what it was the Dave and Hans had been trying to tell him. He had only been back in Charleston less than a half day and already he was feeling hemmed in, too many people, too much noise he wouldn't be happy until he was back in the woods again.

He ate supper in the restaurant and went to bed.

The sun had hardly come over the horizon before Andrew and Hans were on their way to the livery stable. After talking with the liveryman, Andrew figured that it might be best to hire him to buy the horses that they needed. He knew animals, and he knew most of the horse traders in the area. When he explained that he would want between 200 and perhaps as many as 225 horses, the stable man was excited. He saw a chance to make big money, but then he remembered the deal this man had made with him last September and he realized he was no fool.

Finally, Andrew commissioned him to buy as many horses as he could find. He was authorized to pay up to $50 per horse if he had to, but that he should keep it down to around $30 to 35 if he could. Andrew would pay him $2.00 a head as a commission for buying the animals and delivering them here. He was to secure a pasture where the animals could be held until they were ready to leave. As he was preparing to leave he admonished the liveryman, "Now I want good riding stock, not broken down plow horses. I will personally inspect every animal you bring in, and if I don't approve of them, you will be stuck with them. I will also need at least twenty teams of good strong mules to pull the wagons. I want to have enough to double team every wagon and have at least a dozen spares."

When they left the stables, Andrew said, "Hans, I need to go to Sumterville, but I want to get started gathering the wagons. When do you plan to leave with Maggie?"

"We talked about going by stage but it is such a rough journey. We are in luck, there is a ship leaving day after tomorrow for Boston. There is some cargo here that is destined for Philadelphia. The captain said he would put in there and let us off. It will be a much easier trip than going overland. If you don't object, we will book passage on that ship. I will make contact with every wagon builder in the area today and tomorrow. If the wagons are available, I will have them for you."

"Good. I will delay my departure for Sumterville until after you leave, and together we will round up as much as we can. See what you can find here and if there are not enough wagons and supplies, I may go to Savannah. Go on your way. I am going back to the mercantile and start a list of building supplies, tools and food supplies for the winter."

When Andrew returned to the mercantile, it was literally abuzz with activity. The store keeper had evidently hired some additional help and they were hard at work. As Andrew entered, he came forward to greet him.

"Good morning, Mr. Stanley. We are already at work on your order. I have dispatched my assistant to the other stores in town with instructions to buy up all the blankets, knives and cloth that they have in their stores. By this afternoon I will be able to take an inventory and will have your order ready in time."

Andrew said, "Good. Now there are some other things that I will need. I expect to take a party of between 100 and 120 people into Indian country. We will be there for the better part of a year and probably won't be able to get supplies during that time. I want barrels and barrels of flour, meal, salt pork, rice, beans, dried fruit, salt, sugar, syrup, four hundred pounds of coffee and tin plates, cooking pans, utensils and everything you can think of that we might need. I want a good supply of medicine and bandages. We will need tea, cans of food if you have them, or even home canned jars, although I want as few breakable items as I can get by with. I want twenty plows, harrows, sickles, 50 axes, harness for 50 mules, and riding saddles and blankets for 30 horses. If there is anything I may have forgotten, you add it to the list. Will you need more money at this time?"

"Oh no sir. The draft you gave me yesterday will be sufficient for now. Anyway I have no real idea of how much this will come to. It will take me four or five days to get all of this together and total up the price."

"Very well then. I have some other errands to run. I will stop back in a day or two to see how things are going. If you need me leave a message at the hotel."

It was just past 10 and Andrew decided to go visit Peter Georgiades. Peter was in his shop and recognized Andrew when he walked through the door. Peter came forward with a big smile and grasped his hand.

"Welcome back Andrew. I heard you were back in town and buying up all the supplies in the stores. I'm dying of curiosity. Tell me what has happened and where all you have been!"

Andrew launched into his story and for the next two hours Peter was fascinated. He relived the fights with the robbers and the scrapes with the Indians. When Andrew showed him the scar in his hand that had made him a blood brother of Night Hawk, he could control himself no longer. He literally danced around the shop. But when Andrew told him about the land he had bought, he could hardly believe him.

"Andrew, as far as I know you are one of only a very few men that the Indians trust enough to let them live among their people, much less sell them land. You are indeed an extraordinary man. But I have good news for you too. I shipped a small batch of your diamonds and jewels to New York. They fetched a very good price, $75,000. One of New York's finest gem dealers came down to see me and wanted to buy all that I could get like those I had sent him. I did not let on that I had more, but I told him I might be able to put together another batch for him. That night I went through the stones and took out the ones I thought would be the least expensive. When he came the next day he was pleased and though he tried to play down his interest, he was not a good poker player. I have been in this business too long and I could see his excitement. Before he left, he had paid $135,000 for those I had picked out for him."

Handing Andrew bank deposit slips, he said, "I deducted my commission and have deposited approximately $210,000 in the bank for you. I will be sending another shipment to him in New York this month. They want the jewels so they can set them in rings and necklaces for the Christmas season. If each batch sells as well as these have, and I think they should, you should have well over a half million dollars. I don't want to send too many at once. I believe they suspect me of smuggling gems into the country as it is. The man who came from New York said there were no jewels in America that would compare to the stones I sold him and these were some of the least you had. I am saving the best to last and may actually take them to New York or Boston myself and hold an auction. That way the other jewelry companies in the big city can bid on them. I hope you are not in too big a hurry. It may take me another year to turn all of these, and I am having a good time doing it."

"No Peter. I have all the money I will need and where I am going, money means nothing. It is what I buy with it here, the blankets, horses, and things of that nature that have true meaning in the territories. I plan to set up a trading post and trade with the Indians. I want you to be on the look-out for a good solid warehouse that is sound and can be secured. If one becomes available, buy it. I will need someplace to store the supplies that will be shipped in. And it will also house the skins, hides and other items I trade from the Indians until I can dispose of them. I will also want a good honest man to handle my business here. Keep this in mind and if such a person is found, hire him and send him to me."

Andrew paused, thoughtfully. "There is one thing that has troubled me somewhat. Banker Miller treated me with respect and warmth when I was last here. Yesterday when I was in his bank, he was very cool and barely spoke. As soon as our business was completed, he turned and entered his office. You would think with all the money I have put in his bank he would have been happy to see me. Has something happened that I am not aware of since I have been gone?"

Georgiades looked away, and then looked at the floor, not wanting to meet his friend's eyes. When Andrew pressed him, he said, "It is apparent that you do not know. His niece became pregnant and to save the Miller's embarrassment, she moved to Savannah. I think her mother had come there to live. It happened about the time you were here, and although Miller has not said anything, I believe he thinks you are the father. He once told me, before Maria began to show, that she was quite taken with you and he had hoped that you and she might be wed when you returned. She did not seem to care for any of the other men here; and, of course, when he and Hannah found out she was with child, they assumed you were the father. For a man in his position, having a bastard child born to one of his kin was unacceptable to him. Maria left before many were aware that she was pregnant."

Andrew was shocked. The blood drained from his face and he was as pale as any small child. He had to sit down and digest all that Peter had told him. He didn't know how much Peter knew, but he felt compelled to talk with him now. It took him several minutes to get his breath back. Peter walked to his desk and took out a bottle of good brandy and poured him a stiff shot.

When he could speak, he said, "I had no idea. We were two people who were lonely and attracted to each other. We were together only twice and I left right after that. It never crossed my mind that she might have gotten pregnant."

His mind was racing now. This put a different light on everything. He must find Maria and they would be married. He would not have his child being born without a father.

When he could pull himself back to the present, he heard Peter speaking.

"I can understand how these things happen. Is there anything you want me to do?"

"No. I must go see Miller at once and assure him that I will do the right thing by Maria and the child. We will be married. Now that presents another problem though. I gave the ring you made for me to another woman and asked her to marry me. She did not give me an answer but I felt she would accept when I returned. Now I must return and tell her I cannot marry her. What have I gotten myself into?"

It was almost closing time at the bank, and he did not want to discuss this matter in the bank anyway. He returned to the hotel and dressed in his best clothes as he had done once before when going to Miller's house. At seven P.M. he left the hotel and hailed a carriage. He had hoped to find the one who had served him so well last time, but he did not seem to be about. When he arrived at the Miller's, he dismounted from the carriage and asked him to wait.

With dread in his heart, he walked to the door and rapped with the large bronze knocker. The same black maid who had answered the door last time came and when he asked to speak with Mr. Miller, she asked him to step into the parlor. Then she went to get Miller.

He came from the library and when he saw Andrew his face took on a stony countenance. He seemed much older and very sad. Andrew thought that perhaps his hair had even turned a shade darker.

Andrew spoke first. "Mr. Miller, I have a matter of great

importance to talk to you about. May we step into your library?"

Miller turned and led the way. When they were inside Andrew turned and closed the door behind them. Miller did not offer him a chair so Andrew remained standing.

"Mr. Miller, is the reason you treated me so cold today and here tonight, because of Maria?"

"Sir, you have betrayed my confidence in you and you are not the gentleman I thought you were. Hannah and I do not have any children and Maria was the nearest thing I will ever have to a daughter. Your actions have not only ruined her reputation but she will now have a child to rear and her chances of finding a decent man are greatly diminished."

"Sir, I regret I have betrayed your confidence in me, but I had no intention of taking advantage of Maria. It just seemed to happen. I was a lonely man without a real friend, and you may not think so, but she was lonely too. We both thought we might steal a few moments of love without anyone ever knowing. Neither of us had any thought that this might happen. But you can rest assured; I will do the right thing. I will go to Savannah and Maria and I will be wed as soon as I can get there. No son of mine shall ever be called a bastard. You may not think much of me now, but I swear to you that I will be a good husband to Maria and I will treat her good. She shall not want for anything."

Miller seemed to thaw, and a new light flickered in his eyes. "Do you mean what you say? Do you really intend to marry her?"

"Just as fast as I can get to Savannah."

"She is not in Savannah. We told the townspeople that she had gone to Savannah to stay with her mother for a while, but she went to Philadelphia instead. The doctors are better there and we wanted to make sure she was in the best of hands. May I pour you a brandy? Let me call Hannah, she will want to say hello to you."

He poured Andrew a drink and went out of the library and up the stairs. Andrew assumed Hannah was already in bed. However, after a few minutes she and Miller descended the stairs and came into the library. Andrew was a little embarrassed, but Hannah came directly to him and embraced him.

"Andrew, I am glad you have returned safely. Harold said you were back in town and buying up enormous amounts of goods, even rented a warehouse. I hoped you would stop by. What in the world do you plan to do with all the things you are buying? The town is full of gossip about you. You are cleaning out all the mercantile stores in town and the stories going round is that they have ordered additional goods from Savannah for you. Tell me what is going on. I am dying of curiosity."

These were good people, and they had treated him like family when he was here before. He hoped he would be able to reestablish some of that friendship.

"Hannah, thank you for your kind welcome. These past months have been very full. It would take too long to tell you everything, however, I must tell you some of the story so that you will understand why some things have happened the way that they did. Other than some minor skirmishes with robbers and Indians, nothing very exciting happened until about the first week of January. We had left a little village of Roseville on the Mississippi River at the end of the American territories. We had headed north when one night we heard this terrible screaming. Someone was in terrible pain. The two men I had with me and I went to investigate. There had been Indians raiding all over the area, both Indian villages and white farms. They were Shawnee who had come down from the north. When we approached the camp fire we saw that there were eight Shawnee braves. They had one Indian boy spread-eagled on the ground and were putting red coals on his bare stomach. Three other grown men were tied with their hands behind them and around trees. The Shawnee were so intense in their torture that we were able to slip up and cut the other Indians loose and put knives into their hands. Then as we cut loose with our rifles, the freed Indians attacked also. It was a bloody battle and we were about to win when we discovered we had miss-counted and two more Indians who had been guarding their horses joined the fight. I shot one, but the second one got off a shot that caught me in the side. It broke one of my ribs and I was unconscious for almost a month."

The Millers were speechless.

Andrew took a breath and continued, "To shorten the story, the boy we saved and an older brother turned out to be the sons of a Cherokee chief and they were visiting their relatives in the Natchez tribe. They took me to their village and nursed me back to health. When I could walk, the oldest son, Night Hawk, made me his blood brother and we were given safe passage through all the Indian lands. When I could finally ride, in late March, we left to return to Carolina, but by way of the Cherokee village. Night Hawk wanted us to come and meet my new mother and father."

"On the way, we found the most beautiful valley you will ever see. It has a river running through it and is some twenty miles long. The soil is as black as coal and as rich as any I have ever seen. During our visit, it occurred that I might be able to buy some of the valley. They do not understand money, but perhaps they might agree to sell some land for horses, blankets, things like that. Things that matter to them are things they can use to make their lives better. I proposed to buy a large tract of their land expecting that I would get only a small fraction. To my surprise and after much haggling, I ended up with a deed to all the eastern half of the valley, almost 70,000 acres of prime land."

When Andrew revealed how much land was involved, Miller almost choked on his brandy and Hannah couldn't believe her ears.

Miller said, "Seventy thousand acres! Did I hear you right?"

"That is correct. Not only that, but I have negotiated a road through the Creek lands from Birmingham, which is the nearest town, I think. I am to pay them toll for every wagon that goes across their land. The toll will be in the form of blankets, sugar, salt, coffee and things they need but can't get very easily. I also intend to set up a trading post on my land near the river and build a house on a high knoll that is sheltered by the foothills. There were 160 lodges in the two Cherokee villages and 230 braves. I have agreed to pay them one horse for each lodge, two new woolen blankets for each lodge, a new knife of good steel for each brave and a bolt of cloth for each lodge for the women to sew dresses out of. It will be a big job getting that much stuff to them and that is why I am buying up as much as I am. I also intend to buy the twenty black slaves that came on the boat with me, I want to take them and their wives and children to live on the land I have bought. I do not intend to have slaves. If I can buy them I will give them their freedom and pay them for their work. Like me, they do not have a home anymore and I am willing to share what I have with them. I will go to Sumterville before I return to see if Mr. Thomas Sumter will sell them to me."

Now Andrew brings up the subject of Maria. It is embarrassing, but one that must be discussed with Hannah.

"Hannah, I would not have stayed away this long had I known. I heard she had gone to Savannah to live with her mother, but Robert informed me she is in Philadelphia. I must go to her at once and we will be married. I will provide for her and my son as a man should. Will you give me her address?"

"Certainly, Andrew. Before she left she told me how things happened and that you were no more to blame than she was and that we should not hold you accountable. She loves you Andrew, and I want her to be happy. She said she would wait for you, but she would not wait here in Charleston because of the gossip. I tried to make her stay, but she didn't want people to talk about me and Robert."

Andrew said, "I had planned to go to Savannah to see if I could pick up some other items I need, but Hans Brinkman has a lady that was rescued from the Indians. He is taking her to Philadelphia and they have booked passage on a ship leaving day after tomorrow. I will go with them and find Maria."

When Andrew left the Miller residence, there was a totally different atmosphere between them. Both Millers seemed delighted that he was going to marry Maria and make a decent woman of her. They would then be going to this land he called Bright Valley and perhaps no one would ever know that they had been intimate before they were married and Maria had borne a child out of wedlock.

As Andrew lay in bed that night his thoughts returned to the delightful time he had enjoyed with Maria. Little did he suspect that this might be the result. Then he thought of Catherine and how he would have to face her. This, too, he regretted; but it would have to be done. For now, though, he must concentrate on finding Maria and setting things straight between them.

CHAPTER TWENTY THREE

A ndrew awoke before dawn and lay for a while, sorting out the events of the past day. The news that Maria was pregnant with his child had been a shock, one he had not even dreamed of. He never doubted for a minute that the child was his, nor did he consider abandoning Maria and the baby. It was his, and they would be his responsibility. But what was he to do about Catherine? He was sure she was waiting for him to return, and although she had not given him a definite yes, he felt they were betrothed. Now she would feel betrayed. Perhaps he should not return to her and let her think him dead. But he could not do that either. He would have to face her and explain why he would not be able to marry her. First he must go see Maria and reassure her that he would marry her and take care of the baby.

He checked to make sure all his instructions were moving as planned and he then headed out to make arrangements for passage on the same boat with Hans and Maggie. After all, it would take at least 10 days or more for everything to be bought and made ready for the trip.

He met Hans in the restaurant for breakfast and asked how things went the day before.

"I was able to find only four wagons and twenty horses. But I learned of a man south of Charleston, just over in Georgia, that raises mules. They say he keeps a pretty large group and that would be the best place to get the mules. Otherwise, we will have to pick up a few here and there around the farms; and the plantation owners may be reluctant to part with them. They prefer the use of mules to horses for plowing."

"Hans, something has come up and I will be going to Philadelphia with you tomorrow. Maria, a girl I met when I was here in Charleston, is there and she is carrying my child. This has caused me to change my plans. I must go to see her. If it is as I have been told, I must marry her and give the child a name. When I return, I will have to go and face Catherine, but I do not want to do that until I have seen Maria. We need to do all that we can today and let the rest go until I return. Will you ride south today and see the man about the mules? Check with the liveryman and see if he has found any of the mules. If he has not, and the mule breeder has them, go ahead and buy 70 head. Have them delivered here two weeks from today and put in the pasture with the horses. Get as many as you can that have been broke to plow or pull wagons. We will have to work on the rest and team a green mule with a broken one."

Andrew paused in thought, and then continued, "I will check to see if the merchant has secured the warehouse and if he has any questions before I depart. I don't want things to stop while I am gone. One more thing. Ask the mule trader if he can recommend some good mule skinners. We will need at least ten. Tell him the pay will be good. If they want work, have them meet me here two weeks from today. That will be July 20th. I want to leave by July 31st if we can get everything arranged. I will meet you and Maggie for supper tonight and we will go over what you have been able to do."

With these instructions Hans rose and went out the door.

Andrew lingered over one more cup of coffee. It was amazing how the taste of this brew grew on a person. He was going over in his mind what remained to be done. One thing he must do is go to Albert Mueller and tell him how his gun and pistols had worked.

He went first to the mercantile store, and as it had been yesterday, the store was buzzing with activity. The owner spied him approaching and came to meet him.

"How goes the preparations? Was your man successful in getting much of what I will need at the other mercantile stores?"

"Only a small part. I have sent two wagons to Savannah this morning to get the rest of the blankets, knives and cloth. I think we will be able to fill your order for food and staples from what is available here in town, plus there is a ship due shortly with more supplies aboard. The salt pork, dried beans, rice, dried fruit, meal and flour I can get from the local farmers in the area. The salt, sugar, coffee and a few of the other things we do not grow locally I will have to make up from shipments brought in. I am having some of these picked up in Savannah also. I do not anticipate having any trouble filling your complete order."

"Good. How about the warehouse?"

"There is one near the docks that is empty right now. It will be filled with cotton and produce later in the fall, but it is vacant now. I have rented it for one month. We will be able to keep it locked and I will place a guard on it around the clock."

"Very good. I have to go to Philadelphia for a few days. I will be sailing tomorrow and will be gone at least a week, perhaps longer. Proceed with what you are doing and if you run short of funds, contact Mr. Miller at the bank. I will leave instructions to advance you whatever you need. I assume that as you move out the items I have purchased, you will be ordering new supplies. Is that correct?"

"Yes. Your order will practically empty my store. I have already placed orders for replacement merchandise. Some will be arriving soon, while other items may take several months to replace."

"Are any of your suppliers in Philadelphia?"

"Some. But most of my goods come out of New York and Boston."

"If you will make up an order for whatever you want to order from Philadelphia I will hand deliver it to the supplier there. That will cut down some on the delivery time. I am anxious that you restock as soon as possible, particularly with food stuffs. There is a possibility that I will have a work force of 30 or more blacks go with me when I return. If so, I will need to almost double the order for food and clothing I have given you. I won't know until I get back and make contact with some people. If things work as I have planned, I will have a body of more than 100 people go with me when I depart."

The merchant said he could get almost everything from Philadelphia and would have an order ready for him tonight. He would bring it to the hotel.

Next Andrew went to see Albert Mueller, the gunsmith.

Mueller was happy to see him. He said, "Hans Brinkman stopped by and said you were back in town. I was hoping you would stop by."

Andrew responded, "I wouldn't have left town without seeing you."

Mueller was anxious to hear how the weapons he had provided Andrew worked out.

Andrew said, "The only trouble I see with the pistol with the caps is that in the forest it will not be possible to get new caps. If you lose them or get them wet, you are out of luck. Although, I tried wetting a few of the caps, let them dry in the sun; and when they were thoroughly dry, I tried them in the pistol. About six out of ten fired. But this is too unreliable. In an emergency, you can't take a chance on your weapon not firing. Now if they are here in town so one can get new caps, it would be fine. It is a good weapon and certainly can be loaded and fired at a greater rate than the flint-lock type."

Andrew remembered the two times he had to use the pistol, once with the bandits Winslow and Johnson, and the second time with the Shawnee

Mueller spoke, "Then we must find a way to keep them dry under all circumstances, in rain or river crossings."

Andrew asked, "Have you made any improvements since I have been away?"

"Yes. I liked the idea you had of the twin barrels. I have developed something I want you to see." With this he led Andrew back into his workshop. He took a weapon down off the rack over his work bench and handed it to Andrews.

The rifle was of the Ferguson type with two barrels, one on top of the other. Both barrels were rounded smooth and had the spiral rifling inside the barrel as did the rifle he had bought. He noticed that both barrels carried the same shot, a 45 caliber ball. What really caught his attention was that there were two hammers and two chambers for powder and shot. It was a heavy weapon, but Andrew was very interested. He asked for a demonstration.

Mueller stepped outside and loaded both chambers. Then he raised the weapon and fired. Before the smoke cleared, he fired the second barrel. The shots rang out so close together, and it seemed almost like a simultaneous action. Andrew was startled by the rapid reports. While he was still considering the event, Mueller had reloaded and fired a double round again. Andrew was duly impressed.

Mueller basked in Andrew's praise. He was a man who lived for the pleasure of having another who understood guns and shared in his accomplishments. Andrew's ability to comprehend what he had witnessed and to see the significance of the development was praise enough.

Little did he realize that the innovations he was making would, in a few years, lead to a whole new line of weapons, weapons that would be loaded from the breech rather than the muzzle, and would fire metal cartridges that will contain the powder and ball in an enclosed casing.

Mueller continued, "During the time you have been gone, I have worked on the model you took with you and I have made a couple of additional changes. You remember the metal cartridges I showed you? I have developed a cylinder that holds four of these cartridges and I am trying to mount it on a frame that will allow each chamber to fire individually. Come see what I have done."

They walked into the workshop, and Andrew sensed Mueller's excitement. Andrew knew he was about to see something new from this exceptional weapons maker.

Mueller handed Andrew an almost square piece of metal with four rounded holes in it, all about the size of a 45 caliber ball. Then he led him over to his work bench and handed him the frame of the pistol that has been modified in a strange fashion. Instead of the pan and firing chamber for powder, there was a large hole in the weapon.

Mueller saw the confusion and attempted to explain. "The metal cylinder you are holding will fit into the hole in the pistol. It will hold four metal cartridges and after each shot you will rotate the cylinder by hand until a new cartridge is in line with the barrel. Instead of having a flint to strike the powder charge and cause the bullet to be fired, the charge will be inside the cartridge and will be struck by a metal pin in the frame. Like this, you will have to pull the hammer back with your thumb to a cock position, rotate the cylinder until a shell is in line with the barrel, then pull the trigger. The hammer will fall and strike the end of the shell. There is a small charge of powder directly under the pin that will fire, setting off the rest of the powder in the shell. As you will see, the bullet is mounted in the end of the cartridge and crimped. It is water proof and won't hurt if it gets wet."

Mueller walked over to a nearby water well and pumped water over it. "See, I run water from the pump over it and put it in this vice, strike it with the pin and it still fires."

Andrew was simply amazed and stood in awe. He was speechless.

Mueller stared at him with a smile.

Finally Andrew found his tongue. "Why Albert, this is fantastic. Have you been able to fit the cylinder to a frame yet?"

"No. I am having trouble in getting them to match up each time. If they don't match, when the bullet goes off, it will blow up in the hand of the person holding it. It takes a lot of time to fit it, try it, and fit it again. Each time, the cylinder has to be recast and all four holes have to rotate to just the right position before firing. I have destroyed five or six weapons trying to get it right."

He shuffled a bit to his other foot and continued, "Another thing is the cartridge. These are made by hand. You have to pour in the right charge of powder, fit the fight size shot into the end and crimp the neck with pliers. Pliers leave uneven crimps, or cracks that allow powder to escape or water to seep in.

"Also, sometimes the crimps won't allow the cartridge to slide into the cylinder easy. I have to work on a device that will make an even and solid crimp around the bullet, and will allow an owner to make his own cartridges. Otherwise the weapon is useless once you run out of cartridges. You either have to carry a large number of cartridges with you, or be able to refill the ones you have and reuse them I haven't got that worked out yet."

"Nevertheless, you're onto something really outstanding. When you have it working properly, and I'm sure you will work it out, this will be one of the greatest changes in weaponry in history. You are a true genius, Albert." Andrew grabbed him in a bear-hug and swung him around.

When he set him down, Albert said, "I have something else to show you. When you mentioned a two-barreled gun, the idea intrigued me. I have been experimenting with some other ideas."

With that, he reached behind his work bench and withdrew another gun. At first glance it looked like an ordinary rifle, perhaps a little more bulky than most, but a rifle nevertheless. He handed it to Andrew, and immediately Andrew noticed it was much heavier than the one he had been used to carrying. Then he saw the reason why.

Albert had mounted two barrels, side by side. One was an ordinary rifle barrel with the improved pan and firing mechanism that Albert had started putting on all of his guns. The other barrel was somewhat larger and had a similar firing pin on the opposite side of the weapon.

Albert explained how it worked. "The first barrel is a regular rifle and fires just like all the other rifles. The second barrel is designed to carry multiple shot, much like a blunder buss. I call this a scatter gun. The scatter gun can be loaded with small shot much like the blunder buss and propelled with a powder charge back her in the chamber. It doesn't carry as far as the rifle bullet, but it is devastating at short range. It will spread out and hit half a dozen people at a distance of 50 to 100 feet. It will take down two or three birds, such as ducks, up to 200 feet. Beyond that, it is not very effective. As with the cartridge, I am having trouble with the load for the scatter gun. I have an idea for putting a dozen or more small shot into an enlarged type cartridge. With a heavy powder charge, and making a chamber which will take the enlarged cartridge and can be fired with a pin like the pistol cartridge. This scatter gun is not ready for use. I have to do some more work on it."

Andrew commented briefly and then changed the subject. He asked if the other pistol to match his was ready.

Mueller produced a matched pair of pistols. Both had the cap firing process, but what was most interesting was that they were hinged at the point where the barrel and the firing pan were joined. They are the first breech loading pistols that Andrew has ever seen. Mueller was delighted with his surprise and attention. He demonstrated them and then passed them to Andrew.

He said, "These are yours. You gave me the idea of the breech loading weapon and I have made you two pistols. I don't know how well the hinges and the catches will stand up under constant use, but these are the only two of their kind. I want you to have them."

Andrew was very pleased and offered to pay him, but Mueller would not hear of it. Andrew asked if the twin barrel rifle was for sale. They agreed on a price of $100 and Andrew knew he had a bargain at that price. Then he sprung another surprise on Mueller by telling of his plans.

"Albert, I have acquired a large tract of land in the territories. I bought it from the Cherokee and have made a bargain with them to live among them. I will be operating a trading post on my land. I am taking a band of some 100 people with me when I return. We will be leaving in two weeks or so. I will need about 20 of your best Pennsylvania rifles, or Fergusons, if you have them. If you have that many of the rifles you have modified, I would prefer them. Also, I would like all of them to be the same caliber. I do not expect trouble from the Indians I have made friends with, but there are plenty out there that may not be friendly. They may try to run me off my land, or raid the trading post. I don't want a mish mash of weapons. I want them all to use the same powder and shot. I will also want three barrels of powder and 5,000 shot. If we run short I will have the capability of making more shot. Because I'm not as experienced, it won't be as good as I can buy. Some of the people I will have with me will never have fired a gun before and certainly won't know how to make bullets. Can you supply me with these things? If not, I am going to Philadelphia tomorrow and can get them while I am there."

Mueller answered, "I have the rifles but I will have to modify them. I think I can do that in two weeks. I'm sure that you will be able to get powder and shot locally from the mercantile stores. I have only about half of what you requested, but I can get the rest for you if you wish by the time you return."

"Please do that for me. There are so many things I need to purchase. If you can take care of this it will relieve me of a burden."

"When Hans came by did he tell you about the woman the Indians rescued and what his plans were/"

"Yes. He told me of the rescue of the woman from the Indians and that her husband and two children had been slaughtered before her eyes. He also said he was going to marry her. They will be leaving tomorrow for Philadelphia. Do you think he will be happy there?"

"No, Albert. I have travelled with him and Dave Foster these past months and Hans is a frontiersman, not a city man. He thinks he loves Maggie, but I fear it may be more sympathy than love. He feels sorry for her and she is so alone. He thinks she needs someone to look after her. It was a terrible thing that she saw and the things she had to endure. It has left great scars, but Maggie is a strong woman, stronger than Hans may think. I believe she will be O.K. She is a good person, a good woman, she could make Hans a good wife, but I don't think she can make him happy living in the city."

"I believe the same. But he is determined. He is a grown man and I fear that if I interfere, it may affect our friendship."

"Dave and I both have spoken to him of this and he seems determined to give it a try. So there is nothing more we can do but remain his friends. Maybe having a full-bodied, strong woman like Maggie for a wife will compensate for the things in his old life that he will be leaving behind. Only time will tell."

Next Andrew went to the docks to book passage. The captain said they would depart on high tide at 3 A.M. and he was welcome to stay aboard that night if he wanted. If not, he should be aboard no later than 1:30. Andrew indicated he probably would come aboard after supper that evening, but he wasn't sure.

He went to a restaurant and as he ate he reviewed all his plans. It seemed that everything was progressing as planned and there was nothing more that he could think of at that time. He decided to go to the bank and get some more money to take with him. He might need more in Philadelphia.

This time when he met Miller he was a lot more friendly, much like he had been before. Andrew figured that his acceptance of his responsibility to Maria and the child had done much to repair his character in the eyes of Miller. Andrew withdrew $5,000 and asked how much had he spent so far. Miller checked the books and said, "The drafts that have been cashed so far are just a bit over $35,000."

Andrew told him, "There will be more coming. According

to my calculations, the supplies I have ordered, the wagons, horses, mules, etc. will run somewhere close to $50,000 maybe $60,000. When I am ready to leave, I will need a safe and some $10,000 in gold to take with me. I will have some 90 to 100 men who I will have to pay for the trip in. There will be others who I hope will stay and help me build the home and buildings and put the farm into production. I will also want to set up a system of transfers and shipments from here to Birmingham. I will have the items I need ordered and delivered here to the mercantile. They will transfer them to wagons and have them taken to Birmingham. My wagons will come down every other month and pick them up and bring them to the farm. I want to leave my money here in your bank and will draw on it with the drafts as needed. Can that be arranged?"

"Certainly, without any trouble. Do you plan to take Maria into the territories with you?"

"Yes. If she will go. I believe it will be safe for me and my family or I would not risk it. Maria had asked me to take her when I went before, but I did not know what to expect. Now I do. I will not let any harm come to her if I can help it. You can be sure of that."

"I believe you. It is just that we miss her and of course we are concerned for her safety. We hear some very bad stories of the people on the frontier. We will worry about her and the baby, and of course about you, too."

"Believe me Robert; what you have heard cannot begin to convey the true hardships those people on the frontier of the territories endure. They are brave people, and sometimes foolish. I have seen many graves, and many bones lying unburied in the woods and along the trails. It is a hard life, but there is something that someone who has not been there cannot understand. It is a sense of freedom, a fact of being your own man, your own self without any constraints or rules. Out there, your life is always in danger. Yet as you travel the woods and traverse the mountains, it is as if your very soul soars into the heavens."

Andrew paused momentarily, lost in the feeling. "It sounds foolish when I try to explain the feeling, but it has captured me already. I could never live in a town again. It is too confining. As for the Indians it is true they are savages in many aspects. They kill and torture their enemies and think nothing of murdering innocent children. But to their way of thinking, an enemy child will one day be a grown enemy who may come and kill you. It is best to kill them when they are young rather than wait until they grow up and come to kill you. To our way of thinking this is barbarous, but Indians don't understand our customs. I doubt they could ever learn to live under our laws. Yet, within their tribal system, they have their own laws and ways of punishing those who break the law. Most of the Indians I have met are honorable and if they give you their word, you can rely on it."

Andrew excused himself and said he had to go to the Administrator's Office to register his land title. He was afraid it might prove difficult and asked Miller if he would go with him.

When they entered the Administrator's Office they asked to speak to the supervisor. A short man in a stiff collar and a small cap with a green eyeshade came from the back and asked what he could do for them. He recognized Miller and was very polite. Miller spoke first.

"William this is Mr. Andrew Stanley. He is the principal depositor in my bank and he wants to register title to some land in the Territories. I think you will find this a strange situation and he may need your assistance to make sure it is recorded properly."

Andrew produced the doeskin with the drawings on it and the signatures. He explained that he had purchased this land from the Cherokee Indians. It was land generally considered to be theirs and these were their marks on the document. He wanted to register it in his name so that there would be no problem about ownership at some later date.

William was flustered and didn't know how rightly to proceed. This man, Stanley, had been brought over by the most influential man in Charleston, one you did not want to antagonize. So he began in a polite tone of voice.

"Mr. Stanley, I doubt that this would stand up. The various state governments do not recognize Indian ownership in many of the lands they claim. There is general consensus that any title conveyance from them is not valid. In any case, lands west of the mountains were ceded to Georgia in 1787. South Carolina no longer claims any of that territory. You would need to register this in Savannah. But I don't know if that will insure you having good title to the land since Indian ownership is not fully recognized."

Andrew was surprised. He did not realize that the land was now claimed by Georgia. He did not have time now to go to Savannah and get back to sail. His mind raced.

Finally, he said, "Sir, as I understand, almost every one of the colonies have, at one time or another, entered into treaties with the various tribes of Indians. Many of these treaties recognize control of certain areas of land. This recognition of control implies ownership or they would not have needed a treaty at all. Some actual purchases have been made from other Indians.

"Therefore, I am willing to take my chances on the legality of this transfer of title. If it becomes necessary at some future time to argue the matter in a legal context, I want the title duly recorded in the official records of this colony. I cannot go to Savannah at this time for I leave at midnight for Philadelphia. I will go there upon my return, but I would appreciate it if you would record it in your records.

If Georgia later disallows the entry in your records it will have no meaning and all you will have is an entry in your books that is not valid. But at least there will be a record of my attempt to register my interest. Will you please enter it in your books?"

Miller added, "I can see no harm in Mr. Stanley's request. If Georgia fails to recognize the recorded entry in your records, it will have no bearing on your other records and may at some point prove quite important to Mr. Stanley."

The Administrator thought for several seconds and when he could not come up with a plausible answer, he decided to make the entry. What would it hurt? And if it proved of no benefit, he had warned them in advance. But he did not want to face the displeasure of the banker. He had borrowed money from him and might have to again.

As he began to make the entry he looked up and stated, "Why this gives you title to almost a whole valley, twenty miles long and five miles wide. That would be over 65,000 acres. Are you sure these are the correct dimensions?"

"Yes. That is correct. I believe it will actually be closer to 70,000 acres when it is finally measured. And the signs of all the chiefs of the Cherokee tribe are affixed on that skin."

William looked at him again, in a more respectful manner. "Now I can see why you want this recorded. This is the single biggest tract I have ever recorded for an individual. Some government entries have been larger, but this is the largest for an individual and one of the few ever recorded for the territories. I hope you will be able to hold on to it."

Andrew said, very seriously, "I intend to."

When they left the Administrator's office, Andrew thanked Miller and stated he would let him know how Maria was doing upon his return. At this point in time, he did not know whether she would be able to travel at this stage of her pregnancy.

He checked out of the hotel and boarded the ship at midnight. Hans and Maggie came aboard with him. Hans told Andrew he had been successful in getting 55 mules, and the breeder had indicated that he would see if he couldn't get another 25 by the time he was to deliver them to Charleston. The breeder also knew most of the mule skinners who drove for the freighting companies. He intended to spread the word; those interested would meet Andrew in Charleston in two weeks.

Hans said that he had not been able to get any more wagons, but a freight company said they would rent him five of theirs for the trip and would furnish teamsters to drive them. He had signed a contract with them and told them to be in Charleston on the 28th of July.

Andrew was thinking beyond the initial trip into the valley. The four wagons he already had would be insufficient to freight supplies to the farm and to the trading post without making monthly trips. He would prefer having to make the trip once every two months rather than monthly. He was afraid that would not be enough. Even with the five extra he was renting, he was not sure that would take care of all the merchandise he had purchased. When he returned he would see about buying a few more wagons. It was good that Hans had rented some though. This would help him get all of the goods to the valley and he wouldn't be stuck with five wagons he wouldn't need.

The ship sailed on schedule and the trip was uneventful. They docked in Philadelphia the morning of the second day.

Andrew bid Hans and Maggie goodbye and said he hoped he would have the pleasure of seeing them again. To Maggie he said, "Maggie you have a good man here. He is a frontiersman and will find it hard to adjust to city life. Please be good to him and be patient. He loves you very much to make this great change in his life. I wish you both much happiness. Like you, I have seen some very bad things happen to those who I loved. The memories will always be with you, but they will gradually grow dimmer and dimmer with time. The new life I am building has helped me a great deal. I believe if I did not have something to look forward to and sat around all the time remembering, I would have gone crazy. Life must go on, and you are young enough to have another family. Maybe God will bless you with another child. May His blessings be with you."

Maggie responded. "Andrew I know what a big change it is going to be for Hans, and I will do my best to be a good wife and make the change as painless as possible. I also realize that I am not the only one to lose a family. Many others have, and they were not all on the frontier. Disease and sickness in the big towns have probably killed more people than the Indians ever will. But for now, I feel safer among our own kind. I will do my best to be a good wife to Hans and do my best to make him happy.

Andrew embraced Hans and kissed Maggie on the cheek. Then he left to find Maria. Hannah had given him an address. He hailed a carriage, and then gave the driver directions.

Philadelphia was a big city, even in 1791; and it took the carriage the better part of an hour to arrive at the address Andrew had given him.

They stopped in front a large house that was only a few feet from the other homes on either side. It was a solid built home of block and stone. There was little difference in it and the dozens of other homes on the street. The outside was grey from the soot and dust that had filtered down from the chimneys and fireplaces. The streets were of cobblestone and the horses shoes rang as they struck the stones of the street.

Andrew paid the driver and walked up the steps to the door. He banged the knocker on the door three times. In just a few minutes a middle aged woman appeared. She was the spitting image of Hannah. He knew immediately that she must be Maria's mother. She looked at him in a hostile way and for a moment, struck by her close resemblance to Hannah, he hesitated to speak.

The woman asked in a gruff voice. "Yes. What can I do for you?"

Andrew said, "I am looking for a young lady by the name of Maria Santiago. Her Aunt, Mrs. Hannah Miller, gave me this address and said I might find her here."

"Who are you?"

"My name is Andrew Stanley. Is Maria here?"

"Yes, Mr. Stanley. Maria is here. She has spoken of you. Come in please."

She led him into a small sitting room at the front of the house and said, "Maria is resting. I will tell her you are here. Please wait a moment."

She disappeared into the back of the house and Andrew waited. He was very nervous and did not know how Maria would react at him being here. Was she going to be mad at him, or would she be glad to see him?

Maria's mother returned in a few minutes and said, "Maria is getting dressed. She will be out in a few minutes. Can I get you a cup of tea?"

"Yes. If you please."

In just a few minutes Maria came into the room. She was dressed in a large robe and slippers. Andrew was shocked at how big she was. In his mind, he thought, 'Did I do that to that beautiful body?'

Then she came toward him and threw her arms around

him, "Oh Andrew, you did come back. I was so afraid for you and so afraid that even if you did survive, you might not want me. Look at me now. How would anyone want a big cow like me?"

Andrew said, "I have been told that one cannot have a child without getting big. You will soon be able to return to yourself again. When I learned that you were carrying my child, I came as fast as I could. I can't believe that I will soon be a father. Which are you hoping for, a boy or a girl?"

Maria was pleased with his acceptance and by his excitement. She had feared that though they had been very compatible, she might never see him again. Now he had come for her. Her world seemed much brighter.

She said, "I personally prefer a girl, but I hope it is a boy for your sake. Men want sons more than daughters I think."

Andrew said, "A son would be nice. But I don't care, I will be happy with a daughter, if she is as beautiful as you."

Maria's mother brought in tea and Maria introduced them. "Mother, this is Andrew Stanley, the man I told you about. Andrew, this is my mother Mary Santiago."

They shook hands and Andrew felt uncomfortable around her. He didn't know whether she was going to berate him for getting her daughter pregnant or not. He thought it best if he addressed the matter head-on and got it over with.

"Mrs. Santiago, I am sorry that I am the cause of Maria's condition. I do not think either of us thought of the consequences of our indiscretions at the time. But as soon as I learned that Maria was carrying my child, I came to find her. If Maria will have me, I am ready to marry her and provide her and the child with a good home. I have acquired a very large parcel of land in the territories and will be moving there soon. As soon as the baby is born, I will take them with me. I have made peace with the Indians and I am sure they will be safe. It depends upon Maria." He had been speaking to Maria's mother. Now he turned to Maria and asked, "Will you be my wife?"

Before she could answer, her mother spoke. "Do you love my daughter Mr. Stanley?"

"Yes, I think so, Mrs. Santiago. Maria and I only knew each other for a few hours, but I think we love each other."

"That is very important to me, Mr. Stanley. I want Maria to be married and her child to have a father. However, it would be better for her to remain single and rear the child alone than to be in a loveless marriage. Too many men marry a woman out of obligation, and then mistreat them. I would not want Maria married to a violent person who did not love her."

"Mrs. Santiago, I am not a violent person. I have killed men before, but only in self-defense and in combat. I have never struck a woman and do not believe in such behavior. I cannot truthfully say that I love Maria, no more than I think she can say the same about me. However, I do find Maria attractive, enjoyable to be with, intelligent and understanding. While our first attraction to each other was physical, I believe we do have very deep feelings for each other. Having never been really in love before, I cannot say if that is love or not. I do know that I am an honorable man and will do what is right by her and the child."

"Mr. Stanley, I am impressed with your honesty and with your character." Now, Mrs. Santiago turned to Maria.

"Maria, you have told me often of how you love Mr. Stanley. But it is rare when love at first sight endures. If you marry just for the sake of the child, this may someday, cause deep feelings of resentment and cause you both to hate each other. That is not the kind of marriage I would wish for you. I leave you two alone now to discuss the matter. But I ask that before you agree to do anything rash, please think about what I have said, and if you cannot truly feel very deep emotion for each other, that you postpone the marriage until you have time to become better acquainted and get to know something about each other."

With that, she rose up from her chair and left the room.

After a brief period of silence, neither knew how to begin.

Finally, Maria asked, "Do you want to marry me only because of the baby?"

"Maria, I believe I love you, but I don't know for sure. Would you rather I lied to you?"

"No. I have thought of you so much; and I would have gone with you when you left if you had taken me. You have been in my thoughts all this time. When I discovered I was pregnant with your child, I was so happy. If you never came back, I would always have a part of you. When we were together, you made me so happy, such a fulfilled woman. I guess I just expected too much."

"Maria, I do care for you very deeply. Whether it is love I don't know, but I want to take care of you and the baby. If you will have me, we will be married this very day. I am sure that our feelings for each other will grow and become stronger day by day."

Maria was deep in thought. After a few minutes she raised her eyes to meet his and said, "Andrew, I am sure of my feelings, but I want to be sure of yours as well. Stay here and let's spend some time together, get to know each other better and see how we feel in a few days or weeks. How long can you stay?"

"I have to be back in Charleston in 10 days. I wanted to take you back with me. When are you due?"

"In about a week. I think it might be dangerous for me to travel now. Besides, the mid-wife who I have been visiting told me the baby is quite large and I may need a doctor when it is born. I think I should stay here where we can get a doctor if I need one."

"Certainly, by all means. If there is any danger, you must stay here. Hopefully, I can stay until the baby arrives before I have to leave. Then, when you are well, you can book passage to Charleston, and I will come there to meet you."

Maria was in deep thought. "That sounds good. Stay here with us, Andrew. Mother has an extra bedroom and we can spend time together and get to know each other better. Will you do that?"

"If it is not inconvenient. I do not want to be in the way."

Maria called to her mother, and after explaining her plan, Mrs. Santiago agreed and showed Andrew to his room.

He had brought only a small valise. Unpacking, Andrew thought about the strange turn of events. He had come prepared to marry Maria. He thought that would please her and her mother. Now they wanted to wait to see what the couple's real feelings were for each other. He supposed it was a wise move, but it was not what he had expected.

CHAPTER TWENTY-FOUR

For the next three days, Andrew and Maria spent almost every minute together. She tired easily and her mother insisted that she rest as much as possible. During the periods when Maria was resting, Andrew went out and moved around Philadelphia. He delivered the order to the wholesale distributor that he had received from the man at the mercantile. The distributor assured Andrew that all the merchandise would be on the next ship, which was scheduled to depart in seven days.

On one occasion, he took a carriage and rode into the countryside. He was surprised at the well-tended farms after he got outside the city. There were many farms with perfectly straight rows of corn, squash, beans, potatoes and numerous other vegetables growing. He supposed these farmers were the main source of food for the people living in the city. He noted that many were of Dutch or German descent. The little hamlets and villages outside Philadelphia were clean, well-kept; and he was deeply impressed by the friendly attitudes of the country folk. It was much different than in his home country where everyone seemed to be suspicious of any neighbor, and especially, strangers.

It was on one of these trips that he first saw the big Conestoga wagon. It was so much larger than any of the others he had seen in Charleston; almost twice the size. The wheels were larger and had an iron rim around the wheel that was wider than most other wagons. Andrew judged it must have close to two tons of fertilizer on the wagon. It was pulled by three yoke of oxen, two to the yoke. The driver did not sit on the box like most wagons, but walked beside the wagon with a long whip on a stock. He spoke to the oxen and directed them with a crack of the whip over their heads. Andrew was fascinated with the wagons and with the way the drivers handled the teams. He stopped to talk with the driver, and after some discussion, decided he would like to buy some of these wagons. The driver directed him to the place where the wagons were made and he drove there to talk with the man.

There were two wagons sitting in the yard, and the builder and two men were working on a third one. Andrew asked if the wagons were for sale and how much they were asking for them. The builder said only one was for sale; the other had been built for a customer. Andrew examined the wagon and was deeply impressed by the deepness of the body which was made of sturdy oak planks. Over the top of the wagon, hickory strips had been dried and fitted into slots in the body in a bowed fashion. Then heavy canvas had been stretched over the bows and tied down to the side of the body. The rear was hinged and dropped like a tail ramp or gate. Not only would the wagons hold a great deal of goods, but the covers would keep it dry.

The builder told Andrew the price was $350. Andrew asked him when he would finish with the one they were working on. The man said in a week to 10 days. He thought for a few minutes. If he had three of these wagons, Maria and the baby and all of their things could occupy one on the trip to the valley, and he could carry almost twice as many goods in the other two as he could carry in the four wagons he already had bought.

He said to the builder. "Sir, I have a pressing need for three of these wagons. I will pay you $500 each if you can have them delivered to the dock in six days for shipment to Charleston in the Carolinas."

The builder responded, "That is a most generous offer, and I gladly accept for two of the wagons, but as I have mentioned, the one wagon has been promised, and I will not go back on my word."

"Will you contact the other buyer of this wagon and ask him if he will sell to me? I will give him $100 profit if he will let me have this wagon and wait until you can build him another. In less than two weeks I am leading a group of people into the territories and I need wagons like that. Would you contact the other buyer for me and see if he will sell?"

"I will. Can you return tomorrow and I will have you an answer?"

Andrew agreed and rode home to tell Maria. She insisted that she accompany him the next day when he returned to the wagon-maker. Andrew was concerned about the buggy ride, but when Maria's mother did not object, he relented and agreed to let her go with him.

They took a carriage around 9 o'clock, and Andrew asked the drive to take care to avoid any deep holes or bumps that might shake Maria too much.

When they arrived at the wagon-maker's shop, he helped Maria down and proceeded to show her the wagon. He explained how they could pack their things along the sides and lay their bed-rolls in the bottom of the wagon if the weather was bad.

Maria became excited and said she was looking forward to making the trip with him. He had told her about Bright Valley and she was anxious to see it.

Andrew had been afraid that she would not want to move so far away from other white people, but it did not seem to bother her at all. She kept saying, "Wherever you are my darling, if I am with you, I will be happy!"

The wagon-maker told Andrew that the man who had ordered the wagon said he would accept the $100 he had offered and release the wagon. He was in no hurry and could wait until another was built. Andrew paid the wagon-maker and he agreed to deliver all three wagons to the dock in time for them to be loaded aboard ship before it sailed.

On the way back to town, Maria was full of excitement and couldn't stop talking about their plans for the future. When they arrived at the house she went inside while Andrew returned to the carriage. When he got to the house, Maria was still chattering, telling her mother about all the things they planned to do.

She turned to Andrew and said, "Oh, Andrew. I am so excited. I do love you, and I want us to be married. Tell me you love me and we can get married. I will make you a good wife. I promise you."

Andrew was amused at her excitement, and he looked at Mrs. Santiago and winked. "Did you ever hear anything so scandalous, a woman proposing marriage to a man?"

Then he turned to Maria and said, "Yes, Maria. I think it is time we got married. These last few days have been very delightful being with you. I am convinced we can be happy together, and I think our love for each other will grow with each passing day. If you still want me, I am ready to get married. I would like to do so just as soon as we can. The baby is due soon and I want us to be wed when it is born."

She ran into his arms and threw her arms around his neck, pulling his head down to kiss him. Even in her condition, her kiss told him that she was still the warm passionate person she was before and there would be much love and happiness in their future.

When she backed away she turned to her mother and

said, "Mother, do you think we could get a Magistrate to perform the service tomorrow? I do not want to have a church wedding, not in my condition. As far as I am concerned, Andrew and I will be just as married if it is done by a Magistrate as if done by a Priest."

When Mrs. Santiago did not object, Andrew said, "I will go now and see what we must do, how we get a license, and if there is a waiting period. It is only a few blocks to the Courthouse. I will walk there and will return in a couple of hours. You had better calm down now and get some rest. You are tiring yourself out too much."

"Andrew, I am so excited, I cannot lie down and rest. I am so happy to think I will soon be Mrs. Andrew Stanley." She was literally twirling and dancing around the room.

Andrew took his time walking to the Courthouse. He was in serious thought. Maria was not the woman he had dreamed of building his new life with. He had never thought of anyone except Catherine as his wife. But he had seduced Maria and now she was about to bear his child. His honor would not let him abandon either her or the child. She was a very pleasant person, beautiful and before the child swelled her body out of shape, it was one of the most beautiful bodies he had ever seen. He supposed it would be that way again after the baby came, but whether it was or not, fate had thrown the dice and he must accept his responsibility. He did love Maria, maybe not in the same way he loved Catherine, but he had shared very intimate times with Maria and he knew the torrid passion of her nature. He had not made love to Catherine and although there was a strong indication that she too would be an exciting woman to make love to, he could not be sure.

Then as he neared the Courthouse, he shook his head. He must clear his mind of such thoughts. His fate was cast the night he had supper with the Millers and made love to Maria. There was nothing more to be said.

He entered the Courthouse and asked the clerk about marriage procedures. The clerk said there would have to be a license, and a three day waiting period. He further informed Andrew that both the man and woman must apply in person so that the clerk could determine if both people were of age and acting of their own free will. Andrew asked if he could speak with him in private, and when they had entered his office and closed the door, Andrew cleared his throat and explained the situation he was in.

"You see sir. This is a rather embarrassing situation. Some nine months ago, the lady and I had a liaison. I went on a journey and just returned recently. I discovered she was with child and is due to deliver any day now. It is important that we become man and wife as quickly as possible. I do not want the child born without a name. The lady is embarrassed to appear in public and she is so close to delivery that she is indisposed most of the time. We had hoped to secure any legal papers necessary and see if we could find a Magistrate who would marry us in the privacy of her home, with just immediate family present. You understand the scandal that attaches to a woman who has a child out of wedlock. Is there anything we can do so that she will not have to undergo the embarrassment of coming in and publicly exposing herself?"

The clerk listened; and when Andrew finished, he said, "I think I can accommodate you, sir. It is clear you are trying to do the honorable thing. I have a daughter who is 18 and if she were in this condition, I would want to protect her as much as possible from public embarrassment. I must see the lady in person and have her sign the license, but I am an officer of the court and I can perform the ceremony. If you wish, I will bring the license to your house and when the ceremony has been performed, I will affix the seal of the court. It will be as legal as if a Judge or a Priest had performed the ceremony. Would you like me to do that?"

"Oh, yes sir! You are most generous. I will be glad to pay you for your time and inconvenience. When could you come?"

"I must stay and close the office at 5 O'clock. I could come by before I go home. Would you have enough time for the lady to get ready?"

"That is only some two hours from now. I fear she would need more time. Could you do it tomorrow at the same time? That will give her time to get word to any of her friends and relatives she might want to be present. She probably will want to get something special to wear. I think this evening would be too short a time. I am told women like to make a big to-do over these things. Will tomorrow be just as well?"

"Certainly. Give me the address and I will be there at approximately 5:30."

Andrew thanked him and hurried back to the house to tell Maria the good news. Now, he was getting excited, too. Once he had reconciled himself that this was to be his future, he wanted to get on with it and begin their lives together.

When he entered the house, he sensed something was wrong. Instead of Maria or Mrs. Santiago meeting him at the door, there was a strange woman who introduced herself as the next door neighbor. She said Maria had gone into labor and they had rushed her to the hospital. She had wanted to wait for him and even begged to have the baby at home, but the mid-wife was afraid and insisted she go to the hospital. He was to go there as quickly as he could.

Andrew hailed a carriage and told the driver to go as fast as he could to the hospital. In less than 20 minutes, the carriage pulled to a stop. Andrew paid the driver and leaped to the ground on the run. He went to the entrance and asked to see his wife. They directed him to the birthing wing and when he arrived, Mrs. Santiago was standing with her back to the wall. Andrew could tell by the look on her face there was bad news. Andrew asked, "What happened? I did not think she was due for another week or so."

"She wasn't but the excitement of getting married, the trip; her future with you caused her to go into early labor. The mid-wife said the baby has not turned. Normally, a baby turns so it's head comes first. It is an easier delivery that way. But the baby has not turned and it is trying to come in what is called a breech birth. Maria is very small boned and any birth will be hard for her, this type of birth could be very difficult. The mid-wife fears something may go wrong."

"Can I see her? I have good news to tell her. Is she in great pain?"

"Not yet. There are severe cramps and they will get worse, but there are short periods when she is alright. I think you can see her."

Andrew entered the room and there were two other women a few beds away, but he did not pay any attention to them. He went directly to Maria and sat down beside the bed. He took her hand and tried to be humorous.

Maria saw the worry on his face and said, "Don't be so worried. Women have had babies for hundreds of years. I can handle this. I will be alright."

Andrew squeezed her hand and said, "I would take your place if I could. I would bear the pain if I could. To see you like this makes me regret our love-making."

"Do not be silly. Women go through this every time a new life begins. If it were not so, the human race would soon die out. Don't worry I tell you."

"I want you to know I do love you, and I have made arrangements for us to wed. The clerk from the Courthouse can perform the ceremony and he said he would come to our house this evening at 5:30, but I told him you would probably want more time to get ready and I asked him to come at that time tomorrow. If the baby comes tonight, and it is a boy, I want his name to be Stanley. Somehow, I will get the clerk to date the papers today or yesterday. If you feel like it, we will go ahead with the marriage tomorrow at 5:30."

She squeezed his hand and was about to say something, then her face contorted in pain and she clenched her teeth and sucked in a deep breath. The spasm lasted only a few seconds and then she relaxed. Andrew's fingers hurt where she had held them so tightly. She looked at him and again saw the worry on his face. She smiled at him and motioned for him to bend over so she can kiss him.

When he leaned over her bed, she pulled his head down, gave him a long lingering kiss, then she whispered in his ear, "My darling, no matter how painful this is, I do not regret one moment of the time I shared with you. I love you so, and you made me a happy woman. I am very happy to be having your baby. I will have a dozen more for you if you will just make love to me the way you did." Then she pushed him away slightly so she could see his face. There were tears on his cheeks and she took his face in her hands and kissed him again.

She released him and said, "Now you get out of here and let me have this baby. We have got things to do, and I need to get this done so we can get on with our lives. And great lives they are going to be. I love you Andrew. I am going to give you a son to prove it. Now get out and wait outside."

As he was about to release her hand, another spasm hit her and she screamed. Andrew was still holding her hand when the doctor appeared and escorted him out into the hallway.

Andrew and Mrs. Santiago pace up and down the hall; both worried about Maria and the baby. He told her of the plans for the wedding and how he had almost had the clerk come this very evening, but had decided to put it off until the next day. He swore that as soon as Maria could sit up, he would have the wedding; and if he had to, he would bribe the clerk to back date the papers.

Time seemed to drag. Andrew had arrived at the hospital at about 4 O'clock and he thought it must be 10 by now. He looked at his watch, and it was just a few minutes after 5. About 7o'clock, a nurse came and asked Maria's mother if she would come in and sit with Maria for a few minutes. This left Andrew alone and he paced the floor, looking at his watch every 10 minutes. He swore that it had stopped.

When Mrs. Santiago did not return and the doctor and nurses rushed in and out of the room, Andrew became more concerned. He stopped one of the nurses to ask how it was going and she told him, "Not good. The pelvis won't spread enough for the baby to come and your wife has started hemorrhaging. The situation is not good. We will know in a few minutes if we can save them."

This struck Andrew like a blow to the pit of his stomach. Maria was so confident a little while ago, so sure about their future and she would be able to delivery without any trouble. Now the nurse was saying they were trying to "save them." Did she mean both the baby and Maria were in danger? He must do something, but what? He didn't know anything about having babies. But he could not just sit here and do nothing. He got up and headed for the birthing room.

As he approached the door, Mrs. Santiago came out of the room holding a baby in a blanket. There were tears in her eyes, but she looked up at Andrew and said, "Mr. Stanley, you have a son, a big, healthy son!" She handed the blanket to him and Andrew didn't know how he should hold him. He was so surprised, that for a few moments he forgot to ask about Maria.

Then he turned to Mrs. Santiago and asked, "How is Maria? The nurse said she was having a bad time. Is she alright?"

Tears now flooded her eyes; she bit her lip and shook her head.

He did not understand and he asked again, "Is she still in pain? Now that the baby is born, is she alright?"

Mrs. Santiago shook her head again, and in between sobs, said, "Andrew they could not get the baby to come normal, and it was about to die inside her. This would have caused her to die also. The doctor had to cut her stomach open and take the baby out that way. There was no choice. They saved the baby, but Maria had bled so much, they were not able to save her. She is dead."

The shock of what she had just said was so great, Andrew almost collapsed. He had to lean against the wall to brace himself. This couldn't be true. Surely, she was mistaken. But when he looked at her face and the tears streaming down her cheeks he knew it was no mistake.

He walked to a chair and sat down, holding the baby. Although he stared at the child, he was not seeing it. Fate had dealt him a bad hand once again. First it had been his homeland, then his family and his landlord. Now, just as he had planned to have a new family, God had taken Maria from him. The thought jumped into his mind, was it because they had sinned? But why punish just her. It was his fault too. Why had God not punished him instead?

Maria's mother sat down next to him. She saw he was in deep thought and doubted he even realized he was holding his son. His pain had not fully touched him yet; the shock still numbed him. She reached for the baby and told him they had to finish cleaning up the baby, then disappeared back into the birthing room with his son.

Andrew knew he should do something, but what? He could only sit and stare into space. This was the second major change in his plans since he had returned from Bright Valley. First, he had learned of Maria's pregnancy and come for her. Now, she was gone without warning. How could this have happened? A few hours ago he was so happy, planning for his wedding, and now, his bride to be was dead.

Maria's mother came back out and said they were going to keep the baby overnight and they should go home now. Andrew wanted to see Maria, but her mother begged him not to. She said, "Andrew, do not go and look at her now. She suffered much and she does not look as you remember her. Try to keep the picture you have of her, not as she is now. Something else. She asked the nurse to have me come in. She knew she was in danger and she told me to look after you and the baby if anything happened to her. If she did not come out of this, she wanted me to tell you she loved you very much. That if you wanted the baby you should have it for it was your child. If you did not, she made me promise to take care of it. But the last thing she said was to tell you not to blame yourself, that she wanted to have the baby for you, it was part of you and her that could never be separated."

Andrew heard but he only partially comprehended. It was still too hard to accept. They rode home in silence and the next morning he did not have much to say. Finally, after a brief breakfast, Mrs. Santiago said, "We must go and make funeral arrangements, and we will have to go back to the hospital for they must have a name for the baby. Have you given any thought of a name for him?"

"No. I really haven't. I can hardly think. I just cannot accept that she is gone. We would have been married this evening. Now she is gone."

Andrew agreed to make the funeral arrangements while Mrs. Santiago was to see to dressing and fixing Maria. After he had gone to the funeral parlor and taken care of things, he went back to the hospital. The baby was doing fine.

The nurse let him hold the little fellow and Andrew rocked him back and forth. Things had happened so fast he had not really had time to think of the significance of this little bundle in his arms. What should he call him? He had no idea until Mrs. Santiago came out and wanted to hold him. As she rocked him she absent mindedly spoke that it had been a real victory that they had been able to save him.

The phrase struck a memory in his mind. In every battle there were casualties and there were victors who survived. He now viewed the struggle Maria had fought and it had cost her life, but out of the struggle, a new life had come, a victor of the battle of life over death. That was it. He would name the baby, Victor M. Stanley.

He told Mrs. Santiago of his decision and why he had decided on that name. He said, "He is the survivor of a fierce struggle that took Maria's life, he is the victor and that shall be his name. The M. shall stand for Maria. In his young years he can just use the initial, but when he is old enough to understand, I will tell him about his mother and if he wants to use the full name he can."

Mrs. Santiago broke into tears again and said, "I like it Andrew, and I think Maria would have approved."

Andrew forgot to cancel the wedding and at 5:30 the clerk appeared at the door. He saw the wreath on the door, but knocked anyway. Andrew was at first surprised to see him, then he asked him in and told him that his bride to be had died in child-birth the night before and there would be no wedding. The clerk expressed his regrets and departed.

After the funeral, they had returned home. Andrew sat and spoke with Maria's mother. It was impossible for him to remain in Philadelphia. He must sail in four days. He would take the baby with him, but he did not know how to care for it and feed it. She had told him earlier that her husband was on a journey and would not return for at least another month. Andrew asked her if she would accompany him as far as Charleston and teach him what he would need to know to care for the child.

After some discussion, she said she would. She would like to see her sister Hannah; try to make amends with Robert if she could. She would go that far with him and try to get the child accustomed to taking cow's milk since he would not have anyone to breast feed him. Sometimes it was possible to find another woman who had just given birth and she would nurse her child and another if the second mother could not. Such substitutes were often referred to as "nurse maids". But they had no one in mind that could do this, so they would have to try cow's milk.

That was something else Andrew must keep in mind. He would have to have some milk cows taken with them to Bright Valley.

On the day prior to the day they were to sail, Andrew decided to look up Hans and Maggie. It was very difficult to find them, but finally he located them at Maggie's sister's home. They were both glad to see him and Hans wrapped his arms around him in a huge bear hug. Maggie hugged him also. It did not take them long to see the sad expression in his eyes and Hans said, "What has happened Andrew? You look like you been beat with a horse whip."

Andrew said, "Maria is dead." Then he began to relate the story. When he was finished they both expressed their sorrow at his loss. Maggie in particular said, "I know how you feel Andrew. Time will help heal the loss, but it will be bad for a while. You have the baby to remember her by though. I lost all of my family. I don't think I could have made it without Hans to help me. We have become very close. We were married the day after we arrived and he is a lot younger man than he looks." As she said that she poked him in the ribs, and a blush appeared on Hans cheeks.

"Well, I will be leaving tomorrow and I wanted to come and say goodbye. I hope you two have a good life together. May the good Lord give you both happiness."

As he returned to the Santiago house that afternoon he passed the docks and noticed that his three Conestoga wagons were being put aboard ship. It was quite a job. They had rigged a boom from one of the sailing masts and were raising the wagons with tackle. They would not fit in the hole, so they were being tied down on the deck. Andrew had to smile at the trouble he was putting the crew to. He wouldn't tell them who the wagons were for until they were off-loaded in Charleston.

Andrew, Mrs. Santiago and the baby were on the dock at 6 A.M. the next morning, ready to board when to his surprise, he turned and saw Hans and Maggie.

Hans spoke first. "Is that offer of some land in Bright Valley still open?"

"You bet it is. But yesterday you didn't mention anything about going back. What changed your mind?"

Now it was Maggie's turn. "That stuck-up sister of mine and her husband. They treated both of us like dirt and wanted to make us household servants. I saw what it was doing to Hans and I couldn't put him through that. Besides, this town is more dangerous in some ways than the frontier. There are cut-purses and pick-pockets in every alley and street. Some areas are too dangerous to go down a street at night. You have to keep everything locked up tight to keep it from being stolen. On the frontier we expected the Indians to come and take things, and we watched for them. Here you don't know who to watch for. It is not as I remembered it. Hans wouldn't be happy here, and I don't think I would either. Wherever Hans goes, I'll go with him. I'll be nervous back in Indian country, but I'm not comfortable here either."

"That is just great. I am sure glad to have you going with

me. Maggie you know what to do for babies, I'll need your help with little Victor."

"That will be a pleasure. I feel a little lost without a small one around. When we get settled, we may have one of our own. How about that Hans?"

Hans blushed again and smiled. He was a changed man. He seemed more relaxed and calmer. Maggie was having a good influence on him, but he was glad they had decided to go back to the frontier. Hans would have never been happy in the city. Neither could Andrew; he was eager to be traveling again.

CHAPTER TWENTY-FIVE

The voyage to Charleston was uneventful and they arrived late on the following day. As soon as the ship had docked, Andrew and his party disembarked and while Hans was seeing to the luggage, Andrew hailed two carriages. He and Mrs. Santiago and the baby would take one and go to the Miller's house. Hans and Maggie would take the second and go to the hotel. They were to take Andrew's luggage and wait for him there. He felt he owed it to the Millers to tell them about Maria and let them see the baby. Maria's mother didn't know whether she would be welcome at their home or not. The bank was already closed and both of the Millers would probably be at home.

When the carriage arrived at the Miller's house, Andrew got out first and walked to the door. He knocked and the maid answered. Andrew asked if she would call Mr. & Mrs. Miller. When they came to the door, Harold Miller spoke first.

"Andrew, we are glad to see you. Come in man. We have been expecting you. Did you bring Maria back with you?"

Before Andrew spoke, they suspected something was wrong. They could tell he did not have his usual smile and happy appearance.

"Harold, Hannah, I have some bad news. But before I tell you, Maria's mother is with me in the carriage. She would like to come in if she is welcome."

It was Harold that spoke up. "Of course she is welcome. Tell her to come in. This is her sister's house. What is the news?"

"In just a moment. I will get Mrs. Santiago."

When he and Maria's mother returned to the house, she was carrying the baby. She and Hannah hugged and she kissed Harold on the cheek. Then they went inside to the library. The Millers were subdued. The fact that Maria was not along gave them a feeling of dread.

When they were all seated in the library, Andrew spoke first.

"Harold, Hannah I don't know any way to soften the blow for you. I know that Maria was like your own daughter. I hate to bring you this news, but Maria is dead. She died giving birth to the baby. We buried her in Philadelphia two days ago."

Hannah gasped, "Oh my God, no." and Harold sat down as if someone had hit him with an ax. When she could do so through her tears; Hannah asked, "What happened?"

"We had made arrangements to be married the next day and the excitement of getting married, of returning to Charleston and going to Bright Valley caused her to go into premature labor. The baby had not turned and it was a breech birth. It was not possible for Maria to have it naturally. The doctors had to operate to save the baby, but Maria had lost so much blood they could not save her."

Mary Santiago handed the baby to Andrew and went to comfort her sister. They both had their arms around each other and sobbed uncontrollably. After several minutes, Mary said, "Come. Let me show you the baby. Andrew has named him, Victor M. (for Maria) Stanley. Harold and Hannah, I want you both to know that Maria was the happiest girl in the world. She talked to me at length about her and Andrew. She never doubted that he would return for her and she was so happy to be having his baby. I am trying not to grieve for her. Be happy that we still have a part of her in the baby. I know how much you loved her. If Andrew does not object, I would like you to be the baby's God-parents."

Andrew said, "I had not thought of that. I think that is a great idea. Will you accept?"

Hannah looked at Harold and saw the smile on his face and without hesitating, she said, "We will be glad to. Andrew, this will make you a part of the family also. You must allow us some time with our God-child. You cannot take him with you so soon!"

"Mary is taking care of him for me until our wagon train is ready to leave. She is getting him used to drinking cows' milk. He seems to be adjusting. She puts a little honey in it and he has started drinking it quite well."

Andrew continued, "Do you remember Hans Brinkman? Well, he married the woman, Maggie, who was rescued from the Indians. They are going back to Bright Valley with me. She knows how to care for small children. I have asked her to look after Victor for me. I would not think of leaving him behind. But until we leave, you and Mary have him all to yourselves. I will be very busy getting everything together for the trip. Besides, I have to make a trip to Sumterville tomorrow. So you would be doing me a favor if you looked after him until we can make ready."

"Of course we will. Mary, we have a guest room. You and the baby can stay with us and you can tell me all that you have been doing these last months."

Andrew excused himself and said he must return to the hotel and start getting things organized. It was just four days until August 1st and he wanted to depart on that date. Tomorrow was the day he had told the herders, mule-skinners and drivers to be here if they wanted to work. He motioned for Harold to follow him to the door.

At the door he spoke to him in a low voice. "Harold, please draw up a paper acknowledging Victor as my son and lawful heir. If anything should happen to me, he is to get all of my assets. I would like you and Hannah to share joint custody with Mary until he is eighteen. Will you do this for me?"

"Certainly, stop by my office any time after noon tomorrow and I will have it ready."

On his way back to the hotel, he was so tense that he decided to go by the livery stable to see what progress they had towards getting all the horses and mules he had ordered. To his surprise, he found Dave Foster there with the liveryman. Dave was very glad to see him and when Andrew asked about the animals; both men began to talk at once. Finally, the liveryman stopped and let Dave tell the story.

"We have acquired the lease on a field of rye and oats about two miles from town. We were fortunate in getting the 300 horses and they are in the field. However, we were only able to get enough mules for two wagons, two teams to the wagon. I'm afraid we will have to use some of the horses to pull the other wagons."

"Don't worry. Hans bought 70, and told the mule breeder down in Georgia to get another 30 if he could find them. He also rented five wagons with teamsters and they have their own mules. But the best news is down on the docks. I bought three of the large Conestoga wagons up in Pennsylvania and they are on the ship I came in on. They will haul almost three times as much as the wagons we have. Tomorrow, after we talk to the men who have come to drive for us, I would like you to take some of the men we will hire, go down to the docks and bring the wagons to the warehouse. Keep one of them unloaded. Hans, Maggie and the baby will be traveling in it. But you can start loading the other two, plus the ones we have bought. I have to go to Sumterville and will leave just after I have interviewed the men."

Dave spoke up, "Did I hear you say Hans and Maggie were going with us?"

"That's right. They were married and are going back to Bright Valley with us. The girl I went to Philadelphia to marry died in childbirth. She gave me a lovely son. I am taking him to his new home, and Maggie will help take care of him for me."

Andrew gave further instructions on what he wanted done and told the liveryman to have his horse saddled and ready by nine the next morning for his trip to Sumterville. He would ask Hans to ride with him. They would depart as soon as the interviews were over.

At seven the next morning, Andrew, Dave and Hans met at the livery. There were perhaps 150 men there all wanting work. Cash money was hard to come by in the colonies and they had heard that this job paid cash.

When all had been assembled, Andrew climbed onto the bed of a wagon and held up his hand for silence.

Then he said, "How many of you have lost family members to Indian attacks?" About fifteen held up their hands. Then he asked, "How many of you have killed Indians and how many are looking for revenge?"

Most of those who had indicated they had lost loved ones to Indians, again held up their hands. Two did not. Andrew asked one why he was not seeking revenge. The man answered, "The Indians who raided my homestead were renegades. I hated them and would have killed them all. But a short time after they attacked my home my 12 year old boy wandered into the woods and got lost. He fell and broke his leg. An Indian came across him and fed him and put a brace on his leg and helped him back home. They became friends and I learned that Indians are people, good and bad, no better or worse than white people. If I could find those who raided my home and killed my daughter, I would kill them, but I cannot take my anger out on people who had nothing to do with the killing."

Andrew turned to the other man, "How about you?"

"I have done my share of fighting the Indians before. They have stolen horses from me, raided my storage of food and killed my brother more than twenty-five years ago, but I have made them pay dearly for that death. As to the food and horses, I understand this is just their way. The young buck thinks stealing horses is like us stealing watermelons from the neighbor's field. They don't really mean any mischief by it. We play a game. They steal from me; I steal back from them. It is a joke between us. The Indians do not live by the same rules the white man does, but they have their rules just the same. You just have to learn their ways if you go among them."

"What are your names?"

The first one said, "Zebediah Johnson. Most call me Zeb."

The other replied, "William Rafferty."

"O.K. Zeb. You and William will go. The rest who indicated they would kill Indians for revenge, I can't use. We are going across the territory of the Creek and into the lands of the Cherokee. I will be living among them with my family. I have made friends of the Indians and intend to open a trading post in the territories. I do not want any trouble with the Indians. I do not expect they will attack us. If they do we will fight. But I do not want anyone who is out to take scalps. Those that have a score to settle with the Indians will have to do so on their own. I will not be able to use you. You are dismissed. Now, let's get down to picking the rest of those to go with me."

First, Andrew wanted teamsters, those who could drive double teams. He asked all who had experience in double teams to step forward. Almost thirty men came forward.

Andrew motioned that they should go over by the wagons and Hans and the liveryman were to talk with them.

Next, he asked how many had experience handling livestock and breaking ponies to ride or to pull plows and wagons. Another twenty-five held up their hands. Andrew talked to each one individually; then he picked fifteen of them. He told them that as soon as the rest were hired, he would give them their instructions.

Last, he asked how many had experience clearing lands, cutting timber, and building roads. Almost all the rest held up their hands. They were hardy men and would work at almost any job for cash money. He picked thirty-five of the stoutest and motioned them to one side. He told the others he was sorry but this would fill the jobs he had available. He thanked them for coming, and bade them goodbye.

Then he turned to the thirty-five he had just hired. "How do you feel about working along with blacks?"

Several said they didn't like slaves and would not work along with them. Andrew excused them and said that he expected to have some twenty or maybe as many as thirty blacks going with him. They would not be slaves, but they would be blacks. If there were any others who objected to working with them, they could leave now. When he finished there were twenty-two left standing. He told them to have a seat or wait for him he wanted to talk with the other group.

He walked over to where the drivers were and asked Hans how it was going.

"Well, we have about twenty-five good experienced men and probably seven or eight more that have driven some, but are not well experienced. They would do as relief drivers though and might pick up some experience on the way." Andrew told him to hire them and tell them to go over by the others standing by the wagon. Then he went to talk with the group of herders.

When they were all assembled, Andrew climbed back up on the wagon. "OK men. Here is the situation. We are going to take a wagon train into the territories. There will be 12 to 15 wagons and over 300 head of livestock, mostly horses and mules. There will be a few cows for milk and to start some beef cattle, but the bulk of the livestock is destined for the Indians as payment for the land I have bought. I figure it will take us the better part of three, perhaps three and a half months. We will be divided into three crews, one to clear the road ahead of us. The second will see to the wagons and keeping the loads tied down tight. It will be your responsibility to safeguard the stuff on your wagon. We will assign a chief driver for each wagon. He can pick out two more to help him harness, check and guard the wagon, and relieve him from time to time. I will hold that driver responsible for his men and the goods on his wagon."

"The drovers will bring up the rear with the livestock. It will be your responsibility to see that none of the horses, mules or cows are left behind or stray in to the woods. You will also be responsible for insuring that any horses that have not been broken to ride will be by the time we reach Bright Valley. You will also make sure that the mules are rotated between the drivers so that all of the mules experience some pulling and working as part of a team. This will also serve to keep any one animal from being worked every day. I don't want any animal worn out, injured or full of harness sores when we arrive."

"The work crew will be under the supervision of Dave Foster. The herders will be under the supervision of Hans Brinkman. I will look after the drivers and the wagons. Any instructions these men give you is the same as coming from me. If there are any disputes among any of you, take it to these people. There will be no fighting, drinking and no cursing around the wagons. There will be two ladies present and they are to be respected so no swearing in their presence. The pay will be twenty-five cents a day, payable upon arrival in Bright Valley. If we make the trip in three months, there will be another ten cents a day in it for every man. Those people who wish to do so can come back when we reach the valley. Those who want to can stay another month at the same pay and help us build houses, a store and barns for the wagons, goods and animals. If there are any who are unhappy with these terms and conditions, you are free to go."

No one moved.

Andrew turned to Hans and Dave and told them to sign on all those who remained. Then he turned to the new crews and said, "As soon as they have signed you on, you will be free to go home and pack your bedroll. The herders are to be here tomorrow. I want you to start getting the teams in shape. Those working on the road crew will leave day after tomorrow and start clearing a road for the train. You should have at least two weeks start before we catch up with you. Dave will load one wagon with grub and you can also place your possibles in that wagon if you want. The rest of you are to be here three days from now. We leave at day break on August 1st. Teamsters, you come in the day before and make sure your wagons are loaded to your satisfaction. I do not want a spare foot of space in those wagons. Hold out one of the wagons for Mrs. Brinkman and my son. You will also need one for the drovers and other people on the train. I may also need a wagon for the blacks I expect will be traveling with us."

When they had all the men signed up there were 87 healthy, hardy men. Andrew, Hans, Dave and the liveryman rode out to the pasture to look over the animals that had been brought in. Between them they culled about 20 animals that appear jaded, old, sway-back or sick. The animals had been purchased from a number of different owners. Andrew paid each owner and gave the liveryman his bonus. Then he asked him to have two people ride herd on them and make sure they didn't stampede or break out before they were ready to leave.

He left Dave and the liveryman to pick up the Conestoga wagons and instructed them to see if they could locate oxen to pull the Conestogas. If not, the wagons would have to be pulled by mules, and he figured it would take at least three teams. If they were to get in an uphill pull, a fourth team may have to be added. He and Hans headed for Sumterville. It is already past eleven o'clock and Andrew feared they would not arrive before dark.

Hans, knowing he would likely be away overnight, so asks Dave to look in on Maggie for him.

Andrew and Hans rode hard. The black mare had been standing in the barn too long. She wanted to run, and Andrew let her have her head for the first hour before stopping to let her blow, then he walked her to cool off.

Hans rode up beside him. "I wouldn't get too far ahead if I was you. Lots of people have been watching you spend money. They think you are loaded. Someone may get the idea to relieve you of some of that gold."

Han's remarks brought Andrew back to earth. He had all but forgotten the trouble he ran into last time he left Charleston. His excitement for the trip overtook his caution. For the rest of the trip he was more careful.

He and Hans camped just outside Sumterville and the first thing next morning, rode in and asked where they might find Thomas Sumter. They were given directions and rode to where he lived.

Almost all the houses were new and Andrew could tell that this would one day be a thriving town.

Thomas Sumter was a gentleman and gave them a warm welcome.

After the pleasantries were out of the way, Andrew said, "Mr. Sumter. Last year I came to Charleston on a boat that had a group of blacks on it. They were all sold as slaves. You were kind enough to buy one particular group in order to keep them together. The leader of that group was Witambe Morandu. Do you still have him and his people?"

"Yes, I do. Why do you ask? And why are you interested in this group especially?"

"Sir, it would be hard for me to tell you how I feel about this group of people, but I feel a great kin-ship to them. We have much in common. I was driven from my home, they were stolen from theirs. I am all that is left of my family. They are all that is left of their tribe. I came here to begin a new life and start a new family to try to forget the horror I have seen. They, too, are starting a new life, but very different."

Andrew hesitated. "I don't know if I am making sense to you or not. But I have acquired a large tract of land in the territories and will be leaving shortly to go there. Will you sell me Witambe and all of his tribe? I will pay you 50 percent more than you paid for them."

Sumter was quiet taken aback by such a suggestion. "Sir. I do not want to sell any of my slaves, least of all Witambe. He has made a good worker and has kept his people in line. I have the least trouble with his group than with any other of the slaves. Why do you want him in particular?"

"You will think me crazy sir. But I wish to set him and his people free. If you sell them to me, I will give them their freedom and take them into the territories with me. They can either live on the lands I have bought, or they will be free to go their way. I hope that they will build them another village and thrive. They are the last of their tribe. If they die out, their tribal customs and their past will be lost. Just as my country has been wiped off the map, so will this tribe disappear if they are not given a chance to continue as a tribe, together. I want to give them that chance."

Sumter looked at him for a long time. Finally he said, "Man, you must be insane. There are no free blacks in America that I know of. There is much chance that they would be taken by someone else and placed back into slavery again, perhaps under a harsh master. I try to treat my slaves fairly and do not beat or mistreat them. But there are some who do treat them very badly. You are talking about an enormous amount of money, to be just given away without any return."

"Sir, if I can see them free that will be all the return I need. The money will not buy me anything where I am going. If it will buy them freedom, I will be happy. Will you sell them to me?"

"How much did you say you were willing to pay?"

"I will give you $30,000 above what you paid for them."

He was silent while he thought to himself. He did have certain debts that needed to be paid. Building this town has cost far more than he imagined. His creditors did not want to wait until the crops were harvested next summer. And this year's crops were already pledged for last year's debts.

After a long pause he said, "I will sell them to you for $70,000 on one condition. They must want to go with you. If they do not, they will stay here. You may speak to them at lunch time when they come in from work. I will send my foreman to tell all of them to gather at the barn by the stables. You must stay and have lunch with me."

Andrew was elated and couldn't wait until Witambe and his people came in from the fields.

They had a good lunch, and Andrew tried not to show his anxiety and impatience. It would be impolite. But as soon as he thought it prudent, he excused himself and he and Hans walked down to the barn. The slaves from

Witambe's group were all there, the women and children as well as the men. Most of the women worked in the fields beside the men. They were puzzled as to why they had all been called together.

Hans stopped at the corner of the barn and Andrew proceeded to where Witambe was standing. As he approached, he thought he saw recognition in Witambe's eyes but the big black man did not say anything.

Andrew spoke. "Witambe. Do you remember me? I was on the boat that brought us all to America."

Witambe hesitated. He did not know what this was leading up to. Why had this man come here? He had never spoken to him on the boat nor afterwards. What did he want now? Was he here to cause some kind of trouble? Still it was not in his nature to lie, so he nodded his head and said, "Yes. You were on the boat we came on."

Andrew asked, "Are you and your people happy here Witambe?"

Again Witambe hesitated. What was this all about? He was beginning to feel very nervous.

But again, he answered the question, "As happy as we can be, I guess. This is not our home, but Masta Sumter is a kind man. He does not mistreat our people and he permits us to live with our families."

"If you were free and could go anywhere you wanted to, would you stay here?"

Witambe was growing very nervous now and was almost afraid to answer. Finally he said, "If we had our way, we would return to our village and start over again. But that probably can never be."

"No. You can probably never return to your homeland. But if you were given a chance to go someplace and start all over again in this country, would you take it?"

"I don't understand what you mean. We are slaves. We

belong to Masta Sumter. Black people are not free in this country. All that I have seen are slaves. Where could we go that we would be free? And how can we leave? Masta Sumter has paid a great sum of money for us when he bought us from the slave dealers in Charleston. We cannot repay him this money."

"No. But I can. Let me explain Witambe. I feel you and I have much in common. My homeland was totally destroyed and my family all killed except me. Your village was destroyed and the only ones left of your people are you and this group. If I die and do not leave someone to carry on my line, my family will all be gone and so will my history and my customs. The same applies to you. If you do not continue your race, your people will all be gone too. As long as you are a slave you will have no choice but to do what you are told, or go wherever you are sent. And your children will be slaves also.'"

Andrew let this sink in. Then he continued. "I have started a new life way over the mountains in a large valley. I have acquired a great tract of land and will be living among the Indians. They do not have slaves and neither will I. I also have great wealth, money that will not do me much good after I have gone into the territories. I have made Mr. Sumter an offer to buy your freedom and set you free. If you wish to go with me, I will take you back into the forest, away from the white man. There, you and your people can either stay and work for me for wages and live on land I will give to you, or you can take your people and move further on west where there are very few white men at all. That is the proposition I have to offer you."

Andrew paused to allow the information to sink in. Then he continued, "Mr. Sumter has agreed to sell you to me if you wish to leave. But if you feel secure here and do not want to leave he will not sell you. Understand that if you decide to leave, even though I have paid for your freedom, you will not be indebted to me. I am making this offer because I want to and because I want to see you and your people have another chance, as I have another chance. I am not buying you as slaves for I will not own slaves. The decision is yours."

Witambe was stunned. He could not believe what he was hearing. He and his people had reconciled themselves to always be slaves and theirs would be a life of hard work and drudgery. Now this strange man was offering them their freedom. It couldn't be happening. There must be a trick. He looked at the big man leaning against the barn as if asking him whether this man was sincere or whether he was crazy.

Hans came forward and said. "Mister, I never met you before. But this man is not lying to you and there is no trick. I don't understand myself why he is spending all that money to turn you loose. But he doesn't believe in slavery and he wants to do something to help you. He can afford to do so and still have some money left. You stay here, and your children will grow up being slaves too. If you are smart, you will take him up on his offer. No matter how good a master you may have, there is nothing like being a free man. You may never get another chance to be free."

Witambe looked hard at Andrew. He had that penetrating gaze that peered deep into a man's soul. He was trying to see if there was some scheme or trick being played on him and his people.

Satisfied, he turned and spoke directly to his people for several minutes. There was a beehive of mumbles and speech from almost everyone. Witambe was hard put to answer their questions. They kept turning their eyes toward Andrew and pointing toward him. It was very evident that many were suspicious and afraid of what he may have in store for them. They could not believe a white man was doing this without some trick he intended to play on them. For more than a half hour the debate in their native tongue continued. Then Witambe held up his hand and the others became silent. He spoke for about four or five minutes in a deep rumbling voice.

Andrew wished he could understand what was being said.

When Witambe finished, there was only silence. Then one by one they all nodded their heads and seemed to be agreeing. Andrew later learned that Witambe had said he was going to take this crazy man up on his offer, and take a chance that he was being honest. That he appeared to be sincere, but that he, Witambe, would watch him very closely and if he was lying to them, he would run a spear through him.

When he turned back to Andrew, he said, "You have made arrangements with Masta Sumta?"

Andrew indicated he had.

Witambe took a deep breath. "I and my family will go with you. There are a couple of my people who are afraid to leave the homes they have built and have established an attachment with a couple of women from the adjoining farm. They also doubt that you will do as you say. They do not understand the promises you are making and fear this may be a trick. They are also afraid of the Indians. They have heard strange stories about how cruel they are."

Andrew held up his hand and showed them the scar in the palm of his hand. "I saved the lives of two sons of a chief. They made me a brother of the tribe and have sold me ten times more land than Mister Sumter has here. I am going to open a trading post in the middle of Indian Territory. I have a son that is only one week old. Do you think I would be taking him into that place if I thought he would be in danger? Indians are much like people all over the world. Your people will be fairly safe with me."

Witambe turned and related the story to the others, they again shook their heads and he turned back to Andrew. "They have all decided to go. When will we leave?"

"If I can get wagons for your belongings I would like to leave in the morning. How much personal belongs do you have?"

"Only a few things, clothes, a few pieces of furniture that we have made ourselves and some bedding. That is all. It would all fit in two wagons."

"What is the total count of men and women?"

"Counting myself, there are sixteen men, nine women and eight children. We have two small babies, and two of the women are pregnant. They can walk though. They are not very far along."

"Good. I will go make the payment to Mister Sumter and we will go see if we can buy the wagons and teams to get you back to Charleston. There we have enough wagons to take care of what you have to carry. You have your people ready to move shortly after daylight in the morning. We will be back with the wagons."

Then Andrew did a strange thing, something Witambe did not understand. He took Witambe's hand and grasped it between his.

"Witambe, in this country they have a custom that I have come to appreciate. When two people have an agreement, they shake hands. This is a pledge that they both agree to the deal and they are honor bound not to break their word. The handshake is a sign of the pledge and trust in each other. It is a good custom and I now shake your hand to prove my sincerity."

Then he headed back toward Sumter's house. Witambe

stood staring after him and wondered if he had made an error in judgement.

Sumter leaned against the porch stoop had observed Andrew and shook his head in amazement at what had just happened.

Andrew concluded the deal with Sumter, and Sumter writes out an order transferring the ownership of the slaves to Andrew. Andrew asked him to make another order from him granting them full freedom and stating that they shall forever be free men. When this was done, Andrew went to his saddle bags and took out a bag of gold coins and certificates of currency from the bank. He counted out $10,000 in gold and then signed a draft on the bank for another $60,000. Then he asked Sumter where he might find two wagons for Witambe's people to carry their belongings with them.

Sumter agreed to allow him the use of two of his wagons. "I need some supplies that are only available in Charleston. The wagons can take their belongings into town and then I'll be able to haul back my supplies. I will send along another wagon so the men will be able to ride as well. In fact, I will even go along. When do you want to leave?"

"We will need to be on the road at first light. I have two more days to get a large wagon train organized and underway. We will have almost 400 head of horses, mules, and other assorted livestock to drive, along with between 12 and 15 wagons. They were still buying wagons and supplies when I left Charleston. Can the wagons make it into Charleston by tomorrow night?"

"If we push hard, perhaps by midnight."

"Good. That will give them one day to rest up before we depart. There won't be much rest after that for the next two months."

"Man you are outfitting a full wagon train for your own benefit. It sounds exciting. I almost wish I was going along."

He invited Andrew and Hans to spend the night and said he would like to learn more about the place they were going.

After agreeing to stay, Andrew asked Hans to go tell Witambe that they would be using the Sumter wagons, so as soon as they got up in the morning, they should load all their own stuff on the wagons and be ready to go immediately after breakfast.

The evening was pleasant, but Andrew was chaffing at the bit and anxious to be on the road. He had done what he came to do and now he needed to get back to Charleston as quickly as he could. He thought on this all night and the next morning as soon as the wagons were rolling, he asked Sumter to please escort them on into Charleston. He needed to ride on ahead and see to things there.

With that he and Hans rode off and soon had left the wagons behind.

It was almost noon, and they were just getting ready to stop for a cold lunch, when the shot rang out and Han's horse stumbled and fell. Hans kicked his feet free of the stirrups and jumped free of the horse as it sank to the ground. As he hit the ground he continued to roll and when he stopped he was in the brush at the side of the road.

Andrew was lost deep in thought and had not suspected an ambush. When the shot rang out, the black horse jumped, and that movement saved his life. A second shot sounded a slight second after the first. It lifted the hat right off his head and creased his head. Having travelled with Dave and Hans in Indian Territory for almost a year, he had learned to react fast. Before Hans had reached the woods along the side of the road, Andrew was off the black and into the woods on the opposite side of the road. Both men had their rifles in their hands. In this time, a man did not travel with his gun in a scabbard on his horse. It was always in his hand or across his saddle.

Andrew knew exactly what Hans would be doing, and he ran about 50 yards into the woods and turned in the direction the shots had come from. He had learned well from his trainers and from his Indian friends, too. Now it was almost as if he drifted over the leaves and limbs on the ground. He made no sound although he was almost at a full run.

When he came within a few hundred feet of where he judged the bush-whackers were hiding, he slowed almost to a walk, but continued to move in their direction. Then he heard whispering, and although he could not make out what they were saying, it told him right where they were. He detected three voices. He moved in their direction. When he figured he was close enough he went down on his belly and eased his gun along in front of him. Then he parted some branches and there, less than 50 feet away sat three men. They were dressed in ragged clothes and run-down boots. They carried old muzzle loading rifles, but the rifles were clean and well oiled. It looked as if they were the only things they took care of.

Now Andrew was close enough to hear what they were saying. One, who appeared to be very nervous, was saying, "I know I got one of them, I saw him roll off the horse and roll over towards the woods. I must have hit him and then the horse."

"You fool. You didn't hit him. I saw him rolling into the woods and it was so fast I couldn't get a shot at him. The other one got hit because I saw his hat fly off. Looks like we got him in the head but I don't see the body."

The third one chimed in, "Shut your yap. One or both of them are still out there and they may be looking for us. If you keep talking you will lead them directly to us."

Andrew was just about to make a move when he heard a noise on the opposite side of the road, as if a horse is moving around. Then he remembered the mistake he made once before, when he hadn't verified how many Indians there were that night, and the two watching the horses almost cost him his life.

Andrew eased back into the woods and moved until he could see where the horses were. He watched them for a couple minutes and did not see anyone. It appeared that they were tied and without a guard. Just as he was about to go back and confront the three bandits, there was movement near the horses. A man had been squatting behind one of the horses, and he rose up to see what was happening. As he did, a long knife pierced his neck and he began thrashing around, but he did not utter a sound. A second later, he saw Hans rise up and move to retrieve his knife.

Now it was Andrew's turn to take care of the problem on this side of the road. He moved back to his former position and noted that the three men were getting real nervous. The one said, "I don't like this. I'm getting out of here. It is too quiet. We better high tail it from here now."

The others agreed and began to rise up. They were thieves and murderers, but Andrew could not shoot them without giving them a chance to surrender. He shouted, "Drop your guns and lean against that log. If you move you are dead!"

They froze, not knowing at first just where the voice came from. Andrew spoke again. "I said drop your guns. That is the last warning you get. Drop them or I'll drop you."

The bandits made as to lay the guns down, and passed a look between them. They found the man's location by his voice the second time he'd spoken. Next, they wheeled all at once and the one who had been so nervous fired into the bushes above Andrew's head.

If Andrew had been standing, the shot would have

probably got him, but all it got was the other man dead. Andrew's rifle roared and the little man tipped over backwards as if he had been kicked by a horse.

Now the other two knew where he was. They had seen the flash of his gun and they fired where the flash came from.

But Andrew wasn't there anymore. As soon as he had fired he rolled to his left and pulled one of the pistols. As the two rifles roared, he pulled back the hammer and let it drop. The second man fell.

The one remaining was desperately trying to reload his rifle. Before he could complete the job, Hans bounded over the log and brought him crashing to the ground. Hans was a big man. His weight knocked the man down and the breath out of him. He rolled over coughing. There was no more fight left in him. Hans grabbed him by the shirt collar and jerked him to his feet.

"What is your name? And why were you trying to bush-whack us?"

"My name is Billy Bates. Jasper Thompson and those other two guys had been following you around and said you had lots of money on you, that if I came along they would pay me 15 percent of whatever they got off you."

Hans asked, "Shall we hang him here or take him to town?"

As always after a fight, the reaction was sitting in on Andrew now and he felt sick to his stomach. He didn't want to look at the two dead men he had just killed, and he certainly didn't want to talk to this stupid one they had captured. He told Hans, "Tie him on a horse and we'll take him to town. We are only about an hour from Charleston. The sheriff or the undertaker can come back for these two. Or they can stay here for the buzzards to eat for all I care." With that he walked back up the road to where they had left their horses.

Hans's horse was dead. Andrew caught up the black,

retrieved his hat and took a rope off his saddle. He uncinched the saddle and pulled it off the dead horse, then attached a loop around the horse's hind legs and attached the other end to his saddle and dragged the horse off the road. When he had the dead horse out of the road, he untied the rope, recoiled it and placed it back on his saddle. Then carrying Hans's saddle, he led his horse back to where Hans had tied the bandit in the saddle of one of their horses. Hans quickly unsaddled the best of the four animals, and put his own saddle on its back. Then he mounted up. Andrew picked up the reins of the other two horses and led out. Hans brought up the rear.

When they arrived in town, they went directly to the jail and explained everything to a deputy on duty, said they would be at the hotel and took their horses to the livery stable.

Andrew went directly to his room and to bed. It had been a hard day.

Hans found Maggie waiting up for him. He was glad she was there for him. It was comforting knowing there was someone to come home to. He didn't want to tell her how close he had come to not returning this time.

CHAPTER TWENTY-SIX

Although there was much on Andrew's mind, and the thought of the two men he had killed that day bothered him, he finally put it out of his mind and slept.

He arose at day break, and after a hearty breakfast, busied himself with the hundreds of things he had to do to prepare the wagon train. One of his first things was to go to the mercantile and increase his order for more foodstuffs. With Witambe and his people going with them, there would be another thirty mouths to feed. They could expect to harvest enough game to supply their needs for meat, but there would be no flour, sugar, salt, coffee and the like once they departed Orangeburg.

The thought of Orangeburg reminded him of Catherine. She had crossed his mind frequently of late, but things were happening so fast, he had not had the time to decide how he was going to tell her he had a son. One thing he knew, he had to go see her and explain what had transpired, even it if meant she would never speak to him again.

He had missed his appointment the day before with Harold Miller, so now he headed to the bank. The cashier recognized him from before, and knowing he was one of the bank's largest depositors, rushed to get the president of the bank.

Miller had the will and the inheritance papers all ready.

After that was taken care of, Andrew instructed him to place a copy of the papers granting freedom to Witambe and his people in his safe. If they should lose their papers and someone questioned whether they were free or not, he wanted a record they could always find. When they arrived the next day, he would bring Witambe to the bank and introduce him to Miller and explain that this man would always have a copy of his freedom papers.

Now he asked Harold for an accounting of his funds. He was unsure of what he had spent and what was left. Miller told him that Peter Georgiades had made several deposits for him. With the money he had withdrawn to pay for the slaves, and the wagons and outfitting, he had spent over $150,000. But with the deposits, he still had an account balance of just over $300,000.

Andrew was surprised. Peter had evidently made a good profit on the rest of the jewels. He would have to go by and thank him for his skill in negotiating.

Andrew explained to the banker that he would need to take several thousand dollars with him to pay the men and have some cash in case he needed something along the way. They would pass thorough several towns besides Orangeburg before they plunged into the wilderness. If they needed anything they had forgotten, maybe they could get it at one of these towns. He quickly calculated the amount of money he would need to pay the teamsters, drovers and road builders.

Then he said, "I will want $25,000 in small gold and silver coins. I do not want any paper money. Where I am going there are not many who trust paper bills. They are too easily torn, burned and washed out in the rain and elements. I will need some kind of secure metal box that I can bolt to the bottom of one of the wagons and a good strong lock and hasp. Then I want another $10,000 for a money belt that will fit around my waist. I have the belt that I left with Georgiades. It is a good one and fits very snugly."

With his business completed at the bank, he walked across to see the jeweler. Miller had told him they would be expecting him for supper that night. He had not seen Mary and the baby in two days now and he was anxious to see them again. Besides, they would be leaving day after tomorrow and this would probably be the last night they would get to visit.

When he walked into the jeweler's shop, the jeweler looked up and recognized him. A huge smile came to his face and he came forward and crushed him in a big hug. He said, "I heard you were in town and getting outfitted to leave again. I wondered if you would stop by to see me."

"Peter, I wouldn't have missed seeing you for anything. Miller told me at the bank of your deposits. You must have had good luck in selling the stones."

"Very good luck, Andrew. I was fortunate in finding a member of one of the major jewelry houses in New York and they had never seen such good stones. I only offered a few at a time, and told them I might be able to get some more like them, but it would take time. About every two months I would send them a notice that I had another batch, but that each one was a little more expensive. I believe they thought I was smuggling them into the country. But they were never too inquisitive. They bought everything I offered. We still have 5 of the best stones. Do you want me to sell those, or do you have some purpose for them?"

"For now, Peter, please hold onto them. I may have a need for them later and I would hate to have to buy them back for what you are selling them for. I have all the money I will need and don't need to sell any more now. Have you taken your fee?"

"Yes, and I am very thankful. You have helped make me a fairly wealthy man."

"You have earned every penny of it. I owe you a debt of gratitude. I will be gone again day after tomorrow and may not be back for another year. But I will either come back for the jewels or send you word as to what to do with them."

It was getting late and Andrew hurried out to begin checking on the final preparations. Witambe and his people would be in by midnight tonight and he made preparations for them in the warehouse where he had stored much of the cargo he would be carrying. All but a few boxes and crates were already loaded and lashed down for the trip. Everyone seemed to be holding up their end of the job.

As late afternoon passed, he returned to his hotel and bathed in preparation for dinner at Millers' house. He arrived just a little after 6 and he and Harold sat in the study surrounded by all the books and talked. Harold was very interested in Andrew's plans and when he would be back. Then he popped the question he had been thinking about all afternoon.

"Andrew, you have such a tremendous job ahead of you and it is so fraught with danger, it is going to be difficult enough without having a small child to look after. Why don't you leave Victor with Hannah and me until you get your house built and get settled. We would love to have him and you would not have to worry about him. We are very concerned about the danger of going among those wild savages."

"Harold, I appreciate your concern, and the offer to look after Victor, but I will not leave my son behind. The land I have acquired will be his someday and he needs to grow up on it, and feel the intensity coming from the soil. That country will shape him into the kind of man that will be strong and know how to defend what is his. Rest assured, I would not take him if I thought there was much danger to him. I know the land I am going into and the kind of people we will be living among. There are some renegade Indians who would harm children, but no more than there are here in Charleston. The majority of the Indians love children and will defend a small child with their life. I have seen small children that have been taken into a tribe when their parents died or were killed, even though the children were of a different tribe altogether. You also forget, in addition to Dave and Hans and the others, I will have Witambe and 15 of his men, who know how to fight. On top of this, I will have the help of the entire Cherokee Nation. Remember, I am one of them in their eyes, and any attack on me or my men, will be considered an attack on the Cherokees. They roam the forests all the time, and will be keeping an eye out for the marauders. If anything happens, they will come running. We will be safer than we might be here in town.

"Besides, he is my son and my responsibility. He has lost his mother before he ever knew her. I want to be forever close to him so that he knows I am there and he can come to me whenever he wants. If I begin to leave him with one and then another, it may become too easy to get into that habit. Then when he needed me, I might not be there." Andrew took a breath, "No. As much as I appreciate your offer, Victor will leave with me when I go."

Miller said, "I expected that to be your answer. However, I told Hannah I would ask you anyway. I respect you for wanting to be with your son. As he grows up, you will be a great influence upon him and I suspect he will become a fine young man with strong and honest principles. Now, let's have dinner."

The evening meal was somewhat somber as there were many things on their minds. Hannah could tell, without asking, that Andrew had declined their offer to take care of the child. It also came out that Mrs. Santiago would be leaving the day after Andrew departed to return to Philadelphia. She wasn't sure when her husband would return from sea and she did not want to be away when he came home.

Andrew had noted that the child was doing well and seemed to have put on weight already. He was now taking cow's milk with a bit of honey well and didn't seem to mind. When Andrew prepared to leave, he told Hannah that he would ask Maggie to come for the baby the following evening. Hannah pleaded with him to leave him the one extra night, and they would deliver him to the wagon in the morning of departure in plenty of time. Seeing the love in her eyes for the child, he agreed and said good night.

It was several blocks, almost a mile in fact to the hotel where he was staying, but it was such a beautiful night that Andrew decided to walk. There were many things on his mind and he thought the night air might help him work out some of the problems he had to face.

He walked briskly along the road and although there was a breeze coming off the ocean, in a few moments he begin to sweat. He took off the coat he had worn to dinner and slung it over his shoulder.

Deep in thought, Andrew had not seen the skulking figure following him. Nor did he know that the man had been waiting in the darkness ever since he had entered the Miller house. He was delighted when Andrew began to walk back to town rather than take a carriage. He followed close behind, as quite as a mouse. As Andrew passed under a large oak tree, the man lunged at him with a long knife aimed at Andrew's back. It was destined for the center of his back, and if it had been true would have gone straight through and pierced his heart. But instead, the knife became entangled in the loosely held coat and diverted it to the side. It is little things like that which cause miracles. The coat hanging loosely over his shoulder may have saved his life.

Andrew was caught totally unaware. The first thing he knew was a thump on his back and a searing pain along his right side. The coat had deflected the knife enough that it struck a rib and went out his side underneath his arm. For a moment he was stunned and faltered sideways. The man, sensing he had not made a kill, drew back to make a second stroke.

Although startled and injured, Andrew had learned in the woods that if you stopped to take stock of your injuries, the delay may cost you your life. He learned to act instinctively to defend himself, and only after the threat was over, to then look and see how badly you were hurt.

As the man raised his arm to strike again, Andrew stumbled sideways and in so doing, turned to face his assailant at the same time. He saw the flash of moonlight on the raised knife and as he fell backwards, he raised his legs as a defense between him and the attacker.

The man had to get in close now and bend over, for Andrew was lying on the ground. He hesitated just a second, evidently deciding whether to press the attack or, now that he had failed on his first try, turn and run away. His greed got the best of him. He moved forward to strike with the knife again.

Andrew waited for him to get closer and as the scoundrel raised his knife to strike, Andrew kicked with both of his feet. He caught the man in the middle of the stomach and threw him over backwards. The knife went flying out of his hand. Now it was Andrew's turn. Before the thief could get up, Andrew was on him, pounding him with rights and lefts to the face and body and with one swift blow to the side of the head, the man went limp.

Andrew backed off and stood up. There was a savage pain in his side and he put his hand to his side. His shirt was ripped and blood had soaked the whole side of his body and was draining down into his trousers. He looked around. The thief had picked a good area for the attack. There were no houses around this particular area and it was pretty dark. Because of the late hour, there didn't seem to be anyone else on the street. He debated what to do. He had come almost half way from Miller's house. He could go back there for help, but that would just upset them, and they would still have to try to find a doctor.

He decided it would be just as quick to head towards town and perhaps he would see someone who could help him. With that decision made, he leaned over, took a good look at the unconscious man and headed down the street toward the main part of town.

Andrew was in luck. He had gone just a block or so when a carriage came down the street. He turned to the edge of the side-walk and leaning against a tree he hailed the carriage. At first he did not think the carriage would stop, but as it neared, he yelled again, "Please help me. I have been hurt."

The carriage came to a stop and a man stepped down. He came over to Andrew and said, "Do you need help?"

Andrew answered, "Yes. I was attacked by a thief with a knife a few blocks back. He cut me along my side and I am bleeding pretty bad. Can you get me to a doctor?"

The man said "I am a doctor. I am just on my way back from seeing a patient. Come get in my carriage and we will get you to my office where we can examine the wound." With that, he helped Andrew into the carriage.

It wasn't far to the doctor's office. When they arrived, the doctor stepped down, took his medicine bag and asked if Andrew needed help. Although he was beginning to feel great pain, he said no he could make it.

In the office, the doctor lit a lamp and immediately went to work on Andrew. He cut away the shirt and began to swab up the blood. He shook his head and said, "That is a pretty deep gash. It is going to be sore as hell for a while, but you are lucky. It doesn't seem to have penetrated any organs or severed any arteries. If we can get the bleeding stopped before you bleed to death, and you don't get infection, you probably will be alright. He noted the money-belt around Andrew's waist, and said, "Someone must have known you were carrying that and decided to relieve you of it. In port towns like this, there are people who would kill you for much less than you are probably carrying."

Andrew said, "I am preparing a big wagon train to go west and set up a trading post in the territories. We have been buying up a lot of supplies and stuff. I should have known that someone would figure I had money on me and try to way-lay me."

"Oh, you are the fellow that I have been hearing so much about. The whole town is abuzz about the wagons and people you are assembling to take into the territories. If you are the one behind the movement, you should know better than to walk the streets of Charleston at night alone. Sir, all of the dangers are not in the forests."

"Yes, you are right. I have been attacked before by hoodlums from this town. I had just forgotten, and I was deep in thought about things I had yet to do to get ready for the trip. I was just careless."

"Well, it almost cost you your life. Did the bandit get away?"

"I knocked him unconscious but I didn't know how badly I was hurt, so I decided to leave him there and seek help."

"Good thing you did. And good thing Wilbur Johnson's cow was sick. Otherwise I wouldn't have been passing along just now."

Andrew looked up, "You are a veterinarian and not a real doctor."

"That's right son. Most of my patients are animals,

although I do on occasion have a human patient. I've patched up my share of folks over the years. I need to take a few stitches in the cut. Can you stand it while I sew you up, or would you like me give you a little valium to numb the pain?"

"Just get on with it doctor. I've had my share of cuts before. This is a saber cut on my cheek. I took that on the battle field and they didn't have anything to ease the pain there. Just do what you have to do."

"I thought you had the look of a soldier about you. Well, while I get my needle and thread and some antiseptic you take a couple good swallows of this Tennessee spring water. It will help some."

The doctor worked efficiently. He knew what he was doing, even if he was a veterinarian. When he was finished and had wrapped a wide bandage around Andrew, he said.

"You should lay up for a few days and give that gash a chance to heal. If you get out and start riding, you most likely will open it up and you may bleed to death. But like most stubborn mules, you won't listen to my advice, so here. Take these bandages and antiseptic with you. You will need them. You better also get you some good whiskey, because you will need to remain drunk for the next few days to get rid of the pain."

Andrew thanked him, gave him a $10 gold piece and left. He was now within two blocks of his hotel and he made it without further incident. He stumbled upstairs and fell into bed. It was a sleepless night for him.

He had not intended to tell anyone about the attack. However, he was so sore that he could not help favoring his side and he moved with great care. It was Hans who first noticed the way he was moving and the sweat on his forehead. When he came up to Andrew, he immediately knew something was wrong. His face was as white as chalk and he was wringing wet with sweat, although it was early morning. He touched Andrew on the shoulder and he winced.

"Andrew, are you alright? You don't look good."

"I'm a little tired is all."

Hans said, "That is not all. Man I have known you for almost a year and I've never seen you look so white. Level with me. What is the matter?"

Andrew told him of the attack and showed him the wound. Hans let out a writhing string of curses and said, "I knew that me or Dave should have followed you around. You're just like a baby. We can't let you out of our sight for a minute without you getting into some kind of trouble."

Andrew knew Hans was going on so because he really cared about him and was mad that someone had been able to get that close and hurt Andrew without him being there.

After much argument, Hans insisted that Andrew go back to the hotel and rest. He and Dave would take care of things. Andrew insisted that he wanted to see Witambe. They had arrived late last night and he wanted to make sure they were OK. Dave led him to where Witambe and his people were staying. Witambe had a worried look on his face, but when he saw Andrew, he felt better. Andrew explained what they would be doing and asked him to help with the rest of the loading. Otherwise, they were to relax, and enjoy their new freedom. When they left tomorrow, it would be hard travel for several weeks and there wouldn't be much time to relax.

Then he returned to the hotel to rest leaving the final preparations to Dave and Hans. He knew they would have everything ready to depart at daybreak tomorrow. He wondered if he would be ready.

CHAPTER TWENTY SEVEN

Andrew had a restless night and awoke early. This was the big day when they would all embark on their trip filled with adventure. Although everyone was excited, none were more so than Andrew. This was to be the fulfillment of his dream for a new start, a new life, and he looked forward to it with great enthusiasm.

Long before daybreak, he was up and dressed, and had packed his bags. Although his side was extremely sore, he managed to get his gear downstairs and piled on the porch. He would send one of the men to pick it up and store it in one of the wagons. He had breakfast and walked over to the warehouse. He was pleased to see that Hans was already on the scene and most of the wagons were harnessed and ready to pull out. Everyone was scurrying around like mice. As the journey got under way, things would shake down, and once everyone knew what their jobs were, there wouldn't be so much confusion.

Witambe and his people had taken a hand and had all of their gear loaded onto two of the wagons that had been left empty for them and their belongings. The women and children were standing by the wagons, ready to leave as soon as the word was given. Andrew stopped for a minute to speak to Dave.

"Dave, as soon as we pull out, I want you to push on

ahead and take Witambe and the road crew with you. Let Witambe's men have horses to ride and take them with you. I will explain to Witambe that his women and children are to follow with us. Although the women may be uncomfortable being left behind, I will get him to explain that they are going ahead to clear the road for us. They will have their wagons and will be safe in the wagon train. You know the route we plan to take. Push on as quickly as you can and after you leave the better travelled roads, start widening out the trails so that we can get these larger wagons through. If you push hard, you will be two weeks or more ahead of us by the time we catch up with you. I'm sure I don't need to tell you to keep a sharp eye out. If you do run into any hostiles, try to deal with them without trouble. Tell them that the white brother of the warrior Night Hawk and son of the great Cherokee Chief Great Eagle will be passing in a few days with his family and tribe on their way to lands that have been granted to him by the Cherokee Nation. We don't want any trouble along the way if we can avoid it. Keep your men bunched and don't let them get careless with their weapons. I am going to send along enough rifles in the wagon so that Witambe and his men will each have one, although they do not know how to use them. If you have time along the way, teach them as much as you can about the guns and how they work. They will need to know so they can defend themselves after they leave our group. Keep your two best mountain men on horseback all the time reading sign and watching for hostiles. We don't want to be caught napping."

Dave nodded agreement and went to select horses for his crew.

Andrew sought out Witambe and asked him to gather his men. The women, suspecting this was going to involve them, came forward also. When they were all together,

Andrew said, "Witambe, we are going over country that has mainly trails and they are not wide enough to allow the wagons through. This is one of my best friends and a brave man. He is going to move on ahead of us to where the main roads end and begin clearing a path for us to bring the wagons through. I would like you and your men to go with him. Leave one of your men, whoever can speak English and someone you trust, here to help your women and children. They will have the two wagons with your possessions on them and will be safe enough with us in the larger train. We will all help look out for your people. But I need you and your men to help clear the roads so that the wagons can pass freely after we leave the villages and main roads. Will you go and help the men we have assigned to the road clearing detail?"

Witambe had listened carefully and gazed steadily upon the face of Andrew. Was the white man attempting to pull some kind of trick to separate him and his women and children? He did not think so. But he still did not understand why this man had bought him and his people out of slavery. He turned and briefly spoke to his people. It was apparent that some had learned some English and had understood much of what Andrew had said. Witambe's woman gazed at Andrew as did several of the men. Then she turned and spoke to Witambe. Andrew was surprised at how much English she knew. They had learned much in the time that they had been in America.

"You go. We stay with this man and his people. We will be good. We know how to fight if we must defend ourselves. We have trusted this man until now. We have no reason to doubt what he says."

Witambe turned to Andrew. "This is the woman I have taken to wife. Her name is Salliberth, but she is called Salli here. She will be in charge of the other women and children. We will not need to leave a man with them."

Andrew said, "Good. They can draw any food, blankets, or clothing they need from our supplies. In exchange, they can help with the cooking and camping chores. Is that agreeable?"

Witambe and Salli both shook their heads and Witambe extended his hand. "In the ways of the white man, we shake hands on agreement, alright?"

Andrew smiled, shook his hand and said, "Alright." It was good to see that he was accepting the way of the Americans.

Everything was in readiness and Andrew called everyone together. When they were all assembled, he said, "Alright folks, we are ready to move out. If there is anyone who has changed his mind and wants to stay home, now is the time to speak. If we leave together, I expect you to stay on until the trip is finished."

When no one moved to leave, he said, "Good. I hope to make the trip in three months, or three and a half months at most barring any unexpected breakdowns. Our wagons are in good shape. The animals are healthy and our people seem fit to ride with. Dave and his road clearing crew will leave first and will move on as fast as they can to the end of the roads and there they will begin clearing right of way so we can bring the wagons through. The rest of you know what your jobs are. I expect you to do your job and no excuses. We must all depend on each other. If one person falls down on his end of the responsibilities, it may hold all of us up. We don't have a lot of time to lose. It will be getting cold by the time we reach Bright Valley. If we do not get there soon, we may be caught in heavy snow which will make it harder to move the wagons. Also, my agreement is to deliver these horses, blankets and knives to the Cherokee's before winter sets in. You already know that Dave will be in charge of the road crew. Hans Brinkman will be my second in command. Anything he tells you to do is the same as coming from me. Any disputes, fights or arguments will be settled by one of us. If there are no questions, hit the leather and let's move out!"

There was a flurry of movement while everyone rose to their saddles or mounted the wagons. Andrew turned; saw Miller and his wife standing on the sidelines holding the baby.

He and Maggie walked over and said their goodbyes. Hannah and Mary were reluctant to let go of little Victor. With tears in their eyes and dozens of hugs and kisses, they passed him to Maggie. Then Hannah turned to Andrew and said, "Andrew Stanley, you take care of that baby. That is our grandson and Godson. If anything happens to him we will hold you responsible. Come back as soon as you can."

Andrew hugged both women, shook Miller's hand and without any further remark, turned and he and Maggie walked back to her wagon. He held the baby while she climbed aboard, then he handed him up to her. He turned once more to look at Miller, Hannah and Mary; he waved, rose to his saddle and took a position in front of the wagon train. He gazed down the row of wagons, saw everyone waiting on him. As he mounted, a searing pain ran down his side and he could feel wetness as if blood had leaked through the bandages. He would stop at the first opportunity and change the bandages. But for now he wanted to get the wagon train moving. He raised his arm, moved it forward and down in a sweeping motion, and said in a loud voice, "Let's move the wagons out." He kicked his horse into motion, and one after the other, the wagons moved after him in single file. It was barely 7 A.M.

Dave and his work crew quickly pulled on ahead and in

a very short time out-distanced the rest of the wagons and in an hour were already out of sight.

By noon they had travelled little more than 20 miles. Things would go better after they got accustomed to the travel. When they stopped for lunch, Andrew called Hans aside.

"Hans, I have to face Catherine and tell her about little Victor. She is still waiting for me to return. She may not want anything to do with me and I may come back empty handed, but I have to go see her. You are probably a day and a half from Orangeburg, or perhaps more, depending on how the train moves. I am going on ahead to talk with her. If she turns me down, I will return and join you before you reach Orangeburg. Whatever, she deserves to know that I am back."

Hans nodded agreement. "I will watch after things and keep the wagons rolling."

Andrew mounted his horse and rode northwest toward Orangeburg.

Because of his wound, he had to move slowly, and it was almost 3 o'clock in the morning when he neared the Heyward plantation. He decided to rest awhile and not approach the house during the night. He found a small glade near a stream, watered his horse, hobbled her and found a spot beneath a large tree. He wrapped himself in his blanket, with his pistol in his hand, and was soon asleep.

Dawn was just breaking when he was awakened by a strange sound. At first he thought it was an animal rustling in the leaves; but during the past year in the forest with Dave Foster and Hans Brinkman, he learned never to move until he was sure. He opened his eyes cautiously and looked around. At first, he saw nothing. Then he heard the noise again. It was near where he had hobbled Midnight. The horse was acting skittish and he detected movement nearby.

He swung the blanket back and rolled to his feet just

as a figure lunged at him. The thick horse blanket between him and the enemy saved his life. A skinning knife sank into the horse blanket and slowed the other man enough for Andrew to raise his pistol and fire. The bullet caught the Indian dead in the brisket and knocked him over backwards. Without hesitation, Andrew stooped and grabbed his rifle just as a second Indian climbed on the back of his horse. He brought the rifle to his shoulder and was about to fire when Midnight reared on her hind legs and pawed the sky with her front feet. The Indian couldn't hold onto the bare back and slid to the ground, falling flat on his rump. Before he could get to his feet the horse kicked at him with both feet. One hoof caught the Indian in the side and Andrew heard bones snap. The Indian rolled to one side and lay still.

The horse was about to stomp him and Andrew caught the reins and pulled her aside and calmed her down. He turned to inspect the Indian and saw bloody foam seeping from his mouth. He stooped to examine him closer and saw that he was dead. Evidently, when the horse kicked him, it broke a rib and punctured a lung. He never regained consciousness.

Andrew took a quick look around to see if there were any others with these two. Evidently they had seen his tracks and followed them to where he was sleeping. They figured to kill him, steal the horse and take his belongings. He credited the things he had learned while travelling with Dave and Hans for him being alive now. He had learned to sleep light and always kept one ear tuned to the night sounds. When the night sounds stopped, you better wake up completely, or you might not wake up at all.

When he did not see anyone else, he figured these two must have been alone. They must have thought they would be a match for one sleeping white man. Too bad for them, they picked the wrong man. The prompt movement had caused the gash in his side to open and a few drops of blood seeped onto his shirt. He quickly wiped off the blood and applied a new bandage to the wound.

He saddled quickly, and rode out. He would get breakfast later. Now he was eager to see Catherine before school started. He rode into her yard and went to the door. It was just coming full light and as he approached the house he saw her turn out the lamp. She was up and would be getting ready for the children to arrive at the school. He knocked on the door.

Catherine came to the door and opened it. The shock of seeing him froze her in her tracks. Andrew stared up at her from the steps. What a beautiful woman! She was even more beautiful than he had remembered. His heart almost stopped as he wondered what the next few minutes would bring.

Before he could say anything she let out a shriek and came bounding out of the door and down the steps, directly into his arms. She would have bowled him over if he had not opened his arms and caught her. She raised her head and immediately her lips found his. The first kiss was a mere greeting. Then she mumbled how glad she was to see him and kissed him again. This time, it was a kiss that was almost savage in its intensity. It was a kiss that told of her passion and her hunger for him. Andrew could not help but respond and he returned the kiss with quick ardor, hugging her and lifting her off her feet.

After several seconds and more kisses, he set her on the ground and she took his hand and led him inside, as questions began to pour from her. When had he returned? Where had he been? Was he well? Had anything bad happened? One after another, the questions tumbled from her, before he could answer the previous one.

He could not break the news to her now, in the midst of her excitement.

He asked, "Do you have school today? Is it possible we can spend some time together? I have a lot to tell you.

Holding his hand in hers she answered, "Yes. But I am too excited to teach. My replacement is in town and has been helping me with the students. I will turn them over to her today and we will spend the day together. I thought you would never return. I was beginning to fear those awful savages might have killed you. Oh Andrew, I am so happy you are here. Kiss me again." And with this last remark, she came back into his arms and pressed her body hungrily against him. It was as if she was telling him how much she wanted him and now the waiting would soon be over.

Some of the children had begun to arrive and he could hear them in the class room and outside. He was a little embarrassed and didn't want to be caught kissing the School Mar' m.

He explained that he had ridden most of the night and was hungry. She hurried to fix him a breakfast of ham, eggs, biscuits and gravy. When the substitute teacher arrived, Catherine brought her into the living quarters and introduced her. Andrew noted that she used the term "my future husband" in the introduction. He wished he had told her. If she rejected him now, it would be a great embarrassment to her.

After he had eaten and the other teacher had all the children busy in the classroom, Andrew took Catherine by the hand and asked her to walk down to the creek with him. He wanted to talk to her. For the first time she detected something in his voice that she had not seen before. She had been so excited about him coming back; she had not stopped to consider that he may have changed his mind and now may not want her for his wife. More subdued, they walked, hand in hand, down to the creek and sat under the same big Magnolia tree they had sat under a year ago.

Andrew thought about how much had happened and how things had changed.

Catherine noted that he seemed lost in thought and she waited. Finally, she spoke. "Andrew, is there something wrong?"

Her remark pulled him back to the present and he looked at her. He could see the wonder, yes, maybe even fear in her eyes. She knew something was not right. Now he turned to face her directly and took both of her hands in his. Speaking very slowly he began.

"Catherine, I have something to tell you that may make you feel very bad. You are a very sweet person and I do not want to hurt you. But I have to tell you that some things have happened and things have changed from when I left." As he spoke, he felt her tense and tighten her grip on his hands.

Now she interrupted him. "Andrew, you do not have to be embarrassed. We hardly knew one another when you left. You were lonely and perhaps infatuated with me. And I was so excited about being set free; I thought I was in love with you also. You were like a knight in shining armor come to rescue me. I was afraid that the feeling you had would not last once you got out and met other people. I guess I was dreaming that we loved each other and that every-thing would be alright. If you have changed your mind I will understand. I will not hold you to your promise to marry me if you do not want to."

"Catherine, it is not what you think. I love you very much and I too have dreamed of us being wed. Many a lonely night lying in my cold blankets, I would think of you and my body would get warm with just the memory of you."

Now she squeezed his hands even harder and said, "Andrew, do you mean you really love me and still want me to be your wife?"

"Yes. But what I have to tell you may cause you to change your mind. Perhaps you will not want me for a husband."

"If you love me, there is nothing that you could have done that would stand in our way. I did not know whether I loved you or not when you left Andrew. But I have thought about us a lot. Many times when I have been alone I would day dream and plan what I would do to please you and make you a good wife, one you would be proud of. When you arrived at my door this morning, it was in answer to my prayers."

"But Catherine, there is something I must tell you. You were right about being lonely. When I first arrived in Charleston, I knew no one except Captain Joshua Wilson. It is embarrassing for me to tell you this, but I do not want to hold anything back. If you reject me, so be it. But if you do accept me for your husband, there must be no secrets between us."

Catherine said, "Go on Andrew."

"In the process of setting my affairs and selling the jewels I had on me, I went to the bank in Charleston to open an account. The banker invited me to dinner at his house. I needed much information if I was going to strike out into the territories. I accepted the invitation. I did not know that his niece would be there. We struck up a conversation, and after the meal I agreed to escort her home. I won't bore you with all the details, but we became well acquainted, in fact we had a very brief affair."

Catherine gasped and pulled her hands out of his. Tears welled into her eyes. "So you are telling me that you have fallen in love with another woman, is that it?"

"Yes, but no. Let me tell you all of the story. Please remember, this was before I came to you. At this particular moment, I did not know that I would find you, or that I would ask you to be my wife. It was a brief encounter, someone that I never expected to see again. But there is more."

443

"When I returned from my trip, I went first to Charleston to register title to the lands I had acquired and to check and see how much money had been deposited for the jewels. When I entered the bank, the banker was very cold and I wondered why. After questioning, I discovered the girl had become pregnant and was going to have a child. She had left to go to Philadelphia in Pennsylvania. Her pregnancy was my fault and I could not let her have the child alone. So I went to Philadelphia and offered to marry her so that our child would not be borne without a father. Unfortunately, before we could be wed, she went into labor and died in childbirth. To make a long story short, I have a young son that is less than one month old. He is travelling in the wagon train that I have put together to haul supplies to the lands I own in the territories. Hans Brinkman, who you met at the courthouse the day we left, has married. The woman he married had her first husband and all of her children massacred by Indians. Maggie is looking after my son for me. That is the situation and the thing I hated to tell you. I do love you and want you for my wife. But I have a son now and I cannot abandon him. He is my responsibility. If you accept me, you will also have to accept my son. If you can forgive me this indiscretion, I would like you to be my wife and come with me to Bright Valley. But if you cannot, then I will understand and I apologize to you for any embarrassment I may have caused you."

Catherine's face was white as if all the blood had drained from her. A trickle of blood flowed from her lip where she had bit it while he was talking. Tears continued to flow down her cheeks and she starred at Andrew. Finally she turned and put her face into her hands and let the sobs wrack her body. Andrew wanted to reach out and touch her, to try to console her, but he feared it would make things worse. So he sat still until the sobbing stopped. Catherine got up and walked to the edge of the stream. She kneeled down, scooped water out of the stream and washed her face. Then she wiped it with the hem of her dress and stared out across the water. All this time Andrew waited. He had said what he came to say. Now the decision was hers. He could not blame her if she sent him away and told him she never wanted to see him again.

Finally, she turned and came back to where he was sitting. She sat down near him, but not close enough to touch. She sat in silence for some minutes, and then she raised her head and looked into his eyes.

"Andrew, that hurt me very much. I had not even given thought that you might have had other women, and I had no idea that you might have found someone here since you arrived. But you are a handsome man. It would have been surprising if someone had not captured you before me. I am not a very worldly person, but others tell me that it is not unusual for a man to have several affairs before he finally settles down. I believe I can forgive your affair and live it down. The thing that bothers me is if we marry, would it happen again? I would not want to be a cuckold wife. I intend to be true to my husband, and I would not want to think that I might be sharing him with another woman. I could not abide that. If I am to be true to him, he must be true to me and shun all other women. Can you do that Andrew? If we marry, will you be faithful to me?"

Andrew answered, "Yes Catherine. If you accept me as your husband, what is past is past, and I will be faithful to you. Can you also accept my son and help me to rear him?"

"The child has no blame. I love children and I would hope that we would have some of our own. However, that may not be God's will. Yes, he is of your flesh and blood. I will love him and care for him as if he were my own. You need have no fear that I will reject him or treat him badly. When can I see him?"

"The wagon train should be here by tomorrow night or the next day. This is Friday; I would say they will be here by Saturday noon at the latest if everything goes well. We must push on to Bright Valley as quickly as we can for I have a deadline to meet. If you have decided to accept me as your husband, I would like us to get married before we start our journey. Would you want to see if we can be married here, or wait until we are better acquainted?"

"Andrew, if I leave here with you, I want to leave as your wife. Once we are joined I will do whatever it takes to see that we are never separated. Too many things can happen as the days go by. I want to marry here. I think Mr. and Mrs. Heyward would be happy if we were married here at their house. Mrs. Heyward has mentioned it to me several times. Would that suit you?"

"Yes. That will suit me fine." Taking her hands again, he looked into her eyes and said, "Catherine, I was so afraid that I might lose you. I do love you more than you can imagine and I was so afraid my indiscretion might be our undoing. I promise you that I will be a good husband. I will do my best to see that you are never sorry for your decision. Now give me another kiss to seal the bargain, and let's go talk to Heyward. We don't have much time."

With that he took her into his arms and she came willingly. It might be some time before she would be able to erase the incident from her mind, but her love for him and her desire to feel his strong body close to her, made her secretly vow that she would never bring up the subject again.

They separated and hurried to the main house.

When Mrs. Heyward learned Andrew had returned and he and Catherine wanted to be married as soon as possible, she was all in a tither. She sent one of the hands to fetch Mr. Heyward from the fields, and she set the wheels in motion for the wedding. She took complete charge. It would be Sunday immediately after church service. They would ask the preacher to make the announcement at the Sunday service and to invite everyone for the wedding and reception that would follow.

Heyward came in and was informed of the event, and then Mrs. Heyward gave both men a list of small things to do and told them to go away. She wanted them out of the way.

The wagon train arrived in Orangeburg late Saturday. Heyward had the whole train move onto his plantation and camp that night so that they would be close enough to come to the wedding the next day. He had put most of his workers to work preparing to feed the hundred or so local people that would be there plus the folks on the train. The freed slaves and the other members of the train pitched in and gave a hand. This would be one of the biggest events of the year. Altogether, there would be close to three hundred people. Andrew thought, «Just a small wedding huh!»

Heyward was surprised that Andrew had acquired a number of slaves and even more surprised when Andrew told him these blacks were free men and traveling with him of their own free will. He did not question Andrew as to how he had come by the black men and how they were free, He did not think it any of his business. But he did think it was a strange situation.

Andrew and most of the folks from the train attended church and the preacher preached on «carrying the message of God into the wilderness to teach the heathens.»

Immediately afterward, Mrs. Heyward and a gaggle of other women rushed to the Heyward farm. The women took Catherine upstairs to get her dressed. Andrew had brushed up his best suit but when Catherine came down the staircase he felt like a hobo. She was dressed in a long flowing silk gown with a tight bodice and a flowing train behind. She had a small crown on her red hair and she looked almost like an angel. He could not help staring at her, nor did he miss the oohs and ahs from the people waiting for the wedding.

The ceremony was over in a few minutes, although it seemed to take forever. Andrew was nervous and could hardly wait until the preacher said, «I now pronounce you man and wife!» As he kissed Catherine she plunged her tongue into his mouth and bit his lip. When he pulled back, he could see the mischievous look in her eyes and the wicked little smile she gave him. She seemed to be saying, «You›re mine. Wait until I get you alone!»

The reception and the entire event was one of great fun and enjoyment. There was enough food for an army and everyone was in great spirits. People in the country did not have many occasions to gather and many had never attended such a large event as this wedding. When something like this came along, it was if the county fair had come to town. Everyone for miles around, all the parents of the kids that Catherine had taught wanted to come and pay their respects.

Heyward had offered them one of the guest bedrooms, but both Andrew and Catherine elected to stay in her room at the school house. This would be the only night they would have any privacy to speak of. From now on there would not be much privacy on the train and until they could get a cabin built in Bright Valley, they would be sharing the few accommodations with the other members of the wagon train. But for tonight they would have their privacy and consummate their marriage. Both wanted the night to arrive and escaped the party as quickly as they could without seeming too anxious.

As they entered the school house, Andrew picked Catherine up and carried her into the building. He went straight through to the back where she lived and set her on her feet and held her while they kissed. Catherine gently disengaged herself, told him to go into the kitchen and make a pot of coffee while she got the wedding dress off. He offered to help, but she said she would be embarrassed. They needed to get to know each other better. He smiled and said, "That is exactly what I had in mind. After tonight, we should know each other a lot better."

He started a small fire in the stove and filled the coffee pot. Then he took off his tie and coat and removed his boots. Although the wedding was over, he was still tense. He wanted this evening to be very special and he wanted to make sure he did not do anything wrong that might offend Catherine.

He heard the curtains part from the door to her bedroom and he looked up. The sight made him catch his breath. Catherine had stepped from the bed-room and now stood just inside the kitchen. She wore a thin night gown of almost sheer silk. It was cut low and revealed her body beneath the sheer material. It clung to her shapely hips and ended just below her knees and she stood barefoot on the wood floor. He was speechless.

When he did not speak, she saw the pleasure in his eyes and the desire taking hold of him and she was less self-conscious. Now she moved toward him very slowly and spoke for the first time since re-entering the room.

"After you left, I was in town one day and while looking through a catalog at the mercantile, I saw a picture of this gown. I wanted it for when you returned. Do you think it is scandalous?"

Andrew found his voice, "It is lovely, and you are so beautiful in it. It takes my breath away. I am afraid to reach out and touch you for fear this is a dream and you will disappear."

She walks into his arms and takes his face in her hands, "It is not a dream Andrew and I will not disappear. I am yours and you may do whatever you want with me. I have dreamed of this night for more than a year. I love you and want you to love me. I want to please you, but please be gentle with me. I am a virgin, and I have heard some horrible things about wedding nights. But I am ready to become a fulfilled woman. I want you to make love to me."

She clasped his head tight to her breast and now with her this close, Andrew was able to extend his arms around her. He pulled her tightly to him.

She helped him unbutton and remove his shirt. She backed up slightly so that he could get at the belt and buttons on his trousers. For the first time, she became aware of the bandage around his side and backed away with a gasp. "Andrew, what happened?

He explained about the attack and the attempt to rob him. The wound had opened again and blood seeped into the bandage. Catherine was worried and insisted they change the bandage before proceeding any further. She went to retrieve bandage material and assured him she would be gentle. Then, in a brazen move, she decided to have a little fun with him, saying she hoped he was well enough that they can consummate the marriage. She was a little embarrassed that she had been so forward as to suggest that they proceed to make love even though he was wounded.

Andrew assured her he wouldn't stop if it killed him. He had been thinking of taking her in his arms for months and he was not about to let a little cut stop him.

With that assurance she cleansed the wound and rebandaged it. Then she turned her back to him while he finished undressing. She had taken the pins out of her hair and it cascaded down her back almost to her hips. Andrew eased over to her and kissed her on her bare neck.

She felt his hands on her again. She turned around and came back into his arms. She had dreamt of this day; now she was ready to be made a fulfilled woman.

When they had exhausted themselves, she let out her breath and gasped for air. She practically collapsed, feeling limp as a dish-rag. They both remained quiet, holding onto each other for several minutes, relaxing and regaining their breath.

Though this was not the first time for Andrew, the intensity was something he had not expected. He attempted to move, but she held him a little longer.

In a light whisper, Catherine said, "Andrew, I don't know what came over me. I couldn't stop myself once we started. I have wondered so long what it would be like to make love to you. I had no idea making love could be so enjoyable, or that I would lose myself in the act. Is it always that way? I am almost exhausted. I never expected our first union would be anything like that." Then she let out a little giggle.

They talked for a few moments. Then she moved to get up and picked up her gown as she went toward the bedroom.

He cleaned himself, pulled his trousers back on, then approached the stove. The coffee had boiled over and was sizzling on the iron grate. He removed the pot, poured a cup and sat at the table until she returned.

Catherine poured herself a cup of coffee and joined him at the table.

"I hadn't expected to be so sore, I am almost raw. You are a monster to make me do such wicked things." She spoke with a mixture of glee and truth.

"I didn't have to twist your arm I don't think," he grinned at her. "I am sorry that you are sore. That means we will have to wait several days until you feel better, before we do it again. By then, we will be on the train and there will be very close quarters. We won't have the privacy we had tonight."

All she would say was, "Hmmm. We will have to see."

Now Catherine wanted to talk about Bright Valley and what they would be doing. Andrew told her of his plans and of the blacks he had bought and set free. He said he hoped they would stay close and help him build a house and trading post in Bright Valley, but if they wanted to leave they were free to do so.

Finally, they went to bed for they would be pulling out at day break tomorrow and it would be a tough journey for her. He knew she was not used to this kind of travel.

It wasn't too long before they made love a second time that night. She held him close and whispered to him, "Andrew I love you so much. I never dreamed love between a man and woman could be so good. Please don't get up yet. You have spoiled me." She did not want this moment to end.

Andrew raised up on his elbow and said, "Tomorrow you will wish you had never heard of Andrew Stanley. I suspect you will be so sore that you will have to walk spraddle-legged. Then you will refuse me the next time I want to love you."

"I will never refuse you Andrew. You are a terrific lover. I am so glad that you chose me to be your wife. I will be a good one to you, and I hope that I will always satisfy your desire for love-making. You will have to teach me all the things you want me to do. I promise to be a good student."

"I'll bet you will! You already know all you need to know to satisfy me. Now let's get up and clean up so we can get some rest. You have already worn me out, woman!"

She released him and crawled out of bed. When she

returned, she smiled sheepishly, "You were right, I am really sore now. But it was well worth it."

They fell asleep in each other's arms. It would be a long time before they would have this much privacy, and peace and quiet. Tomorrow they would resume their journey.

CHAPTER TWENTY-EIGHT

The wagon train rolled out at day break the next morning. Catherine had risen at 4 o'clock, and after a quick meal, she packed the rest of her belongings. Andrew had left earlier to get things rolling and sent a wagon for her. Once they finished loading, she turned and looked one last time at the only home she'd had since coming to America. It wasn't much but it was comfortable and dry. She wondered how long it might be before she had a roof over her head again. She couldn't help it when a single tear rolled down her cheek. She wiped it away, turned and climbed up on the wagon and they drove away. She never looked back again.

In the days that followed, it seemed she hardly ever saw Andrew, except in passing. He was up before daybreak seeing to things, hurrying people along, helping this one and then that one with equipment, animals or their problems. He would stop long enough to eat and at night, when most others were settling down, he still roamed the camp, making sure all was secure. They were now several days from Orangeburg and seldom saw anyone except an isolated homestead, or an occasional traveler. The third day out, some Indians ran off a half dozen of the horses. Andrew knew stealing horses was like a game to them, and other than that, there had been no trouble. He made sure that guards were posted around the horses every night. No matter how tired the men were, everyone pulled their turn at guarding the camp.

Within ten days, they had arrived at the end of the travelled road and found the place where Dave Foster and his crew had started clearing a path for them. At this rate, they would reach Bright Valley by mid-October. That would give them almost three months to build housing for them before severe weather came. They could not build enough to house everyone though. There would be some who would spend the winter in tents. Andrew sent one of his men on ahead with a message that they were coming and moving at a better pace than he had expected.

Andrew had brought plenty of warm clothing and blankets for all of them. The bulk of the men hired for the trip would return to their homes. Only Andrew and his family, Hans and Maggie, and Witambe and his people, would be staying. Dave Foster had not yet indicated whether he would stay or not.

They travelled northwest, staying east of the Savannah River, waiting as long as they could before trying to cross it. They had been lucky so far; all the streams they had crossed were low and they had not lost any wagons, and only a few head of stock. But Andrew knew that sooner or later they would have to cross the big river. He hated to see that day. Normally the Savannah was a lazy, slow moving river down below. But it could become a roaring torrent after a heavy rain, and the further north you went, the closer you got to the foothills of the Appalachians, the swifter the water moved, even in dry weather.

They had passed the village of Columbia and gone around the headwaters of the western branch of the Santee and the South Fork of the Edisto. Now they were travelling on a sort of ridge that rose between the Savannah on the West and the North Branch of the Santee on the East.

Andrew hoped that Dave had found a good crossing for they would soon have to cross over. The lands they were headed for lay west of the Savannah.

Catherine could see the stress and strain of the journey on him. When he did come to bed at night, he was usually so tired that he was not in the mood to make love. Only two or three times since they left Orangeburg had he turned to her in the night and began to love her. She always looked forward to those times and eagerly responded to his slightest impulse. Once or twice during the night when he was sleeping soundly, she would caress the hair on his chest and snuggle close to him.

During the day when he was away looking after the train she felt a little frightened by the vastness of the wilderness that surrounded them. But at night, when she was next to him, she felt safe and secure. At such times, she wanted to be one with him and hoped he would wake and possess her. Because their love-making was so infrequent now, when he did come to her, she tried to make it as enjoyable as she knew how. She made sure he always knew he could have her whenever he wanted. She teased him and often when they awoke, she would pretend she wouldn't let him get up until he had made love to her. All too often though, they were awakened by some crisis and Andrew would have to tumble out of bed, rushing to pull his pants on before he left the wagon.

Catherine had taken an immediate liking to little Victor and she spent much of her time caring for him. Maggie was a big woman and a hard worker. She did as much as most men. So gradually, it became more and more Catherine's responsibility to look after the baby. She didn't mind. In fact, Victor had Andrew's dark eyes and was a pleasant baby. He seldom cried and slept most of the time, waking only when he needed a diaper change or when he was hungry.

By the end of the second week, she took over full care of the baby and moved all the baby's things into her and Andrew's wagon.

Andrew had bought a small cradle and cleared a place for it in the wagon. As the wagon moved and rolled from side to side over bumps in the road and an occasional log or rock, the cradle rocked back and forth. The baby seldom needed holding. When he was tired they just put him in the cradle and the movement rocked him to sleep. Andrew was pleased that Catherine had taken to the child so quickly. She was growing to love him and it made his mind more at ease, for he had feared she would resent the child and mistreat him. But now, as he watched her cradle the little one in her arms and hum a song to him, he wasn't worried anymore.

By the first week of September, Andrew grew restless. They had not yet caught up to Dave, but it appeared they were getting close though because the trees that had been cut still had green leaves on them. This meant the trees had not been cut for more than a few days.

One morning after the train was underway, he decided to ride on ahead and check on things. As he prepared to leave, Hans waved him aside and in a low voice said, "Take at least one or two of the other men with you and ride with your eyes peeled. There have been Indians scouting the train for a couple days. I think they are Creeks, but I'm not sure. They could be either Choctaws or Chickasaws, although this is a little far east for either of them. I don't think it is Cherokees though. Didn't you make peace with that Creek Chief and make a deal with him to cross his land?"

"Yes, I did. Of course, there is more than one band of the Creeks, and some of the others may not take kindly to such a big wagon train coming into their territory. You better double the guards and have them ride the woods a little farther out, but not so far they could be picked off one at a time. Make sure they stay alert at night too. The train is too big for a small band to attack, but they might sneak in during the night and steal something, or take some horses. I'll be back in a day or so. Keep pushing the wagons along."

He selected two of the best shots to accompany him. They picked out good horses and rode out. One of the men was the one called Zeb, and he had seen injun trouble before. He would know enough to keep his guard up and Andrew felt better having him along.

They rode at a brisk pace and halted at mid-day only long enough to water and grain the horses. They ate hard-tack and drank water from a spring. Thirty minutes later, they were on the road again. Andrew had a premonition of trouble and kept his eyes swinging back and forth, the way Dave and Hans had taught him to do. They approached the big river, and he was relieved to see several of his men working on the near bank. He looked across the river and saw the road leading on away from the river on the other side.

He approached the men, and they were glad to see him also. He noticed that they had cut a large number of logs and trimmed them. Surely they didn't intend to build a bridge across this river. It would take months, perhaps years, to do that; and the next big rain would carry it all away. After greetings were exchanged, Andrew asked the man in charge where Dave Foster was. He said Dave had gone out with the blacks and most of the other white men to flag the next section of road. They were camping across the river and would be back before dark.

Andrew asked what they were doing with so many logs. The foreman said it was Dave's idea. He had instructed them to cut enough big tree trunks of dead trees as they could find. They were to haul them here and stack them on this side of the river. His idea was to lash one tree to each side of the wagons, unhitch the mules and horses, and float the wagons across. They would tie several ropes to the wagons and fasten them to the mules on the other side of the river and as soon as the wagon rolled into the water, they would whip up the mules and pull the wagons across the river. Andrew was pleased with the idea. If something did go wrong and a wagon overturned, none of the people or animals would be lost. The river was fairly swift, but it was pretty wide at this point and the water had spread out and was slower at this point than at some others.

Dave and the work crew returned before dark. Andrew congratulated him and the crew on the good job they had done. Andrew told them they were a little more than half way now and updated the crew on the rest of the people in the wagon train, letting them know there had not been any real trouble thus far. One man had let a wheel roll over his foot and broke it, but he was still able to ride. Another had a mule bite him and took a big piece of meat out of his arm. But for the most part, everything was going good. Almost too good. He told Dave about the Indians stealing their horses and that they had been scouting the train for several days.

Dave nodded in understanding. "Yes, and they have been watching us too. I figure they are real curious as to what we are up to. We have come face to face with them a couple of times. They seem to be very interested in Witambe and his people. Two or three times, they have seemed to be sitting on their horses watching our team work. It is hard to know what goes through their minds. But they haven't bothered us. We keep our guns handy, always within reach, and two or three are on guard all the time. Of course, it is not the Indians you see that you need to worry about."

Andrew asked, "Have you been able to make out which tribe they are from?"

Dave replied, "I think they are Choctaws. At least those

we have seen. I've got a bad feeling that they may not be as friendly as the Cherokees. They have been following us too closely and haven't made an effort to talk with us. Be on your toes. They could be up to some sort of mischief."

Andrew said, "The wagons will be here by day after tomorrow. I would like to have all of your men here to help us get the wagons and live-stock across the river. Witambe will want to spend a little time with his wife and family. They are all well and have fit in well with the others in the train. When we get across, we will lay over a day to rest up. Find a nice valley with good grass for the animals, not too far from the river. We will set up camp there when we get on the other side."

The next morning Andrew headed back with Zeb and the other man. He felt better about crossing the river now. Dave has picked a good location to cross, and the logs were a good idea. They rode about two hours when they rounded a bend in the road and saw six Indians sitting atop their ponies in the road. All three men noticed them at the same time, pulled up their horses, and stopped 100 yards away. Andrew studied the Indians and saw there was something different about them. These were not like the ones he has observed in the distance the last few days. They do not appear hostile. And although they are holding their weapons lower; they could turn mean in a fraction of a second. Andrew whispered to his men without turning his head.

"Keep your rifles handy, but don't raise them and don't show you are afraid. I believe these are friendly Indians, but that could change if they think you are scared of them. Follow my lead."

Zeb said, "I don't know if I can hide my fear or not. I am sweating like a hog and about to pee my pants."

Andrew gently kneed Midnight so that she seemed to turn on her own free will. While his back is to the Indians, he loosened the strap holding the pistol in its holster on his saddle horn. Then he reined the horse around and raised his hand in the salute of friendship. He walked his horse toward the Indians and the other two men followed him.

He hoped they looked unconcerned, but inside he was coiled tight as a spring. There could be lots of blood-shed in the next few minutes if they said or did the wrong thing. When they were about two horse links from the Indians, he stopped and rested his hands on the saddle horn, very close to the pistol. This movement is not lost on the Indians; they were not careless wanderers.

He greeted the Indians in Cherokee, "Greetings my red brothers. It is a fine day for a ride isn't it? A good day for a hunt."

He knew these men were not out hunting, at least not for game. But it was as good a way as any to start a conversation, and as long as they are talking, maybe they wouldn't want to fight.

The Indian sitting his horse just ahead of the others appeared to be the leader; he hesitated. They were all surprised to hear a white-man speak such good Cherokee. Although they had blocked the road with hostile intent, now they wanted to know more.

The lead Indian spoke, "You are not Cherokee, yet you speak their language well. Who are you and why are so many of your people crossing the lands of the Creeks?"

Andrew was relieved slightly. Evidently these were Creeks, but they didn't seem to be that friendly. "I am called Andrew Stanley by the white-man. I am the blood brother of Nighthawk, the sub-chief of the Cherokee, and adopted son of Great Eagle. My Indian name is One Who Sees Far, given to me by the great Creek Chief, Bear Claw."

He stopped to allow this to sink in. He saw that all of the Indians were impressed that this white-man knew so many of the Indian chiefs and had been adopted by one, and given an Indian name by the chief of one of the Creek tribes.

Andrew continued, "I have an agreement with Bear Claw that allows me to pass through his lands unharmed. The Cherokee have given me land on which to live and on which I plan to set up a trading post. I will live between the Cherokee and Creek nations and will trade with all who come in peace."

The Indians remained silent for several minutes before speaking among themselves. There seemed to be no hostility. Then the leader turned back to Andrew.

"You are not on the lands of Bear Claw. His land all lies west of the big river. You are on the lands of the Sweetwater Creeks. Our chief is Running Deer. What will you give us for passing through our lands?"

Andrew knew he must bargain with them, but he was determined that they won't hold him up. "If I am truly on the lands of the Sweetwater Creeks, I am willing to pay fair passage through your lands. Let us smoke the pipe and discuss what is fair." With this he dismounted and reached into one of his saddle bags and took out a pipe that Great Eagle had given him.

The lead Indian hesitated a minute, then he, too, dismounted and joined Andrew on the side of the road.

Andrew lit the pipe and offered it to the Indian first as a courtesy. After both have smoked, Andrew got down to business.

"How far does the land of the Sweetwater Creeks extend?"

The Indian said, "Your wagons have been on our lands for three days. The lands from the river back to the twin branches of the Congree River are our hunting grounds."

Andrew nodded. "Then it is your people who have been trailing our wagon train?"

"Yes. But there have also been some Choctaws who live

south of us watching you also. We have been watching you and them to see that they do not cross into Creek lands."

Andrew nodded. "For safe passage for my people and the wagon train, I will give five horses and ten blankets to your chief. I will also give each of you a new knife if you will guard our animals to make sure the Choctaws do not steal from us in the night."

He knew this was not going to be enough, but was wise enough to start low in any negotiation and leave room to move.

The Indian sniffed and made as to get up to leave. Then he turned and said, "The Creeks are not beggars. They don't want scraps from the white-man's table. It is worth twenty horses and 30 blankets to cross our land."

"I had not heard that the Creeks were robbers of their neighbors. I intend to live on the border between the Creeks and Cherokees. I could not feel kindly to my neighbors if they took advantage of me and charged me more than it was worth to cross their lands. I would not charge you to cross my land when we are neighbors. I will give you 10 horses, ten blankets and each of you a knife. And I will throw in two mules to barbecue so that the Sweetwater Creeks can celebrate the passing of their friend, One Who Sees Far."

The Indian haggled a little more, but when he understood that Andrew would move no further, he agreed.

Andrew informed him that as soon as they reached the river safely he would turn over the goods to the Indian. They agreed, and Andrew prepared to leave. "The goods I have promised are for safe passage across the lands of the Sweetwater Creeks. If we are attacked, or any of our animals are stolen by the Choctaws before we reach the river, I will not pay because we will not have been given safe passage."

The Indian looked at him again and nodded. If he wanted the things he had bargained for, he and his men must make sure none of the other Indians bothered the wagon train. He mounted up, spoke briefly with the other Indians and they rode away. Zeb and the other man with Andrew heaved a sigh of relief.

Zeb spoke up, "Man, was I scared. A couple of those Indians looked down right mean, and I think they have had run-ins with white-men before. They didn't seem all that happy that their leader even agreed to talk to you. I think they wanted our scalps."

"Yes, they probably did. But when they found out they weren't dealing with pilgrims, they decided it just might be too expensive to try to take our belongings. So they decided to negotiate the best deal they could get. Their chief probably won't ever see those horses or blankets. But I don't care. If we get to the river without a fight, that is all I want. Let's ride before they change their minds."

There were no further problems with the Indians. The train was too large to attack without a large number of Indians; and even then, there would be lots of casualties. Indians didn't like those odds.

The crossing of the river went well. They didn't lose a single wagon or a head of livestock. Dave led them to a small valley just above where they crossed. The wagons circled and they set up camp. Andrew announced that they would stay over an extra day to dry out their clothes that had gotten wet in the crossing. The women wanted to wash some clothes too. Just before bringing the last wagon across, Andrew took out 15 blankets, 10 horses, the two mules and the knives he had promised.

He motioned for the Indians, who had been sitting on their ponies, to come forward. He pointed to the horses and two mules and said, "One Who Sees Far keeps his word. We agreed on 10 blankets, but you have also kept your word and no harm has come to any of our people. Therefore, I am giving you five more blankets than we agreed. Please tell your people that I am a man of honor and I will deal fairly with them if they wish to come to my trading post to trade. I do not think that Bear Claw will mind you crossing his land if you tell him that you are coming to trade with me. Go in peace and may the Great Spirit smile upon you and your people."

The Indian looked at him with great respect. He said, "I am Limping Crow. I will tell my people about you. Should you pass this way again and any of our people stop you. Tell them that you are my friend and they will let you pass." He raised his hand in salute and returned to his horse.

Andrew smiled. He had made yet another friend among the Indians. Every friend he made was one less enemy who might steal from him, or worse, attack and kill some of his people. There are enough dangers in the forests; a person didn't need to create any more than he had to.

September wore on, and with October fast approaching, Andrew grew more restless. It seemed the train was just creeping along and in his estimation they should have been making better time. He was afraid that he would not make Bear Claw's territory before the end of October, as he had promised. He also needed to deliver the horses, blankets and cloth to Great Eagle for the land before bad weather set in.

One night, Andrew was discussing the route with Dave and Hans. "Dave, are we heading a little too much to the west?"

Hans responded. "I have planned it this way. Pretty soon we will come on the right of way we flagged to Atlanta from Bright Valley. I did not want to cut another road through Bear Claw's land. When we find the flagged route, we will turn north and build that leg of the road to Bright Valley.

Later, we can come back and open up the south leg of it to Atlanta. This portion that we have been travelling will probably grow up, or the Indians will fell some trees across it to keep any other wagons from coming this way. I am a little surprised that you made it this far without them trying to stop you."

"I was a little afraid too. But I seem to have made another friend in Limping Crow. I don't think we will have any further trouble with the Creeks, although we are leaving their lands at the river and I don't know what tribes are in front of us."

Five days later, they came to the route Dave had flagged to Atlanta. Here, they turned north and headed to Bright Valley. In about five days, they would be on Bear Claw's land.

In the meantime, they were travelling through lands they were not familiar with. Dave knew that they were west of the Savannah River, and there was another river to the west, but he didn't know the name. They were travelling along a high ridge, and although they took a winding path, they had only small creeks and shallow rivers to cross.

Andrew was pleased. Dave and the Indians from Bear Claw's village had done a good job in selecting the route they would be using most of the time.

During the third week of September, Andrew decided to throw all his manpower into clearing the road. He wanted to get to Bright Valley. His impatience took over; in doing so, he became careless.

He had pulled all the men into the work crew but four. These remaining four constantly rode a circle around the train, which remained stalled much of the time now. The train had caught up with the road clearing crew, and the crew could not stay far enough ahead to allow them a full day's travel. Andrew and Dave pushed the men to long hours and when they came in at night they were exhausted.

They ate and fell into their bed rolls. Those selected to stand night watch often fell asleep. They had encountered no trouble and had become careless. Otherwise, the incident might never have happened.

The night watchmen became most sleepy in the early morning hours before daylight, and the two guarding the horse herd were both asleep. One would never wake up. As the late night mist began to rise from the ground, the Indians came sneaking in the haze. Had the watchman been alert, he probably would have detected that the horses were acting up and pulling against the rope corral that was holding them. But he never knew they were near him until a stone axe smashed in his head.

Indians were master horse thieves. They moved with skill and cunning and before you could count to 20 they had their ropes on an even dozen of the finest animals in the herd. Then they slashed the ropes holding the rest of the animals and with a shrill shout that caused the hair on the back of your neck to rise, they were off in a dash towards the west.

The camp came awake immediately. Some rolled out of their blankets in their underwear, holding a rifle, while others dashed for cover, not even thinking to take their weapons with them. They had been lulled into such a false sense of security that they did not expect such a thing to happen. A determined band of Indians, bent on killing them, could have crept into the train and murdered half the people before anyone became aware.

Andrew always kept Midnight hobbled near his wagon and as soon as he realized what was happening, he slashed the hobbles, grabbed a pistol and put it in his belt. With his rifle in one hand, he mounted the horse bare-back, and raced toward the corral in an effort to stop the horses. He was too late. All he could see was the dust where they had run.

Fortunately, the other night herder had managed to cut

about 25 off and herded them into a thick stand of trees. They stopped running. By the time he had them calmed down, several of the other men arrived.

Andrew surveyed the scene and found the other herder.

He turned and barked orders. "I want all the men that can find a horse in saddles in 15 minutes. Bring your weapons and a canteen of water and some hard-tack and jerky. Hans, take Midnight and saddle her for me. Dave and I are going to try to determine how many of these heathens there were. You stay here and organize the wagon. Keep everyone calm. I don't think they will be back, but we can't take any chances."

After questioning the other night herder, who said he had not seen a thing, nor did he hear anything until the Indians shouted to stampede the animals.

Dave searched the ground. He returned and spoke to Andrew. "It was strictly a horse stealing raid. The poor devil over there just happened to be in their way; otherwise he would probably be alive yet. Some young brave is bragging about counting coup now. What is the plan?"

"We have to round up the horses and mules. The oxen won't run. The mules won't go far either. But those horses will be scattered to hell and gone. Pick five of your best rifle men who have had skirmishes with Indians before and we will go after them. We cannot allow them to get away with this or they will be back again and again. The rest will get busy and round up as much of the stock as they can. We will just have to lay over here a day or more until we get the bulk of the animals back. Those extra horses were the payment for the land. If I don't deliver the goods I promised to the Cherokees they can revoke the agreement for the land. We must round up those horses, and in the process, we must run down those Indians and teach them that it isn't healthy to steal from us."

Andrew explained their situation to Hans when he

returned. He had Andrew's second pistol on the saddle horn and a bundle of food hanging from the other side of the saddle. His bed roll and slicker was fastened behind the saddle. He told Hans to explain to Catherine and he mounted up. He was a little surprised to see that Dave had picked Witambe as one of the five men who would be riding with them. But now was not the time to question his decision. As soon as they were all mounted, Andrew told Dave to take the lead. Dave moved out and motioned Witambe to follow him. The rest moved along behind Andrew.

From the sign, it appeared there were no more than five or six Indians. For a short distance, the horses had stayed bunched. Then they began to peel off to one side or another, but one bunch seemed to stay together and continued straight west at a hard run. Dave stopped and conferred with Witambe, then came back to Andrew.

"It looks like this is the bunch being led by the Indians. The others have mostly slowed and are cropping grass, but this bunch is still in a hard run, which means they are being ridden and led. It is too dark to tell for sure, but Witambe thinks there are at least 12 maybe 14 animals, and it appears that four or five are being ridden and the rest are on lead ropes. So this would indicate that this was a raiding party and not a war party. I suggest that we ride along slow and save the horses until it gets a little more light. We don't want to run into an ambush."

"You are in charge of tracking; whatever you say. But we must catch them and recapture those horses, even if we have to follow them back to their village, wherever that may be."

Dave acknowledged and moved out again. They rode at a pretty good pace, stopping every few minutes to examine the ground.

Then just as dawn broke, Witambe slid to the ground,

handed Dave the reins to his horse and set off on foot. Dave didn't move until the black man was almost out of sight ahead of them, then he motioned to the others and they started out at a slow trot. They continued this way for the next two hours. For several minutes, that they would not see the black man, then he would appear in the trail, raise his hand as a sort of signal, and move on again. About 11 o'clock, they came upon him kneeling beside a small stream. Dave dismounted and Andrew could hear part of their conversation.

"There are five of them. They have fifteen horses altogether. Each is riding one and leading two others. They evidently think they are out-riding any pursuit for they haven't left anyone behind so far. They stopped here long enough to get a drink and water the horses. It looks like they may have selected one of the lead horses to ride. If so, they are now mounted on fresh horses and ours are already tiring. We have been riding close to seven hours now. With three horses a piece, they will be able to out run us."

Andrew thought for several minutes. "Dave, as long as we follow them, they will be able to detect us long before we come up on them. And with fresh horses they can run further, and our tired animals will not be able to catch them. It appears that they are headed almost due west. You indicated that they have slowed somewhat and do not seem to be expecting pursuit. What if we rode our horses to the maximum and circled to the north and then cut back? They will probably stop sometime today, or this evening to eat and water the animals. By pushing ours as hard as we can, do you think we could get ahead of them?" Dave replied, "Maybe. But if we guess wrong and they turn and go in a different direction, we will lose them for sure."

"Well, it is a gamble either way. I am afraid they will see us following them and make a run for it. If they feel they have out distanced any pursuit, they may rest and brag about their good luck. This path they are following seems to lead straight ahead. If we ride hard, circle around, we might get ahead of them by night fall. What do you think?"

"It is as good an idea as any. I think you are right about them seeing us and outrunning us if we stay behind them. There is always the chance they may try to ambush us too if they know we are following them. That would really add to their tale back to their village if they could brag that they not only stole the white-man's horses, but took some of their scalps in the bargain."

"OK. Then it is settled. Men grain your horses, rub them down good and give them just a few mouthfuls of water. You eat something too, for when we leave here we will be riding hard to circle and get ahead of them."

When they moved out, Dave took the lead and Witambe brought up the rear. Andrew wondered about that, but he didn't say anything. Evidently, he and Dave had learned to work together and each seemed to know what the other intended to do.

They rode hard for another four hours, stopping only long enough to give the horses short rests and the men a chance to get a drink of water. Each time they stopped, Andrew made the men take a handful of grass and wipe down their horses. The black seemed to be holding up pretty good, but some of the others were beginning to sag and at each stop, their heads sank a little lower. Andrew knew that they couldn't go much more. He saw Dave and Witambe examining the animals and they too knew the animals were about at the end.

Dave came over to Andrew. "I don't know if we are ahead of them or not, but these horses have about had it. We might as well cut back toward the trail now and see if they have passed. If they have, I doubt there is much chance of catching them."

They were beside a small stream. Andrew told the men to lead the horses into the stream, slosh the water over them to cool them off, but not to let them drink more than a couple swallows. Too much water when they were hot would cause the horse to get a belly-ache and give out faster.

While they were doing this, Dave spoke to Witambe and the African started off into the woods at a steady trot, leaving his horse with Dave.

Andrew spoke to Dave, "It seems you have made a tracker out of Witambe. He has learned fast."

"He learned to be a tracker long before you and I met him. This is something he knew from his days in the jungle where he was born. He and I have learned a lot from each other. He can slip through the brush as quietly as any Indian. Since you set him free he is like a different person. He is adapting well to the forests."

"I am glad. I hope that his people will do well out here. We better move on."

They followed the path Witambe had taken and in about 45 minutes, he appeared out of the brush just ahead of them. He motioned them to dismount. Then he told them that it did not appear that so many horses had passed in a group. There were pony tracks, but they seemed to be individuals passing one way or the other.

Andrew instructed Dave to take three of the men and go back a couple hundred yards. If the Indians attempted to turn back, he was to stop them at all costs. He, Witambe and the other two men would wait and stop the Indians in the road. Dave's group was to let them pass and then move quietly up behind them to lend a hand in case there was a fight. Andrew did not want bloodshed if he could help it, but he did not see how that could be prevented.

They waited for almost two hours, and Andrew was beginning to feel they had made a mistake. Perhaps the Indians had taken another path or gone north or south. He would wait another hour and if they did not show, they would camp; and tomorrow, head back to the train.

Just as he was about to give up and moved to leave, he saw Witambe drop to the ground and put his hand flat on the ground and put his ear to the ground and listened. Then he rose up, motioned to the others that horses were coming. They all became instantly alert. Andrew had instructed the men to remain hidden and to pick out their men and hold a bead on him. He was going to try to talk with them if he could. If they made to fight, or run, they were to empty the saddles.

There were indeed five of the Indians. The rode in single file, each leading the two stolen horses apiece. They had slowed; evidently they were also tired.

When there had been no one following them, they figured they had got away completely and were taking their time moving westward.

They came nearer to Andrew's hiding spot and he peered out from behind a big tree at them. He didn't recognize them as Creek, Cherokee, or even Choctaw. He had not seen many Choctaws, but these Indians looked different.

When they were about 50 feet from the tree, Andrew stepped out into the middle of the road with the pistol in his hand and pointed toward the ground. The lead Indian came to an abrupt halt. Andrew did not see any rifles among them, but they all had very ugly looking lances. The other Indians began to bunch up behind the first one and peered ahead to see what had happened. The first one had not moved or spoken since he came to a stop.

The lead raider was very surprised to see a white-man standing in the middle of the trail. His eyes darted from one side to the other, expecting an ambush. Surely this one man was not here alone, facing five brave warriors who had just killed one white-man and stolen fifteen of his best horses. No one would be that foolish. Yet, here he was and he looked unafraid. He wasn't sure if they should ride him down and kill him here, or take him prisoner and carry him back to their village alive.

Andrew spoke. "You have some very nice horses there. They look just like some of my horses that were stolen by thieves last night. I have come to take them back. Will you return them peacefully or must I take them?"

There was some mumbling from the Indians behind. The lead one held up his hand for silence. This brash man must be joking. Surely he could not think that he was a match for five warriors. He looked around again but still did not see anyone with him. He laughed a sneering laugh.

"Does the white man think we will give up our horses just because he says they are his? These are our horses and we will be taking them to our village. Stand out of my way or I will ride over you." With this, he lowered his lance and turned loose the lead rope, as if getting ready to charge.

Andrew said, "Have it your way." And with that he brought up his pistol, leveled it, and fired.

The Indian toppled over backwards as the others began to move toward him. Before they could move a foot, a volley of shots rang out from the bushes and three more fell from the backs of the horses. The fifth Indian turned to go back the way he had come, only to find three men with drawn guns aimed at his chest. He pulled the horse to a stop and sat glaring at the men.

Dave spoke to him, "This is not a good day to die. Drop your weapon and we will not harm you."

The lone Indian hesitated a few seconds more and decided that if they had intended to kill him, he would already be dead. He dropped his spear.

Dave motioned him to get off the horse, then walked over to the Indian and bound his arms behind him, making sure to also remove the captive's knife.

In the meantime, Witambe and the others had reloaded their weapons and came out of the brush. Andrew told three of the men to go back and pick up their horses and the others to round up and catch the horses the Indians had been riding. Then he went to talk with the remaining Indian.

As it turned out, they were Chickasaws. They had been down into the lands of the Apalachees and the Muscogees. They had been returning to their own lands when they saw the wagon train and began to follow it. They had given their own horses over to their friends who had gone on two or three days earlier. They had stayed behind to steal the horses. They had told their friends they would steal some horses or they would walk all the way back to their village near the Big Muddy.

Dave told Andrew that these were Chickasaws and they were fierce fighters. He suggested that they turn this one loose. He would be disgraced as a warrior if he had to walk all the way to his village. Andrew agreed. They set him free and gave him his knife and spear. He would need those to defend himself and hunt game.

Andrew had some last words of advice for him. «I was prepared to let you and the other braves go free if you had returned our horses, but your leader chose to fight me instead. Now he is dead as are three more of your friends. I come to this land in peace. I will not raise my hand against the Indian if he leaves me alone. I will not harm the Indian unless he harms me. But pass the word to all that would steal from me or that seek to do me harm: any harm done to any of my people will be returned ten times over. Anyone stealing from me, I will hunt them down and punish them. I will live among the Creeks and Cherokees. They are my friends and brothers. Do not come back into this territory seeking revenge, lest more of your people die. Now go and deliver this message."

The Indian fiercely turned and walked down the road to the west. He did not look back. Andrew and Dave watched him go.

Dave said, "It would not surprise me if we see that one again. He has been disgraced. Unless I miss my guess, he will rile up the friends and relatives of those four we killed, and they will come back to take your hair."

"Maybe, but I don't have time to worry about that now. Let's get these horses rounded up and head back to the wagon train. We will stop at the first stream we come to and fix some grub."

After eating they decided to rest a few hours. They let the horses graze while they ate and the men took turns resting. At midnight, they arose and headed home. It was the middle of the next day when they arrived back at the train. All but a very few head of the livestock had been found and returned. Andrew told them to take the rest of the day looking for the rest of the livestock, to look to their wagons and grease the wheels or do any repairs. They would be leaving at daybreak. Then he, and the others that had gone after the Indians, turned in to rest.

There were no more run-ins with the Indians, and the rest of the journey was without incident. The day before arriving at Bright Valley, Bear Claw and a dozen of people from his village met the train. Andrew turned the horses over to them and said that he would bring the blankets and other items he had promised to Bear Claw's village as soon as they reached Bright Valley and unpacked the wagons. Bear Claw was pleased and as he left to return to his village, he told Andrew that his mother and Bright Day would be looking for them as soon as they could make the trip to their village.

The next morning, they crossed the ridge and approached the valley. Andrew saddled a horse for Catherine and they rode on ahead. He wanted just the two of them to ride into the valley together before everyone else. He wanted to see her reaction.

When he topped out on the last hill, he pointed to the scar on the side of the hill and said, "This is where our land begins. You cannot see the far end of it. We will ride up there one day. But come over here and look at the valley."

She rode up beside him, and he motioned with his arm. "To the west, where you see the line of trees is the small river that is full of fish. It is the western boundary. To the east are the foot hills of the mountains. The tallest of those hills is the boundary on that side. There in the far distance, next to that peak is where I have selected to build our house. A small stream runs off the side of the hill, it will bring water right by the house. Do you like it?"

Catherine had been gazing out across the valley. Now she turned to him, wonder in her eyes. «Andrew, it is so pretty, and so big. I never imagined, when you told me how much land you had, just had big it was. This is almost like a kingdom. Is this really where we are going to live?"

«Yes. You and I, and little Victor. All of this is ours."

They dismounted and stood with their arms around each other.

She turned to him and smiled. "I have some exciting news to tell you. I did not want to say anything until I was sure. But I think we are going to have a little brother or sister for Victor."

Andrew turned and looked at her and was silent. He couldn›t believe what she had just told him. He hugged her to him and danced around in the grass.

Finally he set her down. "When? Why didn't you tell me?"

She laughed and said, "You have been so busy with

getting the train through, I didn't want to trouble you. Besides, when I missed my first period, I thought it might be due to our activities and the excitement of the trip. I have just missed the second one, though, and I am pretty sure. Besides that, I have been sick several mornings."

Andrew was ecstatic and began to talk about what they would do. If it was a boy, they would do this, but if it was a girl, they would do something else.

Finally, Catherine said, "We will have plenty of time to make plans. For right now, let's get the train into the valley and set up camp. We have lots of work to do. I feel a chill in the air already. I think winter will come in this high country early."

"You are right. We have much to do." He hugged her again and kissed her a long lingering kiss. Not since they had begun the journey, had he kissed her so softly and tenderly. She responded by opening her lips and inviting his tongue. Then, they sank to the ground. When Catherine took off her under garments, she laughed because the grass tickled her bottom. Andrew spread his jacket underneath her, and in seconds, they were in a passionate embrace.

Thus it was that they made love for the first time in the grass of Bright Valley, their valley. It would be a time they would both remember with a wink and a chuckle. The place would come to be known as their secret love spot, and this would not be the last time they would come here and make love.

CHAPTER TWENTY-NINE

The wagon train moved down into the valley, and Andrew directed them to the northern end, the area he had selected for his home. After everyone pitched their camps, he sent word around that they would celebrate tonight. Dave and Hans, and two of the other men, went out to hunt for fresh meat. Andrew asked them to look for a buffalo; they'd roast it that night and feed the entire train. The women picked greens and other wild things and made preparations for a feast. Some of the men and the younger ones gathered wood for a big fire that night.

The evening was one of festivities and prayer. They made the entire trip without the loss of a single life and very few of the animals had perished or were stolen. After everyone had eaten their fill, Andrew stood on the tailgate of one of the wagons and spoke out to the crowd.

"You have all worked hard and pulled your own weight. We are fortunate to have arrived here with such little tragedy, loss of life and only little equipment and animals. I appreciate all that you have done. Tonight, I want everyone to celebrate, dance and be happy. Tomorrow I will take 10 men with me and the two wagons that have the goods that I have promised Great Eagle and the other chiefs for the land. Hans, in the morning I will show you where I intend to build our cabin. I would like you to take charge of the rest of the men and begin cutting and hauling logs for the cabin. You can pick out a site for you and Maggie."

Then turning to Witambe, he said, "I promised you land of your own if you wanted to stay here. You can either build your cabins along that slope to the east if you want to, or you can have 1,000 acres of land at the south end of the valley. You can divide it up any way that you want to with your people. You are free to go or stay. If you choose to stay and help me work some of my land, I will pay you wages so that you can buy things that you will need. I cannot work this whole valley by myself. I would welcome some of your help, but that is up to you. You decide and let me know."

To the other men that had come on the train, the teamsters, the herders and those who signed on for the trip, he said, "All of you that signed on for the trip have earned your pay. I will pay you as I promised in the morning; and those who wish to do so, may return to your homes. Those who can stay for another two or three weeks and help us build cabins, barns and fences to hold our livestock, can earn another fifty cents a day. We have lots of work to do to prepare for winter."

Practically every man stayed on. They had worked hard on the trip and they had come to like this man Stanley. He worked as hard as any of the other men; he was honest and fair in everything he did. They had great respect for him.

The next morning, Witambe came to him. He was solemn. "Mista Stanley, our people talked it over last night, and we are not prepared to strike out on our own right now. We think we would be better to stay close to you and learn the ways of the Indians, and also learn what we can about dealing as free men. We will take the 1,000 acres you have offered us, but we want to work and pay you for it. Just as you have title to your land, we want to have title to ours as well. If it is to be really ours, we feel we must earn it. Since we will need cabins for our people too before winter comes, half of our people will work for you one week. The other half will work for you the next week. We will work six full days, but we have come to appreciate the day you call Sunday. We want that day to spend with our families. The rest of the men and the women will work on building our own cabins and clearing land for garden spots. There are some things we may still be able to grow for food before it gets too cold. Will you pay us the same fifty cents a day you have offered the other men?"

"Yes, Witambe. Also, I have brought plenty of food to stock the trading post. We will set up a credit for your people at the store. They can get anything they need and put it on a list. Then, when they receive their pay, they can go by the store and pay for what they have bought. It will probably be much colder here than it was back in Sumterville, so when you are building your cabins, make them as air tight as you can. We will have plenty of blankets for your people. You are to let me know if there is anything that you need. And one more thing,Witambe, my name is Andrew, not Mista Stanley. We are friends. I am not your master. Among friends, we call each other by our given names."

Witambe smiled respectfully. "There is one problem I am having with my men. There were only 9 women from our village, and one of them, Salli has become my mate, or wife. The other eight women, including the girls that were in the group, are now 15 or older and are ready to take mates. This leaves some 7 men without women and there are already been some fights that I have had to settle. Three have indicated they may seek some of the Indian women and will approach them as soon as they get a chance. If their tribal leaders do not object, I suspect they will take these women as their wives. Two of the men that were with me back on Masta Sumter's farm had been seeing a couple women from one of the other farms at night and would like to go back and see if they could buy them, but they don't have any idea what the cost would be."

He continued, "The other 3 men want wives also and have asked me to ask you if it would be possible to buy other women from the slave ships. They want to go back to Charleston, but we are all afraid that some of the white men will think we are runaways and capture us and return us to slavery. Since there are no other free black men, they probably would not believe them that they had been freed. Would it be possible that they could go back with you when your return to Charleston and see if there are any other black women on the slave ships?"

Andrew considered what Witambe told him. This was something that he had not anticipated. As he thought about it, grown men might go without a woman for a time; but when they began to settle down, it was only natural that they would want a mate to share their life with.

"Witambe, it is now November, and I will probably not be returning to Charleston for at least another three months, perhaps longer. We will have to wait until most of the cold weather has come and gone. It will probably be March before we can make the trip, but, yes, I can take these men with me. They can help with loading and preparing the wagons to bring in new supplies, and I will visit the slave auctions to see if we can find any other women. Perhaps we might be able to buy the two that have been seeing your men at the other farms. Tell them to bid their time and wait out the winter and we will see what can be done. Perhaps there are other Indian women that have lost husbands that might consider taking one of your men for a mate if they could meet them. There are always more women than men in Indian villages. Many of the men get killed in battles with other tribes, leaving their wives without husbands and the younger women without a lot of men to choose from. I will discuss this with Night Hawk and let him spread the word in his village. If there are some Indian women that might want to mate with some of your men, we will arrange a visit to the Indian village for them."

Witambe clasped Andrew's hand and squeezed it hard. There was deep emotion in his face, yet he could not say a word. Witambe turned and walked back to where his people were waiting. He told them of the conversation with Andrew, and the other men shook their heads in agreement. Then he picked out 8 of his strongest people to work with Andrew. He loaded the women into the two wagons and headed toward the land Andrew had designated for them.

Not counting the 10 men who were to help Andrew take the blankets and other goods to Great Eagle, there were almost 100 hundred men working.

Andrew had Hans split them into five teams of 20 men each. Twenty were to go into the forest and cut trees. Each of the other teams was assigned to a specific job. One team would build the barns. Another was assigned to build the main house for him, Catherine and Victor. Another team would work on the Trading Post and warehouse. And the last team set out to build the cabin for Hans and Maggie. Ten of each of the twenty-men teams cleared the sites, removed stumps and leveled the ground to the best of their ability. The other 10 men per team went into the forest with the wood cutters. As soon as a tree fell, they de-limbed it and dragged it to the respective sites they were assigned.

With the clearing and the sites now ready, the teams began to cut and place the logs for the walls.

Andrew laid out a five room cabin for him and Catherine. It consisted of three bedrooms, a sitting room, and a kitchen. The barn was to be a two-story affair with a large loft for hay. There would be stalls for the riding horses and for the milk cows. The rest of the animals would be pastured back in the hills out of the north winds. For this year at least, they would have to take cover under the trees, in the draws or gullies, wherever they could find a place out of the wind.

The trading post was to be the largest of the buildings, and the ten men of each team hauling logs were instructed to haul logs for the post when they finished hauling for the building they were initially assigned. When the other buildings were completed, everyone was to pitch in and help finish the trading post, which was divided into four sections. The front three sections would be devoted to merchandise for trading. One area would be dry goods such as blankets, cloth, and cooking utensils such as pots, pans, skillets, etc.

The second area would be devoted to food stuffs, such as kegs of salt meat, flour, beans, salt, sugar, coffee, tobacco, rice and edible things. The third area for merchandise would be hardware. Here he would display such items as hoes, shovels, plows, knives, leather goods and harness, saddles, axes, and similar items. The last section was to be built onto the back and would have a loading ramp where the wagons could back up and unload. This would be used as a sort of warehouse. It was to have a large roof extending out over the area where the wagons would be stored when not in use. The big Conestoga wagons would be put in the lower level of the barn.

In discussing the type of construction, Andrew wanted to make sure that all of the buildings would be easy to defend. He did not expect any raids, but he would be prepared in case they were attacked. He instructed the teams to ensure there would be a window with wooden shutters on each side of the houses and trading post, and all sides would have slots that rifles could be fired through. All buildings would be placed so that they would be close enough to defend the other buildings, but not close enough that they would all go up in case one caught fire.

He had situated the house near the little spring that came out of the side of mountain behind the house so that water would not be a problem. He intended to enclose the spring inside the walls of the house later so that they could get water without leaving the house. If they should ever come under siege, they would have a safe water supply. As the water flowed on past the house, it would flow through the corner of the barnyard so that any animals penned in the barn would have fresh water all the time.

When everything was moving to his satisfaction, he headed out with the wagons for the Cherokee village. It was slow going and in many places, it was difficult to get the wagons through the forest and across the streams. By the end of the first day, they had not gone but about twelve miles. Andrew was disappointed. At this rate it would take them several weeks to get to Great Eagle's village and almost that amount of time to return. He was eager to see Night Hawk and Burned Belly, and he wondered if Bright Day had taken a husband. He hoped so. Now that he was supremely contented with Catherine and his new life, he wanted everyone to find their life mate as well.

To his surprise, about mid-day of the third day, Night Hawk and more than 50 of the braves from Great Eagle's village arrived. When Great Eagle returned to his village with the horses, he told his people that Andrew was back and was bringing all the things he had promised, Night Hawk insisted on going to meet him. Almost half of the village wanted to go as well. They were all aware of the things that had been promised to them and they were excited about their arrival.

After much greeting and shouting, Andrew explained the difficulty they were having in getting the wagons through the forest. Night Hawk laughed at him and said they would take care of it. He immediately instructed the braves with him to cut travois poles and to hitch up as many of the horses as they would need. In less than two hours, the Indians had all the blankets, cloth and other items that Andrew was taking to Great Eagle as gifts loaded on the travois dragging behind the horses. As they led out towards the Cherokee village, Andrew instructed two of the drivers to take the wagons and extra men and return to the valley. They were to pitch in and help the others until he could return.

Although it was hardly more than a hard day's ride on horseback to the village, with the goods, it took another day and a half to arrive. As the Indians and the loaded travois arrived at the village, there was joyful pandemonium. The squaws ran out to meet them, kids danced around the tents and dogs were barking. Night Hawk instructed that none of the goods were to be distributed until Great Eagle came. The horses had also been held in a bunch.

As was customary, Andrew went directly to Great Eagle's tepee. He was warmly greeted by Great Eagle. Andrew felt as if he had truly come home. The whole village was in a state of great excitement, but custom bade Great Eagle to make everyone wait while they smoked the pipe and talked. When it was over, he arose and went outside and examined all the things on the travois. Since he had returned with the horses he had examined them carefully. When he was done, he turned to Andrew and spoke.

"My son, One Who Sees Far, has kept his word. The blankets, the cloth and the knives will be distributed to my people and those of the other tribes. With a few exceptions, the horses are all good animals. They will help improve the blood lines of our animals." Turning to his son, he said, "Send runners to the other village. We will feast tonight and will divide the goods in the morning. All of the Cherokee

Nation is invited to come and those that doubted the wisdom of dealing with my white son shall see that it was a wise action."

When the business was completed, Little Turtle came and put her arms around Andrew. She was truly glad to see him and insisted he come into the tent and eat. While he ate, Night Hawk and Bright Day sat and talked with him. It was Bright Day who brought up the way he was to live by asking if he had a tepee for the winter.

Andrew hesitated a moment, then decided he might as well let them know his full story. He said, "No. But I have a group of men working back in the valley. They are building barns and stables for the animals I brought, and a big building that I will use as a trading post. There are also some 25 black men and women that were slaves. I bought them away from their owners and set them free. They and their families will live in the valley, at least for now. They may go on west towards the big river later. Hans and Maggie are married and will also live in the valley with me. The workmen are also building a house for my wife and son."

There was a short gasp from Bright Day, but neither Little Turtle or Night Hawk noticed for they were filled with excitement about Andrew having a wife and son. Little Turtle was delighted that she now had a grandson. She said, "It is good that you came to be our son so that I can have some grandchildren. I have told both Night Hawk and Bright Day that it is time they took a mate and made me a grandmother. You must tell me all about your wife and my new grandson."

Night Hawk, also very excited, thumped him on the shoulder and said, "Oh, my brother, you work fast. A mere five months ago you did not even have a wife. Now, in such short time you have managed to find not only a wife, but have a son too. You white men are very fast. It takes an Indian nine months to produce a child."

Andrew smiled at the joking of his new family. He decided he should tell them most of the story. "While I was on the big ship that brought me across the big salt sea, I met a woman who was indentured to a land owner. She and I talked while on the ship, but I thought there could never be any chance for us, because she was sold to another man to work for him. After I left the ship, I met a dark haired woman and we became very good friends. When I returned from my trip, I discovered she was with my child. I intended to marry her, and on the day we were to be married, the excitement caused the baby to come early. It was not ready and had not turned. It could not come naturally. The medicine man, who we call a doctor, had to cut open her stomach and take the baby. The mother bled so much she could not be saved. She died giving birth to my son."

He hesitated and all were hanging on his words. Then he continued, "I thought of the woman on the boat and I went to see her. We talked, and I talked to the man who had bought her. She was willing to be my wife and help take care of my son if we could get her freed from her debt to the land owner. The man who owned her debt agreed to sell her to me, and we were married before we left the white man's village. She is waiting for me now in the valley."

Little Turtle was sad for him, but she said, "We are happy for you, my son and we will visit when the spring weather arrives. You must bring them to our village also so that our people can meet them."

Night Hawk had been silent through all of Andrew's talk. Now he spoke. "My brother, sadness seems to follow you in so many ways. Did you love the woman who bore your son?"

"At the time we were sharing our blanket, we were drawn together as much by loneliness as the attraction of a man for a woman. I had not thought to marry her, but when I found she was with my son, honor required that I marry her and provide for her and my son. Had she lived, she would have been my wife. Now, I have married another. Catherine, that is my wife's name, has agreed to take my son and raise him as if he was her own. I am pleased that I found someone like her."

Only Andrew noticed that Bright Day had not said a word, and now, he smiled at her.

"I am humbled to be a part of your family. Bright Day, did your brother tell you that I have named the valley where we will live in your honor? I call it Bright Valley."

Her face was bleak and she mumbled a quiet, "Yes, he did."

"You were so dedicated in caring for me when I lay dying. And now we are brother and sister. It was important to me that I find a way to thank you. Now, when I tell the story of Bright Valley, others will know you and what a great person you are."

He sensed she still wanted more from him; he hoped this would provide some comfort to her. He was happily married now and she must accept it.

"Thank you, Brother. I am grateful."

She rose without another word and left the tepee.

The men did not think anything of it, but Little Turtle noticed. Now she understood why her daughter had not taken a husband. She was truly in love with this white man, and even though he was her adopted brother, she had waited for him, hoping he would return and take her as his woman. Now there was no hope of that. Little Turtle rose and went out to her daughter and left the two men to talk.

Bright Day sat beside the stream, with tears running down her cheeks. Little Turtle put her arms around her and said, "Now I understand my child. You love him don't you?"

"Yes. And in spite of our laws, I would have gone with him had he asked me to. I had hoped that when he returned he would want me but now that can never be. My heart is broken and I shall never love another as I love him."

"Bright Day, it is better this way. If you had gone with him, you would have been cast out of our tribe, and he would no longer be welcome in any of our villages. To everyone, he is your brother, and you must never let anyone else know how you feel. You must bury this feeling deep inside you and find you another husband who will help heal this wound. But you must never, ever tell your new husband that you feel this way about One Who Sees Far. If you do, he will hate him and always be jealous of him. He will leave tomorrow and return to the valley. I think it would be best if you stay away from the lodge while he is here. I don't believe he knows how deeply you care for him. It is better that he not find out. Go now and stay the night with one of your friends. And remember, he honors you because of the name he gave to his home, Bright Valley."

Andrew and Dave did not wait around the next morning for Night Hawk and Great Eagle to distribute the goods and horses; that was his business to complete. Andrew had kept his part of the bargain and now it was important that he get back to the valley.

He was apprehensive about Catherine and Victor's safety. Although there were close to a hundred men there, only Hans had much experience with Indians. It would be foolish for an open, direct attack; however, a small force could swoop in, do lots of damage and be gone before most of the others knew what had happened.

He and Dave left at daybreak, after saying their goodbyes. Night Hawk said he would try to come see them before the heavy snows came. They rode hard, and entered the valley just after dark. They rode on and within another hour were pulling into the site they had selected for their homes.

Andrew was surprised at what he saw.

They had been gone a total of eight days, and he had not expected so much to get done. As they rode into the compound in the dark, large buildings loomed in the dark and made great images in the night. They neared one of the larger buildings, and a voice called out, "Who's there?" Hans had made sure guards had been posted, and they were staying back in the dark until they found out who was coming.

When Andrew announced who they were, a shout went up. As they rounded the building and moved toward a fire in the middle of the yard, everyone came to meet them. Catherine came running with her hair flying, and he was hardly off his horse before she was in his arms. She felt so good in his arms. They kissed and she teased him with the tip of her tongue, perhaps a promise of greater things to come.

While they ate, Hans told him that the walls of the house were up and the roof on, one of the big barns had been finished, and the main part of the trading post was dried in. They had just moved the goods off the wagons that day and put them inside. With different crews working on different jobs, a competition had sprung up and each crew was trying to outdo the others. At the rate they were going, in another week to 10 days, they would be almost finished. Catherine said they would be able to sleep in their new home this very night. He believed there was more meaning there than what had been said.

It was near midnight when everyone had stopped by and paid their respects. Andrew finally headed toward his new home. Maggie had agreed to keep Victor in the wagon with her and Catherine had gone on to the house earlier. Andrew saw a lamp burning in the front room of the house.

The porch had not been finished, and he stepped up out of the dirt onto the steps leading into the house. As he entered, it was much larger than he had thought it would be. He was very pleased that it was so far along, and was turning out so nice. He called to Catherine, and she answered from one of the back rooms.

He carried the lamp and moved toward her voice. He entered a large room that held a wooden bed with a big thick mattress, a table, and a chest. There were several boxes placed in the room, but there was still plenty of space for them to move around. He placed the lamp on the chest and Catherine came to him. She had combed her long red hair out and it hung down her back to her hips. She had brushed it until it shimmered in the pale lamp light. He had been so intent on looking at her hair and the smile on her face that he had failed to see the thin gown she was wearing. It was not until she was in his arms and he had pulled her to him that he realized that the gown was hardly more than a sheer layer of cloth, and that she had nothing on under it. The thought of her nude made him rush to undress. In less than two minutes, with her help, he was out of his clothes and they tumbled onto the bed. He did not know where she had gotten this material for the gown, but right now he didn't care. He was just glad she had it.

When their passionate lovemaking was over, they lay just as they were, side by side. It was several minutes before they realized that the lamp was still burning. There were not yet any shutters on the windows. Had anyone been passing around the house, they could not have helped but see them. Quickly, Catherine got up, went to a basin of water in the corner, and washed herself. Then she brought a wet cloth to Andrew and wiped him clean. When this was done, she blew out the light and came to lay beside him naked as the day they were born.

As she snuggled into his arms, she said, "Andrew I worried that something might happen to you and you might not come back to me. When you rode in tonight, I was so excited I could hardly contain myself. I wanted your love so much, I fear I may have acted like a harlot, but I don't care. I would do anything for your love. I never want you to go away from me again, not even for one day."

"Maybe we won't have to be parted anymore. I love you and want us to have a family together. You are a passionate woman Catherine, you fill me with desire."

"You do the same to me Andrew. I hope I can always please you and you will never look at another woman except me."

"I promise. I could never find another like you."

Lying thus, in each other's arms, their passions temporarily spent, they drifted off to sleep.

Chapter Thirty

I n the days that followed, the remainder of the buildings went up rapidly; and on the 15th day after his return from Night Hawk's village, all of the houses were completed, not one but two barns built and the trading post was ready to open for business.

Andrew called all the men together and spoke to them. "Tomorrow you will be able to return to your families. I will give you all your pay tonight so that if you want to get an early start tomorrow you can. You have all worked hard and done a very good job. I am going to give each of you a bonus of $10 above your wages."

A great shout went up from the workers. Ten dollars cash was as much as some made in a month or more working, if they could even find work at all.

Andrew continued, "From time to time I will need teamsters to bring in supplies and to haul out things that I will trade for, or that we will grow here. I plan to do much of my trading with Birmingham to the South or with New Orleans on the Gulf Coast. But I will also be bringing in wagons from Charleston on occasion. If you want to mule-skin a wagon, leave your name with Hans and I will look you up when I am in Charleston. The wagons that we have rented will be going back with you. I am going to send half of my wagons back with you also. I will make arrangements to have them stored for me until I return. Then I will load them and have you bring them back here. If everything goes as I plan, I will probably make four trips next year, and three or more the following year. I have work for five men if any of you want to stay. I don't know how dangerous it will be here in the valley, and I want to have a few extra guns in case we are attacked. Are there any of you who want to stay? I will pay you the same wages you have been drawing on the trip."

Most of the men had families or loved ones back home and were anxious to return. However, Zeb and three others said they did not have anyone in particular waiting for them, and they could stay. There was no work back home for them in the winter anyway. They were to build them a separate cabin out to the side of the big trading post. This would be to the south of the post and would be the first building anyone would encounter coming from the south. Andrew's house was the northern most building and would receive the strongest north winds in winter. However, where it was placed it would be shielded from much of the winds by the outcropping of the mountain.

Everyone was up the next morning to see the men off, and it was sort of sad to see them go. Everyone had grown close these past few months and many new friends were made. Those remaining stood in the yard and watched as the men and wagons rolled south to the gap through which they had come.

Finally, Hans spoke up and broke the silence. "What do you want us to do, Andrew?"

Andrew replied, "Hans, there may come a time when we will need all the fire power we can get. I want you to take Dave, Zeb and one of the other men and teach Witambe and his people how to use a gun. Give them instructions, let them fire a few rounds to get the feel of the kick and how to hold the weapons, and have them practice over and over again on loading. As you and I know, too little powder and the ball won't fly true. Too much powder and the gun may blow up in their face. Loading and aiming the gun is perhaps the most important part. When you feel they have the hang of it, issue each of them a gun, 50 shot and sufficient powder. Tell them they must keep these handy all the time, even when they are working in the fields. If they are attacked by Indians, they won't have time to run home and get their guns. Their lives and the lives of their women and children may depend on how proficient they become with the weapons. Get them at least as good as the Indians are with guns"

Dave spoke up, "I worked with Witambe and some of the others a little when we were building the road. Most are not very good, but it won't take them long to learn. They can probably hold their own in hand to hand combat. Even the women can hold their own in a fight."

Little did Andrew know how important this would be before the winter was over.

It was now nearing the middle of December and they were getting settled in pretty well. A few Indians had come to the trading post, but so far, trading was slow. As the word spread, there would be more. After all, it was not as if Andrew was depending on the trade for a livelihood.

Catherine was getting bigger now and her condition was starting to show noticeably. With this, she also became more irritable at times. Maggie was there to help her, and they sewed lots of baby clothes. All in all it was a happy time. Little Victor had adjusted well and was growing fast. If he continued, he would be a big boy.

Andrew kept Zeb and the other men on watch most of the time. They would take turns; two would watch the woods and the other two would work. Then, they would change, and the two who had stood watch would work, and the workers would take over the watch.

Andrew did not want to take any chances. Not only was the safety of Catherine, Maggie, Victor and the rest always on his mind, but he had a substantial investment now in the barns, trading post and wagons. He felt uneasy for some reason. They had come all the way from Charleston without any trouble to speak of. It just seemed too easy. With the 16 men from Witambe's group, things were progressing well and all of the buildings were soon completed.

Perhaps it was the lack of any sign of trouble that lured them into a relaxed posture, and that almost proved fatal.

The first snow fell and was about two inches on the ground one morning. Everyone had just begun to move about. As always, Dave and Hans went first to the stables to feed and water the stock. Two of the hired men had come out of the cabin to wash up and one had headed to the privy. Catherine and Maggie, as was their custom, were preparing breakfast for all the men. Andrew had started to the barn to milk the cow so Victor would have fresh milk. He was half way to the barn when he first sensed something was wrong. The man headed to the privy staggered and seemed to be clawing at his chest. Then he turned slightly and Andrew saw the arrow sticking from his chest.

He screamed one word that galvanized everyone into immediate action, "Indians!"

In spite of his warning never to be caught without his gun, all Andrew had was a wooden milk pail. He dropped it and raced for the back door of the house. As he did, he saw two braves rise up out of the snow and race to cut him off before he could reach the house. They came fast, and he didn't think he would make it.

Two shots rang out. Hans and Dave didn't have to be told what to do, and they had not gone out without their weapons. They had been on the frontier too long, and for this reason, they probably saved Andrew's life. The two braves crumpled into the snow and Andrew didn't hesitate. He leaped over them and raced onto the back porch and in the door. He immediately grabbed his gun and stuck one of his pistols in his belt and slung a powder horn and shot over his shoulder. He returned to the back door in less than a minute.

By now, there were Indian yells coming from all directions. The other three men in the cabin were fully awake and had their guns at the windows. Andrew could not see Dave and Hans, and wondered if they were under attack in the barn. For the moment, they would have to look out for themselves. He did not dare leave the women alone. Catherine had immediately grabbed the baby and retreated to one corner of the kitchen. Andrew glanced at her, and saw her face was as white as the biscuit dough she had been kneading to make bread. Maggie had sprung into action and now had a rifle in each hand and had locked the front door so that no one could get at them from that angle.

Andrew raced to close the wooden shutters. Just as he reached for the strap to pull it shut, an Indian raised his head to come through the window. Andrew pulled his pistol and shot him directly in the face. The shot took the top of his head off and he fell backwards. Andrew closed the window and bolted it while Maggie was doing the same with the other windows. Fortunately, it was cold the night before, and the windows had all been closed. They had only opened two when they awoke that morning to let in light and fresh air.

Andrew raced to the front of the house and peered out through the cracks in the door. There were at least a full dozen Indians racing toward the house and the barn. Shots peppered against the house but the logs absorbed them and none reached into the cabin.

He could hear shots being fired now from the barn and from the cabin. It seemed that they were being attacked from all sides. He knelt and brought up his rifle and as it touched his shoulder he fired. Before the smoke cleared, he re-loaded and he saw an Indian slide backwards in the snow. Just as he raised his gun to fire again, another gun roared beside him. He glanced to see Maggie setting aside one rifle and picking up another. He fired again, and a third Indian dropped. The others veered to the side and raced toward the house of Hans and Maggie. Andrew and Maggie were both busily loading now and they moved around to the side, threw up the wooden shutter and dropped two more just as they went around the corner of the other house. Now they were out of sight. Andrew told Maggie to keep an eye open for them and he ran to the back to take another look toward the barn. Now there were five Indians lying in the yard. He glanced toward the Maggie's cabin and saw three more near the warehouse. But there were no more in sight.

Andrew called out, "Hans, you and Dave alright?"

Dave answered, "Yeh! Hans got hit in the arm by an arrow, but it isn't too bad. We're OK. How about the house?"

"Everyone is OK. Hello the cabin. Anybody hurt?"

"Just Rafferty. Looks like that arrow done him in. He hasn't moved since the shooting begin."

"Four or five went around the other side of Hans's house and I think they are inside. Are there anymore around that you saw?"

There were negative answers from everyone.

"Dave, you and Hans stay put. They may try to run off some of the horses, although they have taken heavy losses, I think they are still around. Zeb, leave one man in the cabin and you and the other race to the house."

A minute later, the cabin door slammed open and Zeb and the man named Clay raced toward the back door of the house. Andrew held the door open and let them enter. He picked up his second pistol and stuck it in his belt and added a short handled hatchet. Both of the other men also carried a pistol in addition to their rifles.

"Look to your weapons and make sure they are primed. We have to go after them in the other house. If they haven't already torn it up, they will and may set it on fire. Are you ready?"

When they nodded, he said, "Let's stick together and protect each other as best we can."

With that, they left the front porch and raced toward the other house. No shots were fired, and they reached the side of the building without incident. They inched up to the corner and looked around the front of the house. Four Indians were just disappearing towards the woods with large bundles of cloth, pans, blankets, and stuff over their shoulders. They were in the woods before they could get a shot at them.

Without hesitating, Andrew shouted, "We can't let them get away with this or they will be back again. Come on!"

He raced after the Indians at a full run and had almost reached the woods before he was aware he had made a big mistake. He had not checked the inside of the house and had assumed that the Indians running away were all of them. He changed his mind when a shot rang out behind him, and his rifle was jarred out of his hand. Zeb saw him stop and swung around. He saw three Indians coming after them from the house. He and the other man fired. Two of them slowed, fell to their knees, and then slowly fell face forward. The third Indian still lurched forward, and now a roar went up behind them in the woods. Keeping one eye on the Indian approaching from the house, they turned to see almost two dozen Indians rising up out of the brush and starting toward them. They had been hiding in the edge of the woods, and now Andrew and his men had fallen into their trap. There was no way they could fight all of these Indians. But first things first. He pulled one of his pistols. As the third Indian from the house rose in a leap, Andrew fired the pistol point blank into his belly. Blood and guts went all over the three white men. They were busy reloading and did not panic.

Andrew shouted, "Try to make it back to the house. We can't stand them off here. There are too many of them."

He grabbed his gun off the ground, and although the stock was busted from the Indian's bullet, he held it at his side and fired into the approaching Indians. The other men did the same, causing a moment's hesitation, before the rest came on. The three men turned and raced for the house. It has perhaps no more than a hundred yards, but it seemed miles; they feared they would never reach the porch.

Zeb stumbled and fell. The other two stooped to pick him up, slowing them more. He had an arrow in his leg. They knew they would not make it and dropped him. They turned to face the racing savages.

The band of Indians sensed they had the white devils now and they were eager to bathe in white blood. They had a grin on their faces.

Andrew drew his other pistol in one hand and the hatchet in his right and prepared to meet them. He had no hopes he could survive but he would at least take another heathen or two with him. Clay also stood his ground and prepared to die fighting. They both fired their pistols and two Indians went down but the rest raced toward them.

The first Indian was no more than twenty feet from them, and they braced for the first contact. Then, a fuselage of fire erupted from the corner of the house. At least ten Indians went down and the rest slid to a halt. Their hesitation caused four more to die as a second, but smaller, volley sounded.

There were only eight Indians left standing and what

they saw convinced them there might be better pickings someplace else. They turned and raced for the woods. Six made it, and two more went down from two last shots.

Andrew turned to see where the firing was coming from and saw Witambe and his men. They were all grinning as if this had been child's play to them. But to Zeb, Clay and Andrew, they looked like angels. They realized that their lives had been spared and breathed a sigh of relief.

Witambe explained that the moment they heard the shooting, he and twelve of his men had mounted their horses and come at a gallop. They entered the fray from the other direction, unknown to the Indians hiding in the woods. Witambe's men saw Zeb go down and dismounted behind the house. They took up positions and decided to fire from the corner of the house.

Andrew was glad they had learned to use rifles. It had saved him and the other two men from certain death. Saying thanks was so little and so insufficient, that they didn't say anything. He just took Witambe by the shoulder and pulled him to him and hugged him as he would hug a brother. All the men knew what was going through their minds and words could not express the feelings of relief of the three men who had given up hope of living, and were now alive, thanks to these black men. From this day forward, they would be as one family, and would defend each other as if they were brothers.

They walked toward the barn and met Dave and Hans half way across the yard. The arrow was still sticking through Dave's arm but it had a bandanna around it and the bleeding had stopped. They would have to cut the shaft on the arrow and pull it on through the arm. It would hurt like blazes, but hopefully, there wouldn't be too much permanent damage. Zeb's arrow would have to be removed the same way. The third man came from the cabin and verified the man near the privy was dead. The arrow had severed a main artery near his heart and he died within a few seconds.

The black men moved among the Indians in the yard, making sure none still lived. Andrew was somewhat reluctant to kill an injured man, but the black men had a different philosophy. This way, they were sure these Indians would never attack them again. When all the bodies were counted, there were a total of twenty seven who would not be back.

This was the last Indian raid Andrew and his people would suffer for several years. In the following years, the Creeks and Cherokees, who constantly travelled the woods, would warn the white people when hostiles were in the area. They often attacked and ran them off before they ever reached the trading center. Andrew set aside a 10-acre parcel as a camp ground for those who came to visit or trade. The Indians considered the camp ground and the trading post a sort of inter-tribal meeting area, neutral ground. They often met there and held pow-wows at the post. It became known as mutual ground and no fighting or war parties were allowed there. All who came were treated friendly and received a fair trade for their skins and trinkets they made.

* * * * *

As the years passed, respect grew for One Who Sees Far, and he was treated as a wise man. He often sat around the camp fires telling stories with the Indians and his counsel was frequently sought by the chiefs. All of the tribes knew him and all of his people. They were allowed free passage through all the Indian lands.

When the new baby came, it was a girl, and they named her Mary Catherine. She and Victor grew up in the wilderness, among the Indians, and with black boys and girls as their playmates.

Victor was a special favorite of the Indians, and they taught him much about their lives and customs. He would become a great woodsman and by the time he was twelve, he would travel in the forest alone, staying sometimes a week or more. Often he would accompany the Indians on their hunts and he took a deep interest in Indian folklore. He would sit hours listening to the elders talk about the past and explain about how they believed in the Great Spirit and Mother Earth. He became adept with the bow and arrow, with the spear and could skin a deer or antelope as quickly as any Indian.

But all of this would follow.

For now, Andrew had found his new land; a wonderful, exciting and caring woman to share it with him; new friends and respect. It was totally foreign to what he had been used to. Now and then, he would remember the family and friends he once had, but this was a new life. He had searched for and found a new beginning. He was happy.

Little did he know that he would begin a legacy and in the years that would follow, his name would become known to many settlers east of the Mississippi and he would have great influence on the affairs of the area throughout his and his children's life times.

But that is another story and will have to wait for another time.